Sword And The Thistle

JAMES JOHN LOFTUS

Copyright © 2012 James John Loftus

All rights reserved.

ISBN: 10:1466387645
ISBN-13:978-1466387645

DEDICATION

I dedicate this novel to my wife who is always there for me. And to my daughter who took the time to help me, and to my son, for his advice.

CONTENTS

	Acknowledgments	I
1	A New Home	1
2	Edgar	35
3	A Wedding, A Death	48
4	Habits Of Monks	83
5	Phail's Return	116
6	Wrath Of A King	139
7	Tainted Love	171
8	Dance Of Death	174
9	The Fugitive	189
10	Clash Of Arms	213
11	The Unicorn	224
12	Leaves On The Wind	260
13	Walter Of Guiyack's Curse	302

ACKNOWLEDGMENTS

I want to acknowledge the many people who helped me get this novel out. Craig Lake, whose eye for a missing comma never ceases to amaze me. Ross Wilson, who gives the best advice, and is a writing comrade. Anthony Edwards for his encouragement. To Adrian Schuster, who was a light in the darkness. Tim Scurr, the competent captain steering the ship away from the rocks and to a safe landing. Amy Pastre, for her support and proofreading. Jean Bishop also for her proofreading. My daughter Jordan, whose talent amazes me. To Mika Sternberg, Magic Unicorn, for inspring a chapter in this book. The cover was a collaboration between my daughter Jordan Loftus and Declan Loftus who I am sure is a relative. And a special thanks to Diana Gabaldon for being a friend. Who knows how many other people helped me, if I have not put your name here, thanks.

A NEW HOME

MORGUND MACAEDH MADE his way to the central keep of the castle where his mother lay dying. His footsteps echoed as he ascended the steps to her chamber. When he opened her door, Mary lay abed too near death to hear his approach or feel his presence. Her hair was a dull, lank grey where once it had shone a bright fiery red. Morgund sat by her bed watching her chest heave, shudder and collapse. Morgund found it hard to reconcile this figure on the bed with the woman he had known his life long. For so many years, she seemed ageless, young of heart and lively - so vital she could barely sit still. That could be said of her until her husband Bran fell from his horse, an unseemly accident, not so uncommon in the wet of autumn but in his case ultimately fatal. Bran suffered a broken back, and died alone, amid the crumpled leaves. A heavy sigh came from the bed. Mary's labored breathing rattled, and sounded to Morgund like the only sound in the world. It was hard to believe things had come to this.

Morgund uttered in a tone barely above a whisper, "My mother will soon be no-more."

As Morgund saw it, the world beyond, was reaching out to lay its hands on his mother. All around him there seemed a heaviness in the air. Rarely given to flights of fancy, he felt that someone or something - not Mary, for she watched no one - was watching him in this room. Perhaps it was Death itself. His eyes moved left and right as if to catch sight of this presence. Naught but flickering shadows cast by the solitary lamp. Just shadows and darkness was all that there was. Dismissing this prickly feeling of being watched as illogical he turned his attention back on his mother. Seeing her like this, seeing how hard it was for her to breathe, tore at his heart and threatened to render it in twain. There would be no relief for the wreck of a woman whose time had come. She was about to go to God as Morgund knew only too well. The priests had come and gone giving her what comfort they could. Realizing there was nothing he could do, he left, leaving her in the hands of the servant who waited outside the door in the sepulchral gloom. Loric, the castle's steward, was with the servant. Whether real or a ghost, for everything and all seemed so insubstantial in his mind, he did not know. Long ago his mother's hair was red and he was a boy and at her side - that seemed more real to him than any of this. He spoke to the figure beside him. "Has thou been here long, Loric?"

A moment of reassurance when Loric replied. He proved to be no phantom in his mind, but flesh and blood. "Not long my Lord." Loric felt compelled to bring a matter to Morgund's attention and made the following statement. "When thine mother falls out of this life altogether they will come for you Morgund, the Morays, and wrest control of this castle from thee."

Morgund registered very little interest in this. "What will be will be."

Loric eyed Morgund somberly. "First in Ross and now in Sutherland thee art cast away to the winds and to the heather."

Morgund gave him a wry smile. "Better to hide in the heather than to lay under it."

"Aye," came the response from that straightforward man.

A glint of anger flashed in Morgund's narrowed eyes. "I have done it once before when I was little more than a child with none but Seward to aid me in my cause. This time I am a man and a swordsman with sworn friends willing to stand by my side. I will take sacks of grain, cattle. I will leave little for the Earl of Sutherland. And you, dear Loric, will stay, will call him M'Lord, will bow your head to this boy who is yet to turn ten. What sort of child he is, I know not. But I pray he be a kind master Loric."

Loric stated it without artifice. "This is my home. I will serve whoever is the master here. I have known no other place, nor ever will."

Leaving that comment unanswered, Morgund made the

following observation, "They waited for my mother's death to lay their claim to this castle, at least."

Loric felt compelled to say, "Some small justice, then."

Morgund turned away from him and his footsteps on the stone floor echoed as he departed to his business.

Watching him go Loric knew Mary would be proud of her son. With much to do, Loric took himself off to his own duties.

Many hours later Morgund returned to his mother's bedside and in the dead of night he watched the lamp on the wall swaying in the wind casting long shadows. The wind heightened and lowered dragging the firelight sideways before straightening briefly again. Then the wind bent the firelight giving all an air of otherworldliness. The air heightened once more and the fire lengthened and bent casting weird shadows on the wall. Whilst Morgund contemplated the unseen force drive the lamplight the wind pitched high and sounded like a multitude of screaming souls trying to outdo each other. There was a second layer to these sounds. The wind called out from the kingdom of Death to Mary drawing her away from the world of living men drawing her to where the angels and the God of heaven reigned, where she need not fear Satan. As a good Christian, it was God who would claim her. Morgund's eyes were upon the deathly pale face on the bed. Mary could not open her eyes nor ask for a drink. Morgund looked away from the tragedy, for no more could he endure it. Morgund would soon take his leave of Skelbo castle. Skelbo castle was recently gifted to the Earl of Sutherland, by the king no less. William Moray the current Earl of Sutherland was the grandson of Freskin the Fleming. Freskin, the grandsire of the current earl, came to Scotland with nothing but his wits and with them alone made good.

When death finally would fell upon Morgund's mother, William, the Earl of Sutherland, would attend with his swordsmen to take possession of the castle. By virtue of Skelbo, the Morays would enforce the king's peace in a part of the kingdom that for many years defied his rule.

"The tide comes in and the tide goes out. As it is in nature, so it is in life." Morgund remembered hearing a man say that and it occurred to him now as truth.

Morgund felt what was happening to him mirrored the plight of the Celts in Scotland. Alexander King of Scots was for the most part committed to promoting the Norman nobility to positions of power within the kingdom, yet, the Normans were newcomers, scarcely in the kingdom a hundred years. The old Celtic nobility, who Morgund counted himself amongst by family reputation alone if nothing else, were for the most part condemned to minor roles within the kingdom. Once they had been the great ones in the land, now any glory associated with their names was but a memory. As the Celts had once been great in the kingdom of Scotland, so too had the MacAedhs. They arose with Aedh, Prince of Scotland, who was the son of Malcolm Canmore; Canmore who had slain Macbeth to gain his crown. When he died, to the consternation of all, Aedh his son refused the mantle of kingship when offered it. That he forfeited his right to the kingdom caused much strife and bloodshed in the years to come. After Aedh declined Scotland's crown his younger brother Alexander became king in his stead. Alexander thought a crown would look good upon his head and so it did. He made an effective king and was nicknamed, 'The Fierce'. In time, Alexander, 'The Fierce,' lay cold in the ground without any heirs, and was thus he was succeeded by a still younger brother, David. By then Aedh's two sons were of age and made a claim for the crown putting forth that they were from the senior line and that the eldest of them, Duncan, should be king, and not their uncle David. David, a much more powerful figure ignored the MacAedh claim. The result was the MacAedhs put themselves up in arms against David. Both sons of Aedh died in the attempt to claim Scotland's throne. The MacAedhs would claim the crown with much commonness, the claimant died for it equally commonly until the only one left with the name was Morgund MacAedh.

An agonizing night did Morgund spend by his mother's death bed until the sunlight streamed into the room. When it did, Mary was gone. Truly alone in the world now because his mother was no longer alive, Morgund bowed his head and prayed for her. The illness she suffered from was known to hammer away at the afflicted until nothing of the person remained, only a mortal shell enclosed in endless pain. Best she had not lingered.

Before the day was out Mary MacAedh was lowered into the ground. Morgund put it out that whoever wanted to come with him should prepare to do so; as a consequence, there was a great clamour whether to stay behind or accompany him. Once the time to depart was upon him, Morgund cast his eye back to such familiar sights as he had grown accustomed to - many old nooks and corners of the castle held memories for him. He dragged his eyes away. This was the past. What was important was what lay ahead.

 Eleven families had decided to follow Morgund. They were on every side of him with their handcarts and donkeys, mules and horses all packed with supplies. Distance from Skelbo brought sights not least the forbidding gloom of the forest. As Morgund led them ever deeper into this kingdom of leaf and root, light vanished from the sky, darkening even further when the sun dropped low on the horizon. With the light dim, they camped in this world of twisted limbs and lichened branches. Though a clear night not a single star could be seen through the verdant canopy. Laying back gazing into the fire considering what was happening at Skelbo castle, Morgund deemed it unlikely that the Morays would mount a pursuit. By Morgund's reckoning they would be immersed in determining the castle's wealth. Nevertheless, he left two men behind to watch the castle to let him know if he was pursued. By Morgund's reckoning if the Morays had wished him dead they would have come for him before his mother's death when there was an obligation to remain and fight to protect her. His defeat would have been inevitable, given the Moray's superiority in men as well as in arms. These Morays, it seemed, possessed compassion to go with their acquisitiveness. When the spider webs of sunlight came through the branches overhead the scouts found him and relayed that the Morays sought property, not Morgund's life. Thus, with the urgency taken out of the departure the pace slowed and great frolics were had by the children as they travelled further. When the dark of night came upon them again by the firelight they felt as one community. With the first pale blue in the sky of a new day and with the dense forest left behind them, Morgund swung wide of the column and took to the deep thick of the ferns that proliferated on these well-watered slopes to relieve the pressure on his bowels. The sounds of travelling soon were swallowed up by the wind in the trees and bird song. Just as Morgund had finished evicting from his bowels that which had stood in his stomach, there was a noise, a cracking of a twig. Four men were making stealthy movements towards him. They were now spreading out around him. They were Norseman by the look of them, big men, broad shouldered and lantern-jawed. Morgund heard the keen knell of swords being drawn from their scabbards. Their eyes lit with a greedy sheen as they gazed at his raiment and the ornate broach set in silver with gemstones pinned at his shoulder. His sword was obviously a thing of great value too, its scabbard inlaid with gemstones. He could feel their avarice. This was to his advantage - it could make them careless.

The rope dug into the flesh of Morgund's neck. At times his captors would cruelly tug the rope to unbalance him, or shove him roughly from behind to unbalance him. His hands tied tightly together, a stumble or fall brought him to the ground, at which his captors would haul him to his feet once more by the rope, leaving him gasping frantically for breath. After being harried in this fashion for some distance, Morgund heard a gruff voice calling from somewhere ahead. Through the thinning trees he heard other voices, and began to discern the outline of a wooden enclosure, an earthen elevation, a hillfort. He would have thought it a pleasant place should he not have a rope around his neck nor these merciless wolves either side of him. Closer still, Morgund saw a blond man watching him from the fortress walls. There was something profoundly unnerving about the fixed stare of this man. When the starring man lit up with amusement, an unspeakable evil lay in his sly grin – Morgund knew no good would come to any let alone himself from this one. His countenance was that of one with his wits dislodged. In the starrer's face there was some likeness to King John. Although Morgund had been treated well by John, that notorious king, was infamous in all Christendom for the harm he had done to others.

"Harold!" A retainer near the gates called to the blond man on the walls. Eager-faced, and red with excitement, he beset the blond man with unseemly loudness, asking if he saw the advancing party. Harold's teeth gritted tight shut in rage. "How can I fail to see that standing as I am on the battlements? Do you think me a fool Oswald? Or blind?" Harold was one step away from slitting Oswald's throat open for his stupidity and impertinence. Harold's worst fear would be to be spend an eternity in hell listening to the grating over-excited voice that berated him now. "I thought you fool enough without you proclaiming yourself the idiot of this hillfort."

The rage in the shouted voice did not bode well for Oswald, nor Morgund who was soon to be confronted with the shocking reality of what had taken place here. When the rising sun illuminated the shadows, he saw unspeakable evil. Heads stuck on the stakes protruding from the wooden gates glared at Morgund as he walked past them. The eyes - he tried not to look at them – belonged to two small boys not long dead. Their mother's head was likewise impaled, lifeless eyes half lidded and silent mouth agape. These slain innocents never lacked attendants. An unkindness of ravens, disturbed from their feeding, erupted past Morgund before taking positions either side of him, as if to contemplate how long before they would feast on his flesh. Never had these birds looked so dastardly the obsidian orbs of their eyes so soulless and vacant. Morgund finally got by them and stepped inside the double gates of the fort to find the blond man who reminded him of King John standing right in front of him. Morgund waited for the red large eyes to do something other than stare - for the man to say something.

Finally, he did. "Who are you M'Lord?" Evidently, something about Morgund spoke of gentle birth - thus the "M'Lord."

To Morgund, it felt like he was looking into the eyes of a devil. Ignoring this impious glare, he answered the question. "Not long since I called Skelbo castle home. Now home is any place where I can rest my head is."

"Obviously thou art of privileged stock. The sword my man Odor holds is of good quality. He had it from thee?"

Morgund nodded. Wealth, perceived or actual, counted for something or else he would be slain already. Those beady eyes continued to stare as if he would see into Morgund's brain. Morgund awaited Harold's considerations as all did wait for him to determine his course of action.

Odor brought forth the sword. Harold's musings departed from Morgund and he gave this magnificent weapon his full attention. His eyes fell from the blade and onto Morgund with a mad glint. Morgund could tell that Harold was tempted to sever his head just to test the sharpness of the blade. Morgund would be dead like so many others in the recent past, his head joining the others outside, just another piece of carrion for the ravens to feast on. Harold's eyes went down again preoccupied with the sword - its fine workmanship, excellent balance, the silver filigree on the pommel - which kept Morgund alive for the moment.

After what seemed like an age, Harold finally spoke. "This is good steel. How came thee to own a sword like this? There would be very few like it in the whole the kingdom of Scotland."

"It was given me by King John of England." Every time Morgund told someone this it led to a wealth of questions. This occasion was no different.

Genuine amazement appeared on Harold's face. "King John of England! To know a king and King John of all kings. Why did he give you this sword?" Harold lowered the sword and his eyes met Morgund's once more

"We were friends." Morgund could not help but notice how much this very strange fellow appreciated this. Morgund could feel his admiration.

A rare relaxed smile rose on Harold's lips. "What do they name thee?"

"Morgund," he answered.

"Morgund ..." Harold repeated it to himself as if the name contained a hidden meaning.

Harold directed Morgund to Oswald. "Take him inside Oswald. Wash him, get him into clothing suitable for a man of his rank. Get food inside him. Go to it!"

For Morgund who only a few moments before expected to feel a sword on his neck it was a dramatic turn of events.

Not long after striding into the hall came Harold. All servants were then smart about their business. They scurried here and there and before long the smell of roasting meat wafted on the air. The lord of the hillfort, Harold, announced the coming feast to honor Odar who had brought such a significant hostage.

When the feast was in full swing, Harold stood, cup held high. "To Odar who has brought such a valuable captive. To one and all, we will have a breakfast to honor our returned heroes. To Odar and his men!"

Harold spoke quietly to Odar. "You lost a man; Guthred is missing?" Harold had noticed earlier but had never liked the man.

He only asked because it was expected of him.

Odar spoke of it thus: "Guthred of the scowling face was killed by Morgund."

"Never mind, you have done well. Go feast with the others." Well pleased with playing the noble host, Harold looked around to see how many men responded to his graciousness; he was more than a little disappointed when he observed that not of them one took any notice of him. Harold's eyes darkened. The affable host withdrew replaced by a brooding tyrant. Certainly, the light left his eyes and the genuineness of his smile evaporated. Those glaring blood-red eyes of his boded ill for any man who drew his enmity upon them. Harold had his eyes on Morgund. Disconcerting to have someone staring at you; to be stared at by Harold was extremely unnerving. Morgund turned his head away from those burning eyes. When he cast his gaze back Harold's seat was empty. Morgund felt an immediate sense of danger and braced himself to feel a sharp blade on his neck. A shiver went up his spine, a sense of dread that Harold was standing behind him with a drawn sword. He only relaxed when he saw Harold was on the far side of the hall.

Although he was safe from Harold for the moment Morgund was quite near other dangerous, drunken and loud men. That his life was in the hands of such scum filled him with abhorrence. Nor was it only Morgund who was at risk. All over the room, women and girls were being taken, some with more than one man upon them.

As if the wanton rape was not wicked enough a Norseman stabbed a Celtic boy to death. Harold gave the murderer his approval with a raised cup satisfied with the notion that his men were like him, without pity, killers all. Although Harold liked the sight of blood indeed would have more of it spilt than wine, there was another reason Harold did not act. To confront the murderer would be to put him at risk, for surely the murderer had sword-brothers. Sword-brothers defended each other to the death. Harold knew if he accosted the man who struck the fatal blow it could cause a spark that could burn his house down.

Some of Harold's men were having doubts about these foul deeds - the murder but being the last and greatest of the crimes. They would kill in battle, not kill innocent children, not those who just happened to be in their power. This was not the Viking way.

Battle deaths, yes, all men respected that. Such acts as were committed here spoke of wanton wickedness. Morgund noticed a knot of men warily watching the rapists give full reign to their low pleasures with the same degree of disgust that he felt. And then he noticed a new man fight his way to Harold's side. "Lord, your sister, the Lady Gudred is at the gates with twenty men."

Harold exploded from his seat, far from pleased. "How dare she attend on me without warning!" he roared, his outrage audible over the clamor of the hall.

Harold regarded Gudred as his father's favorite, a haughty girl who in her twentieth year should have been long married. That she was not Harold could readily understand, given her viper-tongue. Many times she had used it on him.

Harold, curtly gave an order that the twist of bodies in the hall be ceased and the dead boy's body hidden. Gudred would see all this as a deplorable breach of behavior and it would bring forth a torrent of disdain. He despaired at hearing it. Deciding to find something much finer to wear taking himself to his quarters. He wanted to present himself as someone made good. In his room, he put a comb though his hair, donned a fine tunic, then put on a heavy fur cloak and buckled a sword to his waist. To look the part was very important given he would soon face his sister's disapproving eye. Why was Gudred here? The question beset him with anxiety. Gudred thought she could walk right in and take over. These thoughts resonated in his mind: *"No need for Gudred to grapple over fortress walls. If you were Gudred, you just walked right in and took over."* The most galling part about his sister was that she wielded a sword like a man, and like a man well trained.

All too soon Gudred was in the room with a familiar look of censure on her. "What evil did those boys do that their heads are affixed next to the gate, innocent of any crime, yet murdered. That their mother is there with them is beyond belief. Murdering a woman and two small boys how brave thou art Harold.

Her accusing eyes brought forth this from him, "Conquest is not simply walking in and taking over as you seem to see fit to do." He knew he sounded meek and submissive thus promised himself that never again would he be at the mercy of her accusations.

She ignored what he had said instead asking of him, "And once the killing is done, is it any way to behave putting your men like wolves upon those poor women and girls? No honest man would condone the like. A terrible man you are Harold. The children had to die so thee could claim this place, but then, to do the like of that which is happening tonight. No good can come of it. Has thee no pity, no decency? I am a fool to even ask it of thee."

He gave no answer. Harold had allowed his sister to overbear him yet again which exasperated him. Finally, he found the will to respond. "What goes on here is my concern alone. Partake of some sustenance and then take yourself back to my father. Wish him well for me."

Rather than see the sense in this she raged still more against her brother, "I see thee has no sense, as has always been the case with thee Harold." Gudred loved her brother and knew he also loved her but harsh words had to be spoken. "Listen to me brother, the mantle of leadership is beyond thee."

Harold had heard this many times before and it infuriated him to the point that he reached for the hilt of his sword. His anger was such he found a rebuke of his own. "Is it that thee is the only one with a sound head? The rest of us are mere plodders and droolers?"

Gudred felt like grabbing him and shaking him. "What you do here, others can do to you. You came in with twenty men, twenty men cannot hold this place."

"Twenty men it took to take it and twenty men can hold it."

"Twenty men!" She laughed. "What kind of fool are you?"

Being older than Harold, Gudred was not willing to surrender her control. Harold was equally adamant that this was his time and Gudred could be damned for her lack of faith in him.

"You know what kind of fool I am, as do all who listen to you - for you are forever telling them."

She was relentless, "Harold, let this foolishness end."

"I knew I could rely on you to call me witless, but father must see that I have made good here."

"He sees you for what you are, a fool. He sent me here to take you home."

He looked at her joylessly. "Go, please, or risk my displeasure. I am a lord here now and must be treated as such."

"Little brother," she replied in a softer tone, "see reason. Put this behind thee. Stop it. It is part of youth to act without manly consideration as thee has done."

"No!"

"Harold thee is not made to lead. End it."

When Harold heard, "End it," it was Gudred herself he thought of ending. As never before Harold hated her. He was not going to let her win even if he had to slay her. Harold's eyes bored into hers. "The only foolishness is thine own."

"My foolishness is the patience I have for thee."

Gudred used that infuriating smirk he knew – and loathed - so well. His patience was at an end. He felt the blood rushing to his cheeks. He was lord here and she was scolding him as if nothing had changed, as if he was still a skinny whelp under the authority of women. It galled him that she had such insolence.

Dangerously enraged now Harold frightened Gudred. She saw his hand flexing on his sword. "Harold, calm thyself." Gudred felt herself swallow hard. "I am sorry, perhaps that was wrong of me to scold thee so."

"Too late for sorry now," he sputtered out.

She brought twenty men but had entered his room alone. Now she wished she had not. It was time to go.

As if he could read her mind, Harold said, "You can turn around and leave, but your twenty men stay with me. As you know only too well, twenty men are not enough to hold this place."

Unwisely more anger of her own. "How dare you think to take my men from me, to send me home unguarded. Father commanded me to take you from this place where all that awaits you is misfortune."

"No!"

Gudred had heard enough. Momentarily, she forgot herself. "It is the sensible course as a sensible man would know. That thee knows not fails to surprise me."

He took a step toward her. Came right up to her face, and hissed through gritted teeth, "Go. Or stay here and never leave."

Gudred turned on her heels. Out in the hall Gudred was ignoring Harold's direction to leave immediately. When Harold came upon her she was ordering all the other Vikings to leave with her. This level of audacity prompted Harold to make the greatest, and final, mistake of his life, drew his sword on Gudred.

Gudred sensed immediately the outcome. "Harold, put thy sword away!"

Swords were on all sides of Harold. When he took a step towards Gudred, his sword pointing outwards, it prompted his own death. Perhaps he only wanted to say something to her. Gudred's bodyguard could not risk that. Their swords were sharp enough to slice through skin, flesh, and muscle and in one quick stroke and that's what they did. Harold considered that Gudred had an acid tongue, she did, yet his own had made him many enemies which contributed to the gruesome manner of his death.

When the swords fell on Harold, Gudred came to his side to protect him to put herself between the swords and Harold in an attempt to have her men stay their hand. For all her censure of him Harold was her brother and she loved him. But before Ingvar could stop it, his heavy greatsword fell on Gudred and drew forth bright red-ruby blood from her mouth. As she breathed more bright red left her. A fearful high sigh emerged from Gudred's throat, it was the sound of death; then it stopped, and that was more terrible still. The specter of death, that unwanted guest, seemed to have ridden through the gates with Gudred and her men. Many looked around warily, wondering how such a bad thing had come to be. Come night, the Vikings had long gone and taken the bodies of Harold and Gudred with them. They left as quickly as they could for it was obvious after the deaths of Harold and Gudred in such bizarre circumstances that this was a place of demons. The Vikings gone, Morgund saw that all looked to him to guide them. He posted sentinels and before long shapes began to emerge half-seen from the open places beyond the fort. As they came closer Morgund saw it was Seward leading those who had come with him from Skelbo castle.

Once inside, Seward appreciated the quality of the place. "A worthy fortress. And it seems to have a new lord."

"Indeed it does." Morgund's smile was wide. Rather than as the Vikings did, see this as a place of demons he considered it a place of good luck for had it not come into his possession with him not even drawing his sword.

The weeks following the taking of the hillfort saw an influx of newcomers; many were those who had been fortunate enough to be outside the walls when the hillfort was taken, or swift enough to flee. Likewise, a small contingent of families from Skelbo had sought Morgund out, and others still were attracted by his leadership.

Amongst those who came, came a man with nothing to recommend him but the readiness of his tongue. When the interview took place others stood near taking it all in. The new man before them claimed to have known Morgund of old.

Watching with amazement Morgund saw Gregor, for that was this man's name, turn away and say to the others in the room, "I knew him when it seemed he would never learn how to use a sword let alone be one of the greatest swordsman in the land. After all, he was small, inconsequential, unlike so many of the MacAedh's, who were large, soldierly, and proud men if not remarkable for their intelligence. In adulthood Morgund proved to be greater than those before him of his name."

"A flatterer this one. Watch him." It was Seward who made the warning.

True, Gregor had the gift of oratory, Morgund acknowledged that but also that talk meant little.

How is it then I remember thee not?" Morgund asked him.

"Know this ..." Gregor paused as if thinking how best to answer this, before continuing, "Servants are invisible to the great ones. Ask any lowly maid, not a pretty one, a lord takes more notice of a gnat that buzzes than he or she who fills his cup."

"Why has thou sought me out now?" Morgund pressed.

"You are the last MacAedh. The last hope for the Celts. Those of the ancient race no longer have a say in this land now. The most senior and favored at Alexander's court, MacCainstacairt, flies in the face of his people, aping the manners of the Southrons, speaking English and wearing English garb, with no respect for where he came from. Now that thee is thine own ruler I came. Before, I would not, so as to not risk your dear mother. No action towards Alexander could thee make then as it could endanger her."

Morgund drilled his eyes into Gregor. "Little of that made sense to me. How would you serve me that I would like to know? Men who eat here must have a purpose."

Gregor held Morgund's hard gaze. "A loyal servant stands by, offering his protection, as I can."

"I am not at risk. And if I am, others, men-at-arms protect me. It is obvious that you art not a swordsman."

"As you say I am no swordsman yet I would offer you protection. I am of ample wits. With them I can aid you."

"You could probably talk an enemy to death. For the moment I seek no one with that particular ability."

"I am a great reciter, a teller of tales that is true. A bard. One of the greatest in Scotland. All great men need a bard to tell of their deeds, furthermore, on winter's nights to entertain them and their clansmen."

Morgund looked down at him full of discontent. "I find it strange I do not remember thee."

Gregor had nothing to say to that.

"How is it I remember thee not?" Morgund demanded.

"A mere boy you were, with other things to mind, I, a mere servant, was beneath notice."

"I knew most of them."

"I was not notable, not a swordsman, not the kind boys notice. Humble servants who do their job are not noticed. That is the way it is supposed to be. I was good at what I did so was not seen."

"Was it that thee was one of those loyal servants who planned my father's murder? Or left him to die when he needed good men to stand by his side?"

"Kenneth, Earl of Ross, your father was betrayed, on every side of him were conspirators, who advised him to ride to attend the king's summons. Part way there, the enemy fell on him in ambush. Most men in his company with him turned on him ending his life and putting the lie to it that they were ever loyal men. I am no swordsman as you have said, and I know better than to advise an earl. Yet I did, and if he had listened to me he may have lived."

A bitter smile appeared at the corner of Morgund's mouth. "Could it be that thee did not serve him at all?"

"I came to serve I can just as easily not." Gregor's eyes were dark and lively. An aggrieved man unused to such words as he had been given his next sentence reflected this. "None could prosper in your cause but I did not seek to prosper just to protect you."

Morgund called up two men known from that time. He discussed with them in a whisper the truth of Gregor's assertion. Morgund looked Gregor up and down as they whispered until finally he said, "These men do not remember you from Ross."

Gregor came closer and extended his hand to Morgund. Gregor's eyes were reflective of a past that deeply burdened his soul. "I loved Kenneth, but I nor none other could have saved him."

Tears trickled down Gregor's face as Morgund's felt his own tears fall, surprised at how moved he was by Gregor's assertion. Morgund remembered his father's murder and how traumatic it was. Morgund's mind was on the past but he regained his composure. "Serve me well Gregor as thee served my father well." There was quiet in the hall as the deeply meaningful moment held on and on between these two. Morgund finally smiled at Gregor. "Why such sorrow? We celebrate the coming of a friend."

Gregor his own voice rang out. "My kin serving your family for over a hundred years. Memory runs deep, and in my heart, I must honor the MacAedhs. As descendants of kings I can do less?"

That was met with loud applause.

Morgund was on a dark a spiral staircase where he had to feel his way with the knuckles of his sword hand, listening to his labored breathing, his gaze fixed up to the steps that led higher. He went, one step, then on to the next, with treacherous stone beneath his feet. Beyond his own human sounds the wind whistled over the parapets indicating he was nearing the top and the open air. Above, would be the watch-tower, below which the lord normally had his quarters. After three more steps he could see light bleeding down from a narrow gap in the stonework above, a fine mist descending with it. All was very damp. Completely alone,

Morgund stopped for the first time that night, pausing, wondering at the strange circumstances that brought him here. Preoccupied with all that had happened and how all this had come to be, after some consideration deciding it was largely Gregor's doing. Trusting that man perhaps more than he should have. All had happened so quickly that he scarcely remembered how it did. Gregor was the catalyst. That overly wise man predicted young men looking for adventure would come and they had. According to Gregor, if nothing stirring came these new men would go elsewhere to find the adventure they sought. Gregor's opinion was held to be worth something by most in the hillfort. That man, he had a knack for getting others to nod their heads to what he said thus when he had suggested this wild adventure many agreed with him. Those who had suffered under Vikings thirsted for revenge and Morgund had to admit they were close by these Vikings therefore, could not be left to repeat which had lately gone on.

Morgund was nearly at the top of this flight of stairs. It was a good place to have archers waiting ready to shoot whoever came up them. In this case, himself. Showing caution he listened. Nothing. Just the blowing wind and rain. The rain was coming down though the arrow slits. It suddenly occurred to him that he could easily die here like so many others had this very night. Eighteen men came over the walls with him. Gregor of the big mouth stayed behind, stating long and loudly, like he always did almost everything that he would love to be up front sharing the dangers but was physically not up to it. Lamenting the fact long and loudly that they would have to do without him. A worthless statement, all knew he was no good with a sword. Morgund doubted whether he had even held one. His heart raced in anger at the man who by virtue of his tongue had put him here.

Morgund remembered earlier in the night, in the moonless absolute dark they had crept close to the castle walls, some stumbling. Which surely should have alerted the sentries however no alarm was raised. Ladders cut from pines to hand. All of them wreathed in mud to darken their faces to avoid detection as were the ladders also, darkened. After midnight they took themselves up to and then climbed the fortress walls. At the top they peered over the stonework. All was quiet. Once within the castle the alarm was raised and a hot fight took place in which four of Morgund's men were slain. In a lower hall Morgund put his sword on a man's throat, demanding the whereabouts of the castle's lord. The man assailed pointed to the stairs. On the stairs Morgund found the light from the floor below soon disappeared and he found himself in almost complete darkness and alone. When the sounds of the fighting faded and as he climbed the only noise he heard was his own heavy breathing, and his feet moving on the stone steps. At the top of the stairs there was a landing, then, a turn, then more steps leading higher, no doubt which led to the top tower. When Morgund came to the foremost highest room in the castle he found a heavy oak door. It was locked. This room situated where it was surely it was the chamber of the lord? Morgund pondered whether he could call on whoever was inside to surrender to him? A second notion, not so reassuring, came. If whoever was inside came out immediately it would be obvious that he was without supporters withal they would surely attack and overpower him. Most likely there would be a several men-at-arms inside. Perhaps he should wait for others to come up. He thought of another possibility, if the battle was lost downstairs when they came up it might not be his friends who came but his enemies. If enemies appeared he would be trapped and death would be certain. Confounded by what to do he did nothing for the moment. There was a noise, something was happening inside the room, someone was unlocking the door. It seemed that fate was on his side because now he could surprise whoever came out the door. Just as he thought this the door slid open. A boy of seven or eight poked his head out, and as he did, Morgund grabbed him. A sword that was too big for the child dropped to the floor.

    A female voice came from inside. "Pender, I told you not to open the door."

    Wriggling in Morgund's arms the boy shouted. "Mother, I but wanted to see what was going on. A man has me and he is big."

    The woman who appeared at the door seemed amused when she saw how the man who had her son looked at her. Her thick blond hair, twisted in the latest fashion, her becoming gown, all drew Morgund's admiration.

    The woman gazed back at him with as much interest as he did her, "Who are you?" came from her lovely lips.

    The boy did not give Morgund a chance to reply. "Let go of me you oaf. Wait till I get my sword back and I will deal with you. I dropped it by mistake. I am not clumsy. That wasn't fair of you

to surprise me like that. Give me my sword back you!"
As Morgund had hoped the mother spoke up. "Pender, shoosh. The grown-ups are talking."
Her delectable attention was back on Morgund. From those pretty lips came, "Does thee have a name?"
Before Morgund could answer he had his hands full with the boy again. Pender, scowling at Morgund was trying to kick him. The mother took a step closer and he put his eyes back on her. This was not a time for this. Despite her attractiveness Morgund decided he could not get distracted, experience had shown him a safe situation could change in an instant. Often, he had heard of woman manipulating men to their deaths and he did not want it to happen to him.
From her sweet, rose-red, lips came, "Your name sir?"
"Morgund, my name is Morgund." His tone became stern, "Now keeper of this castle. Where is thy lord?"
Interjected Pender, "Let me go or I'll kick you!"
Ignoring the boy continuing talking to the mother, "What of the elder Harold?" Morgund knew something of the power structure of the castle. He knew a man named Harold, the father of he who had taken the hillfort held sway here.
"A very dignified man dead this past week. Pender is his sole heir. Pender is my son. Pender's half-brother, Harold, named after his father, and Gudred, his half-sister are dead." Silence hung heavy in the air thereafter. Some moments passed before she spoke again. When she did it was to say this, "Are all our men slain?"
"Most of them. Some will lay down their arms."
She nodded, looked down, then looked back up, a glint of white teeth when she looked up. "What do you intend to do with us?" With slight flirtatiousness came her next question, "…with me?"
Morgund could not help himself dropped his guard for a moment and thought of something he would like to do to her. It showed on his face and she picked up on it and smiled. He noticed what a wonderful smile she had. Was not expecting her to smile at him like that, obviously, if the boy was not here the bed which was just inside the door would have them both on it and they would be engaged in nothing so formal as what currently transpired.
"What are you thinking?" Charmingly she asked it. Letting

him know what she was thinking.

Morgund just wanted to get closer to her. "I may have to search you for a hidden weapon. It could well be so well hidden that an extensive search is required."

His penis was pressing against his tunic in a blatant manner, and her eyes were down at it with considerable interest. With her eyes still on it she said, "The search better be done privately." Proving what a flirt she was, "If a search is required I would not deny thee the right to conduct it. And as we know weapons may be hidden anywhere."

Morgund was more than impressed with this woman; he could not take his eyes off her. So pretty was she that he was tempted to tease her just to tempt delight out of her. She had that expression that indicated she wanted happiness to engulf her. He had to search his mind to think of another woman as near as fair. Her blondness was as dazzling as sunlight.

Pender was smiling at Morgund having noticed his demeanor when Morgund gazed at his mother. The boy said with a smile, "So you like my mother?"

Morgund wondered why this boy was not afraid of him. For a moment the howling wind above him sighed and groaned reminding Morgund that danger was near and blood had been shed here tonight and more still could be shed at any moment. Eyeing the sword on the floor he realized that comfort and merriment could turn deadly if other men ascended the stairs. Not only Morgund eyed the sword, Pender almost upended himself suddenly trying to get his hands on it.

"I want my sword back!"

Morgund gripped Pender more tightly. If Pender got his hands on the sword anything could happen. At any moment armed enemies could appear then this amicable, comic thing going on could become deadly. Two cuffs to the head shut the boy up. His mother looked slightly shocked.

"He is a handful," Morgund explained apologetically.

Pender sulking, shot back, "Your sword isn't even bloody. What have you done with it, nothing!"

Morgund dangled the boy towards the sword he held in his hand. "No it isn't bloody. How can I rectify that?" Morgund jabbed it at the boy.

A smirk appeared again on Pender's face. "I know give it to

me, and I'll redden it on thee. I'll run you through with your own steel." The child's merriment ran high at this.

Morgund could not hold back his own laughter.

"Not game to fight me that is the truth of it," said the boy.

This caused more laughter in Morgund.

He turned to the mother. "Can he even use the sword?"

"He practices all the time if that counts for anything," she replied

"How dare you ask if I can use my sword, give me it back and find out for yourself. You would not have taken this castle if my sister Gudred was still alive. Those men took notice of her." His voice almost broke, tears were not far away. "They took no notice of me nor mother. They liked us not. But what Gudred told them to do, they did." In a whisper, almost crying. "Until Harold, my brother, killed her. I'm sure he did it, he would commit any crime." Loud sniffles followed that.

Morgund looked at the child smiling. "They liked you not I find that hard to believe."

The regret in the boy's eyes when he said, "I was their lord they should of heeded me," was heart-breaking.

Morgund felt sorry for the boy, thus, said, "They should of heeded you I agree."

The boy looked at him with downcast eyes. "I thought so too."

Morgund asked him, "Do you want your sword back?" The boy nodded that he did. "Surrender to me and I will treat you and your mother as captives and swear to your safety."

"Give me my sword back and I'll consider it."

"Surrender to me child."

"No!" The cheeky imp barked. "And, if I don't surrender, you won't kill me I can see that. And … I can see that you like my mother too."

Morgund gazed at the boy whilst remembering his own past. "When I was your age a bad man tried to cut my head off, he did not care how young I was, nor, that I had a fair mother."

"A pity that he did not, then you wouldn't be here now and I'd still have my sword."

Morgund looked with exasperation at the boy then at the boy's mother. "My lady, surrender to me. Thee, and thy son will be safe. I give you my word on it."

Her reply, "I submit. Pender, I speak for thee too."
Pender looked at his mother and finally nodded in resignation.

Thus, the castle was Morgund's. The castle's stocks of food and ale he made good use of sending messages out that whosoever came to take his food and drink could see what kind of man he was, swear an oath to him, if they saw fit. No harm done if they did not. They could eat and drink what they wanted and depart safely maintaining their independence if they chose. Many responded, some acknowledging Morgund's overlordship.

Less than a week later Morgund marched off together with Pender and his mother. Paten with a small force remained behind to hold the castle. Morgund's two most precious captives Pender and his mother Frida departed with him in good spirits. On the way Pender galloped ahead pursuing imaginary enemies, these imaginary enemies being Scotsman. Pender, killing Scotsman right and left. Not only was he surrounded by Scotsman, he was going to where there were still more of them. Morgund doubted Pender's antics went over well with his travelling companions. Deciding he was not going to put up with it, Morgund, rode to the boy and pulled him close. "Pender, can you refrain from killing Scotsmen. Scotsmen are on every side of you."

"Who am I to kill then?" Pender demanded, defiantly.

Morgund eyed him steadily. "Englishman."

Englishmen now became the victims of Pender's lethal swordplay. Morgund decided earlier before he left the castle that the best way to secure his new possession was to marry Frida. He caught her eye, and when he did, her face lit up with delight. It would not be a bad thing to marry her, she was very fair.

Whilst they were riding, Pender appeared out of nowhere, now at Morgund's side, seemingly erupting from the very earth, whereupon, suddenly he asked Morgund, "Did you kill Harold my brother?"

Morgund faced Pender's stare. "Not I. But his viciousness caused him to die, but not by my hand, he died by the hand of others."

Pender thought about this for a second or two whereafter he replied, "He deserved it I am sure of that." Then he rode off again. Sometime later Pender was back, "I miss her sometimes."

Morgund took it that he was talking about his dead sister,

Gudred. Morgund expected to be asked about her death. Though, whether, she was murdered or it was an accident Morgund could not say. The boy did not ask.

A knowing smirk appeared on Pender's face. "My mother thinks you are very handsome."

Morgund was finding he liked Pender more and more, thought, it was impossible not to like him.

Pender, who was still there, looking at Morgund still smiling, he could obviously read Morgund's expression. "I like you too. We both like you. One day I will be your most stalwart retainer. I will kill many Englishmen with you" As soon as Pender said this he was off again.

When they rode on it could have been the heat of the sun, perhaps the autumn colours all around him that made Morgund's mind fill with happiness. It could have been the contentment he felt being in the company of such a fine woman who obviously found him as attractive as he did her. In the belief that he was alone with his thoughts, with his happiness, thinking that Frida travelled in a cart to escape the heat of the day he sang a song he knew of old. "I picked you flowers, wild roses, buttercups, blue bells, red valerian. I made you garlands of yellow dandelions."

Frida had decided to ride with Morgund for a while and without him knowing it was just behind him. To Frida it was obvious he sang to someone else, a past love. She said from behind him surprising him, "That song Morgund, you were thoughtful when you sung it, does it remind you of someone?"

Morgund knew there was the danger in the question. He dealt with it as cleverly as he could. "My dear it is a day of happiness and beauty. I sing because of the joy you give me."

Frida smiled sweetly. "It is a lovely song I have never heard it before. Where did you learn it?"

"My sweet mother sang it to me when she took me to the wildflowers when I was a boy."

Frida was under no illusion; she knew Morgund wanted her for herself, but also recognized that he would seek to put a ring on her finger because of the Viking castle. By marrying her it confirmed the legality of his new possession. That he would marry her was no bad thing, a woman needed a husband, furthermore, she could do a lot worse than this handsome man. Her last husband the elder Harold was a good man but despite his admirable qualities and there were many of them he could not satisfy the urges that came to her when the darkness was all around her. When the men in the castle spoke of taking her in all manner of ways it made her heart race with excitement. Each time she put Morgund to mind she felt a tingle of sexual charge in her loins. When she thought of what they might do together there was no shame because soon he would take her for his bride. When he rode ahead to see the scouts Frida allowed herself a sinful grin imagining Morgund thrusting into her. The thought of how good it would feel showed on her face which drew others attention which reddened her face with embarrassment.

For a time Morgund rode just to be free from Frida. As lovely as she was he was a man long used to his own company with a need to enjoy solitariness. In amid the visions of earthly splendor, an English girl, Mirium, who once held a place in his heart filled his mind. Edith, who was his first love, she too made an appearance. Finally when his visions for those he had loved in the past fell from him his mind turned to Frida. She matched them all in attractiveness, surpassed them even. However it was not only her looks which he liked, when he thought of her her inner goodness shone like a beacon. He remembered how her lips tilted fetchingly when she first put her alluring eyes upon him. Imagining, the golden patch that dwelt between her thighs he looked forward with pleasure to the sight of it and entering it. His cock quickened at the thought of filling her with his seed. Her fires, he would make them burn red-hot when he plunged into her.

As he thought about her, she rode up to his side. Pulling her hood away from her face, she spoke. It was not a contented, happy face that looked at him. "I heard you say Mirium."

He realized when he had been thinking he must have spoken out loud. She was behind him and had been listening. Mirium had his mind earlier but he was not going to tell her that. "Mirium? No."

Frida looked at him skeptically. "Earlier you said, Mirium? Who is she?"

It was silly to lie, he was not going to. "A witch who saved my life ... many years ago."

"A witch?" Frida held cold eyes on him. "It is great company you keep."

"A novice, very young. Sold to the coven by her mother." A shadow fell across Morgund's face. "Unspeakable practices took place with her."

Frida could not contain her curiosity. "She indulged in what kind of unspeakable practices? Did it require her surrendering to every conceivable urge?"

The undercurrent of humor was lost on Morgund. Mirium's suffering was not a thing he wanted humourised. "She suffered. She suffered greatly. I suffered terribly too until she set me free from the clutches of a high priestess of evil."

Frida gave him a questioning look.

Responding to that look, he said, "Mirium saved my life. I left her in England to return to my mother."

"Did you love her? This girl. This witch."

"Perhaps."

Frida was appalled at the suggestion that he might have. "Perhaps!"

"She loved me that I know."

Frida knew she did not want to hear another word about it. Her mouth twitched in anger. Morgund saw a glistening of tears in her eyes before she spurred her horse away.

"As you wish," he called after her, angry now himself.

From further away she looked back at him wishing she was still at his side. Regretting her jealousy, after all, it was a thing of the past this thing with the witch. How could she begrudge him a past love? Was she not married not so long ago. Frida wanted to return to his side but kept her distance. She was appalled that she had angered him.

With Pender out of the way being entertained by Morgund's men he took the opportunity to enter Frida's tent. There she was, on her furs looking up at him with open lust. Her skin was of a texture and firmness that spoke of an active life, of milk, and honey, days spent running in the sun. Her calves were like carved ivory as they poked out from her blanket. She turned side-on fetchingly letting the blanket slip slightly lower. Her back could not have been more perfect nor that which fell below it. Frida swept her hair back from her face as she turned shrugging off the blankets in the process revealing her full nakedness. Hearing him gasp in awe she giggled girlishly and delightfully. The blond hair evident on her head was but a wisp below and as golden as the sun. He had heard that often blonde locks below are darker than those above. In this case it was not true. Looking down at this lovely woman he knew he was going fill her to the brim with every inch of his manhood. As a bee goes to the honey he went and tasted that which rested between those incredible thighs glistening there. Her moisture tasted like dew on a leaf as he drank deep of it. The long muscles of her arms stretched out taut as he plumbed her depths with his tongue. When she exploded it made her spread her legs wider and as she lowered herself onto this agile instrument of pleasure, his tongue. Frida gasped and sighed. An almost cruel smile of expectation played across Morgund's face - now it was his turn. He stepped back, let his hose drop, to reveal his large quivering member. The look on his face said this was what she was going to get. Seeing its girth and length it made her all the more determined to accommodate it. She had to open her legs wider to do so. Laboring on top of her he rode her like stallion gone mad, a stallion in headlong gallop, a stallion at the peak of its powers. He fucked her half the night before exhausted he fell off her and slumbered by her side. In the morning he left her still asleep with his love bestowed within and without her. He was tempted to wake Frida and place himself inside her once more but unsure of how she would take him waking her, he left her be.

    Rainy skies, thus, by virtue of them Morgund who had been up almost all night slept most of the day. The next day after that brought many stoppages due to more bad weather. When they did move they travelled with the ever-present prospect of rain. When on their way again after a stoppage, Pender rode ahead to call out what lay over the next hill. Riding to the rear then telling them of what he had seen ahead. That he was a good rider was all too noticeable, on Morgund's mind if an older Pender had pointed a sword out at him as he tried to that night at the castle it would not be a thing for laughter. His mind shifting from Pender when he noticed Frida by his side. The jolting of the horse between her thighs brought a smile to her face. Such was the only pleasure she could gain for now but she looked forward to the night when

Morgund could come to her again. Returning her look of lustful anticipation, Morgund let her know he also looked forward to the acts that were to come. He would get her in such a state of wantonness that she would surrender to him in every conceivable way.

Pender, not accustomed to seeing such a dense stand of trees took off toward them with great excitement. As light sank down through the trunks Pender entered a world of dark majesty. Riding amidst these mighty boughs he lost track of time. As rain fell he brought his cloak closer to him. Suddenly what fell became steady and cold. It was almost completely dark in the woods now with the gloomy wet falling. Deciding he liked the soft clomp of his horse's hooves on the leafy soil as well as being in the dim light, these two things together, with dense packs of leaves carpeting the ground had him captive to their particular textures. Enjoying it all so much he rode further and further into the woods far further than he meant to. Splashing through a stream watching the sideways spillage of the water put Pender in mind of shards of breaking ice. As he rode further on into this packed green world it became denser still. He threaded his way through these dark green giants for no other reason than for the love of doing so. There were more and more trees. Attracted by the prospect of experiencing their beauty so he went onward into them when he should not have. Finally coming out of the forest he should of looked for the line of march however he did not. Catching sight of another patch of woodland, he galloped towards it heady with his power to go where he wished. Before he returned to the others he wanted to shoot a deer. To prove that he could. His father had not allowed him to go on the hunt, deeming it too dangerous, telling him that he would not be able to keep up with the men, which Pender knew was ridiculous, he could keep up, he could shoot an arrow as well as any man, enough to kill a beast, even a bear, if he saw one. Said that few if any bears survived in Scotland. Pender brought up on tales of Scandinavia where bears still roamed in numbers did not know this. Now there was no one to stop him not even that old man who failed to appreciate how gifted his son was. Unbeknownst to Pender a similar line of reasoning, to show his father that he had underestimated his son, had gotten his half-brother Harold into the trouble that led to his death. Harold and Pender defied the man who sired them for no other reason than that they could. Forever younger males have defied their elders, for as long they have suffered the consequences for doing so.

Galloping from the shadows into the open skies with the wet falling on him by virtue of the fact that no branches were above his head. Riding until he was shielded from the downpour by the green as before. Continued riding until the arching boughs above him thinned out again and he was instantly bathed in sunshine. Enjoying galloping in the light and shadows. It fascinated him this collision of forces. Then the hectic leaves were all around him once more, therefore, he needed care to ride forth. Heavy vines overwhelmed the timber they grew on. Went between mats of moss, rustled through leaves, skirted trunks, elbowed saplings. There were great boughs with great forks in them which pools of water collected in, spreading roots were everywhere. The hues of greens were numberless. On older trees huge lobes of fungi grew, some of striking colors. Then the trees began to have greater spaces between them. More often than not he saw the sky. When finally the trees thinned out entirely there was a smaller grove still further on, smaller, but no doubt hiding a stream, the willows in sight indicating as much. His horse no doubt was thirsty which was another reason to continue on and ride there. Riding against the wind which rippling through his hair, and snapping his cloak, he felt like a warrior of old on an important mission. On the bank of a new stream about to plunge into it and across it and towards the woodlands when Pender noticed the sun was low on the horizon. He felt an immediate sense of panic. Where had the time gone? Surely, he had not been gone that long. Deciding he must get back before someone wondered where he was he turned his horse around. Cursing himself for his stupidity, of course enough time had passed that trouble would definitely result from his absence, he was never unsighted by those around him for more than a short while so obviously a severe scolding would be coming his way. There would be all kinds of uproar at his disappearance. Anxiety, for the trouble he had caused for it was grave indeed.

As if things were not bad enough, now wolves. Had never even considered himself at risk from them, and here they were. One of them nipped at the rear fetlock of his mount, which made it throw him. When like a fool he had caught the mare he pulled too hard on the reins which made it jerk out of his grasp. Almost instantly the mare was out of his grasp and was away. As if losing his horse was not bad enough, the wolves circled him, slowly creeping in closer. His confidence was gone. Before he felt like a hero on a quest, now, he was no hero, just a boy all alone in the almost-dark, woods. Thank God he still had his bow and quiver of arrows. He raised his bow and a wolf went down howling with an arrow in it. The other wolves disappeared. Pender had made a bad decision riding far from his companions; he did not want to make another, so gave long consideration to his next move. He thought he could try to find the last stand of trees he was in. From there, from one landmark to another, he believed he could find his way back, or thought he had a good chance of doing so. That this was not going to happen became apparent soon enough. Alas, there were no trees in sight. His next idea to follow the horse's tracks was shown to be equally flawed when he came across two sets of tracks going off in opposite directions, one, where the horse was on the way in, the other after the wolves had attacked it, which were coming, and which going, was impossible to determine.

 Deciding to take a chance he followed one set of horse tracks - unfortunately they quickly petered out. Darkness would soon fall. The prospect of which brought forth dread. The boy acknowledged that to surrender to panic was to ensure oblivion. He had heard that when detached from one's friends in an unknown land it is best to start a fire. Someone would come to your rescue, drawn to your location by the smoke. With a flint it would have been possible. He did not have one so to think of a fire was pointless plus in the darkness no one would see the smoke. He walked to the nearest hill to see if he recognized something. Hungry and tired, and although he hated to admit it now terribly scared. From top of the hill there was nothing familiar. It was now noticeably darker and it was colder.

 Out of the darkness came a large silverish streak which reached down from the darkness and seemed to shake the ground itself. With that momentary light that came from the heavens he avoided walking right into a boulder directly in front of him. That the lightning struck when it did it saved him from colliding with this mass appearing out of the darkness. In one way at least, he was lucky, he felt. Used, the rains run-off from the boulder to refill his flask. Once refilled the flask went back onto his belt. He put his lips to the cascade tumbling from the large rock for the sheer pleasure of doing so. Even that moment of happiness was snatched from him when the howl of a wolf pierced the darkness. A momentary light revealing it. A little later, another sudden staggering crack that peeled away the dark for an instant to reveal another wolf. Growls, one to his right, one to his left. Two of them at least. There was just enough light to see a short distance ahead if he strained his eyes to see. After a brief period of walking he could not see at all because darkness was on every side of him.

There was a moment of hope when came to him the sound of rumbling water. Cautious steps took him closer to it. Another lightning flash accompanied by thunder. Light was on every side of him for a moment which revealed that which was to be seen. Over a precipice fell a thundering torrent, over and down, presenting itself to the heavens as it fell. Another flash of light. Thank God there was, for it illuminated a little below him a gash in the rock face. It was a perfect place to secrete himself and seek safety from these predators. So very dark he had to feel his way forward, carefully, torturously. Out of the rain finally tucked in into the cave he felt better than at any time since he realized he was lost. His sword, his bow and quiver were near to hand as he took his ease.

With the new day thinking to put the wolves off his scent he made his way down to the valley floor to the stream below. Amid the shallows a fish knifed through the water. A few moments later he hemmed it into the shallows and scooped it up. He cut of some fleshy pieces and ate them raw. It was a meal fit for a king, a pauper king, perhaps, a homeless king who had foolishly got himself lost occurred to him.

A brighter part of the sky gave him the position of the sun which he could use as a guide to his direction. The sun rose in the east set in the west thus it conveyed a general direction at all times except near the midday hours when it stood directly overhead. South, that was the direction he was heading in because Morgund's citadel was south. Rarely did he miss anything and he did not miss that was the direction they were heading in before he got lost.

Lost, a despicable condition to get oneself in, crossed his mind.

As he walked, Pender's thoughts turned to his mother, how much she would miss him. It was too distressing so he tried to focus instead on her loveliness. It was said of her, he had heard it said often, that she was as lovely as a day in spring. The men who said it respected her and liked her. Other men had lust in their eyes when they gazed at his mother, which Pender did not like and when they spoke of her it was in a way which horrified him and would have horrified his mother if she had heard them. She had heard and it didn't horrify her but Pender didn't know that. They spoke of ravishing her and doing things that were unspeakable. Gripping his sword tight he decided one day he would bring them to account for it. How dare they talk about his mother like that. How angry it made him. To bring them to account he must get out of here. There was no certainty of that, but he told himself if there was a way out he would find it.

A bit further along passing a small stunted tree he noticed a man in a black tunic, a smile playing across his face, such gleaming white teeth it made quite a contrast to the black hose, and black cape, all his clothing was black, even the horse he rode was black. It all seemed to suit the mien of the man, this darkness he wore and his choice of mount. Pender noticed some silver decorative stitching along his sleeves so all in fact all was not black. Soon the man was near, furthermore, eyeing him with an expression of malice. What green eyes the man had with the look of the devil in them. No friend was he. Pender's hand went to his sword and at that the man showed his pretty white teeth again. That angered Pender so he took his sword out of its scabbard, fully.

The man in black sneered. "Put the sword back lad. If thee knows what is good for thee, thee will put it back." Unlike when he was confronted with Morgund on the night the castle fell, Pender had a sense of his own death. It could be forthcoming given that he was a boy and the man in black, was a man. It was not reassuring.

"I can see thee is not artful with that sword."

The man was right, Pender was not so good with the sword he was a lot better with a bow so he took the bow to hand. Again, the man's white teeth were displayed. Everything Pender did seemed to amuse this man in black.

When nearer he came, Pender warned him, "Do not come any

closer!"

Having killed a wolf, to be honest he did not know if he had. He had not seen it die, but he certainly put an arrow into it. This fact heartened him, made him feel lethally accomplished with the bow. Full of determination to make an arrow sing and to kill a man, notching an arrow, Pender noticed the man's smile grow even wider. Any wider and he would aim for his damned teeth. It seemed the man in black's white teeth were his constant companion, so often were they on show. One move more towards Pender and the man in black would learn arrows are very lethal and boys can shoot them as well as an adult. Pender knew bows and arrows to be fatally efficient, knew that arrows once shot cared not from whose hand they flew from, just that they flew and if aimed true that they felled what they hit. It seemed this man must learn this simple fact by the most direct means.

"A boy playing at bows and arrows,"

"You may as well speak soon you will not be able to."

The man in black saw the boy hold the bow steadily, and that the boy's arrow was aimed directly at his heart. Pondering whether perhaps he should turn his mount and ride away. Then he thought it was just a boy. That brought the smile back. Recalling, who it was, that stood before him, he laughed.

Pender brought his own teeth forth and said, "Come forth and see how I play."

The man deemed this a very merry comment. He had in mind to do what they boy told him to and see how in fact this child did play and he almost rode forward. Rather than ride forward he erupted into laughter. He had a pleasant laugh, it softened his otherwise sinister aspect.

Pender said, "Well come on then. I dare you to? Do not let a mere boy stop you."

The man's merriment vanished. The devil glare was back. "I think I will."

"Come on then, take the bow off me show me and tell me what a silly boy I am."

"I will."

Pender smiled no longer. "Tell the devil when you meet him, for you surely will, that I have an arrow for his evil heart too."

The man in black's white teeth were to the fore again. This man must be very proud of them to offer them so readily. It was all a game to this man in black. This fellow did not see a killer, he saw a just boy. Boys did not show adults wisdom it was supposed to be the other way around nevertheless Pender decided to show this man the error of his ways. The first arrow hit him in the shoulder. Although the next arrow was aimed at his heart it missed him altogether. Pender drew back the bowstring once more. The man in black was pulling at the first arrow, seemingly shocked that it had hit him. Soon another came, the third, and sat beside the first. As he continued to pull at the first arrow attempting to turn and ride away, Pender ran up very close behind him and pulled his bowstring back with all his might. Finally, he loosed the fourth arrow. With it in his back the man in black with the very white wide smile smiled no more and never would he smile again. It was shame it was not an archery contest so he could win a prize because it was stuck deeply this arrow he let fly, exactly as he wanted. The pierced man toppled off his horse, dead. Riderless, off his horse galloped much to Pender's regret. That moment of disappointment done with Pender congratulated himself and could not help but display as much devilish amusement as the man in black had shown moments ago. Unknown to Pender his expression was much like the man who had worn the barbs had before he felt the sting of steel.

The man's sword felt good in Pender's hand. As luck would have it inside the dead man's cloak, in his pocket, was black bread. Some hard cheese to go with it. The day was getting better by the minute. After this Pender decided he would try to move while not being seen, before, to his mind anyone he should meet would be coming to his aid now he decided it would be better to hide and see if he recognized whoever was coming. As recent experience had just shown only too well there were men in the wilds who would do him harm.

In his mind as he walked that Morgund's keep would be on high commanding ground if such came into view he would take himself to the top of it to spy the land. There was such a landmark, this sighted, he walked to it.

Atop this wooded hill, mindlessly stepping forth a man called out to him, "Pender thee be?"

Instinctively Pender drew his sword. It was starting to feel good drawing his sword in earnest.

"I mean thee no harm boy."

"Who art thou?"

"Morgund's sworn man and looking for thee as are many others."

Relief washed over Pender as he sheathed his sword. There were many questions from Pender. After answering as best he could the man told him, "Come with me I will show you Morgund's hillfort."

Pender soon found himself in front a crowd inside with a fire blessing him with warmth. The tale deserved to be told to others, thus at Morgund's urging Pender recounted of it.

Pender showed the captured sword to the crowd as he said, "I have a new sword. One taken from a man who tried to kill me. That man who tried to kill me, he laughed at me." A grin came when Pender said, "That caused his death, him laughing at me. That was how I came by his sword." He held it up to show everyone. "He took me for a defenseless boy. In black, he was, as are all those who serve the devil. He was in like garb. This man who tried to kill me, he told me I was no swordsman and should try the bow. I thanked him for his advice which proved to be very good advice and so shot him through the heart with an arrow."

A hush fell around the room as was recounted the deadly duel, man verses boy, the man with close affinity with the devil that was made plain by his black clothing and air of evil. All were amazed that Pender had faced such a one and survived let alone that he had slain his assailant.

All held dark dread when he told them that he had dared the Devil's wrath. "I told the man in black, when you meet the Devil. You will, I told him. When you do tell that dark lord this. When I send you to hell tell him I have an arrow for his evil heart too. And that I am coming for him."

There was respect in their eyes when they looked at Pender. Much later they felt consternation at how such an unlikely event had occurred. It sobered them to think that a boy his age had killed a man. Pender saw how much respect it had gained him, it made him full of pride.

EDGAR

FRIDA WAS WAITING for spring. That was the season of love, the season of flowers, also, the time for Christian weddings. Often in the past before the victory of the white Jesus God over the old Norse gods weddings took place in winter. Offspring do better in the summer months was the prevailing wisdom. Such was the case with paganism, winter marriages, but with the coming of Christianity bride and groom wed after the spring thaw. In Rome where the custom originated, spring or winter, neither season had an impact on the survival of children, however, as this custom became integrated into the wider church the survival rate of children declined. Many places in Europe have very long very cold winters. It was an unforeseen unplanned outcome of embracing the Christian faith. Young couples just getting married were in favor of the new custom because spring after all is a romantic season where love blossoms, when flowers bloom. Europe is extremely lovely then. To many, to marry with the scent of blossom in the air is fitting for the most romantic event in their lives. Frida looked forward to her marriage because this time it was with a young man not an old one. Though the elder Harold was a good man, very unlike his son Harold, who he despaired of, Morgund set her heart racing. He was young and lively. Another fact which pleased Frida was Morgund's affection for her son Pender. Morgund cared for him deeply. She was very proud of Pender. That her son did not take after his cautious father - none would deem Pender cautious, nor was he like the younger Harold with his fits of anger, petty cruelty - was a great joy.

Pender was descended from Arnosson a valiant Viking warrior. Frida thought her son might be alike to him whose heroism still resonated in northern Scotland. In many ways, the ancestor was remade in the descendant for she could easily see Pender as a hero, like, Arnosson. Pender at eight, ate like a horse, seemingly was growing by the day. She had a feeling that Pender's name would be remembered by her people. His love of warfare, his swordsmanship, his natural athleticism, all indicators that he would be a great war leader. Morgund had agreed when they had discussed it. Morgund was wise about such things knowing much of the warrior law.

Frida was pulled from her musings about a spring wedding and what would become of her son by Gregor's booming tiresome voice. She liked it the least of all voices that she knew of. Frida tried to console herself with the fact that without him Morgund would never have taken the Viking castle and would not be now making her his wife. As she knew no good would have come to her and to Pender without a husband's protection, and amongst such men as were in the castle, rape was likely, poor Pender in all likelihood he would have been slain.

Gregor's words carried to her. "Ancient Egyptians once visited Scotland in the time when giants lived here. Hibernia our land was known as then. These Pharaohs departed seeking an easier land to live in, not one they had to share with giants. What happened to the giants no one knows but the stones they used to play games with are there to be seen by all, these stones they moved like chess pieces in an intricate pattern the meaning of which is now only known by a few old men in the outer isles, secretive men, who refuse to tell the meaning of it."

It occurred to Frida that Gregor was easier to bear in the warmer seasons when it was easy to walk outside and get away from him. Winter had her trapped in here with him. That voice seemed to dominate every conceivable corner of the room. Scotland's winter was a time of long nights beside the fire, of bards telling tales, recounting, the genealogies of great kings. Although she did not, others looked forward to winter nights and these long tales. For all his faults, he was one of Scotland's most eloquent reciters, knew a great deal of history and how to tell of it. One of his favorites themes was the death of Macbeth, undone by a wife who sought to rule despite her female status, thus, not ruling at all, for without Macbeth, the source of her power she was powerless. This queen who sought to rule in her own right was undone by her own ambition. Beware the canny wiles of women was the moral of this cautionary tale told by Gregor who she deemed no liker of woman. His opinion, and she had heard it many times before was that they were deceitful and full of guile, almost demonic in their power over men.

Said Gregor, "There did dwelleth in Scotland a king by name of ..."

"... Macbeth," many called back.

"No!" Gregor replied, "Edgar!"

Frida's ears picked up at that. This was a new story perhaps about an Englishman, Edgar after all was an English name.

Gregor picked up on Frida's interest. He had predicted that she would think this story was about an Englishman, thus, that it might appeal to her. In fact it was not about an Englishmen. He would not tell a story about an Englishman. They did not deserve his eloquence.

He told them all, "It is not as some would think that a man with a name Edgar was an Englishman. He was not an Englishman. A Scotsman was this Edgar. Edgar had an English mother, Queen Margaret, known as the Pearl of Scotland, famed for her charitable works. Although Edgar had an English name he was a Celt in his demeanor and allegiance. His father the slayer of Macbeth, king Malcolm, was no Celt at heart being so very enamored of the English that he took an English wife, implementing the style and language of the southerners to the consternation of those who celebrated Celtic ways. By taking an Anglo-Saxon head councilor, Dufford, he drove the country towards a southern style administration."

"Edgar, son of Malcolm, stood in complete contrast to his father. Stood by the old ways despite the wraith of his father as well as the wrath of the Normans. The Normans were newcomers to our land then. Despite this they were a great voice in the kingdom, then as now. The men who wore the tartan who came before the Normans who had served Scotland faithfully for hundreds of years found themselves relegated to lesser roles within the kingdom. Malcolm proclaimed that foreign kingdoms on the continent together with England provided a better example for governance than did our ancient Celtic society."

A quick pause whereafter, "Edgar succeeded his brother Edmund. Both given English names by their English mother, the saintly Margaret. Aedh was the only son of Malcolm and Margaret to have a Celtic name."

"King Edgar of Scotland was the last king of Scotland to be proud of his Celtic inheritance promoting Celtic lords to high office, and dressing often in Gaelic fashion. He spoke the Gaelic tongue. It has been on the downslide since. No other king after Edgar has spoken the Gaelic language and surrounded himself with tartaned men as he did."

Gregor gave a heavy sigh. "I speak not here tonight of the loss of power of the Celts in the land, a brutal reality we are all too familiar with, but the dreadful death that fell upon King Edgar at the hands of the Normans. King Edgar paid the price for defying the Normans and England's king."

"Edgar's younger brother Alexander would become the First, Alexander, to rule Scotland. Prior to his enthronement, Alexander decided for a time to inhabit the English court looking for useful allies there. Many Normans living in England came into the kingdom with him when he returned to Scotland. Needing these knights to help him take Scotland from his brother, and of course Edgar had no idea Alexander had any such intention."

"Alexander though a hardy warrior with a wife seemed not of a mind to put her with child. So enamored of beardless youths was he that he surrounded himself with them all day. They were on all sides of him, and he could not go anywhere but that one of them must be with him. At night too they shared close comfort but it is too foul a thing to speak of. Unlike Edgar, who liked woman and shared an uncommon bond of love with his wife, Margot, a girl celebrated for her outstanding loveliness, showing for her all manner of heartfelt fondness."

Gregor paused then as if his heart would break from sorrow. What had happened to this young and fair couple without doubt gave him great sadness. "This is a tale of murder, of the evil that can befall a man. And it is an account of the most terrible deed the Normans have committed in this land since first they stepped foot here."

Gregor let his words sink in, waited for the sense of expectancy to grow. When it felt very tense within the room and all were rigid with expectation, when the tension had reached a point of high excitement, when all eyes were on him with total rapt attention, Gregor spoke once more of this terrible crime that ended a king's reign. Uttered his words with great solemnity. "On the passing of Malcolm, king of Scots. That very same Malcolm Canmore, that slayer of Macbeth, after Canmore's passing ..." Briefly did he take them elsewhere in his discourse ... "He, Malcolm Canmore, as I have said often was the king who slayed a king to gain his crown, killing, Macbeth. As Macbeth had done before him killing a king to gain his crown, Duncan. When this slayer of Macbeth, Canmore, was dead great division arose within the kingdom as to the succession. Malcolm Canmore had earlier sons to women before he wed Margaret, the English princess who he wed before God, however, these earlier sons to other women their legitimacy was in question. Eventually Edgar assumed the crown after his elder brother Edmund son of Margaret died after ruling briefly. Edgar was the second son of Canmore by Margaret. In a very short space of time Scotland had had four kings, Malcolm Canmore, and his sons, successively, Edmund, Edgar and finally Alexander who had his crown handed to him by the Normans."

"Edgar, although he deserved better, like his brother Edmund, died young, however unlike his brother Edmund it was no natural death that overtook him."

Gregor with his head bowed low when he chronicled the doings of former times. "When William king of England claimed that Scotland's king Edgar owed him feudal service Edgar gave King William of England nothing but a polite refusal. Would have nothing of William as his superior. As he should."

"This infuriated the English king so much he demanded action from his secret supporter, Alexander. A brother should give his brother nothing but loyalty sadly Alexander gave his brother nothing of the kind. A born intriguer was Alexander and suited to acting the good friend when he all the time plotting Edgar's murder. Such an act was foremost in his mind. Alexander and William were close which is not surprising given that two poisonous snakes like to stay together all the better to have double the poison to kill people with."

"Alexander would act for King William to bring about Edgar's downfall. Meanwhile, he acted the good friend and loyal subject to his brother Edgar who in no way suspected him. William, the ruthless king of England would not be scorned by a lowly king of Scots thus would make Edgar pay for his defiance. Acted rightfully did the king of Scots in refusing to humble himself before the English king and acknowledge William as his feudal superior, as both were equal sovereigns. Rather than face Edgar in open battle as would a valiant man, England's king would have Alexander proceed on his behalf with stealth and villainy to unseat Edgar. Alexander, Edgar's brother, whose ambition knew no bounds would do the English king's evil deed for him."

"Alexander, took the king of England's example and found men to do his wickedness for him, men, who would commit any infamy if the outcome enriched themselves or gained them higher rank. The fatal act of regicide was down to the Normans. When the king's blood was shed it was them who had his blood upon their hands. In the dead of night the assassins rode intending to carry out their desperate mission. If only God looked down upon them and took it upon himself to stop what was to come. If only He did. Gregor stopped looked down as if he could not continue. "I feel dread in my heart at what is to come."

It seemed to all those listening that night that the hounds of Hell might appear amongst them in that hall that very night. Gregor looked up, as if seeking divine guidance to deliver his words with the proper grace. These words eventually came from his lips, "Choosing the darkness to act because such deeds have the protection of the master of darkness who is Satan. As all know Satan has his greatest power then when the sun sleeps as do Christians. Thus they rode under cover of darkness and seemingly with Satan's protection. Alexander had no name for honor, nor did those knights of his who were in Satan's service. Edgar, that noble and honest king, died by the treachery of very dastardly men. They heeded no Christian behavior, indeed, it did not matter to them what they did as long as they were well paid for it."

"I will tell more ..." Gregor paused for a moment, took a deep breath, after which his voice rang out in such a way it would raise the spirits of the dead. "The castle where the king was slain is on the border with England in a fair and pleasant place with towering trees and clear, fast flowing streams. Edgar in his boyhood was given this land by his father and he loved it. A Prince of Cumbria was Edgar, a title bestowed by his father. All crown princes of Scotland in those days were princes of Cumbria.

Alexander wanted it as he wanted all else that was Edgar's. Would stop at nothing to steal everything that belonged to his brother. Would take everything of his, including his life."

"A storm of death coming to unsuspecting innocents. Horrible wrong doing about to befall a man who unlike Alexander gave his service to God and not Satan. At an hour when the candles are struck to provide light when the sun has set, a harsh drumming rain began. The rain fell so harsh and powerful it pelted on the heads of the men who would bring down a king as if to punish them. So, to this castle came this party of murderers about to shatter the peace of the night. Upon the heavy wooden gates outside it was no fall from the heavens which rained down upon the wooden gates but mailed fists. The porter opened the gates upon the desperate pleas of knights known to be the king's loyal men, foremost of them, Sir Humphrey de Berkeley, obviously, a Norman by his name, urgent audience of the king demanded from this knight. Unwittingly the porter opened the gates and let it be known he disliked being raised from his rest when night was come and in the wet. The hounds of hell paid him no heed pushing past him, lucky the porter was not to get a sword in the guts for his grumblings. Garbed all in mail, weapons openly in their hands, playing at being the king's men but no honest pleasure would they have at the sight of him."

"Sir Humphrey de Berkeley, the right hand of the king, who was familiar with all the king's apartments, took them to where the king made his bed. As he led them the look in his eyes was mercilessness itself. By prior arrangement, men with the king's safety in their hands were elsewhere that night when Sir Humphrey de Berkeley came to commit his regicide, his twenty men with him. Thus, they made haste to the king's chambers these wretches with all manner of grave sin upon their souls with more yet to come."

All were deeply in Gregor's spell as he told of what occurred that fateful night when a king felt the sharp edge of weapons, when his queen, much loved by all, fell by his side, attacked similarly like he was with no respect given to her gentleness nor regality.

"It was a subtle web of intrigue that brought about this royal spilling of blood." Gregor eyed them all like they themselves were privy to the details of it and were party to it.

Gregor looked about, ensuring all were expectant, waited a

moment longer before his voice was full of energy and power as it had been. "Led by Sir Humphrey de Berkerly to where they found the king getting ready for his bed, sleepy-eyed, and not ready for anything, in fact retiring. All too soon the king's door felt the hammering of mailed fists upon it. This wood all that stood between the king and these men with cold steel in their hands and murder in their hearts. At this vital moment one of their swords smashed the lock off the door and thus they entered the king's bed chamber."

Gregor voice rang out earnestly, "Edgar trusted these men, deemed them honest. These Normans led by de Berkeley, though born in Scotland bore no allegiance to anyone bar themselves. A true Scot, a Celt, would never of left the king's side when danger fell upon him let alone be at him with swords. Any man who knows the Normans knows their kind, devils. They stole England from under the nose of king Harold, 'The Saxon'. Sicily, an island once famous for freedom and sunshine welcomed them, thereafter, fell to their greed."

"When these Normans burst into the king's room with no leave, the king was in his nightgown, seated with his queen and some of her gentlewomen. Seeing them, these fiends from Hell, the queen ran to the door to keep them out, but neither could she keep the door shut nor prevent their entry. The king prayed them to be off. Drawing their swords on him they saw fit to draw his blood and Edgar king of Scots saw that this would be his end, not thinking for a moment that they intended to murder his queen as well."

"There was ugly astonishment in him when he knew them for their purpose, that they were in his bedchamber to put their swords through him. The burning brand on the wall he took it to hand intending to sell his life dearly by virtue of it. Edgar cast it into the faces of those seeking his death whilst retreating to another room and shutting the door closed again behind him. Taking himself within this room the king opened the shutters, his intention was to escape onto the roof. Edgar believed he was the one they intended to kill but hearing anguished screams behind him knew they intended to murder his queen as well."

"The king might well have escaped but his good lady the queen was set upon and he heard her cries thus fulfilled the duty of a Christian husband and returned to her side. His fair lady, hurt and sore sounding, pleading for her life, what man could leave her to her fate. Both of them were young, Edgar, twenty-four, queen Margo no more than sixteen, a girl renowned for her loveliness. Her fair locks were bright as moonlight."

"Edgar called out to the queen's attackers. "What you do is a fearful and terrible thing."

"They were wasted words on these fiends. No pity did they have for her, nor, for her man. The king by using the burning brand and kicking chairs at the Normans remained alive for the moment and valiantly protected his queen. With that, two or more worthy Celtic swords entered the room and the Normans did not have the good cheer they formerly had, indeed, the Normans were forced to fight to preserve their own lives." "Then, by the art of her wits alone the queen, her mantle hanging loose about her so ripped and torn and revealing the feminine beauty she was famed for, made her way to Edgar's side. The others of her gentle sex in corners, lamentable, full of heavy foreboding."

"And then the miscreants fell on these woman with deadly butchery, with blades of death reigning down upon them till all the floor ran red with their blood. A substance that should be within their bodies to maintain life staining the floor making those who moments before were fair to the eye a dreadful sight to behold. Now any thought the king had of escape was made even more remote. He could not stand by and let these ladies be struck down so mercilessly. The brave Edgar took himself back into the fray. Despite his best effort he could not dissuade the Normans of their need to beset these poor ladies as they did. The king called out that they should leave these poor women be. To the Normans everlasting shame laughter was the response."

"By now those Celts who had come through the door earlier crossing swords with the Normans had either fallen or taken themselves elsewhere. So Edgar was alone as he faced those who would have his life and that of Margot his queen."

"A Norman blade would of killed Margo if she had not warded it off. In so doing the sword was dislodged from the grasp of he who held it. Once it fell to the floor Margot took it to hand. She pressed it into her husband's hand thereby the king felt a touch of hope. Perhaps in this confined space he had a chance and he and Margot might yet survive. He was pressing upon his enemies, forcing them back fearlessly."

"One of the traitors fell upon one of the queen's favorite ladies, her screams brought the queen to her side. This dear friend of the queen, having gotten her hand on a dagger fought back. It was then that the king did more deadly work. Such was his good work that bodies on the floor made a barrier between the Normans and the royal couple. If the king had the chance to flee it was at that moment. A lesser man would have left the ladies of the court to die without any effort to defend them. There was no better moment to flee for the Normans had others to deal with, Celts, were defending the ladies of the court having reentered the room. The king could not take himself to safety ignoring the pleas of his loyal subjects. Defending the faithful servants of the crown the king proved himself worthy to wear the crown of Scotland."

"For every Norman that died three Celts fell. There was a good reason for this. Of course the Normans were armed for war and the Celts expected nothing more than by the by to put themselves to their beds, martial garments and accoutrements of war were not upon them as they were upon the Normans.

'Come hither,' said Edgar to these devils in human form, he now with his sword, and the queen too did swordplay finding upon the floor one dropped by a wounded man. There were in fact four of them. At their back, a maiden held another blade ripped from a dying knight's hand. Not very old this one but despite her youth willing to sell her life bravely. Not forgetting the queen's special friend who earlier had armed herself with a dagger."

'Come forth tyrants and traitors,' said the king. Life-long glory did Edgar win by his sword's edge even though he was death-doomed but this did not in any way diminish how gleefully he dealt with them. Suddenly the girl who had wrestled the sword from the dying knight's hand, froze, and the sword she held dropped to the floor. When young girl's eyes showed that life was no longer inside her it was too harsh for Edgar to bear."

"Said the king, 'Maids thou art after the blood of maids because thee knows mine is too hard to come by.'

"The nature of the king was manly strong. He defended himself and his lady like a lion; the matter at hand though grievous in no way curbed his willingness. By now, he was wounded, blood blazed down both his arms. Despite this, fight on, did he. His lady wife now very bloody and was staggering. The sword she held fell to the floor, her innards spilled to the floor with it to her horror and consternation. Her dress once very white had no trace of white left at all, all was red. When Edgar looked down at her on the floor that knowledge that she was killed in truth made him completely heartbroken."

"With that, the odious rogue Sir Humphrey de Berkeley swept down with his sword and Edgar waxed faint. Mores the pity was that he slipped on that bloody wooden floor. They would never of brought him down otherwise. In that fatal moment when his legs went from under him, beheaded was the king, with a battle-axe carried by Sir Henry de Lisle. Edgar had once called de Lisle a friend. De Lisle was the worst traitor of all that night, yet he, de Lisle to cause the royal head to fall was not the least of it. A pack of wolves they truly showed themselves to be, these Normans, worse was to come, those the vile scum the Normans rained their swords down on the already dead king foremost among them de Lisle, the king's former friend besetting him with the battle-axe."

"With the king dead one of the ladies beseeched them for the life of the queen for within her was the faintest heartbeat. And herewith the same deadly weapon, the battle-axe, Sir Henry de Lisle brought that said battle-axe down on the said queen's neck casting aside her head from her body. De Lisle had in fact often shared pleasantries on many occasion before this day with her yet he committed that act. He cast aside Queen Margot's once lovely head from her body without a care. No amount of pleading in the eyes of those who loved the queen swayed him. It happened then that a multitude of blades cut her body to pieces."

"Unto death were both man and wife cast. One head beside the other, in death, brows touching, one to the other. As if all that had happened was not enough to confound the minds of ordinary men, what was left of their heads tilted as by accident so seemingly they were looking at each other. If there was any life left within them at this moment most definitely the last sight they had was of each other. For whatever reason, it is beyond the ken of mortal man to know why, or how, the heads that touched inexplicably turned towards the pack of wolves who slew them."

"Listen well for what I now tell is fit to horrify the hardest soul. It was the king who said it. 'Look at these slayers, these deceivers with the mortal blood-royal on their hands.' "Those words came from the dead king's mouth."

Gregor could weave a spell with words no doubt of it at all

and all in the hall had their hearts in their mouths when from his lips did fall: "That is not the end of it. The king did then put his baleful eyes on those who saw fit to end his life, as well as his young queen's. He spoke from beyond his mortality. The dead eyes of the king of Scots, yes, his dead eyes were on the Normans to their consternation. Edgar king of Scots said to the numerous Normans who had his blood on their hands and were just lately congratulating themselves on the measure of their success, it is reported true, many did hear him say, 'Vengeance shall be done for a worthy king so cruelly put to death. Even though I die of deadly wounds in diverse places upon my body, and my head is cut of, none too neatly I might add, another will come to take my place to uphold this kingdom's honor and to put this grave injustice to rights. Justice will be done in my name. He who will come will send you Normans out of this land, back to where you came from, Hell.'

'And you, de Berkeley,' the king fixed his dead eyes on him, 'On your head, on your sly face, shall fall the sword, as yours fell often on others, including my own, so shall a sword fall on thine and strike thy head to the ground.'

"One day years thereafter a man, Duncan MacNab, who had argued with de Berkeley snuck back into the hall from where he had been banished for his threats. As Berkeley lay asleep head on the table, much besotted with strong liquor, MacNab drew his sword and sent it speeding down with much grievous violence onto that head that lay on the table drunkenly and clove it at the neck. The effect so bloody and unwholesome that the man who held the sword sent the head one way and the body the other. A mighty slice it was and not only cut through the neck but the table of strong oak, also. The severed head was raised by he who had severed it and thrown into the fire. That man, MacNab, held a grudge.

Thereafter, the de Berkeleys, declined, no longer the great men in the kingdom that they were. When the sword came crashing down to end de Berkeley's life people remembered Edgar's final words to him. This man, the murderer of de Berkeley, was said to have drawn his sword at the slightest provocation and many said that de Berkeley was a fool to anger him. The murderer fled and escaped to Ireland where he himself was murdered, no doubt as a result of his feuding ways."

"But this is a story of a king who though bold, strong, gruesome when he was wroth, playful with his bride, deep-thinking and of good conscience, God-fearing, who, never fled from any battle but often sought clever ways by which to get his way without resorting to war, was cut down despite his value to the kingdom."

The silence which followed was long and heart-wrenching until more came. "Thus came to an end the rule of king Edgar and the life of his young lovely queen, Margot. Then came to rule Alexander, 'The Childless', they called him. He was a king who did not like the sight of a woman's nakedness. I am guessing he did not mind the sight of a young man's nakedness at all."

Despite her dislike of Gregor Frida had to admit to herself that this story was as good a one as she had ever heard. She could not get out of her mind the image of the two young beautiful people made ghastly, without heads, furthermore, touching, brow to brow. As horrific as that was, more dreadful still, the king's head, all manner of gore upon it, turning, and from beyond his mortal life damning the Normans.

That night she tossed and turned, saw, that queen beset on every side by slashing blades. The horror inside her head gave her a drenched brow, a sheen of sweat across her skin. In her dreams, a flood of blood brought forth. Seeing before her the young queen's not yet dead eyes looking up beseechingly at one of her attackers. Then it was herself looking up at the steel axe poised above her own head. Rather than pity her it was a hideous grin that her suffering induced in the man who held it. Then the flashing blade descended. The grinding, as the axe parted bone to make her head a thing apart. Then opening her eyes to see her own head fallen from her body rolling along the floor until it lay beside Morgund's own. She remembered Gregor whilst speaking with her complimented her on her pretty neck and looked her dead in the eye and told her it was said of Margot the murdered queen that she also had a pretty neck.

A WEDDING, A DEATH

MORGUND AND PENDER were riding out to deem if those on outlaying farms were safe over the winter when a sudden and vicious storm struck. Snow started blowing wet and heavy. In the open spaces between the trees the wind howled in a great gale. The icy blades felt like to flay them alive. Shouting above the wind Morgund called to Pender, "Let us find shelter!"

A gentle descent led to a basin of pine and moss. Evergreens climbed the slope in the dull light looking like warriors in file hunched over against the wind taking themselves higher. In the hollow they escaped the screaming wind which roared over the top of them. The unseen power above their heads bent trees over. When it lulled for a moment Morgund told Pender, "We will have to wait it out here."

Pender said nothing his eyes were fixed on the wind whipping the snow through the air.

A moment later Morgund filled the snowy air with his voice, "How goes it with thy tutor Gregor?"

"Gregor can never find me so it goes well."

Morgund stared straight ahead, anywhere but at the boy in case he laughed, which he shouldn't.

Pender decided to tell Morgund about something he had seen. "Gregor was talking to an old man with a hardwood staff, clothed in brown, a hood covered most of his face. When I asked who it was Gregor told me to mind my own business or he would give me concerns enough that I would not worry myself about what others did. I heard Gregor call this man, Duibne. When Gregor told me to be off this Duibne shot me such a glare it chilled my blood. His eyes were as sharp as knives."

Morgund thoughtfully replied, "His eyes are very sharp."

"Who is he?"

"A man in league with Satan." Morgund would know more of it. "Where was this?"

"Outside the fort, in the trees."

"And when he told you to be off what did you do?"

"I ran off."

"That is not what you usually do?"

"I did then he frightened me."

"How did you find these two in the first place?"

"I followed Gregor. I knew he was up to no good."

"Of course. Is that not his constant habit to be up to no good?"

Pender's voice broke through Morgund's musing a moment later. "I saw them together a second time."

"A second time!" When Morgund spoke he sounded very concerned. "When was this second meeting?"

"A week ago. Again in the trees."

Although Morgund gazed at Pender he was deeply inside his own mind. There were some secrets here, secrets to be uncovered. How did Gregor knew Duibne? By Morgund's reckoning Gregor was nothing but trouble. The longer he stood with Pender, the longer it would take to hold Gregor to account for his mischief. To have this out with him he must return. This prompted Morgund to say, "Despite the weather we are riding back."

Pender could see that the matter with Gregor held great importance for Morgund.

Once inside the fort and out of the shocking cold, Morgund had Gregor sent for. Part of Morgund still remembered how much Seward was in the thrall to the same dark forces Duibne gave himself to. Had to admit that felt a good deal of resentment at it. When both Seward and Morgund were held captive by the witch-queen in England Seward had that he woman's especial favor. Such favor given him because Seward had the gift of the second-sight. Often he saw that which was about to be. Now Duibne had come back perhaps to tempt Seward to the path where only darkness dwelt. Strangely Seward appeared unmoved when Morgund recounted the secret dealings between Duibne and Gregor. Listening in total silence, not a word escaped his lips. Morgund mulled over his apparent almost complete lack of concern.

Finally, Morgund said to him, "Duibne, is a man of the underworld and appears to be a friend of Gregor's, thus, he too is pray to the same dark forces." Delving deep into Seward's eyes trying to decide how he stood on the matter. "I will have Gregor cast out into the snow. There is no place for a man like that here."

Morgund did not intend to go that far, in the grip of winter Gregor would not survive a night in the bitter cold. After getting no response at all from his friend Morgund excused him none the wiser on his opinion. Morgund sat in silence waiting for Gregor. When that man appeared he wore an expression of bored disdain. An expression Morgund was all too familiar with having experienced it from him many times before. Gregor had his eyes raised as if to say what was he doing here, as if, it was beneath his dignity to be sent for.

Morgund asked him, "Well what says thee about this meeting with Duibne?"

Morgund's question brought forth a sneer with this reply, "Duibne, I hardly know the man." Gregor appeared to think carefully about what he said next before he intoned with his usual haughtiness. "We went into the forest to pick certain herbs that I know the whereabouts of. Wild plants have many uses, they help the heal sick, heal wounds. Pender made a nuisance of himself, no wonder as he usually does everywhere he goes. As thee knows thyself the boy is beyond good governance."

Morgund's fist slammed down hard on the table. "You are here to answer what went on with Duibne!" A cold stare followed. "Answer me, what were you doing with him?"

"I see the boy will have no manners having the example set for him by you."

An exasperated Morgund stood up, was near to slamming Gregor into the wall. Gregor noticed and appeared milder, thus an explanation passed his lips. "Duibne passed me some herbs, I passed some to him, that done, he was gone. We share a common interest in such things." Gregor couldn't help himself a certain level of impertinence even as he tried to avoid a blow. "There is a

herb for anger perhaps thee should partake thyself of it."
 Morgund's penetrating gaze poured dissatisfaction into Gregor. "So innocent was this meeting that it was in secret, away from the eyes of other men. He is a man in thrall to the powers of darkness that man and thee met with him and discussed plants like two garden maids. I doubt it." A heavy silence fell between the two only broken when Morgund demanded, "Why was I not told?"
 Gregor replied, "I did not see it as worthy of your attention. If take a piss do I have to tell you what color the piss is which issues from my dick?"
 "I want to know why you met an enemy of mine in secrecy?" Morgund's eyes bored into Gregor. He was a moment away from striking him. "Answer me now!"
 "I was not to know that he was an enemy to you, to me he is just another man. I saw Seward earlier, perhaps I should of told thee about it in case he had angered thee without my knowing it and thus he is now thine enemy."
 Even if Gregor thought it was fit for mirth Morgund did not and his eyes were icy. "I see. It was not noteworthy."
 There was amusement in Gregor's reply, "Well, I did not know thee would find any issue with it. Meeting someone to discuss plants is hardly a cause for wrathful words. I spoke to Paten just yesterday on the weather perhaps thee wishes more details on it. He considered it very cold and I agreed with him." Gregor's tone changed, adopting a coldness matching Morgund's own. "May I move onto a matter of more importance?"
 Morgund could not believe the man's arrogance. Stating to himself with disbelief. "A matter of more importance?"
 "I have had enough of being spoken to like a child. I must bring up Pender, he is impossible. I want permission to beat him."
 "Beat him, of course not. Do not raise a hand to him."
 Gregor raised his eyes in displeasure and made as if to turn and depart without having Morgund's leave to do so. Only a sword could end Gregor's haughtiness Morgund realized. Morgund raised his voice, "I am not finished with you!"
 He could stand still till dawn for all Morgund cared, the mere sight of the man sent his heart racing in anger. Gregor rather than let the fire in Morgund's eyes diminish before he put forward more intemperate words pushed Morgund's forbearance still further. "I must insist, the boy, has had no strong hand of guidance, and

would benefit from one."

Morgund could not believe he would ask this again, his request had been denied and yet he dared to repeat it and attempt to have his way. "No, have I not already said no. If anyone needs beating it is thyself."

Morgund doubted that Gregor could in fact carry out any punishment on Pender so the matter did not concern him over much. Gregor had to catch Pender, the negative prospect of that brought a little smile to his lips and took some of his anger from him. Seeing his expression Gregor looked at Morgund like he was a fool. Seeing this Morgund's cold fury returned. From now on Morgund would have the man watched. He was nothing but a burden and come spring he would have him gone. Morgund flicked his wrist dismissing him.

Subsequent to the matter of Gregor meeting Duibne, and the conflict that resulted from it, Pender noticed a change in Gregor, the glint in his eye when he saw the boy a sure sign that Gregor was furious with him. Nor did he acknowledge the boy as he formerly had done. It was more of a relief than anything else not being spoken to by this strange man, however, when Pender got more of those fixed glares it began to worry him. To Pender it spoke of disorder of the mind, which made him all the more want to keep his distance from him. There was a conflict in Pender's young mind with regard to his former tutor, mixed with this dislike there was a certain amount of admiration because he loved hearing about kings of old. That king's talking head particularly was a story Pender liked. A shame he thought that the other head, the queen's head, did not speak as well when the king's head did. A more horrific vision one could not imagine. How frightful it would be if both heads spoke together like any married couple but with heads alone, no bodies to go with them. Sometimes Gregor told a story to him when no one else was with them, a real treat. Recollecting such moments whilst regretting they would never happen again. By Pender's reckoning, although Gregor knew a lot of stories, that was not a reason to put himself above other men as he did. Despite what was good about him there was much that was not, and just because Gregor acted so important did not mean that he was. Gregor had nothing but contempt for Morgund and Seward, and they were far bigger men than he was and were good with swords. Gregor did not even know how to hold a sword as far as Pender could tell. Pender decided most of the tales told by Gregor were make-believe. That king's head from long ago, he was sure that it did not speak but was glad he was not there to find out if it did. Pender thought there was violence in Gregor, not manly soldierly violence which all knew was a thing of virtue, but the unpredictable sudden rage of the weak and disturbed. Pender decided when he saw him to keep his sword close to him. That said, Pender would not dare to hold Gregor's eyes with anger. Whilst Pender disguised his distrust of Gregor, that man contemptuously dismissed his former pupil with a look of his disdain whenever he saw him.

At the same time he was dealing with the bard's discomforting behavior, Pender found himself given a new name, the new name being, Phail. Pender was obviously a Norse name and Sueno the cook, a good lady, declared he had been with them long enough that he should be considered one of them. That he was the holder of a barbaric Viking name was an affront to the Christian folk amongst whom he was. The small ones must fear for their safety with someone with such a name within the walls. Phail was a good Celtic name. Accept it he must to please her insisted the cook, furthermore, called him Phail every time she saw him, and others took to calling him that too. Thus Pender with hair like snow became Phail of the fair hair. A valiant warrior from long ago was the original Phail This original Phail came from across the sea like the Vikings themselves had done, but before them. A tow-headed foreign warrior from a land of many lakes very far away from Scotland. Said of the original Phail that he had fought Finn MacCool on the island of Lewis. The battle between them lasted many days and at the end of it there was no clear winner. With his fair hair and foreign origin the ancient hero Phail reminded Sueno of Pender and thus she named the boy after that famous warrior. Ancient towers on the north coast were reputed to be lookouts to warn of raiders. This of the Vikings might not be so new occurred to Pender's friend Sueno the lady cook. Nevertheless there must have been an abbreviation on their onslaughts or else such accounts would go further back than they did. Whatever the truth of this and Sueno and her young friend she took to calling Phail pondered on it often. They had to admit it was unlikely to be solved. The hillfort folk were happy the blond lad had a good Scottish name that was not the least bit heathenish nor unusual to the ear. It was a sign of acceptance and affection, and the boy once named Pender, and now named Phail, liked it. He felt more at home here than amongst the moody often dangerous Norseman who had often looked at him like they would like to put a sword through him back at his father's castle.

Late in winter, soon after Pender's name changed from Pender to Phail, the boy went to visit Gregor. Would not have seen such a thing as remotely possible weeks before, however, lately Gregor had taken to nodding at him in the corridors on passing. At his friend Iain's urging, they were on the way there despite the late hour. As they walked Phail thought again about how Gregor had looked at him after he had disclosed the meeting with Duibne. The danger soon after that was so obvious that everyone must know Gregor meant him ill, that some plot of revenge was at work in Gregor's mind. There was no doubt of it. When he asked Iain if there was any danger to him, Iain had laughed and told Phail not to be silly. Iain went on to tell Phail Gregor thought of him as he thought of everyone else, which was to say, despised him slightly. There was only one person who Gregor truly liked, Iain. If Phail was in danger his friend Iain would surely warn him and not invite him to a place of peril was the reasoning within Phail's mind as he took himself to Gregor's door. Phail reassured himself with the fact that his friend surely would not do him wrong. Iain and himself trained in weaponry almost every day, side-by-side, sharing comradeship. Despite the fact that Phail was only just nine years old, and Iain was eleven, Phail was unlike any other nine-year-old boy Iain had ever seen, precocious with arms, and very strong.

That Phail had a sword the right size for him made a tremendous difference to his ability. Morgund had seen to that. By Morgund's reckoning anyone who trained as hard as Phail did could not help but one day be a very good swordsman and Morgund had decided he would do all he could to help the boy. Seeing him at work often made Morgund smile for he too had trained as hard before he grew into a man's body. Phail pushed himself until sword and boy were one. Just like Morgund had. Yet, as often as he thought well of Phail for his commitment he wondered if he had made a terrible mistake because he could not take a step hardly without the boy waving his sword at him. The worst thing was every time Morgund took on Phail, as he often did, the boy was that much better, actually at times Morgund felt genuinely tested which defied belief.

Walking beside his friend, Phail, felt that tonight was a test of character. Felt sure that in the future he would face greater tests than this. If he faced down his fears on this occasion so too could he overcome other tests of courage in the future and with the life he had chosen for himself, the warrior's path, such tests were sure to come. When Gregor's door came into view Phail asked himself why he was doing this. It was partly to impress his friend that he went along with it. He felt sure that Iain was trying to get back at him for besting him in sword-play, to have Phail show his fear of Gregor. Phail decided he would not give Iain the satisfaction. There was no way Phail was going to back down. Alert and very quick of mind as he of foot so if there were any danger he was convinced he could get himself out of it. Reassuring himself with this reasoning he maintained his pace. But as he continued some inner voice told him that he should not take a step further, however, he kept on, with a part of him wondering why he did. Trying so hard to impress a friend was childish, no reason to endanger himself, although he knew having his friend laugh at him was not a big thing he could not bear the thought of it.

Iain asked with a slight smile, "Do you have fears?"

"I fear not." Although Phail said he did not, his stomach was tied in a million knots.

Iain considered him with an infuriating smile. It was natural that they spent time together Iain and Phail having both committed themselves to the art of swordsmanship and both being boys. It seemed in Iain's case despite his best efforts he would never be any good. What was unusual was that Iain and Gregor were so often together. So often seen together that people were talking about it, most with an air of condemnation. Iain abruptly took Phail away from his musings, Iain's words seeming to echo in the dark passageway, "Gregor has a crwth. Has thee ever heard one played?"

Phail shook his head.

Iain continued, "The Welsh play them. It is an instrument somewhat like a lyre. This instrument is favored by the Welsh and is exceedingly melodic to the ear. We will see it and learn to play it."

Phail kept walking with the constant nagging doubt in his mind until they were at Gregor's door. The long dark corridor that led here had given Phail too much time to think. This room, Phail had never noticed until now how isolated it was. Gregor lived very much alone. In Phail's mind he saw those shiny black pinpricks of eyes of Gregor's, so far seeing. They looked right through a person. The occasional childish chuckle he affected, his put-on good humor which came from a deep void, trying to convince you he liked you when it was very obvious he did not. Something felt wrong about this. Phail felt he should turn and leave while he still had the chance to. Be damned if he would and have Iain's laughter ringing in his ears.

After a brief knock they entered. A lit hearth was in one corner of the room. Hot drinks, milk with crushed berries were passed onto them by their good host. Pleasant warmth blazed at them from the fireplace as they played the crwth. It was obvious to Phail that Gregor was trying to ease his fears. But after a little while any feeling of contentment vanished. Phail noticed a secret communication was ongoing between Iain and Gregor. Phail thought seeing them together was decidedly odd. A comment once made by Iain came to mind which made Phail think he did not really know his friend as well as he thought he did. Iain told him that two men could join as one in sexual congress. Phail thought nothing of it at the time. It was such an outlandish statement that it could have no relationship to fact. Seeing them two together it was only too easy to believe.

Iain like he could read Phail's mind asked, "Is all to the good Phail?"

Avoiding Iain's suspicious inspection Phail gazed at Gregor who shot him a look of hate. The atmosphere in the room dropped markedly which prompted the suggestion from Phail that he leave. A benign smile came from Gregor then and he asked, "Is our company not to your taste?"

"I am tired." With that Phail proceeded to yawn trying to be convincing of exhaustion, wanting an excuse to escape them.

His comment was regarded like it was never said. Neither would stand that he might call it a night, insisting he enjoy himself with them still further. For now Phail agreed to. There was something unmistakably odd about the way these two looked at each other when he agreed to, it was like somehow there was a secret pact between them.

So the night rolled by and Phail thought about Iain's statement about two men being together in sinful nakedness one atop the other enjoying immoral congress. He remembered Iain saying that Gregor was more than a father figure to him. What had that meant? Phail thought he knew all too well as distasteful as it was to contemplate. Taken from his thoughts for a moment when Iain handed him a small hand drum. His hand stayed on Phail's followed by a long seemingly sensual look. Phail decided it was time to leave he had had enough. What enjoyment of the music he had had was not enough to keep him within sight of these two, and from bad to worse things had gone for now his friend Iain was acting towards him like he wanted to have immoral congress with him.

Iain, sensing Phail's restlessness played a tune that he considered Phail liked. For a time Phail's unease left him. It was a good tune, he wanted to hear the end of it. The playing of the instrument was very pleasing; Iain was in fact skilled. More time rolled by playing until the simple fact was that it was very late, tiredness dragged Phail's eyes down thus he decided he must be off, dawn was near. Now the crwth, the reason for their appearance which had kept him here until now had lost its magic. He was rather sick of it.

Gregor called out to him. "Is it past your bedtime little boy?"

A laugh of close confederacy between these two set Phail's teeth on edge. "You can sleep here." Gregor gestured toward a small bed. It was a horrifying prospect. With none of his usual reserve rather a barely hidden eagerness Gregor had pointed to the bed. Phail gained a sense that there were all sorts of hidden dangers, all sorts of secrets best kept between those of like mind. The kind of hidden things he did not want to know about. Some places generated evil and Phail could sense it here, he had the impression that this unholy power was growing. Just as his heart was racing Gregor brought forth another crwth, a handsome wooden instrument.

Gregor said with some excitement, "The fingers taken back and forth across the strings produce the most gorgeous sounds."

Gregor was as good as his word and made a tuneful melody with a somewhat hypnotic effect. Midway through the song as if responding to an internal clock suddenly Gregor glared at Phail, narrow-eyed. A disturbed somehow other-worldly voice echoed in the room. It seemed to come from Gregor's mouth though no voice of man could have such a sound. "It is the hour when the powers of darkness are at their mightiest. Just before dawn."

Just then what was no human sound came from the rumbling chamber of Gregor's mouth even odder than that which had occurred moments before. Phail felt the hairs on his neck stand up. It was like a demon possessed Gregor. Even though he felt like flying he would not show his fear in front of this despicable man. The seclusion, the late hour, that no one knew he was here were suddenly critical factors. With Gregor's wickedness there was no telling what might happen. Phail looked at the door estimating how long it would take him to get to it if he ran.

Gregor came closer, the crwth still in his hand. When Gregor plucked a note, he laughed. Phail noted how heavy the crwth was. That it could be used as a weapon if he could get his hands on it. Earlier he had put his sword down because it had interfered with his playing. That too could have been planned. In fact, surely it was. Someone had moved his sword away further when he had put it down. That was no accident. If Gregor took another step forward Phail could reach out and take the crwth out of his hands, and with it, he would best Gregor, Iain too if need be. With great reverence Gregor placed the crwth down, then took a step back. Phail's eyes darted to the crwth, a quick grab and he could swing it at this hateful man.

Two small rows of malicious white teeth rose from Gregor's mouth in a deadly expression. "Did you think to blacken my name with no retribution?"

Phail remained frozen to the spot. Suddenly Gregor turned away from him and where Gregor was moments before was empty space. It did not take long for Gregor to reappear with a black blob beside him near his hip. Phail, seeing this shadow wondered what it was. Whatever Gregor brought forth from the dark space behind him was not for Phail's benefit that he knew. Then he saw it. At Gregor's hip was an enormous demon-dog. Phail thought that he had never seen such a frightening beast. Released, the beast-dog shot towards the boy. Phail quickly shoved the crwth into the gaping jaws that were about to bite him. Iain stood motionless his eyes glazed over in shock. Phail jumped up on the table. For a moment he looked at Iain with pleading eyes. However, the coercion by which Iain brought him here was of it itself evidence of his involvement in this plan to do him harm. The dog went straight for him which meant it was obviously under command of its owner. Catching a beam overhead with his hand Phail swung his legs up away from the hound. Hanging from the beam, trying to keep his legs away from the dog. It was everywhere jumping snarling, incredibly muscular. A scan of the room revealed Gregor standing to one side, a delighted smile evident on him. Obviously Phail was drawn here to be murdered. Another fact as inescapable pressed itself on his mind. Gregor watchful now could just as easily decide to go get a spear to run him through. If he were to survive he must do something before he fell into those razor-sharp teeth. There was a fire over in a corner of the room with a log in it that was narrow enough to fit into the dog's mouth. Swaying to one side of the table using his legs to draw the dog away from the direction he intended to go. Phail swung hard right, then swung hard left, let go, fell onto the table rolled off it, sprinted to the fire; not fast enough because the dog caught him. It had his hand in its mouth biting him. Blood streamed down his arm. The fire was at his back. Despite the intense heat involved, the immense pain, he reached back, took the log out and thrust it deep into the dog's mouth. With a high-pitched squeal the dog ran off in agony. Phail took his chance, pelted out of the room and down the corridor.

Morgund heard a rapid heavy tumultuous thumping on his door, a voice he hardly recognized as human calling out, "H-e-l-p me. H-e-l-p, me, help me. H-e-l-p, me."

Bursting up, leaving Frida uncovered, Morgund sprung to the door to find Phail laying in a pool of blood. Taking him into the room laying him down, Frida used a sheet to stem the flow of blood whilst wondering what on earth had happened to her son. An accident of some kind was the first thing that came to mind, but at this hour?

Feeling a soft bed beneath his back there was an overwhelming sense of relief. Somehow he had survived. It all happened so quickly for a while he thought he was still in the grip of that demon beast dog and had not left the room at all and all this was a momentary vision. He could take great comfort from the fact that in amidst of it all his good sense did not desert him. The decisions he made saved his life. Tired though he was, he was also pleased with himself. A badly gashed arm was his biggest wound. It took over thirty stitches from wrist to elbow to close. Despite the seriousness of it Phail felt elated that he did not lose an arm. His burns were painful too and in the days following even more so. Morgund was waiting, impatient for Phail's wound to be treated so he could get his hands-on Gregor.

With Phail's injuries seen to it was time to get his hands on that serpent who saw fit to murder Phail. That it happened in the depths of night made sense given that Gregor was at his most powerful when darkness reigned, thinking himself under the protection of Satan. It was obvious to Morgund now that Satan was who he truly served. Dawn had broken. See how potent he was in the light of day when his master had slunk back into the underworld. Morgund's mind raced ahead to what Gregor would say, how he would explain himself. That man would have excuses, he always had excuses. In his mind imagining the back and forth between them, the smug denial of any wrongdoing from him.

Others thought Gregor must be given the chance to explain himself. Morgund did not want to listen to whatever he said to cast the blame off himself. Morgund took himself in haste to Gregor's door. Arriving at it, he kicked it down. Entering Gregor's chamber, several men-at-arms at his back.

When Morgund stormed through the door, the bard's black eyes blazed with rage at the intrusion. "What are you doing here?" Rather than display remorse Gregor stood proudly with the dog. The dog had its teeth bared at Morgund.

Morgund could not believe this. How many times must this man confound him with his belligerence? His very cold attentive eyes rested on Gregor then on the dog. "Is this the killer dog?"

Some of the rage went out of Gregor when he gauged Morgund was but a moment away from slaying him.

Gregor tried hard to give the impression that it was all a misunderstanding. "Of course it is the dog." He tried to soften his expression, Morgund doubted whether a smile had ever passed his lips, this was the closest he could come to it. "The matter with the dog was a simple matter, a mistake. I hope that Phail is well? It snapped at him I admit that. The dog does not like strangers."

The whole room filled with the sound of Morgund's rage. "Evil, vile man!" Morgund kicked out leaving Gregor grounded on the floor. It was then that the dog reared up with a mouth full of ugly razors. Mid leap, Morgund gave it one thrust through the side, then it was on the floor, dead.

Morgund breathing deeply was trying to get his head together. He could easily slay Gregor. However the lucid thought in his mind that he must be seen to be just. To kill the man made him no better than the deranged Harold who killed on his whim. These people had suffered enough under one brutal ruler, he would not have them think him another. In his mind, as severely as Phail was injured he was alive. Gregor did not murder Phail so he would not murder him.

Finally feeling more in control Morgund said, "No one knew you had such a savage beast. Why did you have it?"

With the utmost poor timing Gregor picked this moment to regain his former arrogance, never far from him. "The dog is mine and I should of decided what happened to it, not thee. There are many dogs here and mine is singled out for this kind of brutal treatment, it is unforgivable!"

Morgund despising the man spoke quietly keeping his voice in check. If he allowed his anger to rise again he knew in a moment Gregor would be a dead on the floor along with his precious dog. "A secret, Gregor? Another one. Why? Why have this kind of dog? One so dangerous?"

"When I gained him he was a puppy. I never knew he would grow so big. I had him as a companion. I am not married. I get lonely."

All could see no sane man would have such a thing as a pet. It was not fit company for man or woman. Terrible anger flowed from Morgund. "As ever thine words are clever but with no sense."

Gregor could not help feeling sorry for himself. "To you he was a killer, to me he was a loyal and gentle friend."

Morgund had heard enough. "You are evicted from this fort as of this moment."

"Where will I go?" Gregor looked bewildered. "In winter? It is impossible. Have you no shame?"

With teethed clenched Morgund intoned, "You go, or you die, which one you choose is up to you, I care not."

Gregor called out to all others in the room, "Where would I go?"

Morgund almost cut him down that instant, instead said, "You have an hour."

Gregor rose from the floor with as much dignity as he could muster. "A day or two to arrange things, I insist on it."

That this man was not having his own way this time was written heavily on Morgund's face. "Outside the fort in an hour or I cut your head off."

There was a slight return of Gregor's habitual haughtiness. "An hour ..." His voice went up in register, his anger obvious. "It is impossible." His tone dropped back a notch, "In a day or two perhaps."

Morgund realizing he was dealing with a madman thought he should just cut him down and be done with it. Morgund said, gripping his sword tighter, "An hour!"

"All this is a mishap between a boy notorious for trouble and an innocent animal slain for protecting its master. Your entry to my room uninvited I must say is beyond all decency, to storm in here like that it is most inexcusable."

Morgund could not believe the nerve of the man when he heard him say, "I will have compensation for the damage done to my door, and the dog is my property too and I will be recompensed for it also. Who do you think you are?"

"Count yourself lucky that you are still alive," Morgund said.

"A true knave's answer that. I must insist. I will have payment. And you have leave to depart my room now. I must do some tidying up. Look at the mess done by your ill-considered handiwork, blood everywhere, a faithful dog, like carrion on the floor."

Morgund put his hand to Gregor's throat and applied pressure. "If you are not gone in an hour you are dead." Morgund drove his fist into Gregor's chest casting him into the wall where he lay all askew.

With eyes full of hate Morgund told him: "In an hour I will be back. If you are still here I will cut your head from your body and we shall see if it speaks still. I think it may. If it is the only way to shut you up, though, I doubt it, I will gladly cut thine head from thine shoulders. I simply want to see your head cut off, as simple as that. On consideration, if it speaks I will then smash it to pulp until no sound comes out of it. I doubt even cutting away thy vile head will give us rest from the sound of your yelping nonsense."

Not a murmur from the figure on the floor now blood spattered. Just as well because Morgund did not know if he could stay his hand given another word from Gregor.

In an hour Gregor was gone, Iain gone with him.

White water glided down from the heights it spilled from. The most glorious moisture fell upon the faces of those present. A pleasant piney scent wafted from the tall green heights above them on three sides. Wild roses cast out their beauty from between the grass, their shimmering colours peeking out at them. A multitude were assembled for the wedding of Morgund and Frida. The beautiful blond Frida a child of the Scandinavian north had a sense of expectancy. Although she had been wed once before as a very young girl this time it felt entirely different. She might be a bride for the first time so joyous was it. In a very pale yellow gown, all eyes were on her, all woman and girls admiringly, the men certainly projected affection and respect. The pale yellow gown went so well with her Scandinavian blondness that none could not imagine her wearing anything else that was so becoming. Morgund was in dark green, with slight red, blue and brown check of tartan. At his breast, a heavy ornate gem studded brooch. All in all he looked like a hero of ancient legend. Morgund was as enthralled by the superb beauty by his side as were all the others who stood witness. So absorbed in each other were they that when they gazed into each other's eyes it was as if they were the only ones on the face of the Earth. Both bride and bridegroom went barefoot connecting themselves to the glorious earth as did all others in this sacred place have naked feet. A Celtic custom to be unshod on your wedding day and outside touching the Earth Mother. It was also the custom to conduct the rite of marriage near clear fresh water where a single yew tree grew. The darkly glorious yew, an evergreen, symbolized everlasting nature and love and, long life, and health. Others of this botanical family grew further afield, almost or in fact touching. A great human circle surrounded the field which the officiating priest and the bridal pair were in the middle of.

The priest's voice rang out in the crisp morning air, "Frida and Morgund do you feel God's love?"

When they nodded that they did the Celtic priest proclaimed to all, "We are all made up of this earth. It is a sign of simplicity and humility to be barefoot. We stand upon the ground that nurtures us. The circle of goodwill around us gives us power."

Then he said to the witnesses, "Love is powerful, ours for them, theirs for us. The love they share for each other is the most powerful love of all." Then he looked back at the two lovers and said, "A ring is a circle. A ring has no beginning and no end. The circle of the universe is eternal like a ring. We feel the love of our ancestors long past, they share their love with us from afar." His words came on the wind to the attendees. "Made in God's image was the first man Adam."

Frida and Morgund never heard another word of it. They were lost in each other's eyes, not even the priest who officiated claimed their attention. They were in a world of delight and joy that was all their own. When the priest made them unite hands they felt the outside world intrude on theirs once more. They witnessed their friends delight in what went on here which gave them much joy.

The priest directed first from Morgund, "Morgund, express your love for Frida."

When Morgund responded and said, "I love you Frida." He had tears in his eyes when he said it.

Frida did not need to be prompted immediately saying from the heart, "I love you too Morgund."

"Morgund, do you take Frida as your lawfully wedded wife?"

"I do." Morgund's voice quivered with emotion. Captured by

the gravity of the moment every word was tremendously meaningful to him.

It was the priest who spoke next. "And you Frida, do you take Morgund for your wedded husband?"

"Yes." There was a slight quiver in her reply.

From the priest, "Morgund take the ring and place it on Frida's finger."

Morgund turned to his best man, Seward, took the ring from him and slipped it on Frida's finger.

"Say after me, Morgund, with this ring I thee wed ..."

As Morgund was told he did. "With this ring I thee wed ..."

The priest then turned to Frida. "Frida take this ring and place it on Morgund's finger, and say after me, Morgund, I take thee for my lawful wedded husband."

As the priest told her to so she did.

Morgund felt a wedding ring placed onto his finger and a broad look of pleasant satisfaction was on his face because of it.

Then the words that commenced their married life together were proclaimed by the priest. "I join thee both together in holy wedded matrimony."

A moment later much rejoicing from all celebrating this wonderful event. Amidst all the merriment Morgund spied Paten talking worriedly to a Norseman from the Viking castle. Morgund knew this late-comer was obviously the bearer of bad news from the message-bearer's behavior, and from Paten's reaction to it. Paten immediately looked at Morgund as if to say he must have word with him urgently. From the alarm on his face Morgund knew he must find time to speak to him to discover what was amiss because something surely was.

But consumed by the gaiety of the occasion Morgund quickly forgot Paten especially after imbibing the strong uisge beatha, the lively-water, that was so much a feature of Celtic celebrations. Many cups of it were offered by well-wishers. It was a day of full revelry, including horse races, foot races, wrestling, melees, where men fought with blunt swords the aim being to cast an opponent to the ground by a wrestling maneuver, or to strike him with the safe soft flat face of the sword, thereby scoring a point. There were also fights with wooden staffs. For Morgund and Frida the day meant, eating, drinking, dancing, in addition to being attendees at all these games and sharing the joy of the day with all their friends until finally they departed.

Rather than enjoy the beauty of his wife that first night married to her Morgund filled with tiredness and uisge beatha barely had enough awareness to fall into his bed. Frida who was just as tired as he was slept just as soundly as he did. The next morning though nothing could part them. Morgund's arousal took Frida aback, flattered by his rampant demonstration of desire she responded giving as good as she got. His commanding domination of her when he took her from behind made her heart race with excitement.

They stayed together in bed with their bodies rubbing up against each other again and again in sexual ecstasy. It seemed like not a thing in the world could spoil their enjoyment, until, someone was pounding on the door. What was so urgent that someone would disturb them now immediately occurred to Morgund. The matter obviously so urgent that someone had found a key and was now opening the door. Morgund took himself off Frida as quickly as he could. Just as the door opened Morgund looked out at Paten again with his Norseman bodyguard.

Paten spoke, "Sorry my Lord, there is a matter ..."

Morgund was astounded that now of all times he should be interrupted. Morgund looking at the deeply concerned cast to Paten's face subdued his outrage. "What is it?" He fought back his displeasure. "Go on tell me what is it?"

Paten came to the point. "The same morning after I left the castle Gregor arrived, the boy Iain with him. The man I left in charge, Donchadha had speech with the wayward Gregor. Gregor told Donchadha that he was in transit to the north and would have two days of rest within the castle. He said that you had commanded that it be so. The dog biting was no longer an issue of disharmony between you, all past disturbances were put to rest. Gregor said it was your wish that he was to have the freedom of the castle."

Morgund had to keep the anger in check for he was about to kick a chair or a table over. He did not wish such an act of anger on his first day after his wedding so he restrained himself. Trust Gregor to find a way to turn a wondrous event on its head. "Not a word of it is true!"

Paten tried to keep calm despite his grievous error in letting Gregor inside the castle. He continued, "It could be that he sought shelter for a night or two, intending, to be gone before I got back. It would take some time for any word of this to reach me. Of course, when I had speech with you, the lie would be uncovered. Under those circumstances no harm done, that he be sheltered for a day or two, then gone. The only way in was to use your name my Lord. He would know about the wedding thus he could seek such shelter as the castle offered for a day or two before what he said was uncovered for a lie. He is clever."

"A clever fool." Morgund was full of pent up rage which he still sought to subdue as he eyed Frida. "He will pay for this."

Paten stayed silent waiting for Morgund to fill the silence which he soon did.

"He misused my name. What is he up to now? Some matter of mischief goes on. It is often the case with him that a thing involving him is fraught with chaos. Have you had any further news of him?"

"No. I left instruction should anything of note to occur to send another messenger. None has yet arrived."

"Ride forth Paten, and if still Gregor is at the castle. If he is, keep him there until I arrive. If he has flown I would be informed where to. Send a man back to me immediately whichever way it goes."

Leaving the gloomy greenwoods behind him Paten saw the Viking castle rising ahead of him. With Gregor's guile he could easily take the castle, a stupid notion Paten immediately decided after it came to him. Gregor could not hope to take possession of the castle, not even a man of his talents could dupe those within with so much to lose if they let his devilish charm overcome them. All Gregor could hope to achieve was his own death in attempting it, but Gregor was a strange man with much slyness and silliness, which made the idea not so unlikely after all which when Paten gave it consideration made him decide he should ride forth warily. Approaching the walls he heard a whirr. Then another whirr. From long experience he knew what those whrr's were, arrows.

Wrenching his horse around as more arrows came at him. What manner of devilments went on here? This question was on Paten's mind as he left the castle speedily. With more consideration, knowing what kind of devilment went on, Gregor had taken the castle. Morgund must know of this immediately. Any of the twelve arrows that were stuck in the ground behind him could of killed Paten.

    The castle air was thick with arrows. The men from the curtain wall releasing them were men that not so long ago Morgund had spoken with in friendship. When he pulled his horse around it elicited a ragged cheer from the castle walls. The air was full of arrows. With arrows raining down every side of him Morgund had expected to have one find him. Tears of rage in were in his eyes when he was safely beyond their range. Gregor's life was forfeit after this. Morgund was enraged with himself for showing mercy to that vile snake on that earlier occasion when he had set that demon-dog on Phail. Obviously the man did not deserve such gentle treatment. It was poor judgement and he was paying for it now. Nearly paying for it with his life. It was madness for him to ride upon the walls like he did expecting them to fall just because he wanted them to.
    Like Knut, king of England, demanding the tide to halt just because he commanded that it must. He was as big a fool as that English king to undertake it. King Knut had famously demanded the tide to stop coming in and seated himself in its path to defy it. This was not so much his idea but that of his courtiers who suggested he held such power. Knut turned to those who believed or said they believed such nonsense and said to them, 'Even a king has a limit to his power. I have been made humble by a greater monarch than myself, he who governs us all, God.'
    Morgund had held the mistaken opinion that the arrows shot at Paten and his men were meant as a warning, not meant to kill. He could not believe Gregor would do something so drastic as try to kill him or his men. Expected it to be some kind of bargaining

device to be taken back into his service. Now he knew this for what it was, an act of war. Seven of his men were dead, more arrows raining down upon them as he watched. These arrows to make sure they were truly dead. Perhaps a man amongst them had been wounded, not now. Even though they were surely dead still more arrows rained down upon them. A waste of arrows, no good commander would spend them like that. As he thought of it the arrows stopped. Someone, probably Gregor, had some good sense to refrain from firing further arrows at dead men. What to do now? Perhaps he should sneak up and climb the walls like he did when he first took this castle. Frustrated at the horrendous outcome so far, Morgund spent what was left of the day full of anxiety and slow burning anger deciding his next step. When night came the walls were alive with men and woman. Woman were spotters calling out to their menfolk the targets below. These women must be from surrounding places because few women were in this castle when Morgund had originally taken it. Morgund could see that taking the castle was not going to be easy. By morning the arrows that had been shot had been recovered, retrieved in the night by work parties, significant of someone with considerable efficiency behind all this. Taken up with how best to proceed when there was a face he did not expect to see but on second thoughts was not so surprised to see after all. Suddenly gazing back at him was Phail. Even though he was left behind and ordered to stay at his mother's side, a part of Morgund all along expected to see the boy for did he not on all other occasions be wherever he was supposed not to be, always, appeared where the action was, or, more truthfully was, more often than not, the cause of the mayhem. Responding to Morgund's questioning eyes Phial made his explanation, "I rode after you." What Phail said next had Morgund with his lips pursed in thought. "I brought a large chest which will solve your problem."

"How?"

"The chest I bring will give you Gregor and allow you to take the castle with little effort."

Morgund knew Phail was no fool so it must make sense once he had explained it.

Morgund lamented Gregor's treachery. "I admit I could not see something like this happening ... him trying to kill me." Morgund then turned to a matter that must be attended to. "What does thy mother think of thee coming?"

"Mother probably thinks me still in bed."

The clever Phail, indeed he was. Although only just turned ten, with that sword at his belt Morgund pitied anyone who thought it an article of fashion. Morgund wondered what usefulness the chest had. There would be a plan, there had to be a well thought out valid plan because that was Phail's way. The sharpness of his mind was matched by his uncommon adeptness with a sword, altogether, making him a force to be reckoned with. Phail sparred three boys at a time and those boys could only just manage him.

Morgund gave Phail his full attention. "The chest, out with it, how does it solve my problem?

"Gregor often asked me about treasure thee had taken from Skelbo castle. I think that is why he came to see you. Treasure amassed by Earls of Ross, also added to at Skelbo, when thy good mother Mary married her late husband, a man said to be very wealthy. That was the sum of Gregor's reckoning that thee had this vast wealth in thy possession. I told Gregor I had never heard of your wealth. He asked me to look into it. If I could bring the subject up with you find out where it was hidden. I never brought it up, having no interest in it. When he kept asking me I laughed at him. I told him there was no such treasure and he was a fool to believe in it."

Morgund's face shone with subdued mirth at the idea that Phail had called Gregor a fool. Then he focused on the absurdity that he was a very rich man. "My sword and scabbard are the full measure of my prosperity. They were given to me once long ago by king John. I took from Skelbo all I have, horses, cattle, sheep, grain. I own a jeweled brooch. The hillfort of course is mine. He could hardly hope to take that!" As he said it Morgund realized he might have something of the like in mind, after all, was not this castle once Morgund's and now was Gregor's. "Gregor has me as rich as Solomon." Morgund almost laughed at it and would have if there was not so much anger in him. He was a baffling man Gregor, full of contradictions, not least, his silliness and cleverness mixed together.

Phail made this point then, "Gregor thinks thee has this treasure. And he is a greedy pig. Make him believe he will get his hands on it and his reason will desert him. He will be at your mercy."

Morgund looked at Phail, appreciating the subtle mind contained in his young head. "You have done a good deal of thinking about this."

"Aye," came from Phail.

"And how is this to work? I am sure it has it all been assessed."

"Have two men ride with the chest just beyond arrow range. Have a man under a white flag approach the castle. Have him declare the chest is for Gregor given so he leaves the castle. That there is gold in it. The gold in exchange for the castle. Leave the chest on the ground and have the men who delivered it, depart. I will be inside. When Gregor opens it as he surely will I will spring on him catching him by surprise. Keep in mind he will have no other man near this hoard of wealth as he thinks it to be. Once he opens it I will have a dagger at his throat in an instant. At the same time send in horsemen. In the confusion we will have the castle. The gate will be open with Gregor without."

Morgund looked around at the tent walls trying to weigh how this would work. "Won't others be near to protect him?"

"Grasping greedy man that he is no other will be anywhere near when he opens it," Phail replied.

"I see the truth in that."

Phail spoke once more. "Tell Gregor the intention is that it is in exchange for surrendering the castle that he gets all the gold. I can just see his greedy eyes, see him rubbing his hands with glee. I know the heavy oak door of the castle gate well. It is locked by a large key. It will take a while to lock once more after being unlocked whilst Gregor is without. It takes a good while to at any rate."

Both were silently thinking until Phail had an excited animation on his face that was not there earlier. "I might have to kill Gregor." That last comment, "Might have to kill Gregor," caused a vicious smile to appear on the child's face that was spine chilling to see in one so young.

Warming up to his theme Phail's words became even more animated. "The porter is old, he needs someone to tell him his every action, his wits are addled. It might take some moments for him to decide that the gate must be locked again despite the urging of others to do so. The porter, to urge him to take action makes him the more fumbling. No one will shoot arrows at me with Gregor near me. All eyes will be on Gregor's neck with my dagger pressing close on it. The key will stay unmoved in the lock when you ride through the gates. Or, any attempt to lock them, will be incomplete." Phail gave vent to his passion. "Here is a surprise indeed for him to find me where he never thought me to be and with a dagger at his throat."

Morgund came to the consideration uppermost in his mind. "What will I say to thy mother when this goes wrong and you are murdered by Gregor. He so nearly succeeded not long since?"

Phail was prepared for this. "There is no other way. Mother will understand. Do this, it will work."

A grin appeared on Morgund's face. "Is that knowledge gained from all the battles thee has fought?"

"I have fought battles Morgund, lest thee forget. With the dog. With the man in black. Have fought with my life at stake, on two occasions and won both."

Morgund stated the obvious, "Most warriors are not ten!"

"That is why my plan works. Gregor expects nothing inside the chest only what he imagines, gold. His greed will be his undoing."

"I have fought in many battles and they seldom go to plan."

This came from Phail's lips in response, "I am ten but have already killed a man in single combat and he was mounted and I was not, yet he is dead and I am not. How many others could escape that hell hound which attacked me? It is because of my quick mind and sound reasoning that I did. As thee too will have success, if thee follows my plan."

One of the fighting men who had entered the tent and having heard some of Phail's discourse laughed at him. Which drew this response from Phail, "Laugh at me all you want, but did you kill a man by my age? And remember well the man I killed, he laughed at me just like you are now and that was the reason I killed him."

The man's eyes narrowed, he looked affronted, but Morgund had no doubt if Phail was slightly older this man's life would be in peril. Morgund motioned for the newcomer to be gone.

Morgund thought for a moment and then said, "Tell me how this will work?"

Phail tried to keep the excitement out of his voice as he did. "Gregor believes in this treasure. He thinks to have it, he will not bear another to be near in case in some way they claim it for theirs. He will be outside the castle, the gate kept open in case a hasty retreat is called for. He pulls up the lid, in that moment I am out and on him, a dagger at his throat. In the confusion you ride through the gates. No arrows coming in. No arrows of course in case they hit him." Trying to keep calm in case he sounded childish, "Thee knows how fast I am. He will not have any others near in case they are overcome with greed and contest with him for the gold. Few other men are as greedy as he is, but to his eyes all men are as greedy as he is. He thinks most men want what is his, or, what should be his. He might have Iain to hand, only him. I will keep Gregor alive until you ride by. Or, if I have to, I will slay him." When he said that he might have to slay him the vicious smile was back.

Morgund contemplated in silence or a while.

Phail could see Morgund could do with some more convincing. "Ride through the gates with utmost speed. You will ride straight through them."

"Can no other lay in the chest?"

"You have seen it? No, no other can fit in it as I can."

Morgund resigned himself to this course of action. He knew what manipulation felt like. Gregor, was the foremost exponent of it, the difference here was that he agreed with the sense of the proposal put to him. Morgund respected Phail's brightness. Looked into his step-son's thoughtful eyes as he said aloud testing the idea, "In the confusion I will ride straight in."

Phail tried yet more convincing. "With Gregor held, and none to give the orders, none will shoot arrows."

Silence until Morgund admitted, grudgingly, "This might work."

There was a hopeful edge to Phail's words when he continued, "With Gregor outside the walls with no else to give the orders all will be confusion."

The castle loomed large in Morgund's memory; he remembered the powerlessness he felt beneath its walls. Here was the thing if he let Gregor hold the castle he could expect more trouble from him. Phail could suffer at Gregor's hands. Gregor hated Phail. The man was ingenious, dangerous, and stupid all at once. So much of what he did caused consternation to Morgund but if he knew one thing it was that Gregor was dangerous. One aspect of it more than any other worried Morgund, how did Gregor convince these men to cast in their lot with him in a so short a time? That showed considerable ingenuity. Morgund was determined to take this castle or die trying. As usual, as young as Phail was he was worth listening to. Morgund realized Phail surpassed him in power of mind and told him so. "You have cleverness and intelligence beyond your years, canny wits even beyond my own. I am going to do it."

Phail bowed deeply in acknowledgement of the honor done him.

Inside the chest, it seemed like a dark tomb, which it could be if no one opened it to free him from its stifling atmosphere. Phail heard voices, heard, a dull booming voice giving orders. Of course it was Gregor. Phail felt the chest being dragged away. Despite what he predicted Gregor was bringing the chest inside the castle before opening it. Then he heard a war horn. Morgund was coming to his rescue, or, at least trying to. Phail could feel the ground trembling with the movement of horses. Suddenly the chest was opened to the light and he gazed into the surprised face of not Gregor, someone else, a man-at-arms. He thrust his dagger up into the man's eye. The man immediately fell back out of sight. Outside in the sunlight, Phail was blinking away the effects of the darkness.

Seeing Gregor with his back turned to him Phail ran and hit Gregor and sent him flying. Gregor was old and slow and had little fight in him. His breathing was labored and after receiving Phail's dagger in his back, he gasped for air. Men ran at Phail with swords drawn. Before they could reach him Phail got his hands on Gregor again. Phail felt the soft flesh give way stabbing him in the stomach. Afterwards, Phail's his head was pressed into the ground. Out of the corner of his eye he could see a battle raging, arrows being fired from the walls. All this he saw until a heavy blow took away all his senses. When he awakened someone was dragging him somewhere. Some part of the attack must have been successful because Phail saw Morgund's men inside the walls in actual combat. Then he wondered if what he saw was not some vision caused by blows. It could not be gainsaid that the fighting had a distorted reality. In his pain and misery Phail tried to find the reason for what had gone wrong with his plan until his head filled with nothingness. It was like he was inside the womb so far did he feel from anything. Distant voices, he heard men debating what to do with him. Someone said Gregor was dead.

There was a period of darkness and then Phail was where he thought never to be, locked in a cell. A torch on the sconce wall outside was the only source of light, it flickered red and gold trying to cast back the dark shadows around it. There was dried blood inside his mouth and in his nose. When a chair scraped on the floor he turned his head to it. A jailor sat at a table, a plate of meat and vegetables in front of him. There was no light bar that on the walls that shone down meekly. It could be day or night, it was impossible to say. When his father held this castle the dungeon was hardly used, and rarely, had he been in it. Phail asked his guard, "What occurred with the battle? Did Morgund survive?"

The jailer answered, still eating. "Gregor is dead that I know. The battle is over, Morgund is dead, an arrow through the throat. And the day after tomorrow you are to be hung." The man seemed to find this was very funny.

Phail went back to his pallet, gazed at the wall, until blackness overwhelmed him and he was lost in time and space. A hand on his shoulder awakened him. It was Torkill his friend of old, a man who was loyal to his father. "Do you lack for anything Pender?"

At first when Torkill called him Pender, Phail wondered who Pender was, it had been so long was it since someone had called him that.

Torkill for his part thought the boy was still dazed, thus, he repeated the question, "Pender art thee well?"

It was so reassuring to look on a friendly face. However, that said, it could not overcome his gloom at the fact that he was to be hung on the morrow. "I am filled with dismay that my life is soon to be taken from me."

"Brighten then. For thee has a long life still ahead."
"What?"
"Some here would surrender to Morgund."
"Morgund is dead. Is he not? I was told he was."
"What?" And what Torkill said next brightened Phail

considerably. "No, he is very much alive."

"The man before thee who served me as jailor told me Morgund was dead and I was to be hung."

"A poor jest."

Phail asked, "How did this come about, Gregor, and the taking of all?"

"First, he entertained, told stories, he is very good at doing that. Then he spoke of some of the Vikings of yesteryear who would never fall at the feet of a Scotsman. That by his own assessment the castle could be ours with but eight men, and more from outside who could be snuck in. He cajoled. He persuaded. Spoke to one then another, then, two together, then, three together. Before we knew it the castle had fallen, and all of us somehow, were presided over by Gregor, the talker, ever the talker."

When Torkill brought food Phail ate he supposed well. Very much later or so it seemed to Phail came the clamor of men barging down the corridor, and at the head of them was Morgund. "I want to see the most dangerous prisoner you have." Soon Morgund stood before Phail with merriment in his eyes. "Your plan worked well."

Phail in no fit state for humor missed Morgund's attempt at it.

"How?" Phail asked Morgund.

"The castle has fallen to me despite thee."

"Tell me true," Phail asked, "What happened?"

"They surrendered after I said I would starve them out and kill each and every one of them when they came out, which they would be forced to do eventually through hunger. They opened the gate to me under sufferance that their lives not be taken from them."

"What of Gregor?"

"Dead."

"And Iain?"

"Dead too."

A month later, south of his hillfort Morgund met a man all in green. As he stepped out from beneath the leaves he looked like a woodland king with a crown of leaves. Giving himself a self-important air the man all in green, declared, "Do you know who I am?"

Studying him closely Morgund did not venture a guess. A large heavily built man with features that were intensely unnerving. The impression was of a dangerous man, which he was. It was made plain however that also he was a possessed of goodwill. Morgund's eye went to the sword that he had his hand on. Morgund then put a hand on his own. It was always a good habit to do so. Amid the trees to the south towards Skelbo he met this fellow, in a place Morgund went to infrequently. Being so near as it was to the Morays it was a place of potential dangers. He did so now because of a lost horse of good quality and reports it had been seen nearby. Amid the green was this fellow whom he met. He made Morgund think of the Green Man. It was said of the Green Man that lurker of the forest that no one must follow him or be lost in the forest for evermore. Although this man wore green, still, he was not made of leaves. Green Man, or real man, either one could be dangerous, so Morgund took care. This Green Man spoke, "I am a friend. I come in peace with only good will for thee, and a message. I was on my way to find thee. It is nothing but chance that we meet here."

Morgund kept his hand on his own sword. "Out with it?"

"The Earl of Sutherland is still a boy, only ten, thus, his uncle rules him. The master of this child, Andrew Moray, his uncle, knows of thy success. That thee has found a place for thyself, a place of safety and a following. We of Moray mean thee no harm, in fact Andrew wishes thee success. The boy William wishes you well, as much as his uncle does."

Morgund nodded.

"King Alexander is set to visit Skelbo castle. Alexander is well known to thee. As thee is well known to him. His ill feeling towards thee is known to all. The king has an entourage, many lords from the south with him. The young, ambitious, Lord Cunningham who is much at the right hand of the king and has ambitions to gain land, he might decide to ride north, he may choose to ride close to thee. We of Moray do not intend to tell him that thee is but half a days ride away." That said, the man slunk back into the undergrowth.

    Perhaps it was the Green Man himself who had warned Morgund so unusual was it, either way, it was a warning. With this news on his mind he hurried back to the hillfort. With provisions and retainers he returned to where he had met the man in green and then on further until he was in the forest, and within sight of Skelbo castle. Indeed, Alexander was there as reported and attended by many worthies, that young man referred to in particular resplendent with much adornment of his person. Perhaps twenty, he had fair hair, with the swagger of one who knows he is fit company for any, even for the greatest in the land. The man Morgund took to be Cunningham was in fact the young Earl of Buchan.

    Morgund acknowledged the very good favor done to him by the Morays. Such a debt must be repaid one day. They owed him nothing but for the sake of kindness extended warning. Yet despite their best efforts Alexander might still learn Morgund was nearby, therefore, with expediency, he returned at the gallop to his home. Yet more preparedness was needed, so he trained his men, set about arming them better than he had done. Morgund found after capturing the Norse castle he had wealth, many more cattle than before, owned more land, had, in tenure men who gave him service who caught him fish, tended to his cattle. If need be, they would wield a sword for him.

    By summer Alexander and his entourage had left for other climes. By then Morgund had a small army. Armies often find battles to fight and so too would this one.

    There was a fire going. It spat and hissed as it devoured dry wood. Laughter floated in the air as several almost-women peeked in through the open door at Frida's young and handsome husband, swooning over him. Any one of them could be her replacement if she failed to bear him a son. Morgund gave them a wave that set them to giggling again. *"God help her, already."* But then Frida had to admit that more than a year of marriage had gone by without a child. She slammed the door evoking more laughter from these evil nymphs. She could hear the girl's affected by the excitement running down the corridor. It was apparent by his speech and looks that Morgund was not as other men, much better looking, and sharper of mind with much humorous wit about him. Frida was pleased with Morgund. She hoped he was pleased with her. Up until recently she took it for granted that he was. She no longer did. What had been good between them to Frida's mind was not as good as it had been and to her mind there was one reason for that. Morgund was the last of his line and she knew how important it was to him that he have another after him to carry the MacAedh name on. Recently Frida saw Morgund smile at a rosy-cheeked girl in a most lingering way. She was not the only one, another girl had caught his eye too.

With this on her mind Frida walked past those very same giggling girls who had flirted with Morgund moments before which set them off to giggling again. First chance after that Frida took herself away from them all to outside the fort. In her hand Frida grasped a small idol of the Norse fertility god, Freya, intending to make an offering that would make her womb stir.

Her yellow-blond hair was blowing awry in the wind. Nothing could hold it out here beyond the pines. In Frida's mind's eye the two beautiful girls Morgund had flirted with, one small, with grey eyes in a perfect face and the blue-eyed girl who always got attention from men. What they exactly saw in that blue-eyed girl Frida was unsure of, she was lovely but so too were many others. Either one of these two could become Morgund's mistress. She remembered only a week before the grey-eyed girl with the lustful eyes had the nerve to evaluate Frida as she walked past her as if to say soon your husband will soon be mine. That she had been married more than a year and had not fallen pregnant resonated over and over in Frida's mind.

Outside the fort, that night, so as not to attract notice it was done in the midst of the darkness, having arranged earlier with the gatekeeper to have the gate unlocked at a certain hour and making sure before she left him that Morgund was deeply asleep. Looking out into the blowy night, a little speech she had out here in the darkness with the fertility goddess Freya. Afterwards, Frida left the goddess a gift, a gold necklace. Intending to tell Morgund she had lost it. Perhaps he would not notice, after all he was looking at her less and less often. This thought caused tears to gather at the corners of her eyes. Later that night, back in bed that night her hand went to the necklace that was no longer there.

The next morning Frida noticed one of the woman in the fort, Caera, watching her with questioning eyes. "Did you lose this?" Frida's gold neck chain was in her hand.

Frida was not quite sure how to respond. Caera offered her the necklace back.

"You have my thanks," came from the seemingly calm Frida. Only a very keen eye could see the tremor in her hands.

"Forgive me,' Caera said, "I do not want to appear forward, I may be able to help you with your problem."

Frida's eyes shot right and left to make sure no one was listening. They were not. "Does everyone know my problem?"

A small smile followed by, "Meet me tomorrow just after the dawn. Outside the gate."

"How did you know about my necklace?"

"I saw it missing and set my mind to find it, as you have already guessed, I know much about many things. You should feel no shame that there is no child yet in your belly. I have a feeling you shall yet have a child and I am very seldom wrong about what is to befall."

Frida turned away from the burning eyes, so blue. She was a good-looking woman this Caera. It seemed to Frida that she was surrounded by good-looking woman, far too many of them.

The next morning at the prescribed hour Frida was there and so was Caera. Turning her back Caera started walking away. Frida knew she was expected to follow and did. After they walked a considerable distance there was on a hill a solitary tree, standing tall. The witch made a sign to it with her hand a kind of blessing.

It was obvious to Frida that Caera was a witch. After that it was a solid hike through the forest to a series of small hills. They walked into a small circular clearing below one of these hills. There, they stood at the mouth of a cave. Tucked beneath a ledge overgrown with vines the cave walls danced in the light of the morning brightness. The witch's melodic voice bounced off the craggy bumps and smooth planes of the cave. "This has always been a place of power. Woman seeking to be with child have always come here. Thus it has ever been." They entered it, upon doing so feeling an immediate sense of magic. Inside the cave were paintings a burnt brown in colour. "Blood was used for sacred drawing to pay tribute to the goddess whose influence was sought." Thus spoke the witch.

Frida looked around her in wonder, one painting stood out, and the witch noticed Frida's eyes on it.

"It is Morrigan, the Celtic goddess of war and death. She is greatly feared. Some say she can be seen washing the clothes of those who are about to die in battle. That she flies across the battlefields, lands, to take the skulls of the dead to build her dreaded palace of the dead. Morrigan is also associated with strength, independence and fertility and can have a woman pregnant if so it pleases her to."

Frida looked elsewhere. "Some of these paintings have three faces connected to one body."

"She is the threefold goddess, Morrigan, often seen as a beautiful maiden, a great mother, and a bloodthirsty crone. She changes shape at will."

Frida laughed. "Men say that of all women that they are a multitude in one."

"You could come here to cast a spell on a full moon, paint your blood upon the walls, paint a child, to represent the child you want to have and paint the goddess herself. Morrigan might hear you and accede to grant you that which you wish for."

With that Caera left. Frida staring the walls did not know that she was alone. When Frida looked around for Caera and did not find her she made her way back. It seemed a long way and it rained part way forcing her to shelter under that same tree Caera had blessed. It was a strange tree. Frida had the feeling she was being watched by it.

On a subsequent night, Frida snuck out weaving through the woods by lantern light until she came to the cave. Deep inside the dark womb of the cave in the middle of the night it seemed more cavernous. The place seemed alive with spirits. "I don't think this is a very good idea," she said to herself choking back panic.

Fighting back tears Frida prayed to Morrigan, "Dear goddess, fulfil my dearest wish and have me with child."

A strange wind then sprung up, whistling: "You want a child?"

The pain was sudden and sharp when she drew the dagger across her arm. With her blood she painted a child and the threefold goddess on the cave wall.

Again in the whistling wind, "You shall have your child but not as you would have it be."

HABITS OF MONKS

STILL AFTER MORE than two years Frida was without child, thus, Phail remained Morgund's sole heir. Phail was twelve with that in mind Morgund decided to do something about the boy's education. With the benefit of learning he might grow even more wily of mind. Monks could teach him to read and write, determine figures and learn the mysteries contained in the Bible. Learn Greek and Latin, of no use whatsoever in everyday life but as a means of sharpening the mind they worked very well. Morgund knew this how well having been taught these languages to some extent in England by monks. Morgund decided monks could enrich Phail's mind with all manner of learning. Taking advantage of the temperate August weather Morgund and Phail rode towards Pluscarden monastery. Phail felt great excitement on the journey for it was the longest he had yet made. Morgund and Phail rode along in such pleasant country that it made Phail stare at it in wonder. At the golden leaves over his head and at his feet bewitching him with their beauty. The autumnal the effect of the sunlight on the coloured foliage was most striking.

    A full day into their ride they met folk who claimed to have known Morgund as a boy. Not only had they known him, they were related to him, or so they claimed. Morgund was of the opinion that there were none in the world who could make that claim. After initially knowing no such thing this is how they decided that such was the case. Before we get into that, why were these folk Morgund met, far from their original homes and wayfarers? Those who gave their allegiance to the MacAedh had been cast out when MacCainstacairt took over Ross. As loyal supporters of the MacAedh they had suffered for it. Any sorrow attached to this was immediately dispelled when the rare fact was explored that they were of one blood with Morgund. Said one of them, a darkish woman, Daerna, "Morgund thou art the very image of Mary, thy mother, and thee has the look of many in my family. As my family often said Mary had our look." The woman took Morgund's hand. "Your mother did look like many of us."

Initially, it had occurred to Daerna that she had the same colour eyes as Morgund had, as Mary herself once had. Perhaps Morgund was a cousin. If he was he was distant because she had not heard he was of her blood. Not that there was a formal legitimate link by marriage but such similarity in the looks told the tale. Perhaps no blood did they share but then again there was something in his eyes that reminded her of her own eyes as well as many of her kin. Morgund noticed how closely the woman stared at him.

Another, an old man, thought the same way Daerna did. Saw much between that they had in common. He decided that not long before they had a common ancestor. "Morgund you are related to her beyond doubt."

Morgund responded with an obvious degree of skepticism. "My mother never told me we had cousins."

A wise comment came from Daerna. "Perhaps she did not know. Blood has a way of appearing where it is least expected. Beds often find men and woman in them who should not be in them."

Morgund was very pleased that he was not alone in the world and had kin, no matter how tenuous the link, or illegitimate.

Daerna conveyed to her children, "A man of royalty is related to us."

Morgund thereupon showed his perfect teeth, "We obviously are kin and I am glad of it. I claim thee all as my cousins. All of you."

Daerna who deemed her eyes were the same colour as Morgund's own brought this up once again. "See our eyes are alike."

Phail was brought into it having to attest to the great likeness between this woman and Morgund. Indeed, he agreed there was something of one in the other. That Phail could see it brought great delight to all.

To my cousins Morgund said, "So good to be among my kin
Daerna who had noticed their similarity to begin with said, "Morgund you have changed so much since I last saw you." She shook her head at it. "Who'd have thought it, such a strong and able man you are now."

The old man said, "As a lad thee seemed not liable to become so big."

These people treated Morgund very well, with every deference. That they deemed him a worthy successor to the ancient kings was beyond doubt; that he was made in the image of those ancient Scottish kings who performed heroic deeds and made sound decisions was obvious. Handsome and virile, he bore all the traits of those who had made Scotland great.

Told this, Morgund was suitably impressed, pleased, and in joyful spirits. Phail and Morgund spent the night by firelight making much of their shared ancestry. There were notable warriors and heroic figures who were of Morgund's blood, many tragic ones too. Told were tales of them. Phail had never heard them and he was grateful for them.

When the next morning came their parting which was full of affectionately made farewells, mutually congratulating each other on their dawning friendship and kinship, and promising to meet again, furthermore, these things, though often said are seldom fulfilled and such was the case in this instance. With the parting Morgund felt a moment of genuine regret.

Deep in the tangled green they were. A scatter of pearly light filtered down through the trees to drop shifting bubbles of light onto them. The flickering sunlight cast a wondrousness on all until the branches over them strangled this wondrous light out. Just emerging again from darkness, from the enclosing branches overhead, it was almost like a sign, that the darkness became wonderful brightness as they sighted their destination from atop the crest of a wooded ridge that overlooked Pluscarden monastery.

With its mill, brew house, and stables, the monastery embraced by pines existed in contemplative serenity undisturbed by the rigors of the outside world. So far inland that it had never known the menace of Viking attacks. At the birth of a new day the bells sounded the call to matins, at twilight the swallows glided down, at other times these swallows called to one another as they sought their pleasure.

Once inside the walls the Abbot told them this was no place for swords and Morgund nodded and thereafter Phail surrendered his weapon. Morgund had too many enemies to ever think of surrendering his own.

Phail, bemoaned the fact, "Morgund, you keep your sword with you. I will be kept here without mine."

Morgund considered Phail and smiled, after all, what manner of threat could befall him in this place of God. "I will keep it safe. It will not lose its edge." Morgund's smile revealed that he considered there was no risk to Phail here.

Before Phail knew it his simple meal was over and he was in bed. Morgund, was quartered elsewhere from Phail who felt very much alone. Found himself lying awake replaying an event that happened earlier in the night. Morgund sitting beside him noticed nothing and heard nothing. A brother said the strangest thing to him, a thing that instantly reminded Phail of the sly friendship that existed between Gregor and Iain. "You have such a lovely face." The brother had whispered this to him before rushing away.

Not knowing what to make of it Phail kept the matter to himself. It was but the beginning of all manner of strange events because in the middle of that very same night this same brother woke him attempting to get in bed with him. When Phail pushed him out the monk landed heavily then ran off. Phail still felt the roughness of his course brown cloth which had brushed against his face. The man had tried to hold his hand. The brother had soft hands like a woman's. A leering look before he ran off. The look stayed with Phail preventing sleep.

Early the following morning Phail was awakened by a young novice monk not much older than himself. After a hurried parting with Morgund the gates were shut. Morgund, who had been his protector, was no longer with him. When the gates were shut Phail found himself surrounded by the monks, amongst them the leering one who was again leering. Looking at him it immediately came to mind that what Gregor and Iain shared together, immoral congress between males, was known to this monk. Phil felt a moment of panic, because the way the others looked at him, the leering monk was one of many. At a nod from the Abbott Phail was taken inside by a brother not the leering one and left with clothes and towels.

Enjoying a hot bath until he felt a hand on his neck. It was that monk again, the goggle-eyed one. This man could not stop bothering him. "I am Fionn. Here to assist you. Remain calm, I know best how to increase thy pleasure."

Phail used to bathing amongst others found lack of privacy had never worried him before, on previous occasions bathing was often a communal event with much nudity, but here before this man he felt dangerously exposed. The young monk's eyes hungrily searched his body, its make-up obviously delighting him. Embarrassed, Phail covered his penis with his hands. A slight tuft of hair proclaimed his almost manliness. It was soon hidden from view, like all else that proclaimed his sex.

"You need a hand there?"

The monk's hand came down towards Phail's penis.

"Take that hand elsewhere." Phail smacked the hand away.

Fionn leant near to inspect Phail's penis. He extended his hand as if to touch it.

"Stay, thy hand. What is thee at?"

"I might test the water as to its heat."

Phail felt confusion perhaps the monk had good intentions, and was attempting to test the water. He did not know the habits of monks but even so he would not take the risk. "The water is fine."

To Phail's surprise Fionn turned his back and went. When he did Phail got out and dried himself listening to his own ragged breathing and feeling a nervous flutter in his chest. The memory of what had just happened was confusing. Thinking of what he would do if molested his hand went to where a sword usually was. It was not there. That it was not reminded him that without a weapon he would find it difficult to overcome an assault should it come to that. He must have some kind of weapon. Telling himself that and that if he had to he would slay the monk. He thought of going to the Abbott and telling him about all manner of strange events but remembering that man's beady disingenuous eyes knew he would find no support there.

If they were contemplating making him their plaything these monks were much mistaken. He had slain men, would easily slay monks. Not fighting men they would be easily killed, if, and this thought was again uppermost in his mind, if, he had a weapon. That he did not have one was something that he had to rectify and soon. Monks were soft and stupid and would be no match for him, again, if he had a sword. He knew now why they took them off boys coming here. The more he thought about it the more he decided what had happened with the monk was an attempt at unnatural perversion. There and then upon accepting this as a fact deciding the first chance he got he was escaping. To do that, he must have food, find himself a mount and a weapon if he could. By midnight he was still awake listening in case the monk returned. By the time he finally did get to sleep the first rays of the dawn sun were upon his skin.

Phail's gaze was drawn from the writing tablet on the table in front of him to an annoying voice: "Phail if thee please, I asked thee what is the noblest passion of Christendom?"

"To spread the faith among the heathens and bring God's word to all mankind."

Around him they were snickering. Often he was without an answer. This time he recalled what he had been taught though it did not seem to impress anyone. A sarcastically bitter laugh came from the rear of the room, it was Fionn, the monk who had the weird fixation on him, who had intruded on him in the bath.

This shameful man addressed Phail, "Thee has found for once some wisdom so rarely in thee. There has been much discussion amongst us, your teachers, considering the fact that if we took a cow from the paddock, had it sit amongst us, if in it, we would find more thoughtfulness than thee has."

Responding to the laughter all around him Phail could feel burning shame upon his face. His cheeks flaming red revealing to all how the barb had hit home.

Fionn was not done with him yet. "At least thee has no need of a steel helmet if thee finds thyself in combat with so thick a head."

Emboldened by this cruel witticism the boys could not have laughed harder. Twenty pairs of eyes glowed with gleeful malice at Phail. Phail was not going to take this. He stood. "I have slain grown men for less than that!"

Fionn was unimpressed at this farcical statement. Phail despite his height was twelve years old. Fionn laughed at him.

Offended by Fionn's laughter Phail repeated his earlier statement: "I have killed grown men and one of them he laughed at me and died for it."

"Of course he did." Fionn stared at Phail with a mocking expression then looked to his left over Phail's shoulder. In that direction he nodded.

A burley brother came at Phail and held him around the waist crashing him to the floor. Blood spilt from Phail's head as a result of this.

Fionn stood over Phail. "How dare you stand and confront a brother? We will teach you manners. If you do not curb your brazen tongue we will have it cut out altogether."

Phail whilst being dragged away managed to gasp out, "Where am I being taken?"

Fionn looked down at him with stony eyes. "A child of the devil must be taught what happens to Satan's minions. To Saint Andrew's Chapel to pray for strength to cast evil spirits from within thy body."

Their motives were not as stated but black and evil. Once there three brothers dragged Phail to a room behind the Chapel. There unspeakable acts of deviance were committed upon him. In this room he was shattered in every atom of his being. After they had finished with him blood dripped down his leg. Barely, he made it to his bed. His fists tightly clenched by his side listening to every sound in case they came to assault him again. Lying there bathed in hatred, he knew then he would kill all three of them. They had been inside him, finding their satisfaction by causing him intense pain. They would all pay, he promised himself, Fionn, Nechtan, that smug smiler who told him he was the stupidest boy ever there was, that Thomas, who also kept at him on how oafish was he. Obviously all was planned goading him to speak back then springing their trap. But he was not a rabbit to be snared. This time it was a bear they had trapped not a weakling without the ability to fight back. In time, they surely see how unfortunate for them it was to have treated him the way they had.

He found out the other boys knew all when their knowing eyes were directed at him, making him even more determined to kill those who had assaulted him. All of them would rue the day they saw him as a victim. He needed a map, he needed supplies to go forth with. He would do all other things necessary to be free of his tormentors. He must get a weapon, preferably a sword. Then he thought of something he already had. His best weapon was his guile and he intended to use it to best effect. Although he would kill these monks outright he would do it when no one could put his name to it, could prove it was he who had slain them. Anyone murdering a monk would be hunted throughout the kingdom until brought to justice, such justice being the hangman's rope. Even though the monks called him a simpleton he was cleverer than they gave him credit for. He knew his own cunning, and they were going to find out how cunning he was.

For a while nothing happened allowing Phail to feel somewhat better in mind. Needing strength to return before he tried anything he resisted the temptation to run at the first opportunity. It was difficult save for he had decided to do it well this escape when he did it. Weakness in mind and body would make him easy to catch thus there was no way he was going without being vigorous enough to undertake it. Almost he began to think they would never return to harm him again until deep on a subsequent night laying in his bed he heard cautious footfalls. He must of fallen back to sleep because the next thing he knew there was a nudge on his shoulder. A nudge on his shoulder could only be a very bad thing this late at night. It was Fionn. Moving his hand slowly he took Phail member in his hand and jerked on it. Phail's penis was unmoved by the hand that would kneed it to life. Phail was not made to like this but he did nothing to resist knowing resistance was futile. Knowing to have it over with, to comply, was better than being bashed once more. Another bashing could kill him. Fionn could easily get his two friends to hold him down to repeat what had happened in the chapel, which would be even worse. At least Fionn was alone. So he lay on his stomach meanwhile taking his thoughts a long way away. Trying to ignore the agony of being torn in his behind.

Before he left, Fionn said, "One night the Abbott himself will come to visit thee."

The next day again bruised and just able to walk Phail took himself to the chapel, and committed his allegiance to God. Although it was very difficult for him to, he knelt. On his knees he prayed that he be given the strength to overcome all his enemies. Phail knew if he remained here he would lose all vigor, for he would not have time to recover, be made more and more degraded and wounded, day by day, until all the fight was taken from him, this being the case, he decided to undertake his escape immediately before such a level of degradation overcame him.

There was a quiet mare he gave salted bread to. It would remain quiet whilst he edged it out of the stables. The stables were beyond the monastery's walls. Going over the plan in his mind, a favourable factor came to mind, a part of the wall had collapsed, it should be easy to jump twenty feet to the ground below from that part of the wall. In his mind that it would not be so easy to get back over those same walls when returning. He would return, to kill the men who were on his mind. He would need a rope and grapple-hook for that. Then what lay ahead had his attention. A knife, or a sword, if at all possible he was going to get his hands on one.

As if God had heard his prayers, word came to him of two noblemen staying at the Abbey. Perhaps one of them could avail him of a sword. They had kept their swords on them these two. All adult visitors were allowed to. Phail would steal to their room and somehow take a sword off one of them.

The agonizing slowness of time fell heavy on him as he waited for darkness to fall. Finally those hours he sought came and he stole silently to their door. Outside, waiting for an opportunity to make an entrance, his mind racing because he needed a reason to enter the noblemen's quarters. Momentarily Phail moved away from their door thus to the kitchen and took a jug of wine. Alone, with his thoughts he decided he must move things on, in that endeavor Phail made his way to the room again whilst still holding the jug of wine. When the wooden door appeared before him, knocking on it, forced the door slightly.

From within, "Aye?"
"A servant with wine."
"Enter."

Once he did, scanning the room. On hooks on the wall two

swords still in their scabbards. Typically for noblemen they took no notice of him. Both of them lazed near the fire. Although Phail seemed to leave, away from the light he crouched low giving the door a nudge to make it look like he closed the door behind him. Seeing the door almost closed, assuming he had left it half-closed when he departed they complained about it loudly and like most nobleman did with much damning criticism of those of lesser rank. They drank, moved around the room, complained over the fact certain notables in the kingdom got preference over themselves. One of them got up and closed the door fully. Much later the talk slowed as weariness overcame them. Finally, they were deeply asleep, the fire burned down. It was then that Phail went to the hook where he silently took a sword, took a scabbard, a moment later he opened the door and slipped out. His next stop was to the walls where his natural agility took him safely to the ground. After that, to the stables. At the stables, all went well and without incident and he left with the horse.

When dawn came Phail crossed a broad valley where the warmth of the late autumn sun lay like a golden haze upon his brow. Phail felt good after so easily leaving that place so full of hateful perversion that he was lulled into unwariness. With the monastery many miles behind him and pondering his success when he was shaken out of this contentment upon spying four outlaws in the distance on runty horses. That they were outlaws was evident by the way they urged their horses towards him. No doubt weapons were in their hands. Responding to some deep primeval instinct Phail kicked his mare toward them at a gallop. For far too long he had been the victim, he was determined never to be the victim again, rather to be the aggressor.

Realizing he was charging toward them they steadied. One of them called out to him. "Hold you!" It was confusing for he was charging them.

It was splendid to have something to charge at. Phail laughed heartily seeing their confusion. It might be his last laugh, and that it could be, did not concern him at all. For some reason he could not even say why he found it a thing of great merriment and laughed more heartily still. His sword was sharp and they were going to learn how sharp it was. They surely did, when its edge fell on the biggest of them. Another fell by his hand thereafter, that man, the last expression he wore stayed with Phail, an expression which spoke of consternation that a mere boy killed him. Once on the ground this man lately slain stared up fixedly at nothing. Looking down at him thinking this man was number two, two kills in combat. It did not do to lose focus so he drew his thoughts back to what was in front of him. Just because all this had gotten off to a good start did not mean the end result would favor him. Before he completely stifled introspection he allowed himself another moment of joy at his success. Suddenly the ground rushed up to meet him and he landed heavily on the ground. It had rained earlier and he felt the wetness at his back. The high grass waved placidly in the sunshine. He decided it was very relaxing laying here being surrounded by it. Directly above him the sun looked down at him benignly. It was his friend this sun. It had darkened since this melee began, there were clouds to one side of the sun. Soon the brightness of this golden orb that ruled the sky would be stifled when clouds overcame it, came to mind. It might rain. There was the hint of moisture in the air. At this time of the year the sun rarely shone so well, it might be the last warm day before the real cold began.

Awakened from his dream seeing a sword thrusting down at him from the cloudy sky above. Rolling away from it at the last possible instant. The robber died with his neck skewered by Phail's counter thrust. Obviously his senses were taken from him by the fall and he had recovered them just in time to save his life. There was another man somewhere; Phail cast his eyes around to sight him. His eyes lit on the man staring down at his dead friend with confusion. Phail decided it was time to rid himself of the last of these men who thought it good work to attack a lone traveler. The last robber staring down at his dead friend - the first man killed by Morgund - was shocked at how truly well this boy had fought. He was not now in a good state of mind, in a void of nothingness that occurs when there is an abrupt shift away from the reality one is used to. So disengaged was he from the present that he seemed not to feel the sword thrust which killed him. He just opened his eyes wider then died.

The fight was over resounded in Phail's mind. Unfortunately, the birds in the trees were the only witnesses to his feat of arms. He had so little to celebrate lately that he allowed himself to feel the full pleasure of it. Self-indulgence soon over, he carried out an inventory on what possessions the robbers left him. He had two extra horses, two had escaped being captured, he had some food, some coins. Coins were so rare he had hardly seen one before today. They were gold coins. He thought, that perhaps he should be a robber. It occurred to him, that he was a robber, for did not he receive all this by force of arms. Upon a complete inventory, no weapons worthy of the name, a sword that had seen better days, three chipped daggers. Although the weapons were not very useful other things were; two ropes, one long and thick to capture the horses with, the other, used to straighten a tent. There was a canvas that could be used as a shelter. There was even a bow and a quiver of arrows. In this country if he did not shoot a deer he did not deserve to. One of the robbers was small and his clothes fitted Phail. His inventory done, he went over the battle with the robbers. He decided the robbers would have been better off hiding beside the track at a turn in the road and shooting whoever came around the corner. If he was a robber that is what he would have done, use concealment and shoot arrows on the unsuspecting, then he reminded himself again that he was a robber which brought forth a chuckle from him.

With the coming of night he slept long and deep. It was the first real sleep he had since his arrival at Pluscarden. In the morning he got moving again. In the forest, he came to a small pond nestled in amidst the pines. Erecting his tent, tethered the horses, where there was ample water and grass. It did not take him long to learn that whoever these men were that they had good taste in food. They had bread, and cheese, and even some small cakes. Lovely and delicious softness entered his mouth when he ate those cakes.

Staring into a fire, musing on Pluscarden, Phail's bitterness rose. He never learned anything there, he could only recognize a few written words in Latin. What good was it, Latin? They were correct in naming him slow at learning those things that they considered the measure of a man. They had learned these things better than he ever could. They said scholars were mightier than swordsmen, scholars ruled, despite what kings believed. That is what they had told him. He laughed when he heard them say it, which they did not take very kindly to - did they take kindly to anything? He thought it defined their sort of arrogance. They wore their conceit as ostentatiously as their dignified poses. The real world needed to affect them deeply and if he had any say in it, it surely would.

The next day was a day of rest in which he did a good job of depleting his stores. He slept a lot making up for the sleeplessness he had endured at the monastery. Seeking more feed for the horses he moved further into the woods the next day. There was a secret meadow further into the forest. With the horses tethered and grazing he took his bow and explored the woods to see if he could find game. Despite many signs there was no sight of the animals themselves. In the afternoon he took the horses down to drink at a small pool where the horses drank their fill after which they picked at lush grass.

Whilst the horses grazed, Phail lay back casting his eyes at the towering pines on every side of him. Gazing at them gave him the most restful and peaceful feeling. He breathed deeply, drawing in the rich smell of the woodland. Sensing the pulse of the living earth beneath the mouldering leaves that existed under him.

After another day his bread was gone, the cheese, little of it remained. It had not escaped his notice that without something to eat his stomach would soon pinch. Such was the reasoning that caused him to venture out of the forest seeking more to eat than what was available to him where he was. He experienced sweet delight leaving the darkness of the crowded leaves. The indescribable benevolence of nature stood before him. The sun's brightness fell on a body of water. The woods and their leaves bestrewn with their morning colours, russet and gold, were split wide, at the depths. The shore was composed of a belt of smooth rounded stones. On the farther shore, trees hugged heights that rose sharply. He looked at the stones that extended row upon row to the water. It was pure water, of well'like character. There were ducks and geese, fish. A shelf-like path led him down to the loch. Serene, contented, transparent waters. Perchance, he could avail himself of some fish. To delight him more than everything he looked at, he did. He trapped three salmon with his bare hands chasing them into the shallows. The taste of the fish toasted on coals went deep inside the ghost that was his stomach and returned it to peace and contentment. That was only the beginning of his luck because a deer appeared almost at his side. So as not to scare the animal away he raised his bow very slowly. Thereafter his arrow flew and the deer staggered with the arrow its side until it fell.

The deer gave him enough meat to last many weeks. He would have to smoke some of it or it would spoil. Fortunately, he knew how to do that, being nosey and forcing himself upon the people who do those tasks served him well. Often, he done so at the Viking castle and at Morgund's hillfort. Not much went on that he that he did stick his nose into, wanting to know everything and himself be a part of it. This was the first deer he had seen in the wilds let alone shot, like so much that had happened to him there was no one to witness his glory lately done which caused him a moment of sadness. Those who knew him would not be surprised at his success.

His hardihood was well known to many yet not to those secreted monks who did not know him well. They saw a young boy with scant Latin and a scrawly writing. He rued the fact that even with delicious food in his mouth the monks had found a way to reach into his mind and ruin his happiness. These monks, their evil, would not reach him here in the forest he decided and eventually his anger at the deeds done to him for the moment fell away.

Phail spent the rest of the day watching and listening to the wind blowing through the trees, watching the leaves streak through the woods driven by the wind as if the wind was chasing them and the leaves were determined not to get caught. Then the wind dropped. After it did, listening to the peace and contentment all around him, listening to the sounds of silence. As the night began to fall he made a large fire that blazed warmly. He was sure there were wolves here, had seen sign of them, and as always fire provided comfort and safety from predators. Directing his gaze into the fire he followed the vibrant colors of the flame with his eyes going with it wherever it went. Reflecting on it all he decided it was a splendid if lonely existence, one he would miss once he returned to where, lords, knaves and graceless men beset others with their lack of charm, wit and honor, not to mention men who committed ghastly crimes.

Determining by counting the sword cuts left in a tree that a full month had passed since leaving Pluscarden Phail set about making his return. It was time to make those who made him suffer pay for their foul deeds. To go about avenging himself on the monks of Pluscarden. Knew he needed something to use as a grappling hook to get him over the monastery walls, coincidently with this to mind, he heard a hammering that could only be the work of a smithy at his trade. Following the sound to a blacksmith shop which sat beside a stream, a substantial wooden building was close to the forge, stables along with living quarters close by.

The smith saw the boy riding up with two horses in tow. He determined the fair-haired lad to be perhaps twelve or thirteen. In a red tunic and sandy hose, a sword evident in a scabbard around his waist. A disconcerting smile the boy had, the look of a danger about him. Something in his eyes told the smith this one knew how to use that sword with an ableness than many men let alone boys rarely had. The smith decided he must use a light touch with him. "What is it I can do for thee my young man?"

"I wish to buy a small ploughshare." Phail had decided not to say a grapple, a strange device associated with war, furthermore, associated with scaling walls. Phail was thinking of the event that was yet to come, the slaying of the monks who had wronged him. Word would get back to the monastery not so very far away that a grapple had been bought nearby making that person who bought it an immediate suspect matched with his description an accurate conclusion almost certain. A ploughshare on the other hand was a common farm implement unlikely to arouse suspicion.

"Son, forgive me, thee does not look like a farmer, more a soldier in the making."

Phail liked that but responded warily. He knew enough of men not to trust their words. Phail looked into this man's eyes. He saw nothing but honesty, the look of a simple man of labor. Phail said with what he hoped was good humor, "The implement is meant for friends. I buy it at their request."

"Then you have come to the right place."

The smith downed his tools and took a long drink of water, splashing more on his face. Drank another brimming pitcherful of water. Phil wondered at his thirst but soon felt the heat and thus understood the blacksmith's need. The tradesman directed Phail to inspect the implements that hung on the wall. Phail saw the one most suitable for his intended task and paid for it with some of the coin he had taken from the robbers. The smith took the coins and handed over the farming tool and shook hands with Phail and made himself busy once more. Watching the boy ride away the smith decided the boy looked good on a horse, altogether a mounted warrior in the making. The smith who had been around many dangerous men in the presence of this youth felt that he had met one as dangerous as any of them.

Deep in a thicket near a small pond of clear water, near the hated house of the sinful monks, a storm passed over, though, not so much as a drop of rain fell on him which Phail took to be a good sign. He hid the horses, hid all his gear, after which he sat waiting for the hour of deepest darkness. Finally when that hour arrived, he picked his way towards the wall until he stood at the foot of it. To his amusement a cart full of bales of hay aligned the wall. They did not take any precautions at all to forestall a raider these monks. They did not because they had never had one. The cart and hay up against the crumbling wall made it easy to get over the barrier. Once over the curtain wall he merged into the shadows. Should he meet anyone in priestly garb who had done him harm they would meet their executioner tonight, the cast to the boy's face was convincing of this. When he thought how much he would savor the shock and fear written large on them when they saw who it was who had them in the brutal embrace of death, he looked pitiless.

He took himself to the path that led to the chapel where midnight mass was held. It would be like a wicked ghost in the night had floated in on the breeze to rain death on those within. Mysticism was second nature to these monks so it should be easy to believe the like, or some other such wondrous nonsense that they spent their lives mystifying themselves with. Only such was fit to fill their foolish heads. The heads of fools did not deserve to sit upon their foolish shoulders. See how much Latin would help them when they met him with a sword in his hand. In the absolute velvet darkness there was one clear note of sound, a call to prayer, the midnight mass. The monks would be coming soon. Along came a monk without a companion, from his gait he could tell who it was, one of his oppressors who liked to rape him. Fionn was in the habit of walking alone, tonight, he would wish he did not.

Fionn walked the well-trod path humming a little song to himself as happy as a bee buzzing near it's hive when something from the blackness reached out and grabbed him. Twisting his body around so he could see who it was. It was someone he thought never to see again, Phail. Be damned if a mere boy would beat him. Fionn was struggling more than Phail thought possible. Fionn recalled Phail's comment to him that he had killed grown men, it felt like a stab to his heart for now he believed it to be true. As there often is, there was a reversal in the course of the fight. When Fionn thrust out with his fist Phail dropped his sword. Phail rather than panic kicked Fionn's shin hard. With Fionn clutching at his shin Phail again took up the sword. Phail ran at Fionn and landed heavily on top of him using all his body weight to force down his instrument of death. Fionn fought to draw a breath as he felt the life drain from him. When Fionn stopped moving Phail gave him another deep wound to the heart to make sure of it. Then he dragged Fionn's body into the total dark, and moved again to wait. Some cowled monks passed him disappearing into the night no harm done to them. Heard more voices, ones he knew, he had no problem with them as he had none with the previous monks so let them pass by. Two more came and went, they too met no evil fate. He watched, biding his time. They would pass, those he came for, he just had to wait for them, those devils in monks habits. Every night they came this way he knew this because he had watched them often. Those he hated shared fellowship on their way to mass. They also shared fellowship in committing acts of rape as well. Those rapes would never happen again, nor would those committing them survive the night. It was frustrating seeing others and not those he sought. It seemed to Phail that the devil was protecting his own. If he saw them not this night surely it demonstrated that the devil did look after his own. Phail thought Satan himself did not have as much hatred and murder in his heart as he did. He recognized voices coming his way. They were running late. Closer, closer, unaware that death was about to claim them.

  Phail raised his sword and with it he sprang forth from out of the dark and stuck deep into Nechtan's side. Whilst Nechtan fell, the wide urgent eyes of Thomas, no look of conceit and low cruel wit in them now, in fact, he stared back at Phail with an almost pleading expression which was caught in the light of a nearby torch. He looked bewildered. Thomas took a quick step back, not far enough to beat the steel that came for him. Thomas's life was gone, it was as simple as that.

  All had gone as planned. Phail had watched them, knew their ways. It was the key to his success. Know thy enemy all the better to kill them such was the wisdom he had learned here and the only thing of value he took with him from this place of deceit, hate, and terror, was that. Phail had proved that he was the king of Death's devoted subject. Instead of gold he brought that Dark King, bodies. Phail liked the tingling sensation of the power he had in his fingertips when he brung on death. It was a feeling he savored and he looked forward to killing more men who deserved it.

Far to the north, Morgund was in a stone tower in audience with one of the most powerful nobles in the highlands, Ewan MacDougall, Lord of Argyll. The MacDougalls were a family with a long illustrious history to rival the MacAedhs own. The difference being, the MacDougalls maintained their position as one of Scotland's premier families whilst the MacAedhs fell far from grace. Although, MacDougal of Argyll - like most of the others in this room - would like to bring Morgund to their cause, and to have his aid against the Normans despite this he eyed Morgund with wariness. A considerable part of the highland leadership and ancient Celtic nobility were alarmed at the rapid rise and ambition of the Normans. But for one consideration Morgund would be considered a valuable ally in any future conflict with the Normans. The reason for this wariness was that stories were repeatedly told of the MacAedh ill luck. Morgund could see them considering whether or not the curse of the MacAedhs, if curse it was, would it fall upon them if they had connection with him? Wondering if this last MacAedh had turned his family's fortunes around, and, furthermore, the curse, if there was one, was a thing of the past?

Argyll came to the crux of the matter. "Much has been said of the MacAedh ill luck. It began with this Aedh the priest. He was an unlucky man your forefather. Being unlucky was not his only failing, rather than fulfil the role of a father he took himself elsewhere of his offspring."

Morgund felt he had to defend this man who after his wife died had left his two small boys with his wife's relatives. Rarely, he saw them thereafter. "Aedh, the son of King Malcolm was the father of the two boys with a loving wife." Morgund imagined his pain. "One day his wife was there and then she was gone and there was empty space beside him in the bed. Prayer gave him comfort, enabled him to sleep at night." Morgund described the events of a hundred years before with some words he had heard Gregor use. "Vital she was when she went to bed, alas, as the night progressed Aedh looked at her face in the candlelight, her face getting paler and paler until it was almost translucent, until it became a death mask and no human face at all. The longer he looked at it the more it did not look real and looked even less so when in the morning the worldly glow left her as the greyness of death made plain that she was dead."

Argyll shrugged his shoulders. "At least he found his peace with God."

Morgund nodded.

Another man, one of Argyll's allies, not so versed in the story put it to Morgund, "What became of the two boys?"

Morgund answered him, "One of them, Duncan, challenged for the crown and died for it. His brother younger Malcolm, remained living until he became old, and from him I am descended."

Argyll spoke with sourness. "Luck is alien to your family. Is it not true that Skelbo castle, a castle once yours, no longer is?"

Morgund reviewed this idea aloud. "Does luck rest on us MacAedhs?" A moment later he resolved it in his favor. "It does rest on me." I took a hillfort. Survived, great danger to. All I have I obtained, I gained by my own hand. Therefore I believe I can call myself lucky."

The Lord of Argyll decided Morgund might be a better ally than first thought. At least there was some cleverness in him, indeed, Argyll acknowledged Morgund had made good through his own efforts.

One would think a shared Celtic affinity should make these two natural supporters of each other but in many ways the history of Scotland ensured both were opponents. Morgund's clan were never close to those who ruled Scotland, whilst, Lord Argyll's clan had in the past been close supporters of the crown. Such closeness between the MacDougalls and Scotland's kings was now a thing of the past. This came about thus: The division between the north and south from at least the time of king David in the 1120's had led to bitter hatred between the factions divided by geography. The northern Gàidhealtachd opposing the supplanting of the old Gaelic culture in the south where an ascendant Anglo-Scottish way of life had taken hold. Southern Scotland - the new political heartland - enamoured of chivalry and the trappings that went with it had turned their backs on the ways of their uncouth forebears embracing a new Europeanised world view. The Celtic Scots were seen as inferior, culturally, socially and racially. Much English and Norman blood now flowed in the veins of the Scottish kings, so it was easy to see the highland Celts as a race apart. Also, already, a percentage of the southerners were Anglo-Saxons when first the Celts entered the south centuries before. Refugees from the recently deposed Anglo-Saxon court in England added to their number and were given ready welcome by Malcolm Canmore. Their advancement at court, English was the court language to please Malcolm's wife, was assured by the English women Margaret, Malcolm's queen. In the last hundred years many Norman knights added to the southern influence for these Norman knights also came from England.

As Argyll considered the man in front of him, the man he considered, likewise, took stock of Ewan MacDougall, Lord of Argyll. About thirty, Argyll, carried a lot of weight in his shoulders and arms which bespoke of practicing combat for many hours daily. He had a wayward confidence that so often complimented competence at arms. The current Lord of Argyll, Ewan MacDougall, was very dark of skin, hair and eye. Dougall means dark stranger in the Gaelic so it was a fitting name for him. Once in the distant past Viking parents whilst producing the usual crop of fair haired children had in their midst a very dark one. He was the black stranger to his Celtic nursemaid. As often happened a Gael looked after the children of the Norse being in service to them. The name given by the nursemaid, stuck. This Dougall had children hence a new surname sprung to life, MacDougall.

Next to Argyll was his friend Muieadhach. As with many in the kingdom of Scotland at that time Muieadhach had no surname. A famed swordsman was this man. When Muieadhach looked at Morgund his lips rippled in mirth at a secret joke known only to him. Apparent, that he did not think well of the new-comer. His eyes had danger in them. Morgund looked at him assessingly. Muieadhach's body was designed for action.

Many deem themselves gifted with a sword, few are. Muieadhach was gifted with a sword or so many said. Also said of him, which Morgund could easily believe, that he was even more exceptionally talented at finding trouble. In the art of wielding a blade as in most things those who put in the extra effort reap the rewards. Morgund knew how much effort he himself had put in. He wondered if Muieadhach had worked as hard. It would be an interesting contest if it came to it Morgund decided and he knew if he continued to draw these amused looks from Muieadhach, full of contempt, a clash of arms would occur in this very room very soon between them. That Muieadhach failed to respect him was not something Morgund was prepared to tolerate. Muideadhach was denying him his due respect as a guest, as a member of a distinguished family, not to mention the common courtesy entitled to all. When Muideadhach gazed at him with his sneering amused expression Morgund was itching to draw his blade on him.

 Argyll, seeing the likelihood of bloodshed signaled that food be served. If Argyll wanted to test Morgund's metal he had done so but a dead ally is no ally at all so Argyll intervened to have both men made safe, also, it was bad luck to have a guest slain beneath your roof. Young men and swords thought Argyll. They shared bread and salt, a custom in the highlands, which prevented bloodshed, a good thing or else angry hands would be often on swords and blood spilt more commonly than it was. Most times food was enough to bring about better feelings. Not on this occasion. Here and now this man provoking Morgund, Muideadhach, kept his glare going to the point Morgund was about to draw steel on him and Argyll had in his mind that all good work to calm things down would be to no avail.

 Apart from Argyll, and Muieadhach, the others in the room were a motley collection of highlanders. Only one amongst the multitude of them stood out, Ewan of the Blackspot. Hardly deserving a place here and yet here he was. Seventeen, Ewan was too young and too inferior in rank to behave like he did towards Morgund which was to say mirroring Muieadach, with glares and low mirth. Before this day was out Morgund thought he might spill some of his blood. Receiving another long glare from him he now intended to paint the walls red with it.

 Whatever else could be said of the young man, Ewan, he was

well informed. "I have heard thee has been to England and at court of that noted tyrant, John, King of England. That king, dead and mourned by none gave thee a sword. I have heard it is one of the best in all of Scotland."

Ewan of the Blackspot eyed the weapon in its scabbard.

Muieadhach, who had been quiet for too long and who had to hear the sound of his own voice very often to feel important made this comment with a sneer: "The sword is a masterpiece too good for the likes of thee."

Morgund shot back, "The blade is of the finest toledo steel. It is too good for me, for you, for all of us."

Argyll mused, "Of a kind rarely seen in the highlands."

Muieadhach rudely interrupted, "Show me the blade entire MacAedh."

"You dare to ask that?" Morgund shot Muieadhach a look of hostility. "And if I do not?"

Muieadhach loud voice directed a threat at Morgund. "If thee has the gumption to show me your steel withdraw it now. It is dangerous for you not to."

Morgund liked what he said next, was pleased with the wit of it. "I can show thee very close if thee would like?"

Something about Morgund's statement made Muieadhach wary, which was unusual for him.

A slip of silver came from Morgund's scabbard.

Argyll, curious about this blade would see it revealed fully. "Withdraw it slowly Morgund. Muieadhach take a step back and do not get excited at the sight of it and withdraw thine own. Argyll requested kindly, "If M'Lord Morgund does not mind, out with it fully."

"As you wish." With a flourish Morgund swept out the blade. Waving it at Muieadhach who involuntarily pulled his head back which made others laugh at him. Even Muieadhach's close friend Argyll could not resist finding amusement at Muieadhach's close shave. Not content with that Morgund stabbed the blade towards Muieadhach. Again Muieadhach jumped back causing alarm and more laughter. There was no mirth in Morgund's action. It was the act of a fighter who would have the other man take out his own blade and see which of them had the right to call themselves the better swordsman.

Argyll abruptly stood, cried out, "Enough! Enough! Must I

bear the misfortune of having a guest slain under my roof?"

At this Morgund sheathed the sword. Unlike those about him his face remained passive. Many were impressed with him. Before this Morgund had met flat eyes and now there was the light of merriment in many of them. Of course one man was deeply disturbed, Muieadhach.

Part of Argyll wanted to see the sword again but daren't ask. Ewan of the Blackspot had it in mind to see the weapon again also. There was not a man in the room not so disposed. Some of them, Muieadhach included, had a measure of respect for Morgund now.

It was not only the men who Morgund had impressed, the women liked what they saw from the moment he walked in the room. One of them, Argyll's daughter, Edana, thought his frown when he gazed at Muieadhach was adorable. That Morgund was so bold sent her heart racing. That his ancestors were kings was all too apparent in his noble bearing and blessed good looks. God's favour heavily fell on him by virtue of his features and build. His muscular arms were a sight to behold. His close presence performed a kind of magic on her. That he had noticed her too she did not doubt. Edana thought he gazed at her with special appreciation. That she had caught his attention pleased her so much she looked at him with all the more interest. Argyll noticed Edana flirting with Morgund, but given the imminent danger - he judged Morgund and Muieadhach were one step away from killing each other - put her misbehaviour aside, as a secondary consideration, a failing which would cause him grief, no less than it would Edana. Edana was a maiden, it worried her that other girls her age had already had a lover whilst she had never had one. Small for her age, pretty some said, but with small bosoms. Of course a man would not worry about that when it was dark and sinful passions had a hold of him. Her own eyes glowed with suppressed lust. Such immodest and delicious notions entered her head that it was apparent to all that she was in the throes of contemplating taking Morgund for a lover. Although Edana knew Morgund was married, however, she considered that no impediment. It was passion she was after not commitment. As it often is with young girls it is all about themselves. She guessed he would have her if she came to him at night. Morgund was sleeping beneath her roof this night as her father had told her. Looking at Morgund too long whilst leaning over serving him drew her father's ire and Edana moved away.

Argyll addressed Morgund, "Come next spring we will move against the Normans. Are you with us or against us?"

"Certainly not against you. Perhaps, with you," Morgund replied.

Argyll could not contain his anger. "Perhaps? What do you mean, perhaps?"

Morgund put it simply. "If I go to war with Alexander I would have confidence in the men with me. I have found anger and threats not such as would have me without I fear the blade that finds me is from behind me and not from those I face."

Morgund's eye fell heavy on Muieadhach, Ewan of the Blackspot at his side who seemed to think that everything Morgund said was a cause for a curl of his lip. The young Ewan, no more than seventeen, with the black spot, he was a minor retainer as such he should not of been considered worthy to speak, let alone make mockery of Morgund. That he was here at all, was down to his willing tongue and supposed cleverness. The only thing by way of ornament on him was his sword. That it was a second rate thing had not escaped Morgund's notice. Despite his lack of rank and wealth, the young Ewan was good at making himself the center of attention and did so now when he strode forth making this accusation on Morgund's motives. "He came to see our plans and pass them on to his friend the king."

Morgund had an accusation of his own for Ewan. "Alexander is no friend of mine, perhaps of yours. It seems to me you are both alike, you and him, two dogs with sneering grins." Morgund looked at the others in the room, Argyll too, "As are you all sneering dogs." He took Argyll's eye and held it.

The goodwill he had earned earlier had vanished when Ewan had nominated him the agent of the king.

Argyll stood and remained standing. "Morgund you are no friend of ours!" Whatever earlier attitude of friendship he felt for Morgund had withered and died when he refused to commit himself to the combined Celtic action he was contemplating.

Muieadhach's came to the center of room all voice and rage. "This man came here to find out what he could for his patron the king. He has done that. The question is what do we do with him? We cannot afford to let him leave to tell what has been said to the king."

Argyll shifted his gaze from Morgund onto Muieadach. "We came here to discuss the Normans who are like wolves. Let us remember we are not wolves." A moment later he said, "We are not here to contemplate murder. Morgund came in peace he goes in peace."

The next voice that spoke was old and croaky. "They come here a few in one place and a few in another, marrying a Celtic heiress. Being granted lands elsewhere by the king's favour. They build so many castles now that soon we will not be able to see anything but Norman castles about the land."

Not to be outdone, Ewan of the Blackspot made this statement directly to Morgund. "And here he is as brazen as Satan."

It seemed to Morgund there could not be a moment go by but that the annoying youth must not have his say. Morgund saw nothing which had impressed him so far as cleverness went with him.

The sage-like man that spoke earlier cast his baleful eye on Morgund. Then the man took his eyes away from Morgund and put them onto Argyll. "Somerled, tried to stop them and they came upon him in the night under cover of darkness, using it, the darkness, taking advantage of it. So by the unwariness of his men they murdered, Somerled. He who is thine own ancestor, Lord Argyll, him, who they killed, this man they killed in cold blood was of your blood. That is the make of the Normans to kill a man they were in treaty to."

Morgund looked at the faces around him, a stupid lot they all were. He would find no suitable allies here. Wanting no further communion with them he looked at the door planning to take his leave.

The same sage voice spoke again. "We came here before the Normans. They crept in on a low tide and they will sweep us out on the turn."

Morgund decided they deserved knowing what the king made of them. "King Alexander once told me of the Celts ..."

Muieadhach interrupted, full of scorn "... And what does the mighty king of Scots say?"

Ewan of the Blackspot insolently interjected, "Alexander has him in his confidence for does he not now admit to it! Close confederacy between them for do they not engage in intimate discussions."

Morgund wanted to split Ewan, head to navel, for saying that. He must leave soon or have some of their blood on his hands. Before taking his leave of them he would tell them what, Alexander really thought of them. He had to admit the king's sentiments were not ones that they should want to hear. His voice raised, a sneer to go with it, "He despises you and sees little value in you. The Celts are the most troublesome folk of all in a realm, full of discontent." A snort of disdain. "The king deems all you are good for is making plans that you will never fulfil."

Lord Argyll digesting this had a bitter tone when responding to it. "How pleasant a king he is then to condemn his subjects like that."

Morgund said, "Those, with the misfortune to know him well, know this, make no mistake about it, he is a man of rare cunningness."

"Explain the manner of his deceptions?" It was Argyll.

"My kin have mistakenly trusted him to their misfortune. To fight him is to court disaster. He is that kind of man who finds ways to achieve all he sets out to."

Ewan Blackspot proclaimed to one and all, "So says this worldly man, who knows all, whilst we know so very little. Are we not the men Alexander refers to as full of discontent and who according to Morgund are making plans that will never be fulfilled. I know something despite what Morgund thinks. I know I will not sit idly by, doing nothing whilst evil rejoices. We have fought the Normans all our entire lives yet we are but dumb beasts without eyes or ears. The king is close to him so of course he counsels caution." Ewan of the Blackspot cast his eye out amongst the throng. Incensed, were those on every side of him. Young Ewan flicked his eyes around the room then on Argyll. "He is Alexander's dog."

Ewan's statement outraged Morgund. "King Alexander hates me like he does few others."

Argyll said, "To the contrary. Your family's importance has passed. The king would not give thee a thought." Then Argyll's eyes narrowed as an idea came to him. "You say your success is due to your own efforts but perhaps a greater hand then thee has helped thee." Lord Argyll's eyed narrowed still further. "I can see you consorting with that crafty king. These Morays perhaps deem thee a useful ally to consort with, seek to befriend thee so they have you report to them; thus, the king is informed. I have heard that good will flows from thee to the Morays. Is that so?"

Morgund knew with their lazy relaxation he could cut many of them down before they could defend themselves. Muieadhach would go first because he was the most dangerous. Morgund eyeing him decided Muieadhach had done enough to deserve to die. Morgund was a moment away from drawing his sword on them. Why just show it to them, why not have them feel its worthy edge. Looking at his close retainer Seward, he saw that his friend would have him leave. The moment of madness passed for surely he would kill many of them but in the end numbers would tell and he and his retainers so few of them as they were, would die.

Before he left he would warn them of his feelings towards the Morays. "When I was with my mother in her castle they could of besieged me, the Morays, with all their strength. I with but little. Yet they did me no harm when it was in their power to. The Morays can count me amongst their friends. Be they Normans or not, I care not."

From Argyll. "Whoever does them wrong will feel your sword, is that it?"

Argyll's comment met Morgund's cold disdainful eyes. A thoughtful Argyll, "May I ask you a question? "Would thee engage with the king if he invades?"

"Aye. If I could. Of course if I am outnumbered badly I would avoid him. I could do naught else."

"I see," Argyll replied.

There was anger in what Morgund said next. "Alexander is my sworn enemy. If he should come into the highlands I will ride upon him whether you do or not. If the Morays ride with him, they take their chances along with all others who align their cause with his. However, if I have small numbers and if the king is the greater in strength, to do so, is only to repeat the mistakes of the past."

Argyll smirked. "So the Morays at one moment are thy friends, and the next, if they ride with Alexander thee will kill them?"

Morgund could not believe the idiocy of this man. "Anyone

who is by the king's side takes his chances. I see by your reckoning all things are straightforward and without contradiction. Only children see things that way."

Ewan of the Blackspot applauded Morgund with sardonic humour. "It is obvious to me that we are all dithering idiots with childish senses. The error of our ways is made plain to us by the sober adult Morgund tutoring us, the jabbering children."

Morgund had had enough of them all. "I am going."

"As you will," Argyll replied.

Muieadhach farewelled Morgund in his own fashion, "Good riddance to you MacAedh."

Morgund nodded to Argyll and was soon mounted and riding away. Morgund had expected to sleep in the tower and now darkness would find him on the road. Morgund would not put it past one of these men from the tower to find him and set upon him. Glorious autumn sunshine lit his passage and time marched slowly on along with the growth of long shadows. As he rode Morgund turned to his ablest companion Seward. "These men, we must watch in case they cast some form of malice upon us."

Knowing Morgund did not require an answer Seward did not give him one. Rather than respond Seward looked into the trees searching for a hint of unnatural movement out there. Certainly, there was enough dense undergrowth to hide armed men. It itched at his mind that some harm befall them at any moment. Images and faces in the movement of the leaves, in the shadows. Did his mind deceive him or were they really there? The more he looked the more he saw them. On closer investigation they were natural features.

Morgund looked to his friend questioningly and Seward responded. "I see nothing. That does not mean they are not out there." Seward thought he saw movement in the undergrowth again. His eyes fought to regain an image of the man he might of seen. Heard a noise, what it was he couldn't say. It could be a bough that had creaked on the wind. Ought he to warn the others? He was not really sure there really was anything out there. If men fell on them he would never forgive himself if he did not warn of them thus he surrendered to his urge to speak. "I am almost sure they are out there."

Morgund looked to where Seward was looking and said, "I think that it is the wind in the trees."

After a few more moments of intense concentration on the greenery before him Seward said, "Morgund there are men out there."

In gestures and words Morgund readied the men for action. Seward's own misgivings vanished when he withdrew his sword. Now he looked forward to using it on whoever it was that came at them from the forest. Then, from amid the greenery Edana rode out alone. When Morgund allowed her to, for at first Morgund thought she was a decoy to disarm the wariness of his men and himself, and bid her be silent. After a while with no attack forthcoming Morgund allowed her to speak. She informed him that Ewan of the Blackspot had left the tower to waylay him.

Morgund grabbed her wrist. "Tell me more?"

She was surprised how hard he grabbed her wrist - it hurt. Distress obvious in her reply, "I do not know more. I must go back. I took a great risk coming to you."

"Why do so?"

Her face was aglow with embarrassment. "Because you pleased me in your looks. I must go back before I am missed."

"That is no reason to help me? Why did you?"

"As I said because you pleased me with your handsomeness." Calling back over her shoulder as she was departing. "Good luck Morgund. Go with God. One as handsome as thee does not deserve a bad fate to fall upon them. And I, despite what others think, think, that you are very lucky."

Watching her trotting away Morgund appreciated the smile she gave him. A feeling of power and wellbeing came to him from that lovely smile from Edana. This very good feeling, he cast it away and restored order to his mind. Men were on the way to do him harm. With this in mind, he said, "We should disappear into the forest, leave the road."

Entering the deep woods the darkness fell on them like a dense black cloak. With the black also came white flurries of snow. The snowy glow in the sky lit their way. With the white falling down upon them, under this sky-fall, Morgund played out his worst fears. Morgund had hoped to find some friends amongst those he had just lately parleyed with. Rather, they gave him their hatred, Argyll's daughter notwithstanding. When Alexander came north, as surely he would, Morgund as a significant man would likely to draw the king's attention.

Without the aid of others it was a dire prospect. When Morgund called a halt tiredness overcame him and he closed his eyes and laid back on his furs. It seemed like he slept for moments only before the light of the new day fell upon his eyelids.

Meeting very dense forest too thick to travel through they decided to turn back.

Riding back whence they had come deep in the shadowy black woods a man held his bowstring taut. The archer was no other than Ewan of the Blackspot. His arrow sailed past Morgund and took the hand of one of Morgund's men. Ewan did not get time to shoot another. Running, when he saw Morgund dismount and begin to chase him. Ewan amongst heavy foliage with Morgund at his back.

He heard, "Ewan I see you. When I catch you I am going to cut you in half."

Ewan thought to kill Morgund, moreover, escape, without harm being done to him, not in this current predicament, being chased through the woods like a fox. It was a pretty place. Having all the pleasantness commonly a feature of Scottish forests. None of that mattered. What he was thankful for was the possibility of escape with heavy cover. When stuck in the tangled undergrowth he heard a sound behind him like a twig snapping under foot, a moment later a crashing sound like someone had lost their footing. Someone had indeed fallen. It was Morgund who had slipped down a bank. It took Morgund some time to climb back up giving Ewan time to gain ground on him.

Having lost Ewan Morgund trekked aimlessly until he came to a meadow. Leaving the meadow, the thickness of the forest closed in around him. He passed tree after tree, all of them so without distinctiveness. Morgund had it in mind that he might get lost. In a short period of time these two almost stumbled upon each other. Ewan doubled back on his own track without realizing it bringing him close to his pursuer. Another sound of a twig snapping underfoot told Ewan, Morgund was near. Ewan ran, and made better time than Morgund for to Ewan's front there was less thickness of growth, Morgund had yet to get to this more open ground.

Walking, out of breath now, thinking, was Ewan. A second-rate sword and nag of a horse was all he had to his name. So he took a risk to better his life. Knew if he had killed Morgund Alexander would have rewarded him. Now he could not even fight if Morgund caught him. His sword was somewhere behind him. He had dropped it somewhere. If he knew Morgund was alone and he still had his sword he might have waited to take him in ambush. He was no coward and handy with a sword, however, he had seen how easily Morgund made use of his in the tower and besides several men were in all likelihood with this man who sought his life.

Fighting a stream's power until coming out the other side onto slippery rocks, slipping and sliding on them, aiming for the better footing until finally with stable ground beneath him he looked ahead whereupon his heart leapt in his chest. A cliff above him wept water, a gushing torrent came crashing down. Surging, in powerful sheets, throwing a weighty flood onto the rocks below. The forceful song of it was not a tune of jollity and gaiety. To Ewan's ears it was a dangerous and treacherous song that caught at his heart. Going to the base of the falls for a moment he hesitated there at the foot of them wondering if climbing up was the right thing to do. No point in worrying about that now he thought though it hung heavily in the back of his mind that he should not, but the fact of the matter was there was nothing else to do, behind him was Morgund, how far behind he did not know, better to risk climbing than to risk Morgund's sword.

The cliff walls were sheer, wet and slippery, icy with spray. Any moment he might fall to his death reverberated in his mind. Near the top, easing himself over the edge he climbed no longer. Thinking to regain some strength, he sat. Minutes later Morgund's head suddenly appeared only a few feet away from him. The shock to Ewan was greater than any in his young life. His heart pounded so hard in his chest it actually hurt. He did not even have a sword to defend himself with. His eyes were filled with tears as his running footsteps took him on. A sharp drop suddenly was there in front of him. Below, was a vast forest, a long way down. The whistling wind at his back he noticed had the hint of snow in it. As the currents of the air knifed along his back he heard small rocks drifting down from behind him no doubt kicked. It could only be Morgund coming down to kill him. There was a narrow ledge further down, below that, a vertical cliff and the trees far far below that. Whatever else existed off this cliff did not bear thinking about because he had no way to get to it without wings. The ledge was a temporary reprieve but such is the instinct to preserve one's life that he took himself there jumping down onto it. Ewan had come as far as he could go. He stood stock-still, expecting any moment to feel an arrow slice through his body. He should have been content to own a dog, own a sword, own a horse. He admonished himself with his idiocy.

Then he heard, "Why did you try to kill me?"

At least he would live a moment longer for a man did not ask a question without waiting for an answer. There was another good thing about this, being asked to speak gave him time to think. Falling to his knees, pleading, "I but wanted to feed my children. They starve. I am hard done by in my house, dogs eat better than we do."

Morgund was incredulous. "Children? You are but a boy yourself!"

"They are my brothers and a sister, so much younger than I that they call father. I have no father, nor do they. I am their father. If I die, they die. Do you want that upon your conscience, the death of these poor fatherless children?" Ewan was clever at coming up with reasons to live. Seeing a momentary doubt in Morgund's eyes, he filled the air again with his anguished beseechings. "They are very young." Ewan was piteous. "Wee bairns they are. Are you that cruel you would have them dead before they have had a chance to live?"

Morgund was merely waiting to regain his strength before coming down to kill Ewan with his sword. The climb had been long and arduous. His quiver was empty after firing two arrows at the retreating back of Ewan. Most of the arrows had fallen out on the climb. At one point the quiver had spun and then the arrows had fallen out. May as well use the sword and make it clean. There were other ways, he could throw some large rocks and dislodge Ewan to his death. That way, however, did not have the elegance of a sword, there was nothing better to kill with than a sword. The death it caused gave a particular kind of pleasure to the killer. Morgund imagining steel in Ewan's belly then had a deadly facial expression. Seeing his look Ewan knew that death was about to take him. Regaining his breath Morgund calmly slid down the ledge, once on it, walking toward Ewan with his sword out.

Rather than die in such a gruesome way Ewan cast himself off the cliff. Had never imagined he would die this way, killing himself. For a second it did not seem he was falling at all. Then the wind made its presence felt grabbing at him, buffeting him. A glint of sunlight on the water below caught his eye. Rocks were one side of him. Closing his eyes to avoid the horror of them. In deep water he realized he was alive and not from this world gone. Little, did he consider how lucky he was, dropping like a stone he did not have time to think about it but a few feet either way whilst falling and he would have been smashed to death by rocks. After a quick swim to the bank he climbed out onto it. Thereafter, into the forest. Amongst the pines he looked back and up at the gradient that Morgund would have to negotiate to come down after him with a sense for the danger involved. Deciding, no man, nor a goat could find a way down there. Ewan skirted the edge of the water as he walked so as to prevent walking in circles.

PHAIL'S RETURN

PHAIL BIDDING HIS time making for home fearing what he would tell Morgund and his mother about the monastery and what had befallen him there. With bitterness of winter upon him he could delay no longer so finally he rode north. On his way, rode into a little village towing his two captured horses behind him, some children appeared to the left and the right of him. A young woman who looked unwell, who had a baby in her arms, held out her hand in supplication. He kept riding leaving her behind. A little girl walked out to look at him, behind her a step or two, her infant brother sucking his thumb. Phail found him a funny little fellow and stopped to talk with him. "Hello boy, what art thou called?" "Aiden, and thee?"

"Phail."

The boy eyed the sword. "That is a big sword for you. You look silly with it."

The little girl scolded her brother, "That is rude, Aiden. And stop sucking your thumb."

He did stop sucking his thumb long enough to call out in a small voice, "My sister thinks she is the boss of me." He then plunged his thumb back into his mouth. Leaving Phail in no doubt he was his own man.

"Take your thumb out of your mouth," the sister said to him again, but he did not defiantly sucking on it all the harder.

Phail's horse shied at some mangy dogs that ran behind it. There was loud noise of shouting up ahead, of a fair, or market. A woman with red, filthy hair, red distant eyes, stared at him.

Phail asked her, "What is going on there?"

"A horse market?"

"Oh aye," replied Phail.

"They buy horses," she said eyeing his horses. "They might buy yours." The laughter that followed was an ill sound with no mirth in it. Whatever the joke was Phail did not understand it and thought perhaps the woman was from her wits dislodged.

Another man red of face reassured Phail. "They pay good prices for horses." A good natured laugh followed that. The red faced man spoke again. "Oh yes they pay very good prices." This time he did not laugh but looked at Phail with an unreadable expression. Phail looked at his face and had an unsettling sense that they did not buy horses at all but murdered people.

A hearty fellow patted the horse he rode. "Does thee wish to sell this horse, if so it is to there thee must go."

"I will sell those two behind me not this one." Phail made to move on.

Phail meant to leave but propped when he heard the red headed woman once more. "Does thee like our village?" The redhead asked it of him scratching her lice ridden noggin.

Morgund was reprieved from rating the muddy shambles when other words were said. "Will like it even less if he stays," said the older sister of the red-haired slag. Alike to her sister in every detail except that her hair was streaked with grey, and not red but a muddy brown. Like her sister scratching her head but so determinedly as if she would tear a hole in it. When she laughed missing and rotten teeth were a fitting accompaniment to her overall hideousness. A crow watching from a high tree cawed with a cry that sounded like contemptuous laughter. All in all Phail decided it was as ill-omened a place as he had ever seen.

The little girl whose brother was the thumb sucker approached. "Phail no good will be done to thee here. Go whilst thee can. They will take your life."

The red-head now with eyes narrowed to slits, said, "Pay her no heed she is just a silly child thee will be welcome at the market."

Rather than be quietened the little girl wanted to know of him, "Are you with anyone? With armed men?"

"No."

"Then turn and flee. "Eight men came here but a week past and every one of them was slain."

The man red of face smiled trying to appear benign and failed. "She is overwrought with nightmares and delusions from a bump to her head." He went to hit her in the head again but the little girl ducked away. "It is unfortunate. We despair of her ever recovering her senses. Go to the market and obtain a good price for these horses you wish to sell."

Phail hurried along having had enough of these oafs and sluts.

Behind him he heard the man say, "That young fellow, sword, horses, his life, all will be gone within the turn of the hour." He laughed with the kind of deranged hilarity which the red-headed sister had displayed moments before.

The little girl chased him. "Don't go. Turn from this place. Flee!"

Phail looked back at her, stopped for a moment and considered whether he should take her advice. How could he turn and confirm that he was afraid to face down those who would harm him? He was sick of wicked men and wanted some wickedness to fall on them. Death could come to him as a result of these actions he was about to undertake, no doubt it would, one day, and perhaps, even this day, but that was no reason to turn from the prospect of it. Thinking about death, something told him that it would not claim him this morning, he felt too good, too confident in his sword-arm. Had he not he beaten odds before. Had not others underestimated him before today and died for it. He had seen death, tasted death, and dealt death. Death was his friend and would not claim him rather needed his assistance. A strange notion, the kind one keeps to oneself. As strange as that notion was, another, even stranger occurred to him, death, could not claim him, because he was death.

Their ugly faces were disgusting, if given the merest excuse, Phail would start slaying them, hacking into them. Would like to do that or give each of them a good bath. It was easier to kill them. If it was his fate to be Death's servant he was pleased to stock his subterranean vaults with the carcasses of those on earth silly enough to find a vulnerable boy in front of them and not what he was, truly, a killer. He was not a weak he was someone born to wield a blade and born to make his blade sing on the flesh of knaves. Those with eyes that did not see that would learn what he had in store for them. Remembering how good a sword felt in his hand, how good it felt to kill. Recalling the exhilarating thrill of danger. These thoughts, curled his lips into a smile as he kicked his horse forward into a trot toward the market. That was where the fun would be, where he could make his sword sing, the market.

The little girl caught his reins. He liked little girls their prettiness and innocence appealed to him. It was in the same class of likeness he had for flowers and dogs. He cast his eyes down at her. She eyed him with all the sobriety of someone telling him going forward was to die. He noted her pluckiness, liked her. Her skinny boyish frame would please the monks although her sex left him in some doubt whether they would choose to inflict pain on her. If they did, they would crack her open like a little nut and rip the juice right out of her, when they were finished a dry shell of hurt and pain would be all that remained. Knowing this, it made his heart race in anger. He shook her off and proceeded. These evil men with murder in their hearts would learn the cost of living sinful lives.

She did not give up easily shouting after him, "My good young lord beware!"

He waved her off angrily. Phail wanted the pain in his heart to stop and how better to stop it than to stop an evil man's heart. The thought of such an act, have them be evil to him, and he punish them for it pleased him a great deal. Very much hoping these violent men would bring the fight to him, that they would tempt his sword into action. He was distracted for a moment by the girl who looked after him with beseeching eyes. She looked very disappointed that he was not taking her advice. Perhaps he would ride back later and present her with a severed head as a gift to dispel her concern about the poor boy with the sword that was too big for him, which looked silly on him according to her brother. What would the monks make of her? He wondered if she could learn Latin, if, the monks would call her stupid. Her boldness would displease them; they would definitely dislike her for it. Thinking of the pain they had caused him made a glare appear in his eyes, a warning to whoever wronged him that it would bring on violent retribution.

It was a comic image, an angry boy with a sword which seemed a little large for him advancing into danger until one looked harder. Little did those around him know the quality of his swordsmanship. They saw a boy with a swagger about him that appeared ridiculous.

Phail soon found others staring at him, their scraggy loose hair, dirty beards, dry cracked lips, wolves all, he thought. Ever since the monks dire treatment of him an instinct to defy evil men had welled up in him. All around him, he saw wickedness. A reckoning that would dispel his pain was in the making. Should he unleash his sword on them? Make it sing the song of death on their flesh. Their limbs, should he let them fly? Make their heads fly? A ghastly image for many it was a most pleasant prospect for Phail. He saw nothing wrong with it at all and it made him wonder who was the more black-hearted, he, or they? Arriving at this answer, they both were. At least in his case no innocent would ever feel his sword. Of those around him, bar the children, he saw no innocence, what he saw was bloodlust, and was joyful in heart at it. They wanted blood. He would give them blood, their own. He was in the right place to revel in that dark substance. A smile flitted across his face like the devil had come to visit. As he felt their hostile eyes on him he felt the reckoning coming.

From the point of view of those watching him, all they saw was a boy with a sword overlarge for him. They thought him witless for coming in amongst them when warning had been given him. Just as they were certain he was about to die he was equally certain before the day was out these people would have cause to redress their opinion of him. He felt his friend Death was near. Let them meet Death.

A big horsey looking woman with the smell of horseflesh on her smiled pleasantly at him, "Good day young sire, come for a visit?"

Her protruding teeth and long horsey face might confuse the horses, a second thought occurred to him, might it comfort them having one of their own amongst them. He felt like asking her if she minded looking so much like these animals that were sold here but so far she had been polite so he did not.

She asked him, "Do you like horses boy? We have many fine animals."

"Yes, I admire them very much."

The stares Phail was getting he was mightily sick of them. A grimace appeared on his face. His small white of teeth clenched together. He cast malicious glares at the starrers. "Your relentless gaze is wearing thin on me."

They sustained their looks because a boy posturing with a sword was silly. It was the horsey faced woman who spoke next. "What bring thee amongst us?"

"Did one of your horses give you its face?" He could not help it. She had been civil to him so far but the comment erupted from him before he could help it. Again, surrendering to this urge, telling her, "I could get a good price for you. Perhaps I could enter you in a horse race."

He saw their hands going to their weapons, those that had them. The horsey faced woman obliged him with a mixture of regard for his gumption and perhaps a touch of admiration for his yellow Viking hair so rare here amongst the Celtic folk of this region. Hounds barking, some nipping at his horse's forelocks making it kick out. The dogs sent scurrying by the kick from his mare.

"What art thee staring at?" Directed at the multitude of scum. His sharp words to them, made them draw their eyes into slits and be more fixed in their scowls. "Has thou never seen a boy on a horse before, or, a boy with a sword?"

Phail felt surrounded by a pack of wolves and wanted to send them scurrying with the flat of his sword, like his horse had sent the dogs, scurrying.

He withdrew his sword such as an act of boldness they deemed it beyond belief. His face was lit fierce.

The spell was broken when laughter rang out amongst them. They obviously thought him a loon, telling them not to stare, it was fit for mirth and withdrawing his sword no better than an act of madness given that he was surrounded by wolves who would kill him in an instant.

Something nagged at the back of the horse woman's mind that there was danger here not to him but to her and to all of them. So improbable seeming that she dismissed it, however, not entirely, something about the boy made that impossible. This boy had the eyes of the devil and was well used to making use of that sword, it seemed like a part of his body, he withdrew it with such ease and held it so well. From the look in his eyes he had killed before. For all that the boy was well outnumbered, and obviously lack-witted to provoke violence when he had small chance of coming through it unscathed.

Although, a ragged bunch of scarecrows mostly Phail noticed some had better clothing and had quality swords at their belts, or in fact, now, had them to hand. It might be some of this weaponry belonged to the slain eight. He would watch those men particularly carefully.

The big robust woman made no first move, she continued inspecting the strange child.

Phail noticing her intense gaze more for his own merriment than anything else, said, "Would thee like a carrot? Perhaps an apple? I could gallop thee across the fields." There was laughter at that from many but not from her. She did not like the laughter it took alertness away from her men, diminished the respect they had for her. Phail called out to all of the dirty oafs. "She certainly has a head like a horse."

More laughter.

This smart-arse boy was going to die here and soon if he kept this up. Phail spun his sword in the air and caught it. Some of her men laughed at that too, the knaves.

She decided she might as well find out what it was he wanted. Something had brought him here. "Give our guest some room and to cast laughter on him is not fit for a guest." She said the laughter was at his expense when it was at hers. That was something she could not bring herself to admit. That her own men laughed at her was something that would bring her wrath onto them when she had finished with this boy. For now, she looked at Phail with a look which said she meant him no harm. "You would sell me some horses boy?

"For the right price."

An expert judge in horseflesh she took in their quality, one particularly was a superior animal, the others less so. "How did thee come across these fine horses, in fact, the one you ride is a quality animal."

"The one I ride is a fine animal and is not for sale, the other two it is I wish to sell. How I got them is my own affair and no concern of yours."

She was taken aback by his rudeness. She had heard enough of it. This was the last time it would be tolerated. Gritting her teeth in anger she said, "Mayhap boy, I will take thine horses and take thine head too."

"Did the horse comment rile thee? Never mind, better a head like a horse, than a head like a pig."

Spontaneous laughter erupted from crowd. Their mirth had Phail laughing along with them. Indeed, that he was a very strange child occurred to her. With him laughing along with the others she began to think he was simple witted. She had to admit his laughter was infectious. Despite herself found her own lips twitching in mirth. Her wondrous wide expression made her look pleasant but Phail noticed that although her eyes were wide and mirthful she was planning to murder him. She rolled her eyes, a look which almost made him decide to not kill her. Then she signaled to her closest stalwarts. Before they came on, a man separated himself from the others and came close to him. Phail found himself being poked in the chest. The man who poked him was dressed in a dark red cloak, his face seemingly contorted by a permanent anger.

After poking him the man in the red cloak, said, "Those horses are all ours, count yourself lucky we do not take your head."

Phail sent the man flying into the mud with a kick. He could just as easily of stabbed him and made that red cloak he wore bloody. A pity he did not, then he could see if red of blood was alike to the red of cloak. He took his eyes away from the red cloaked man. Men fanned out and blocked his way out. It seemed the battle he had wanted had come. Should he be afraid? Perhaps he should be, but he wasn't. All he felt was the pleasant expectation of combat. Like the horse lady he knew himself for a strange child.

The woman chuckled, "Does thee still find this a thing of lightness?"

To her great consternation he showed all the signs that he did. All those around her had the signs of humor on them confounding her senses which she felt gave this all this a feeling of unreality.

Still laughing the boy told her, "I will laugh heartily when your head flies off your shoulders. No doubt the horses will mourn the loss of one of their own."

His composure, it caused a glint of nervousness in her. But it did not stop her from calling out to him, "I mean to give you nothing for your horseflesh. Not a coin."

"And I refuse to give you a carrot."

A half dozen threadbare clothed folk, bleakly staring, and their humor gone from them. There was a different tone in the air now, the sniff of death. Their expressionless faces Phail found so irritating, he wanted to stick his sword into one of them just to see a different aspect on them. Perhaps if he stuck his sword in them it would rid them of their angry, dumb, looks. Phail saw the girl, with her, her thumb sucking brother, unlike the others she looked worried for his safety. Taken from his thoughts when he heard her call: "You should of listened to me. I bet you wish you had."

The horse woman giving him a blank hateful stare said, "And we'll take the blankets, saddles and bridles. With your sword."

"And I get?"

"Your life."

"I will pass on that deal." He queried her. "Was it the carrot comment that made you so harsh with me? Be of good cheer because I will still give you a carrot. There is a field outside your village I am sure I can find a carrot there."

"Are you mad?"

Phail met her glare with his own intense stare. "Who knows."

He threw back his head with hilarity after deciding he was. She laughed along with him, all the while knowing no one could defy such odds as faced him, and survive. The genuine laughter that erupted from her was convincing of a kind woman, kind to all, a Christian. But what she said next put paid to that. "I like you boy. It will be a pity to kill you and wrest your heart from your chest for that is what I shall do and then throw it to my dogs for them to sup on."

Although her minions laughed, no smile touched her lips, she had had enough of this tormenting boy. An expression that had frightened many men before took hold of her face. It seemed to Phail she was not like a woman at all, more like one of Satan's handmaidens, if not his bride. A notion occurred to him. That chief adversary of God, Satan, he, who ruled in that dark kingdom underground was someone he would like to meet. He had half a mind to ask her where to find him. If anyone would know, she would. Intending to seek him out and send him to wherever it was Satan went to when he was slain for that was what Phail going to do, slay Satan. After he slayed this wicked horse-headed woman though, she had earned an immediate death.

The horse woman addressed him in earnest. "I am going to take that sword from you and use it to cast your head away from your body."

Her threats were beginning to bore him. "I will not give you my sword. And you will have to take it off me. For that to be thou will have to beat me. I cannot see that happening."

Her voice was without humour now. "I want, and will have your head."

"No," he replied with a jolly look. Then his scowl matched her own. "Yours, I would like to see from your neck departed and amid the earth and if thee makes any move towards me my sword will sing a merry tune on your neck."

Then he laughed again convincing her of his witlessness.

"Boy, in truth, in a moment your head will laying apart from your body."

Phail addressed himself to the filthy peasants. "I warn thee to be gone if thee values your life and a place on this earth."

If they did not think he was deranged before they did when they heard him say this:

"Now look closely upon the horse woman, look well, in moment your mistress will be dead, her head in the mud."

He turned his gaze back on her, smiling at her, and she hated to admit it, his smile was now beginning to terrify her. She fought down her panic.

"Remember well to pass on my regards to Satan when you meet him for you surely will, and tell him I am coming for him."

The horse woman addressed the peasants. "A young boy with

a sword thinks he is a swordsman." She then said to him, "It is not toy a boy."

"Now you are becoming tiresome. You surely will soon learn when your head is cast aside from your body whether I can use this sword."

The woman almost let him go. Her instincts had always served her well in the past and he was far too willing to fight for her liking.

What happened next was very fast and very lethal. Phail cast his hand to the cache of gold in his saddlebag. Spilling the gold forth out amongst the throng. Whilst they were bent over picking up the glittering gold coins in the mud, and the horse woman was damning them for their foolishness, Phail rode at her and chopped her head off. He could afford to lose the gold and his two lesser horses, what must be must be, but he was not leaving the horse woman with her head upon her shoulders.

She and her malice were in a good place, the mud. She could keep her malice and take it with her to Satan. He would not miss her too horsey face. The hate-filled eyes settled in the mud with a look of shock in them. A shame he did not have a carrot so he could of thrown it down to her. As he looked down at her now frozen eyes he hoped she had a moment to know how wrong she was to misjudge him. "Of course I can use a sword!" he said to himself. The girl, he saluted her with his sword bringing it to his nose, thereafter tossed her a gold coin. Then he rode off happy at how he had spent the morning.

Meg kept hovering above the hens and chicks she loved throwing them corn from her bucket. Her hard nimble hands busy at their chore when the shape of a boy on horseback, about thirteen, expanded from behind the stable. To see a stranger came with a moment of fear. At times there wandered through this region men with a propensity for finding or inventing trouble. When she saw this boy gazing down at her with his solemn eyes she felt an urge to flee. This stranger was well armed with a sword. He was well mounted. There was the look of danger about him.

"Where do you come from sir?"
"From the south."
"Are there many with you?"
"I travel alone."

The boy saw her fear and smiled at her trying to allay those fears. "I will not hurt thee. I but seek a cup of milk if you have one, a handful or two of oats for my horse."

She got his milk and fed his horse. Whilst she did, he did not speak, he seemed a very quiet dour fellow. As she was about her business she felt his eyes resting on her it gave her an uneasy feeling. Then he was gone riding away without giving her another look.

When he had departed suddenly she realized she had liked him and a silly girlish grin took hold of her face despite her best efforts to suppress it. She wished she could see him again, this quiet youth, who looked like he was moment away from drawing his sword. Even though he had cold dangerous eyes of a swordsman she thought he looked kind. She felt a jolt of something hit her heart. The rest of that morning she went about her duties with lightness and spring in her step. She played over in her mind his few words. *"I will not hurt thee. I but seek a cup of milk if you have one, a handful or two of oats for my horse."* She pondered if he had travelled far. Heard again his words, *"A handful or two of oats for my horse,"* and, *"I would care to rest my horse and care to have a drink of milk."*

It split her lips in a grin from ear to ear these thoughts of him. She found herself saying words to this mysterious handsome boy she now wished she had said, in her mind, passing these words to him with flirtatious smile, like a girl would give to a suitor, "I reckon I could give thee a cup of warm milk with some crushed berries in it. But there is more I can give thee?"

In her mind he told her, "I believe I have never seen a lovelier girl."

Her pleasant thoughts were taken from her for suddenly she saw them, filing solemnly around the water trough near the barn. Aden, her father, stopped turning the crank on his grindstone. These six men had weapons, one a sword, the others rough spears, or bows, or the farm implements so often used as weapons. Eilidh, her mother, appeared in the doorway. Meg held her feed bucket to her chest her heart racing.

One of them obviously the leader sneeringly shouted, "Get some good strong drink for us."

Aden stood with his axe, he had been sharpening it on the grindstone, "We have none here."

"We'll have a pound of beef then. For myself I'll have three hard boiled eggs. My men, what say thee, what will thee have men?" His eyes travelled over to Meg, "I think I know what else I will have."

Aden's answer was, "Yee will get naught of anything here."

Eilidh came to her husband to have him put away the idea of displeasing these men. Her eyes went to Meg she would very much wish her away. Eilidh indicated with her eyes that Meg hide herself.

Aden stood sedately, axe in hand, looking at the six men who loomed nearer. "Hold ye," said Aden.

Without realizing it Aden had taken steps back to the croft's doorway, Meg and Eilidh were behind him now. They halted by the indefinite edge of the trampled area at the croft's doorway. Then the grinning leader of these men made a lunge to grab Meg who shrieked and pulled herself inside. Aden and Eilidh soon followed her inside the croft with Aden doing his best to keep the door shut with all this pressure on it from these men. Aden had finally pulled the bar across locking them in, but by the sound of the din outside, soon the door would break and these devils pour in. Eilidh and Meg crossed themselves in the steady candle light of the croft's interior semi-darkness. Inside they sat close, looking into each other's eyes, the resignation of death upon them.

Phail who had ridden by earlier was once again out in the yard bearing witness, and decided he would bear no more of this and got off his horse. Phail came rapidly to the first man. Whissk, off went his head. A second man made his rapid exit from this world. Their leader, made a rather pathetic pleading gesture before Phail cut him down. The last three took to their heels.

Phail called out to those inside, "Those who would harm you, three of them are slain, the rest have put themselves elsewhere. It is safe to open the door."

Recognizing his voice Meg opened the door before her father who thought it could be a trick could stop her. Looking up at the blond handsome warrior now smiling at her Meg decided he was the most handsome boy she had ever seen. She asked him, "Why did thee ride back?

"I wanted to talk to you again. You are rather pretty. And I thought I could do something to help you, some kind of work. It looks like I have."

Meg looked at her mother. "By virtue of my prettiness we are saved." Meg had not known a man for many months and wanted him even though he be a boy and a year or two younger than her. "I think you should stop the night."

Aden got a word in, seeing it was going to be hard to part these two. "I thank you for stopping here sir. To best six men whilst alone thee is a wonderful swordsman, and far from being a grown man, if you don't mind me saying so."

For all the notice they took of Aden he may as well of not spoken. Phail did not take his eyes off Meg nor did she take her eyes off him.

"I think I will stop here."

Phail gripped his hand with hers. An undeniable mutual attraction flowed from one to the other. Aden looked to Eilidh and she to him, an unspoken communication going on between them. That night Phail and Meg lay entwined together blissfully on the straw in the barn unaware of anything outside of themselves. Time had no meaning for them, and thus it was until Aden spoke from the doorway sometime that night. "I am thankful to thee lad, but my girl will wed before she is bedded?" Little did her father know she had been bedded many times. Already, twice by Phail.

When Phail returned to the hillfort Morgund was elsewhere having left with Seward and William MacRuarie, where to, no one knew. Phail gave his mother the excuse he left the monastery because he had heard from Norman knights staying at Pluscarden that the hillfort was to be attacked, this, being the case, he had left in all haste. Strangely so it was.

Turbulence and fearful weather was a cause for hope at the hillfort that it might dispel these attackers from staying out in such bad weather. Although still autumn, a mid-winter-like wind whistled down from the frozen north between the blacker-than-black wall of woods that surrounded the hillfort. Thin alders and birches bent before it. Needle-point ice crystals rode in on the freezing air. With this winter-like weather had come men with weapons, dangerous men, Norman knights, with their men-at-arms. Word passed through the keep like a tinder on dry twigs that Phail was intent on riding out to take on the men who ringed the fort, and looking for others to join him. All of thirteen years he looked older, sitting defiantly on his warhorse. A mere boy though he was no player of games, this boy. There was something about Phail that spoke of his being born to spill blood. Many lads full of excitement, full of youthful ardor, were out the gate before Malachi Morgund's man supposedly in charge of the hillfort in Morgund's absence could temper their recklessness. Watching them go Malachi felt Phail's unwavering thirst for war would spell his doom. Death waited patiently outside the door, furthermore, when you left the door ajar, in it came, always it came, always, and left, taking you with it, to the kingdom of everlasting darkness. Phail seemed to think he was immune from this fact. After what subsequently transpired Malachi thought perhaps he was.

Phail had the good sense to take a white flag with him, waving it in plain sight to convey peaceful intentions. His sword, everyone knew how good he was with it, it seemed too, that he was good with his mind because this allowed his contingent to get close to them without facing attack. It was immediately obvious to Malachi that to use this ruse defying the rules of combat meant Phail might be a good general if he lived long enough to display more of his tactical mind.

When he met the enemy the white flag was cast aside. It began at once then the melee. Phail hit the enemy hard; the blood ran thick thereafter. A head lay on the grass with no a body attached to it sent flying by Phail's sword. That Phail put another head beside the first proved it was no fluke, his deeds bringing cheers from the those watching him from the walls. Even from so far away Malachi saw Phail's gleaming smile. Malachi would see it in his nightmares, that smile. Phail was obviously a lover of death, a harvester of souls. That smile, all who saw it admitted an inescapable fascination mixed with horror at the sight of it. For Malachi's part there was a loathsomeness to it. Phail must be a great a liker of killing to smile like that. Phail was now killing right and left and so freely and with such glee it put one in mind of Satan and all his terrible power. For no reason, it was beyond the ken of Malachi, by some incredible slice of luck Phail with his twenty-five, eight of whom had fallen, turned away the Norman host.

On the coast of Ross disembarking horses and mules furthermore, once that was done, Morgund, William MacRuarie, and Seward, rode at night to the site of the infamous ambush where Morgund's father, Kenneth Earl of Ross, met his end. Here too, many years before, William MacRuarie discovered a cache of gold. William was the sole survivor of those who rode in support of Kenneth that night when tragedy befell Kenneth. William MacRuarie was buffeted by men on horseback and plunged over the cliff only to be caught on a tree that grew outward further down. The cave containing the gold was near this tree that had saved his life and prevented him from falling further down the mountain to his death on the rocks below.

William MacRuaire thought, back then, that perhaps the cave would shelter him until the rain passed and from inside it he could more easily get up to where he had been before he had fallen. Inside the cave, he had observed rain drizzling down from above and decided there and then that if he ever wanted to return here he could through the top of the cave if he could find this place where the rain came in.

What had happened to Kenneth, Morgund could feel on every side of him in the dank wetness, knew, that sorrows were all around him in the night-air. Morgund had never thought to be here nor wanted to be. The foul murder of his father had haunted his dreams since the day it happened. Despite his misgivings, he was driven to come by the need to arm and provision an army. A dread malevolence held sway in this place, twisting and turning shreds of miasma filled the empty night spaces, such subtleties of the air turned into shapes and at times soldiers. These long dead men held shields, held spears. They had come here and died here. By virtue of the coins found in the cave, Roman coins, Morgund knew Romans had once been here. They seemed to be watching from the edges of the gloom these spirits of the dead. For a moment the faint cries of wounded men inhabited the air. There was much that defied explanation. A dense hard rain began to fall. Suddenly, the wind blew like it wanted to blow them off the mountain. A hundred ghosts came out of hiding. Morgund's father's spirit, if it was anywhere in the world it was here. Trapped by the endless memory of him Morgund saw nothing and everything in all.

Morgund with a start felt a touch to his shoulder. "What are you looking at?" It was Seward. His friend had a serious cast to his features.

"There is much out there that defies logic, too much, "Morgund replied.

William MacRuarie upon noticing Morgund's un-calm eyes, found himself giving voice to his deepest fears. "I feel whatever it is out there means to kill us. I felt it twenty years ago and it is here now." William passed his two friends a look of dread.

Morgund made no reply just stared out into the night. Once the mist turned thinner, furthermore, when it did, they were out there in front of him the men who had served his father. Of his father's retainers some were now dead, some of them were being slain in front of his eyes as he watched.

Knowing he owed his friends something of his mind Morgund said, "I have never seen this place. Never been here, yet, I feel like it is a part of me." Morgund shuddered. "The ghostly figures from the past fall undone by the bloodshed done to them by vicious men. What happened when my father met his end is now before my eyes."

A sudden gasp of terror came from Morgund for what he saw now was the face of his father.

From Seward, "Tell me what you see Morgund?"

Morgund's reply came, "Kenneth, Earl of Ross, and daggers, many daggers in many hands. Daggers falling on him. I see my father and the clansmen of that night. My father, his chest beset with many treacherous blades." Morgund's eyes filled with tears. "Enemies surrounding him hacking him left and right."

And as shocking as that was more shocking still, was this, his father's long dead voice erupted out of the dark. "Go, leave this place whilst you can Morgund."

The voice both Morgund and Seward recognized as belonging to he who had been once Earl of Ross. The words came from the spirit world. That man long dead warning his son from beyond his mortal life. Morgund saw him for a moment. Then the Earl was gone. Where he had been Morgund saw only liquid air. Knowing by his stare that Seward had heard the voice of his father, Morgund thought it well to ask William if he had also heard the earl speak too.

Came William's reply, "There is no doubt that there was something. A call to get off the mountain." Having heard himself say it William thought it sounded ridiculous and too strange to be said aloud. "Contained in the wind, perhaps, in the wind alone or in my imaginings was it."

Morgund knew it was a true voice that spoke for he had heard it many times before, they all had.

"Come Morgund," Seward said pulling his friend away.

A brilliant flash of lightning lit up the sky. The ground shook for a second or two and night became day. Rather than go Morgund insisted they stay. He would have his father reappear. As much as Morgund would have loved to have sight of that man, such was not to be. As powerful as the urge was to see his father, there was a second reason to remain. They had come for the gold and Morgund had it in his mind that he would.

They separated to cover more ground. Once that was

done, higher up, MacRuarie digging with a long spear trying to punch through the earth at his feet disclosing that which they sought, the cave. At first the spear hit nothing but rock, but then his spear hit nothing at all, which meant there was a crevice and perhaps the cave. "Here it is!" he called out to his two companions.

The sky lit up even more luminous than before. Lightning crashed to the ground as if to break through the earth itself. Seward and Morgund took themselves to MacRaurie's side. Thrusting burning brands into the dark mouth of the cave Seward dropped a stone. It echoed and clattered below. When lightening flashed and thunder cracked overhead it gave them a better look at the airy chamber below.

They brought ropes from their mules. Quickly, a rope was attached to Morgund at the waist, and he was lowered down into the dark chamber with his torch still in his hand. When Morgund's feet touched the bottom he cast the torch about to reveal ripples in the cave walls. Darkness, half-shadows. Electricity cracked in the night sky overhead and he got wet from the gap in the stone above. Moonlight came in with the rain, and due to the collaboration of water and light the rain shone phosphorescent. Little streams cascading down the sides of the cave created pools of water. More lights came down spluttering in the rain as the two others joined Morgund.

Seward asked his friend when he reached him, "What now?"

They had found the cave, entered it, yet, they had still to find that which they sought, the gold. Seeing Seward was still waiting for his answer, Morgund thought William a better man than himself to answer it thus turned to William, "Tell us MacRuarie?"

William MacRuarie looked into the hidden dark clefts that blended Morgund's face into a dark-red, pagan-like mask.

Unrecognizable from the face William knew. It was almost like some dark force had taken over Morgund and talked with his voice. MacRuarie shook off his feeling of otherworldly possession of his friend to say, "I hope we can find our way for we could easily get lost, these caves are large, how large I cannot say, but each step could lead to a chasm beneath our feet so be careful."

MacRuarie to avoid getting lost used his burning brand to put a burn mark on the cave floor, doing this, over and over, to ensure they did not lose their way as they proceeded. Just behind them would be the mark and they could retrace their steps if they had to. Came to them a change in the consistency of the air. They felt a rushing breeze on their faces and sprinkle of rain telling them above their heads was sky and not solid rock. The walls closed in around them again and it got darker. Carefully, gingerly, in case they were engulfed in a sudden drop they moved slowly forward and did in fact find the wind-swept ledge and the lucky tree that had saved William's life. It still stood where it had many years before. MacRuarie thought he knew exactly where he was now and, when they were again in the cave's vastness William thought of the way he had once went and went that way again. MacRuarie just to make sure he was not mistaken still occasionally dubbed a burn-mark on the floor. Wholly open to the sky now light danced in the air making a lighter smudge in the black light above them. Not much further there was an echo from one of the underground passages of flowing water. Not just rain run-off, an underground stream. MacRuarie directed them to it.

Striking on ahead, MacRuarie slowed listening to the stony roar of the water as it grew louder. Floating, misty-wetness danced in the air around them. A stream of liquid-silver, made so, by the moonlight striking it, flowed near their feet. Particles of light jiggling about seemingly gazing at them like tiny dancers. As if the internal water that had led them here was not spectacular enough the now gentle rain falling made a spectacular light-show with the moon glow emanating down behind it, making this place a silver realm. The underground stream flowed foamy with the rush of rainwater. In amongst the deep chill of the wet, being careful to protect their torches from the drizzle, they shone light directly onto things that did seem to be made of stone. With the light they were seen to be metal chests. Opening them there were heavy gold coins.

    Seward stayed by the chests whilst Morgund and William MacRuarie made their way back to the ropes. Arriving at them, they climbed back up. Once out in the open Morgund and William set to get the mules. Seward, from inside the cave kept up a series of yells so they could hear him. Locating his voice they called back down to him. They then sent down first one rope, which was immediately followed by a second. After attaching the ropes to the chests they were hauled up. Leaving the mountain they rode to their ship taking with them the gold.

WRATH OF KINGS

WITH ARYLL WAS his close friend, Muieadhach, Ewan of the Blackspot, and Gilleasbaig, another highlander,. Those mentioned were in attendance upon King Alexander the Second of Scotland recently up in arms against him and now bowing low before him. At thirty-six, Alexander was one of the most able and intelligent of all European rulers and he looked every inch a man of superior mental faculties as he gazed down at the four men on their knees before him. It was not only his obvious intelligence alone which marked him out as a king, he dressed like one. In a velvet doublet with a regal pale blue embroidered with golden thread at the hem, sleeves and collar, his mantle was ermine at the shoulder with and red and purple gems aligned with the wrists. His red hair was immaculate and his red beard trimmed to perfection. It was not wise for a ruler to eschew the trappings of wealth for power in no small measure flowed from such trappings and Alexander knowing this, wore the wealth of the realm upon his person. Looking down at the knelt highlanders, Alexander indicated that they rise.

The king addressed them,"Stand ye men of good faith? Although I do not know the truth of that I have good cause to discover the truth of it."

"Your Grace," Argyll gave a nervous reply, "it is to demonstrate our loyalty that we came to have any misdeeds of the past put to rest by knelling at your feet in supplication."

Alexander had a smile that promised much and delivered little. Men did not trust this smile even Ewan MacDougall, Lord of Argyll had the sense to know it did not signify goodwill. Alexander laughed, whether it was at Argyll, Argyll was not sure. The highlander thought perhaps his reaction to the king's amused expression had made it, or that Alexander picked up on his sense of anxiousness and decided to laugh at him.

Looking down at Argyll and his companions from his lofty throne the king proclaimed with fitting regality, "My Lords thee art welcome and it is good to see thee. So good of you to come to me in peace." The king decided for the moment to calm their fears. He had cups brought to them and when he smiled it was not lit with an inner threat, it was calming. "Thee must trust that goodwill can be found amongst us."

When he wanted to Alexander could charm anyone as Argyll and his companions were finding out. The king encouraged them to sip their wine, have a moment to taste how good it was. The regal wine was known to be the best in the kingdom. The benign smile of a fatherly figure was cast out at them. "I am a king however also a man just like yourselves." The very idea that he was as ordinary as they were was a cause for mirth and made a genuine smile play across his face. "We are all equals under the sun, beloved as one of God."

Alexander made this statement because he would see how they took to it. Often highlanders were said to think themselves better men than they were. He wanted to know if these men of the highlands thought themselves his equals. The king had another reason for doing what he did, what this reason was, and the machinations of his mind will henceforth be told. It was obvious to the king that two men saw themselves indeed as his equals. Ewan with the prominent black spot was an exception. He knew who was king and how better a man Alexander was than himself. Alexander could tell that at a glance. Argyll just looked nervous.

Only an accident of birth had put Alexander on the throne. Alexander had heard such a view from highlanders in the past, that rather than it be right that he was king by virtue of the grace of God, that they, or others like them who were able men would do as well, or better. Alexander knew if the mystique of kingship was drawn away from the crown-wearer he would not wear it for very long. These men would not take his crown, however, others, if they thought they could, might. The king saw these men before him remained at their ease. Few men felt comfortable with him, these men did so because he had disarmed them.

The king thought perhaps they were too comfortable with him thus concluded some unsettling was called for. Talk of them being his equals was meant as a courtesy as far as the chamber was concerned; unfortunately, for some, they believed it. These men revealed themselves for fools. Looking down at them the king thought how dare they appear before him with such impertinence. It was time to take them up on their presumption of equality. The king intended to take their composure away from them. Even his admirers agreed that the king could be difficult. Alexander was going to show these highlanders just how difficult he could be. He had seen it in their eyes, they did not have the wit to hide it, they thought themselves as good as he was, two of them. Their presumption offended his sense of his royal dignity. To these men new to his presence Alexander responded with obvious humility, not normally his way, any accustomed to him would have been on their guard. The tone was calm and it was hard to pick the sarcasm but it was there. "Tell me is it not said in the highlands amongst your own that you are like kings?"

Gilleasbaig responded with no sign of understanding the danger. "In our lands we are not held to be like kings, we are kings."

It was immediately apparent to Alexander that this one was an complete idiot. Alexander's smile was back but not now so gracious, with it appeared arched eyebrows. The king peered down at Gilleasbaig. The man now had his full attention. Alexander suddenly laughed good naturedly. "We are fellow kings then. Until now the only other king I had met is he of England, my brother-in-law, Henry, an unkingly man if ever there was one. Of us three, Henry of England, me, and yourself, who is the greater of us monarchs?" Not giving Gilleasbaig time to reply he spoke, now though the friendly tone was gone. "Though thee art at my feet like a dog, but a dog has been known to bite the owner and one king to fall and another take his place, kings are as changeable as pieces on a chess board, do you not agree?"

Even Gilleasbaig saw that to agree to that might endanger him and thus remained silent.

A sudden heavy silence had engulfed the room which was

pierced by Alexander's sudden and impressive voice. "That was how Scotland came to determine their first king, he was chosen by our forefathers to be the first among them. I am no better than any of you, but as our forefathers knew only too well, one of us must lead. Which means others must follow. Equals do not follow equals, Gilleasbaig. Kings lead and I am I your king thus I lead you. There can only be one king in Scotland. Not two, nor several."

Gilleasbaig thought he must give a reply and thus gave one, a bad one. "Aye. I just meant in our country in the highlands that great respect is done us by the simple folk. That they look up to us as they would kings."

Sir Hugo de Montgomerie pitied this Gilleasbaig who gave voice to his stupidity, thus, decided to give this course and vulgar highlander seemingly for the first time in the company of civilized men an example of the kind of behavior expected in the king's presence. What the king heard next was exactly what a courtier who knew his business would say. "Definitely, Sire, there is no better man to rule in the realm than thyself," said Sir Hugo.

The king nodded. "Sir Hugo, they are the words of a wise man. A man of manners." Alexander turned his attention back on Gilleasbaig. "Because thee is my equal perhaps I should get another throne and put it beside mine." Alexander looked down at Gilleasbaig with dangerous narrowed eyes. "Without thee be anointed by God to be king it is like a cat wearing a crown, or a crow, or a cow, meaningless and silly."

Gilleasbaig made an apology of sorts. "I am just a simple man unlearned in the ways of court."

The king was not finished yet. "As luck would have it a crown just fell from the sky and landed on my head but with another gust of wind it could just as easily blow elsewhere, even perhaps could come to rest upon thine own brow." Alexander looked him in the eye coldly. "Do you seek my crown?"

Gilleasbaig replied, "No, your crown is thine by right of birth."

Alexander looked at him with a wry smile. "Are not all babies born of woman and because of that fact, therefore, the same? A baby prince shown to a woman who does not know it is a prince thinks of it simply as a child. Is that not true?"

"I know very little about royal births, princes, and ordinary children, and the differences between them."

"Nonsense, I asked a question answer it if you are man enough, answer it! Is not a royal babe and an ordinary child the same to whoever sees it if not knowing from whence it came?"

"Yes a royal babe is the same in looks as any other babe."

"Even of a servant?" asked the king.

"Yes."

"By every word you speak you proclaim your willful ignorance."

"I just responded with the truth."

"Did you not say that in your own land it is you they deem king? There is only one king in Scotland, whoever else claims to be is a traitor and must die a traitor's death."

"Here is a long way from where I live, so far from royal decree it is natural that our people look to us to lead them."

"Have they a king?" asked the king.

"Aye."

"Who is it?"

"Yourself Sire."

"Finally you prove yourself not a complete cretin. And well remember it. What caused you to say such a thing, that thee is considered a king? It was foolish."

Gilleasbaig agreed, "It was foolish."

"It was a lie." The simple man from the north got a long cold glare from the king, "And your ignorant serfs they at least are excused their misconception, being led to it no doubt by thee. Has thee encouraged them to see thee as a king?"

"No."

"Explain then how they got such a notion?"

"You speak a language they do not. And sit on a throne in a place they have never been."

"I have heard enough, Gilleasbaig is king of bogs and bracken, and dogs and cats. Perhaps of cups." Alexander turned to his courtiers, acid in his voice, "He is the king of liars, that, I do know." Alexander saw Gilleasbaig's anger rising. It prompted more from his tormentor. "Gilleasbaig is king of turds." A sword would be drawn here soon if Alexander did not relent on Gilleasbaig. Alexander had no intention of doing so. "Oh what a fool you are. King of Fools, the Fool King! You stink so perhaps it is better to name you the Dog Turd King."

The whole hall was in fits of laughter and Gilleasbaig did not know how to react, he had never experienced such ridicule.

The High Steward curled his lip in contempt at Gilleasbaig. "Was it not only months past you were up in arms against His Grace?"

Gilleasbaig had his eyes fixed on the floor so the High Steward turned to Argyll. "Argyll is that not true?"

Argyll replied uncertainly, "Not us. Unruly men without conscience."

King Alexander cast his attentive glare onto Argyll. "Have I caught thee out in a falsehood? Argyll, those men were redoubtable supporters of yours who rose against the crown? I have heard thee was amongst them to the forefront with all kinds of treason upon thy lips."

Argyll admitted it, "Aye."

Gilleasbaig who would have been better served to keep his mouth shut, however, decided to enter the fray thinking to support his friend, Argyll. It would have been better had he chosen his words with more care. He had been belittled so much he didn't care whether he lived or died but would prove he was a man worthy of respect. "Does not the wolf ever chase the sheep?"

The king stood. "Who is the sheep, Gilleasbaig?"

Alexander did not have to wait for his answer. Gilleasbaig unfortunately chose to produce a defiant smile. All the courtiers believed that smile would cost him his life.

"Art thee art so very clever Gilleasbaig that you can grin at me like a deranged cat? You will soon learn the price paid for cleverness. Dogs will feast on your mangled corpse before the day is out. I might send your head back to your wife that she may lament the moment of madness that overtook you and blame you for her widow's lot."

This caused a look of alarm to shoot out from one highlander to the other.

Argyll said, "I am sure no harm was meant Your Grace, he smiled at his own unfortunate jest that proves he is not worthy to be in your presence."

The king paused for a moment with a hint of consternation upon him. "He said, does not the wolf chase the sheep. A sheep ... me? The king of Scotland is a sheep. " The king looked at Argyll, askance. "Argyll does thee think me a sheep? Am I the sheep and Gilleasbaig the wolf? Perhaps Gilleasbaig is the king and I am the peasant. In truth, it must be so, or, he would say no such a thing. Argyll?"

By now Argyll and all the others bar one wished they'd never chosen to come.

"Such an idea is ridiculous," Argyll reassured the king.

Argyll was addressed then by he who sat on the throne. "Unlike others of your company I can see thee being alive at the end of this day." Alexander gave his attention back to he who originally began his rage. "That a man like you considers himself a king? I would rather give my crown to the most despicable turd on the face of the earth than thee." The king considered Gilleasbaig with a sneer. "Thee has done enough to be hung."

Gilleasbaig challenged this statement. "Hung for what?"

A tight smile from Alexander as he replied, "Gilleasbaig, do you want to hang? Every word you speak tells me that you do."

Alexander cast his eye out to include all. "Has he said any word to dissuade me from hanging him? He deserves to hang?" He looked at Muieadhach. "What do you have to say in his defence?"

Muieadhach, like Gilleasbaig, thought the king was unjust and would never forgive himself if he did not say a word in support of Gilleasbaig. They had fought battles together Gilleasbaig and he, sharing comradeship. His life had been in Gilleasbaig's hands on the field of battle and the man had never let him down. Unfortunately Muieadhach had no art with words as he duly showed. "I agree with him. Hung for what? "I thought kings were men of honour?"

Alexander looked at Muieadhach his wry smile back. "I see." Alexander had not finished with Gilleasbaig and turned his vitriol back on him. "You are not a wolf, that I know. Perhaps a cat, or a pigeon but not a wolf, definitely not a wolf, perhaps, a ... dog turd."

Muieadhach dared to speak over the top of Alexander. "He is your subject and as thus is entitled to have mannerly conduct from thee?" King or not, all men deserve respect.

The king's voice fell upon Muieadhach like an axe. "If I hear you again without I give you leave to speak I will have your head. We have already established that kings have no honour. And that you are treasonous. So consider your head is now mine. So do not speak again, your head, it is now my head, and I will choose when it speaks. It is not yours. I own it, like I own this castle."

No other man in the chamber bar the newcomers held themselves anywhere near the king in intellect and canny wits. The rest of them cast each other sideways glances waiting for the retribution should Muieadhach or Gilleasbaig forget themselves and speak hastily again. Argyll had already shown himself cowed, the young man beside him, Ewan of the Blackspot, was quiet from the start.

The king spoke to Muieadhach. "Muieadhach, I am a king that I know and that thee is a knave that I also know." A moment of silence before he turned to that other man who had caused him great anger. "As for thee Gilleasbaig, a wolf, that is laughable." Alexander's eyes narrowed to the merest slits. "If thee is a wolf Gilleasbaig think ye what happens to wolves when in the hands of men?" Muieadhach nor Gilleasbaig ventured not a comment at that. Looking at two silent men elicited this from Alexander, "And moments ago as noisy as larks. I believe the cat has got thy tongues."

Evident in scowls, in dour faces, in the stunned expressions on them that their lives could be forfeit if a word fell from their lips unsuitable for the king to hear. Alexander now enjoying himself had a disquieting smile that many others knew so well. The oppressive silence was too much for Gilleasbaig to bear. Gilleasbaig could of done his best to ingratiate himself and undo his offence, rather than do that he spoke like a desperate man and a stupid one. "We came under vows of safety. It seems they mean little to you?"

"One word and my men will hang you from the walls all your life gone." Alexander looked to his personal guard as if he was about to order just that.

Gilleasbaig gazed at the Normans around him with a sneer, his hand on his sword seemingly ready to raise it at the first man who came towards him.

Alexander drew himself up to his full height. "Norman swordsman are renowned throughout Christendom. Of exploits, unequalled. Doest thee think thee are their equals? You are equal to myself we already know that."

Gilleasbaig's mouth was his ruin, he decided he was already dead so had nothing left to lose. "These Normans faced with good highland swordsman, run." A grunt of disgust, "I have caused them to run often enough."

"Of course, I forgot, thee art a wolf." Alexander raised his voice to include all in the room. "It seems as if I am the fool and this man in truth is the king. It seems fitting that I must give him my crown." Alexander lifted his hands as if to take the crown off his head. For a moment Alexander eyed the Celts assentingly. It was obvious he considered them poor specimens. Then he said, "I see two men whose tongues wag like dogs and two men with much less to say." After a thoughtful pause he continued, "If you put four men in a room in most cases three will be wise and one a dunce. It seems to me in this case we have two silly and two wise." Words, there must be words with Alexander. He loved them and he was ever artful with them as now. "Art thee in agreement Argyll? You look at a loss. Or is it with thee Argyll that thee is so without wits that thee cannot think of a word to say and Ewan is the only one among you with any intelligence? No doubt thee was full of clever speech when inciting men to violence against the king of Scots, inciting treason like a knave."

It was Gilleasbaig who spoke next. "Though thee sits higher than us it is not kingly to put other men down because they come from far away and are not familiar with your ways."

Even The High Steward was taken back by this. He wanted to beat Gilleasbaig with his fists. "Do you not know how to behave, to speak only when addressed. To address His Grace like this is to invite death, is like putting a noose around your own neck."

Gilleasbaig met the king's glare with a stern one of his own. "You are a tyrant?"

That brought the king to his feet. "I doubt thee wants to live another day," said the king. "They tell me it is a good view hanging from the castle walls, or, so I'm told. I think thee will find out. I will ask thee, and then thee can tell me, if, the view when hanging from the walls is fittingly gorgeous" Alexander directed his next words to The High Steward. "Take them away I want to see them dangling from the castle walls."

Gilleasbaig's anger was obvious to all his black eyes glaring out everywhere but at Alexander which he knew would ensure his death, he regretted now letting his anger get best of him. "So we come with a safe conduct and it ends thus."

Said the king to him, "Enough bleeting like a sheep I thought thee a wolf."

The young Buchan had his say then, "I see nothing but a worm sire. Two of them Sire, two worms."

Muieadhach turned to the young earl. "I will show thee Buchan what a worm looks like when I draw my sword on you. You will be on the floor and have your sarcastic lips cut from your despicable face, they will look like worms on the floor."

Alexander smiled at Muieadhach like an indulgent father. "How much like a wolf thee art." He shot Gilleasbaiga a look and said, "Gilleasbaig do you see this? One of you at least is a wolf."

While Alexander's attention was on Gilleasbaig, an angry Buchan took a step toward Muieadhach with his hand on his own sword. "If lips are to fall highlander they will be yours."

Muieadhach drew his sword and it seemed blood would be shed in front of the king, a capitol offence.

At this, some of the Norman lords in the chamber stepped forth naked steel in their hands. Alexander took a sip of wine to hide his amusement.

Gilleasbaig took his friend's cause on as his own and sent a warning out to the Normans, "Even though we are but two we will sell our lives dearly."

Both Celts had their gleaming steel taking the light as did the Normans. Time for Alexander to put a few dogs on leashes or these dogs would tear each other apart.

Alexander said mildly, "Enough. How much of this must I endure? I am king of Scots. And thee art ... what ... two highland brigands, and any of the men who inhabit this castle know better than to withdraw a sword in my presence, for to do so means death. My blood boils, my patience shortens, but as thee has drawn steel, so too have my knights, so, if I hang thee, I must hang them." Alexander's eyes floated onto his own Norman knights who quickly sheathed their swords. Then his eyes were back on Gilleasbaig. "Be gentle Gilleasbaig, I your king demand it of you."

Gilleasbaig's steel no longer showed, having slipped it out of view, nor, did Muieadhach's weapon hold the light.

Gilleasbaig put it to the king, "It is your Norman dogs who need to be instructed for no part of this is my fault. Nor Muieadhach's."

Alexander looked at him askance. "Who I censure and who I

do not is down to me, and not you. The crudest brute knows not to instruct a king."

Gilleasbaig could not keep his resentment to himself. "It is true my sword left its scabbard but only because I have been subjected to great provocation, that said, I apologize for drawing steel in your presence, Your Grace, forsooth, we came in peace and have not been shown much of it."

"Is thee in such a high estate as to instruct me? I think not. The land is full of scoundrels, but I see the greatest of them has come to visit and lecture me, come to tell me my duty as a king, and to confound me with his stupidity."

Alexander cast his gaze out onto his personal bodyguards, well armed men all. Watching it all terrified was Argyll. Argyll saw Gilleasbaig was about to be arrested. Argyll thought he better speak up or Gilleasbaig would be dragged away and executed, Muieadhach with him. Did not want it said of him that he did not say a word in their defence. After all, they were his friends and allies.

With this in mind Argyll addressed the king. "Gilleasbaig meant no offence Sire, he is unused to the ways of court. It might be best if we ask for leave from the royal presence, men as ignorant as ourselves do not deserve your royal consideration."

Ewan then addressed the king. Ewan of the Blackspot rather than seek to defend his former friends saw an opportunity to show the king that he was a man of judgement. "At no time have I caused offence, Your Grace, nor put a hand on a sword. If I did so, it would be in your service, not against you, but rather to defend you."

Alexander asked the young Ewan, "What think you of this swine Gilleasbaig who thinks fit to lecture me?"

" I would advise him Sire."

"Do so," directed Alexander. Alexander was finding Ewan had a tongue on him and a canny wit to go with it.

Ewan addressed Gilleasbaig. "When we are in the presence of the king we must keep our peace."

The king called down to Gilleasbaig, "Do you hear that you dog?"

"I stand corrected." Gilleasbaig's eyes were full of hate for Ewan. No man in the room failed to see it.

Buchan, the young earl drew Gilleasbaig's attention. A high

sarcastic laugh came from Buchan.

The young earl full of scorn found himself scorned. Gilleasbaig said to him, "I deem thee food for the worms if thee ever gets away from your protector, the king."

Buchan gave Gilleasbaig the evil eye, and whispered to him, "Thou art nothing but a knave, Gilleasbaig."

Gilleasbaig glared at Buchan. "We will meet again and when we do we will see how much of a swordsman you are. If I have the chance I will make you pay for your wit."

The Earl of Buchan responded with hilarity. "Challenge me, thee art a fit match for the kitchen maid and naught else."

Buchan had the temerity to raise his voice before the king. To speak in the presence of the king in such a manner and without leave was insolent in the extreme. In due course, decided the king, he would have to deal with the young Earl of Buchan. The Normans had to be managed carefully or one of them could challenge for his throne. That they had not thus far was down to his own wiliness and ability to divide one of them from the other. These men in front of him, the Celts, he would use a similar method against them.

Gilleasbaig had hand to his weapon a moment away from withdrawing it as he had before. "I have killed better men that thee Buchan."

Buchan's voice was merry. "Weak men threaten. Talk, talk, talk. All words. Words mean little. I am weak I threaten when nothing may come of it. Here thee is safe from my sword." Buchan looked out at the multitude. "I can match myself with Gilleasbaig, or, I may fight a kitchen maid. I will take on the kitchen maid thus for the better contest."

Gilleasbaig put forth his own brave words. "Where I come from I am held to be a great swordsman. Count thyself lucky I cannot show thee the measure of my ability. Before the king I must keep my sword by my side, at home, it is different."

"Then go back where thee art considered a wolf, thee art nothing here. I am sure thee is greatly feared there, considered a wolf." A mocking laugh followed.

"Easily proven by point of sword," countered Gilleasbaig.

Alexander's eyes glittered with rage. "Enough!"

Chief among the king's retainers was Walter fitz Alan who was the High Steward. Fitz Alan was responsible for the king's day-to-day affairs thus he was, The High Steward. The surname Stewart would begin with this fitz Alan. His surname, fitz Alan, would eventually become Steward, after the office he held and Steward, would become Stewart, ending in, a, t, and, not a, d, in later generations. Some final versions of the name were, Sturt and Stuart. Sturt, the result of pre-literate and non-cohesive spelling, and Stuart being the version of the name derived from the royal French court. That was the preferred spelling in France and helped to differentiate the royal Stuart family from the numerous non royal Stewarts because by the later middle ages there were numerous branches of the Stewart family who were not royal. Stuart, the royal version of the name is much rarer and those with it most often have it as a corruption of Stewart and are not royal. The Royal Stuarts would rule first Scotland and then in the fullness of time, England.

Walter Fitz Alan, the man whose descendants would have the above mentioned, surnames, spoke up. "Come gentleman both of you henceforth parley with gentleness."

The young Earl of Buchan appealed to fitz Alan, "M'Lord, other gentleman understand gentleness. This roach before us would parley with threats. Empty threats as menacing as a mincing French stager. I am waiting for him to anoint me with his sweat smelling water so fashionable among his kind."

"Those shrill maskers who entertain alike to them is he!" Alexander considered this hilarious.

The High Steward saw Gilleasbaig's sword partly out again prompting this warning "Parley in peace as I have told thee before Gilleasbaig."

It was too late, for Gilleasbaig had endured enough. Eyeing Buchan, Gilleasbaig drew his sword fully forth again. "Understand, Norman I will parley with you with this!"

The deadliness in Alexander's voice now could not be missed. "You put the noose over your own head. You will die." The king corrected himself the better to avoid a melee endangering himself. If swords met in this confined space he did not trust one of these Normans not to run him through. In the confusion how easy to slip a blade beneath his ribs. "You may yet live. Put that sword away and yet have some chance of a further life. If not, I will command my men to cut you down, Gilleasbaig."

Muieadhach put his hand over Gilleasbaig's sword hand,

helped him put his blade back within the scabbard. "Stay thy hand Gilleasbaig."

The king was deadly-voiced. "One of you has some sense at least, the little good it will do you. I will have both your heads." With a flick of the king's wrist Gilleasbaig and Muieadhach were surrounded, no hope now of making any kind of fight of it, halberds held at their breasts.

"We came under truce," Gilleasbaig responded to the rude steel placed on him. "It seems it means little to you."

Alexander looked to The High Steward. "Take them away."

Seemingly The High Steward had no pity for Gilleasbaig nor Muieadhach. "You heard the king, move dogs."

The king stopped The High Steward for a moment. "Not Argyll he has not offended. He shall stay." The king then spoke to the other man he saw a use for, Ewan of the Blackspot. Alexander had noticed how cunning Ewan was. As always it was a sought after quality when linked with ambition. "Thee too Ewan." The king focused again on The High Steward. "To the dungeon with them. A fit accommodation must be made for men such as them."

Any solidarity that had existed between the four highlanders when they entered the royal presence was forever destroyed when Muieadhach and Gilleasbaig saw themselves evicted and being taken to a dungeon whilst their former comrades Argyll and Ewan remained with and were favored by the king.

Muieadhach made the comment, "I came here believing a king has honour. I leave knowing that he has none."

The Steward laid hands on Muieadhach turning him back away from the king.

When the backs of the two evictees were turned away from Alexander he began to engage the other two, Argyll and Ewan, in pleasantries. "Oh the task of the throne is hard, to keep the blood flowing in the legs after a long day seated that is also hard. To keep that blood calm when others would have it boiling is hardest of all. What is this about angry words, hate filled voices? Come forward, kiss me. Embrace your kind and gentle king."

Consequently, Alexander accepted Argyll's embrace and kissed him. Ewan hung back.

"Thee watches me with concerned eyes, fear not."

Thinking Ewan's quietness a criticism Argyll excused him for it. "He is young and in esteemed company perhaps he is not aware of the honour done to him, Sire."

Ewan's inbuilt wariness kept him silent. Ewan considered the king. Recognized what manner of man he was, how dangerous, and also, the opportunity in front of him. His every action and every word must be considered. Alexander could set him on the road to riches if he did well.

A hint of a smile from the king watching Ewan's contemplative eyes. "Am I not fit to speak to? It is easy to believe it seeing you standing there mute when addressed by your king." The king looked at Argyll. "Is the lad simple?"

"I beg forgiveness Your Grace." Ewan came forward and took the king's extended hand. One kissed the other. "It is not every day one meets the greatest sovereign in all Europe."

The king commanded a page. "Bring two chairs." The chairs were brought and placed near the two. "Gentleman take thy ease." Alexander pitched his voice pleasantly to them. "Argyll, you are now my Constable in Argyll and the West Highlands, not only that, I create thee Lord of the Western Isles. Whatever other land you can take acting in capacity as my Constable will be part of your lordship."

Argyll replied, "These titles far exceed my worth Sire."

"Not at all. You will bring the king's peace to a land, godless and lawless."

Seeing Alexander sitting there benevolently it was easy to believe he was the sun that shone, having experienced his earlier persecution of the two banished highlanders, to Ewan, it was equally obvious he could be the storm that destroyed all in its path.

At the far end of the chamber shaking off accosting hands Muieadhach who was near enough to hear Alexander's regal tones echoing down the hallway seemingly meant for the ears of those lately evicted - they were not, but so it seemed to Muieadhach - thus he shouted back to the king. "A king who is unjust is no king at all."

Ewan his former friend, now seemingly no friend at all had these words for him, "Has not your tongue gotten thee in enough strife, Muieadhach? It is time to shut up."

Alexander raised his voice now much higher, it was now meant to carry to the two highlanders just recently evicted from the royal presence. "Above all others Argyll you will bring justice to them that need the king's justice, deliver it where there is none.

Obviously, with the likes of such men, that is no surprise." Alexander now spoke for the benefit of those close to him. "Those two, just moments ago gone from my presence, they could do with some justice and I intend to give it to them."

In the outer corridor Muieadhach reached for a sword that was no longer there. Remorse fell on him then like an iron fist taking all the breath out of him. Turning the events of the day over in his mind he did so with these words, "Argyll and Ewan are treated well when by contrast Gilleasbaig and Muieadhach are treated like vermin. Argyll given land, given titles. The king's sweet words to Argyll sicken me."

It enraged Gilleasbaig enough these goings on, that he committed the biggest folly of the day, he shook off his holders, turned on his heels, ran to the king. There he stood before the king and shouted. "Here I stand before you despite your foul order to have me hung."

Immediately, the king pushed himself off his chair, stunned that Gilleasbaig stood there glaring at him. Regaining his composure, he, the king addressed Gilleasbaig with all the authority of his office. "I see the banished has come back. It seems my commands are as meaningful as a crow's call." The king's voice was heavy with sarcasm. "And I thought thee a fool! I know now, I am the fool. I am wearing thine crown and thee has come to claim it back. Someone look for my scepter, this man must have it too."

The men in whose custody he had been were appalled at his audacity, knowing full well he would not get within striking distance of the king. Gilleasbaig, although holding no such certainty, thought he could reach out to the king, but knew to lay hands on him was death.

Alexander had this to say. "Death awaits us all one day but you are not willing to wait for it but you must run to meet it. I will make sure you will meet it. As soon as I can I will prepare a hangman for you. Obviously, you desire is to be hung, so hung you shall be. Do as I say now be a good lad and turn around and depart in peace, if you do not, your limbs will be torn off before your hanging ever takes place."

The highlanders never came another step closer to the king. Muieadhach had followed his friend. Muieadhach following his friend again showed that he lacked wits. Arms came right and left of them and held them close. Both had swords pressing at their necks. That man who took himself back when banished had the eyes of a demon boring into his. The king's eyes bore a similarity to those of such a being.

A moment later, Alexander continued on in the same melodious air he used earlier. "Thy sweet worth Argyll, no gift is too far above thee. Kneel now and feel my sword upon thy shoulders and I will dub thee knight." A moment later the king said, "Arise Sir Ewan MacDougall, Lord of Argyll, Lord of Lorn, Warden of the West Highlands and Lord of the Western Isles."

It was done, Argyll was Alexander's man. The four Celts who came to the king's court that day came as friends and comrades, such was not the case now, divided from this day forth. They were pawns on the king's chessboard and he was a master player. Alexander did in fact play chess and his wily mind ensured he was one of the best players in all Scotland. There was much to admire about this king and still more to abhor. It was done so easily, dividing them.

This king called, 'The Fox', obviously was well deserving of it. Henceforth, from this moment on the balance of power in the highlands had shifted. There could be no accord between Argyll, Muieadhach and Gilleasbaig. Ewan of the Black Spot counted for less but Alexander would find a use for him and a lesser man promoted above one of higher status was always proven to enrage the man not favoured. Ewan, that he had done and said almost nothing and yet had profited by it took Muieadhach and Gilleasbaig's common sense from them, little enough of it they had to begin with. Alexander sat back smiling at his friend The High Steward. Divide and conquer a maxim as old as time with Alexander the ultimate exponent of it.

Alexander with a disdainful gesture, bid the unruly highlanders be from his presence gone. Thus, they were hurried along to the dungeons.

He turned his attention to MacDougall. "Tonight thee art my guest Argyll. Within the castle a room will be put at your disposal." All manner of courteous speech was made to each of these men, Ewan and Argyll. "Dear Ewan, some accommodation must be made for thee too."

A nod came with Ewan's reply. "Yes, Sire?"

A pleasant smile of dignity from the king.

Ewan would know this from the king, "What shall be done with he just lately gone and who returned despite dismissal?" Ewan felt a degree of guilt at how badly things had gone for Muieadhach and Gilleasbaig.

A look appeared on the king that The High Steward found so disconcerting. "We stand on a cliff, take them to the edge of it and see if they can fly. Hanging is too good for the likes of them."

The High Steward knew the king meant no such thing, he thought, it was said in jest, however, he had to clarify every word the king said. "Pardon me Sire, throw them off the cliff? Thee will be condemned for breaking safe conduct"

Alexander's eyes narrowed in displeasure. "Condemned by whom?"

"The Church," replied The High Stewart.

"Let them, I care not." But despite his words Alexander paused thinking. He thought out what he would do, through his introspection, said, "I will be wrathful on those two frightful intemperates." The silence which followed fell heavy on the two remaining Celts who by now were thankful it was not themselves faced with the king's displeasure. An ill word or two and it could of been themselves faced with the king's censure.

"Walter," The High Steward's questioning gaze prompted from His Grace, "hold them in the dungeon until I decide their fate. I doubt they will ever see the light of day again. They shall die in bolts. If they struggle use all the force you must use including death to calm their intemperance the like of which we are all too familiar with."

Gilleasbaig saw how foolish it was to have stepped into the king's presence after he had been bade gone. It was more than imprudent, probably fatal. If he stayed it would of galled the king more so he had allowed himself to be taken away. Many paces from the great hall the two Celts were disturbed, humbled, fearful. It seemed such a desperate situation it made all their lofty arrogance fall away from them. Of the two, Gillesbaig displayed little of his former willfulness and Muieadhach was deep in the marrow of his own suffering. Finally the sight of the dungeon that was to hold them appearing before them dispelled this lethargy and resignation to their fate. Panic seized them. Gillesbaig with a sword pressed up against his breast held his ground and glared into The High Steward's eyes. The Steward had newly arrived after having the king's advice. The High Steward stepped away quickly once the king made his commands known and caught up with those in custody.

Gillesbaig faced The High Steward. "What does this mean? Am I to die here so far away from my loved ones? Why?"

"You say that!" His ignorance of wrongdoing astounded The Steward. "You have disturbed the king's peace and must pay for it."

Gilleasbaig flared up, "You say I have disturbed the king's peace and I must pay for it, surely not with my life. With words spoken in anger."

The Steward felt his own anger at this man, rising. "One does not get angry at a king!"

Protesting, likewise was Muieadhach as had Gilleasbaig moments earlier. "You have numbers. You have too many numbers."

Gilleasbaig contributing again, "You Normans are like flies on a shit."

The High Steward found he could only muster a smile at that. "The only shits in here are you two."

One of the men-at-arms said, "I dare say M'Lord these men will not escape dungeon walls and die here."

Replied The Steward, "What happens to them is the king's business."

Gilleasbaig knew what the man-at-arms said was true. They would never see the light of day again. Muieadhach, too, was certain of it, his sense for these things was rarely wrong and he wished he had kept his temper in check and realized how much danger he was in when in audience with that red-haired devil, the king.

Muieadhach downcast voice broke the silence. "Amongst a more devilish brood of evil doers I never thought to be."

The High Steward felt disgusted at Muieadhach's self-pity. "Hold thy peevish tongue, it has brought thee enough woe."

"I wish I never came here," shot back Muieadhach.

Gilleasbaig pleaded, "Will I be jailed for nothing? I stand here accused while that villain Argyll is made Warden of the West Highlands." Dark thoughts circulated in Gilleasbaig's mind creating somberness beyond measure. "Who would of thought it, I, here in a dungeon whilst Argyll is at the right hand of the king!"

Muieadhach passed Gilleasbaig a look so desolate. "We may never see home again Gilleasbaig."

"No more," The Steward told them. "None are interested in your sad bleatings."

Muieadhach responded to that telling The Steward. "You are a tyrant like your king."

"I'd rather be a tyrant than a fool," declared The Steward.

Muieadhach could only say, "You are a man without pity."

The Steward shook his head at Muieadhach. "Will your head still yap when it is from your body parted, I believe it will."

Muieadhach's pitiful eyes bored into The Steward's. "What did I say that has wronged you so?"

The Steward almost felt sorry for the man. "Well may you ask?"

"Tell me then?"

"Did you not insult the king?"

"No."

The Steward berated him. "It is lie. I heard thee."

Muieadhach shot back. "It is you who tells lies. Did we not come here in safe conduct and now find ourselves within a dungeon!"

"Better thee dared not speak a word to me, nor to the king." Walter, The High Steward had some pity for these men but dare not have Alexander know it. All the men near him would report any word of support, so he was at them harshly more than he would have been without the distrust he felt for those around him.

Gilleasbaig with more hope than confidence asked, "Will we have a trial?"

This caused The Steward to laugh with bitter humour. "You will have a trial at the end of a rope. Gilleasbaig you are a fool. Always be on your guard when in the presence of the king. Take to my words if ever thee has cause to kneel at his feet again. That is, if your liberty and life you value." The Steward decided to educate these ill-informed men for all the good it would do them. "I am The High Steward to the High King of Scots. The King of Scots rules the realm, rules you, rules me. He rules the realm. You should rule your tongue it is your ruin."

Muieadhach stared into space realizing a lot of what The Steward said was true. The lot they were in was down to themselves.

Urged The Steward to the jailors, "Keep them locked up soundly."

The Steward then left them to it taking himself away to inform the king that the prisoners were secure. Behind him he heard Gilleasbaig shouting after him, being hurried into his cell at last he saw reason. "I admire your loyalty to the king. I realize my mistake and would correct it. I would throw myself at the king's feet and beg his forgiveness."

It did Gilleasbaig no good. His friend Muieadhach was enclosed securely with him. They stared at bars that surrounded them without hope, two condemned men, together.

On his way back to Alexander, The High Steward wondered what Alexander would say. Often things were not as they appeared with Alexander, and Walter, The High Steward, suspected this was one such occasion.

When the Steward found the king in the audience hall now it contained only Ewan, and a few bodyguards. These bodyguards were nearly always in attendance upon His Grace. The Steward was surprised that Ewan seemed deep in the king's confidence. It was not feigned the king saw something in this youth. What it was The Steward could not say, for himself, he judged the boy sly and untrustworthy. The Steward stood where he was and watched them together for a moment. Ewan obviously had the gift of making himself likeable.

Alexander noticed The Steward, thus included him in the conversation. "He is no gentry and the fitter for it."

"Sire?" asked The Steward.

"Our friend Ewan is no gentry."

"Sire?" Ewan himself appeared momentarily nonplussed. "The fitter for?"

"For not being nobly born." Although the facial expression was one associated with happiness, cold eyes like barbs drilled into Ewan.

Ewan, repeated, "Sire?"

Alexander dove to the heart of the matter. "Never mind that. I have a question for thee Ewan."

"Yes, Your Grace."

The king continued. "Can thee do my bidding?"

"Aye."

"Why would you do my bidding?"

"I serve great men to better my own circumstances and in my state of lowliness have few other pathways to success."

"I see, as would any wise man serve a man who can better his circumstances." Thoughtfully the king added, "And who better to serve than he who is the highest in land!"

Ewan agreed. "Indeed so!"

The king was impressed with this answer.

The High Steward thought it was like witnessing two spiders weaving interlocking webs, attempting mastery over each other. This Ewan of the Blackspot was no match for his monarch, but something told The Steward that only a very foolish man would underestimate this Ewan despite his youth.

Notwithstanding what The Steward thought the king did not particularly like Ewan. Alexander saw in front of him one who could fulfil a purpose, saw Ewan for what he was, an ambitious social climber without scruple, obsessed with advancement, such men could labor in his cause successfully if they were of ample sits and Ewan seemed to be well gifted with them.

In the morning in his bedchamber the king sat at his desk attending to his business. He was stiff for he had been sitting for far too long. When he rose and stretched his legs, his loose white linen shirt fell beyond his waist. He opened the shutters to give sight of the sun. It was early September and unseasonably warm. In bed, he continued to look over his daily business until there was a knock on the door. "Enter," called out the king.

Robert, a lad of twelve who was Alexander's personal page entered. After admittance he stood ready for the king's direction.

"Robert," a kindly Alexander requested, "water please."

"Yes Sire."

The boy poured water from a stoneware jug into a cup and brought it to Alexander. The boy was quick and smart and able like all who served the king. Those servants who were close to him were not simply pawns in his strategies. Those who truly served him saw a man of simple tastes not ill humored, not cold-hearted,

however, always the king.
"How is the swordsmanship going Robert?"
"Very good Sire."
A pleasant genuine smile from Alexander as he rubbed the boy's head. "I will cross swords with thee later and attest to that. Now I have a job for you, get down to me Donald Brid, Lord Of Perth, have him come to me in all haste but not so as to be seen. I would have him come here unsighted, in secrecy. Do you understand?"
"Yes Sire."
"Then be off with you."
The page sped. As with all his other tasks it would be matter of routine that what Alexander expected was done and to a perfect standard. With the boy gone Alexander washed his face, changed, put on a robe more suitable for state business. Later, reviewing documents when there was another knock on the door. Without, was Alexander's page, Robert, calling from beyond the door. "My Lord Brid is here Sire."
"Send him in Robert."
Donald Lord of Perth was a proven enabler so Alexander entrusted many of his most delicate tasks to him. When he entered the king's presence the king had the following conversation with him: "M'Lord Donald I would have you deal with a matter involving those two malcontents in the dungeon. In the dungeon they can commit no mischief and it would suit me better if they were free to commit greater mischief elsewhere. If the highlanders are at each other, they are not at me."
Donald Lord of Perth bowed his head in answer. Knowing Donald for the clever man he was the king was satisfied and bid him be gone.

Night, and Alexander was with Fergus Cunningham, the heir to the Cunningham lordship on the castle walls. Cunningham, a boy of seventeen was well mannered and Alexander liked him. Of ancient Gaelic stock, his family were noted for their steadfastness to the crown. For over one hundred and fifty years the Cunninghams had served Scotland's kings. Malcolm Canmore, the king after Macbeth, was the making of the family. In the year 1050, on the same day that King Duncan was slain. The same King Duncan referred to by Shakespeare in his famous play, Macbeth, Warnbald, a lowly farmer met the lately slain, king's son, Prince Malcolm. That said prince was being pursued by Macbeth's retainers after he escaped the battle where his father was slain. The prince was wounded, and the pursuit not very far behind, and was catching up. The pleading eyes of the young prince persuaded Warnbald to save his life. For no reason other than pity he assisted the fugitive prince. Malcolm's horse he let loose scaring it away. It galloped off with a stone after it. Moments later, one of the pursuers looked down from his horse at Warnbald who was tossing hay on the hay bale which hid the prince.

Said the man in Macbeth's service to Warnbald, "Farmer, has thee seen a prince, that he is one thus obvious by the rarity of his armour and harness, and that he is on a good horse?"

"I have indeed seen him. He rode onwards but looked like to fall at any moment. He is badly wounded."

"Which way?"

Warnbald pointed off away. The horseman without bidding Warnbald a word of thanks galloped off after the prince. Those other men of Macbeth seeing him galloping off sped after him. Thus Warnbald saved the life of Prince Malcolm. The said Malcolm returned to Scotland a conquering hero two years later, an English army at his back. Malcolm became king and gratefully granted Warnbald the lands that he worked on as a farmer. Warnbald became known as Warnbald Cunningham. Cuningham being the name of the lands he had once worked on and now owned.

The family's motto up to this day is, 'Over, Fork, Over', referring to the act Warnbald performed when he had saved the prince, the motto also reminiscent of the farming origin of the family, and the day which made the family fortune. Like his forebear, Warnbald, Fergus Cunningham, was favored by the king. Fergus Cunningham wondered at it given how much cleverer and accomplished were others compared to himself. Often he asked if Alexander would be better served bringing other men closer to him, with Fergus being regulated to a lesser role in the king's fraternity. Doing this, made the king like him all the more, it was so unselfish.

Alexander an admirer of nature loved to sit back and watch plants grow, furthermore, to watch a youth grow was of considerable interest particularly with himself being a part of that development. Steel is formed in the hottest furnace and so too is a man's character. Challenges would bring forth the boy's inner resources of intellect, skill and ingenuity. With this in mind, Alexander put him in the company of men who tested him. Alexander could see that he had the potential for great loyalty. To Alexander, it was like throwing grass seed with a mind to have it grow. When you threw it some caught and sprang to life, some withered and died. Nature took its course as it always did. Just put things in place and accordingly things happened if they were meant to. Intuition played a part in this decision to advance Cunningham. Congratulating himself on the fact that some of Fergus's potential was already noticeable.

Some men are men of sand, the men Alexander built, indeed, the men he could rely on, were men of stone, and the foundation of the kingdom. Fergus could be one of those men the king relied on. With courage much can be accomplished and the boy had courage. When he was engaged in trials of combat, despite every hard knock he kept on with no diminishment in his determination. Although the boy considered himself a useful swordsman he was not as yet. That would change with time and experience. Surrounded by able men who would develop a keen edge to his blade. Each time he put himself to test with these men chosen by Alexander he was a little better than when he had last crossed swords with them. He was persistent, another good trait. As a negative, his parents had cosseted him in Aye which had not helped him. There was another reason to advance him, men of Cunningham's ilk balanced power within the kingdom. They, of the old Celtic lowland nobility were a counter to the Normans who were very powerful in the land, perhaps too powerful. The Celtic nobility of the lowlands provided a much needed counter to the Norman ascendancy. The highland Celts were the remnants of an antiquated culture no longer relevant in Scotland. They represented Gaelic Scotland, and the king and all the kingdom south of the highlands looked toward Europe for cultural and governmental ideas. Scotland had to be a modern kingdom. In fact, the kings of Scots and the lowland nobility now spoke a dialect based on English and considered the northerners and their language, barbaric. Those southern Gaelic speakers, Cunningham's folk were a cultural anomaly, loyal to Alexander but like their northern kin Celtic in their culture. Fergus was bilingual, all men of the court were.

That night on the battlements was very still. The king and Fergus Cunningham stared out at the sky in silence until the autumn air provided light and movement in the heavens. It stirred Alexander from his thoughts and brought speech to his lips. "Watch the elements Cunningham. They make a mockery of a king's power. Do they not young Cunningham?"

Fergus decided to leave the question unanswered. Although he felt the power of the heavens were greater than any king's, it was more than it was worth to admit to such to a man as prickly as this king. Like so many others who served Alexander a part of him was wary of a man who was so sharp of mind, of tongue and action as he was.

After a while it was almost as if the king forgot Cunningham was there until he said, "Cunningham?"

"Yes Sire."

"So peaceful."

"It is indeed Sire."

"Indeed it is." The king responded not to Cunningham but to himself. "To stand here it is easy to believe the deeds of men do not matter at all."

"Aye."

"It is weighty matter to be a king, Cunningham. I am afraid lest once I die the kingdom will have no heir, as a result war take the land."

Cunningham made no answer, knew the king did not expect it of him.

After a long silence Alexander spoke again. "Know you this, when I stand here I am no king, just a man. Just like thee Cunningham."

"Just like me?" Cunningham could not believe that.

It brought forth a soft, gentle laughter from the king, "Just like you."

When the king laughed it was with genuine affection. What the king said next had a serious tone to it. "If I fail, my failure effects a kingdom and countless lives. Therefore I must ensure that I do not fail. I must have an heir."

The king put his eye on Cunningham. Fergus Cunningham had such a guileless face, all the boy wanted was to serve him faithfully. If only all of them, each and every one of his subjects was as loyal to him as was this lad. At times the arrogant Normans wore him down. They despised his inclination to get his hands dirty in the earth; too wise they considered themselves to lower themselves to delve into the soil like some kind of farmer. As far as the king was concerned he had a special appreciation for workers of the land, far from being despised, they were worthy men, who brought life to the soil and to other men through their efforts. Strangely enough, that was another reason he liked Cunningham. That his people were once farmers appealed to him. He saw the Normans look at him with their barely concealed contempt for working his hands in the dirt. However much they held such scorn of him they kept their opinions to themselves. They did not understand his fascination with plants and growing things, however, they recognized a dangerous and powerful man when they saw one. For his part, Alexander noticed how much these Normans supported one another. They were dangerous. He did not include amongst those he deemed a threat his closest confidant, Walter fitz Alan, The High Steward.

A young knight scrambled onto the battlements trailed by The High Steward who said, "Sire the two Celts have flown, they got out of their holding."

Alexander seemed to all intents and purposes, shocked. The rage that followed was a sight to behold. The king claimed he was surrounded by incompetents, traitors even. "Men shall hang for this!"

Such a good actor that all were initially completely taken in, even The Steward for a moment, after which, Alexander held his eye for long enough to know this behavior was for the benefit of the others, it was a sham. Others by now appeared, men at arms, knights, members of the king's guard. Just then The Chamberlain made an appearance, red-faced trying to compose himself readying himself to try and make an explanation for what had occurred. Came upon them too the young Earl of Buchan with considerable haste. Buchan had several men at arms with him. He rarely went anywhere alone. Seeing him, Alexander passed The Steward a sly wink.

It was The Chamberlain who had the ear of the king next. "The villains hath escaped."

Like so many Norman lords Buchan was loud and stridently outspoken and spoke over the top of The Chamberlain. "Ill done work. These knaves who let this happen need a sword to sever their necks."

The king scoffed at the young lord's assertion and informed him, "It is not for thee to say whose neck is to be severed."

Buchan glared at The Steward before addressing the king again. "He, The Steward, I expected better of him." Buchan shook his head at The Steward. He glared at The Steward. "This is down to him." Buchan obviously was not pleased to see Cunningham and Cunningham got the treatment he was accustomed to. "I see young Cunningham is by your side, as ever the lap dog."

"Cunningham stayed with me to protect my person. He feared for my safety with men of that ilk at large. Came to me when he heard of it. As to him being a lap dog, better a loyal lap dog I say, eh, Buchan, than an disloyal dog just waiting to bite the hand that feeds it."

Buchan asked the king, askance, "How did Cunningham know of this with me coming straight from the scene, the escape just newly made?"

"Sounds to me like he knew his duty." A level cold stare directed at Buchan made the young earl's heart beat faster. "He was the first to make me aware of this, in haste, made his way here to tell me long before thee. And now thee arrives. What do I make of that? What, nearly an hour later? I deem thee poor about thy business, Buchan. Cunningham has my ear because of the knowledge he often has before others, like thee."

Lord Cunningham asked the question with his eyes, he knew he told the king nothing of the kind.

Buchan was too heated in anger to pass over what he saw as criminal incompetence. "The jailors, how were they overpowered by two men in shackles?" The look on his face was disbelief.

The Steward growled back in answer, the suggestion it was down to him this wrongdoing, riled him no end, brought scarlet to his cheeks. "It is a mystery. No doubt one that will be solved when those responsible for keeping them there are put to the rack."

Buchan thought that was rich coming as it did from the man who ultimately was responsible for their custody, who had placed them within the dungeon in the first place. "Indeed those responsible should be put to the rack." Buchan made it plain to The Steward by giving him sustained eye contact that it was him he was referring to.

The Steward snarled, "How dare you ..." The Steward's hand went to his sword.

The king interjected. "Wherever Buchan goes, hands go to swords." "No one will draw a sword here. Hardly a day must go by that someone flashes steel in my presence. There has been enough of such nonsense? Buchan you will plead forgiveness for your rudeness."

The king threw a heavy eye on Buchan until Buchan said, "I take it back, sometimes my intemperance is hard to govern."

The Steward looked briefly at the king before saying, "How could such a thing come to be?"

Cunningham took it upon himself to say, "These men no doubt had help."

Buchan considered Cunningham far below him in rank and took exception to him being included in the conversation, furthermore, acting like an equal. Which brought forth this from Buchan, "I speak because I am an earl, one of the premier earls in Scotland, the Earl of Buchan. The Steward for all his ineptitude is the right hand of the king, you are only an heir with no clear title to the lands your family holds. Although the king finds thee worthy to speak before the highest in the land, himself even, I do not deem thee worthy of my ear. Please do not speak in my presence again, "Buchan was not the only one who considered Cunningham undeserving of the favor given him by the king. Buchan knew many other Normans felt as he did.

The king rebuked Buchan, "Is it any wonder men draw swords on you, Buchan?" A roll of the eyes and then his attention was elsewhere. To The Steward the king put the next question. "How did this come to be?"

The next voice the king heard was not The Steward's as requested, but Buchan again. Speaking when given no leave to speak. Again, as was his way his words had some rudeness attached to them. He said, "I thought Cunningham knew all, is privy to all kinds of information. Why not ask him?"

That the king had asked The Steward to speak and Buchan had spoken, it was almost fatal rudeness to a king to talk over the top of him, very few others would take such liberties with Alexander and Buchan was soon to find the king's patience had its limits.

Not missing a beat more from he who could not stay his tongue, Buchan said, "It was obviously done through treachery."

Cunningham intervened, "I believe the king asked The Steward how it was done, not thee."

"I did not give thee leave to speak, knave. If I have cause to remind thee again not to have speech with me it is the flat of my sword that thou shall meet."

"The king gives me leave, I need no other to consider me worthy."

Buchan took his glaring eyes away from Cunningham. He was biding his time with him and intended to deal with Cunningham in the suitable moment when he was away from the king.

The king had his turn then. "May I speak Buchan? Does thee deem me worthy of speech? I would see what thee makes of the matter."

"They caught the jailers unaware," was Buchan's reply, "Obviously!" That was in itself rude.

The king put it to Buchan. "These jailors, what kind of injuries do they have?"

"None," replied Buchan.

"None!" Full of sarcasm was the king at that. "No doubt they resisted very manfully to have not a mark on them."

The Steward felt the weighty gaze of his sovereign. "Walter, have them hung from the battlements." The king's eyes turned to flint and steel and then he said, "I want them dead, the jailors."

Ewan of the Blackspot appeared amongst them, and asked, "How long past did they go?"

Buchan said to Ewan taking a step forward. "How dare you talk to the king without thee be addressed!" Buchan turned to Alexander. "If he says another word I will drive my sword into his guts." Buchan addressed those around him. "He is a lesser man even than Cunningham and Cunningham is no man at all." Buchan addressed the king turning his back on Ewan. "Do we pursue them, Sire?"

Alexander knew Buchan would love to ride after them as he was a lover of all kinds of action. Alexander answered the impetuous earl thus: "Buchan no doubt you would love to fly over the moors on horseback on the chase making a jape of the king's justice, demonstrating to one and all how easy it is to escape from my jails. Men who defy me or perform acts of treason just walk out of my dungeons. You are going nowhere Buchan."

Buchan met the angry eyes of the king with his own tempestuous eyes. "So we wait here letting them get away for the sake of appearances whilst men are hung from the walls, the jailors, in plain sight demonstrating to one and all that the escape has happened. Will none question that?"

"I will not have one mistake compounded by another. And question my judgement again Buchan and I will hang thee beside them."

The Earl of Buchan was not cured of his outspokenness. "My fellow lords would have something to say about that."

Although the king's smile would make a lesser man than Buchan tremble, Buchan stood where he was seemingly unconcerned, however, he was given cause for concern at the king's next words. "Buchan one more word and I will have thee arrested and I know what your peers will say, they will say what a twit thee was to defy me."

Buchan noticed his men at arms had stepped away from him, distancing themselves, others, the king's men were ready to arrest him. One word from the king and they would do so. As he watched his own men now further from him he bowed his head. "Your Grace my words were in anger they were because of youth and stupidity. I would beg your forgiveness."

A tight smile from the king, "I would hate to hang you Buchan, you provide me with such entertainment, but do not think that I will not do so if you treat me as a lesser man than I am."

The High Steward sought official sanction. He would have it repeated, the hanging order. "Hang the jailors Sire?"

"Do it now, all three of them. See how easy thereafter it is to flee my dungeons. Someone always hangs, if not the prisoner, it must be he who hath lost him."

Alexander had known for some time his jailers could not to be trusted, that they were taking bribes. It was only a matter of time before they allowed someone to escape who the king intended should not escape. His agent, Lord Perth, paid them to let the prisoners out. However, the jailors did not know about Alexander's involvement. Obviously such men were a risk to him. Also, disturbing rumors of bestial abuse came to the king. Alexander had no time for men as would commit these acts. However he would not make it known he hanged them for those reasons. Few realized the extent of his enterprises. To all intents and purposes he tolerated no man to fail in his service and for this reason alone he would have it known they would hang. The king expected obedience and loyalty. And all should know how dire the consequences were if one did not meet the king's high standards.

TAINTED LOVE

MORGUND HAD ONCE summoned Frida at night pulled her under the covers and had at her like an animal burying himself into her depths until she let out high-pitched cries. Ladies were not supposed to cry out like that but she could not help herself. It was at times like this that her nails clenched into his back. Thus it had been for a long time. She had expected Morgund to look elsewhere for entertainment long ago, rejoicing that he had not. Although the acts done to her by night were fully satisfying to them both, that no pregnancy had befallen her after so long was cause for concern.   In the past, the girls who made it their business to gain his attention, he gave very little attention to them. But now, when night fell, her bed was empty and remained so for the duration of the dark hours. Now, she could say for the first time since marrying Morgund that she felt dissatisfied, thus, when Morgund was away her eyes wandered onto other handsome young men. Sometimes they looked back with the same light in their eyes that she had in hers, sharing the same idea, find a quiet spot and be passionate together. Seward was one who returned those looks. That he did surprised and pleased her. Thus it came to be that when Morgund was absent they began spending evenings together, these two, talking.

Once after dark, Frida seated herself beside him at the table, their legs touched which brought forth a wicked and delicious feeling of desire in her. Part of her was curious that if she moved her legs apart whether he would look up her gown.

Bending down and crouching after a spoon she had dropped the look he gave her crutch gave her much pleasure when she presented it to him. It seemed the minds of men more often than not were on woman and lust, indeed, they thought of little else was made plain to her when he looked at her with open wanting. She knew then when she saw how he had reacted to her legs spread, him hungrily devouring her, that they would be together, very carnally, and very soon. She had often in the past taken a moment to admire his masculine beauty. His white blonde hair fell to his shoulders, his fringe just above his eyes. It was the kind of hair recounted in old fairy tales, so pale and glossy. In the courtyard with his shirt off muscles on open display she had watched him. A part of her was driven mad with lust. Frida was full of resentment that Morgund had neglected her of late. Those parts of her body below her belly throbbed with need, longed to feel the rhythm, the motion that caused the heart to beat faster. Without question it was a disastrous course of action and if she had any sense she would of not of pursued it. Sometimes those fires down below burned so hot the only way to put them out was to quench them with her fingers. When she did, on those nights, it was Seward who entered her mind. Often in those lurid dreams he plunged into that fiery place that kept her awake at night. Logic is calm and considered and alas neither one of them was, before tonight Seward had looked in her direction either full in the face or with soft sliding glances that showed his appreciation of her. Others began to notice those looks passing between them which should of worried them. That it did not said much for how past caution they were.

When Frida had parted her legs she revealed all for Seward to see. She wore no undergarment. A blond, she showed herself to be, truly blond. This very forward act, stirred him to action and he took her to her bed. When both were together on the bed he drove into her with a rhythm and anger that made her surrender to his madness. After it was over Seward began pacing up and down, that he was worried was very plain to see. She was not, not at first, she had done this with him many times in the secrecy of her mind. It took her a while to acknowledge that this was different, that something had changed, suddenly she felt fear at what they had done. Such was the measure of her self-control that the next night she turned him away, unfortunately, that self-control wilted when he reappeared again the night after that. When he touched her hand she felt her heart beating in her chest too fast, felt the heat in her loins heavy and urgent so she took him inside.

    When Seward left to hunt one morning she collected her thoughts and put some reasoning to this. On the whole Frida loved being Morgund's wife. The time was near when Morgund would return thus she knew this could not go on. It could spell death for both if they were caught. The next time Seward sought her eyes he found the back of her head. Such things as had happened between them ended. She made herself faithful to Morgund by using her fingers to delve and explore and calm her passions.

    Frida sat in her small garden watching the snow falling with turmoil in her mind, her monthly cycle was a week overdue. The blood which usually spilled did not. Moments of contemplation taken from her when there was a commotion in the courtyard. Morgund had returned. She stood her head throbbing, wondering what she would say to persuade him that this child was his. She must be with child, she was never late.

    Morgund approached; she stood for several moments panting, listening to her rapid heartbeat. Noting the strange dizzy angles at which her eyes met the whirling faces of those around her, with that mercifully she fell losing consciousness. Morgund, carefully held her forehead, seeing the glazed look in her eyes when she opened them he thought it was a fever. When she came to, the wind whistled, it was an ill wind she knew, as she knew she would have to face the reality of what she had done.

DANCE OF DEATH

A LITTLE RAIN a little sunshine on the day a fancier of the old religion made mock of Morgund. Also, that day this same wicked man foretold of Morgund's ruin. Such lamentable predictions, foremost among them that Morgund would die if he ever lifted a hand to Alexander King of Scots. It seemed there was little hope for Morgund. Foretold by this sayer of things to come - if that was what he was - that if Morgund did not fight king Alexander, dying in poverty, lamented by none was the prediction for him. Foretold too that he would have a son; however, this son would not be of his own making, in Seward's likeness would he be.

Morgund was deeply regretful that morning. Chief amongst his regrets that in a fit of passion he had made a girl pregnant and rather than fulfil his duty to her, left her to suffer the fate of having and bringing up a child in England, alone. Never did he learn if Mirium, for that was the girl's name, bore his child. Shutting his eyes he made a prayer for her safety, for the safety of the child if there was one. Then his eyes snapped open as he fastened onto a new idea. They could all be together in Scotland, Mirium, the child and himself. The child would be eleven years of age by now.

Why had he left them and never given it a thought until lately was perhaps down to his greater maturity. As well as the fact that he had no child of his own although he had been married for over six years, thus, an heir was uppermost in his mind. His pressing preoccupation was the continuation of his line. Part of the reason he had abandoned Mirium was the burning desire to return to

Scotland.

When he had left as a boy after the murder of his father he fled like a dog with its tail between its legs, furthermore, that fact galled him and he would have those who forced him away know that he was a swordsman and more than capable of having his revenge on them. An outstanding matter still far from accomplished after more than ten years back in Scotland. Remaining alive was a kind of success, for the king of Scots and many others would have him dead. He took joy in the fact that he was not dead and that they took none in it. The secondary good cause was to see to his mother's safety. That should of come first in his reckoning but if he was honest with himself it played little part in his decision. Women seldom were under threat within the kingdom of Scotland as the men controlled the land and the worse a woman could expect was a forced marriage or to be placed in a nunnery.

No, the most pressing reason for his hasty departure from England was a wish to have his enemies fear him, furthermore, that, although he had left the kingdom as a poor boy he returned capable of smiting them. To win acclaim for feats of arms was important to him. Too important, more than was Mirium and the child. The shame of it he would carry with him to his grave. It made him want to cry, the very thought of it. He had come to learn that a man's reputation does not just rest on feats of arms alone, doing justly by those who are of your blood is a sacred contract which a man must honor. This child if it was born and it still lived it was one of a very select few with MacAedh blood in its veins. It struck him that his name would die with him if he did not find this heir. As it stood there was no ther to carry his name on after him. That he had been negligent in his duty, failed to do the right thing up to this point in his life, was a heavy burden on his soul.

'Mirium'. 'The child.' 'Mirium'. 'The child'. Like a nail being hammered into a single spot but failing to insert it drove again and again into his mind, he fretted over what had happened. How wrong it was to do what he had done, and that he could have a son, or daughter for that matter, out there, who was unknown to him and perhaps suffering. Although in his mind he was committed to Frida, however, conceding that after many years there was no sign of a quickening in her womb. Mores the pity for without a child the MacAedhs would be like leaves on the wind – withered and dead, their strength and vitality crumbling into infinity. His thoughts turned to the mother of this perhaps-child, Mirium. The girl-witch who subscribed to the old beliefs believed in magic, used it. Even though a simple girl she had wisdom beyond her years. Although Mirium did not inspire fear some of her ancient beliefs were worthy of the black reputation that made folk fear them. Like the dark priestess who claimed Mirium's allegiance and for a time held Morgund in her power. The arch priestess of Miriam's coven was loathsome. Just to think of her, even for a moment, brought Morgund out in a cold sweat. As her prisoner, suffering terrible woe at her hands. That monster had terrorized him to the point of total mental disintegration. Any sense he had of himself, any relic of peace-of-mind, was ripped from him by that evil crone. No doubt she performed all many of perversions to sate the demons that governed her wretched soul. One thing was certain she had a great appetite for horrendous deeds. The sins that could be attributed to her, not only included murder, torture, rape, think of a crime and you could put her name to it. She performed acts upon him that were like black butterflies flying just beyond his sight any moment to fly in on him dragging him down into terror. Horrified at seeing her eyes fixed upon him anew. The ill usage by that evil hag intruded on his mind and made him feel sick to the pit of his stomach. No matter how far from her he was, nor how distant in time her sovereignty over him had been it felt like a heartbeat away. It felt like she was just nearby and if he turned his head he would see her. He was relieved that priestess of hell was but a memory. Reminding himself of this truth his breathing returned to normal, the sweat on his brow no longer fell as heavily, his heart no longer felt like it would explode in his chest. Her long tapered fingers could not reach him now he told himself.

    It must be a day for doubts and misgivings, for Alexander then took hold of his mind. With the king becoming ever more active in the highlands sooner or later Morgund would be forced to defend himself against his power. With the Normans advancing and he being a long time enemy of the king it meant trouble for him. Wherever they went they sought to dominate. Whoever was a prominent man and an enemy of the king would have to deal with them. Moreover, the king was committed to taking the Celtic north, which would bring many Norman knights wanting to acquire land, and his, would be ripe for the picking being as it was productive and extensive and held by an avowed traitor.

Upon hearing his friends calling out to him to eat with them declining to join them for he was still absorbed in his considerations. Such was the despondency on his mind that not until the sound was quite near did he hear it. For a moment thinking it a dream in his mind this tune he heard playing. Very tuneful and joyous to the ear it was. A piper played who was uncommonly skilled. Deft musical patterns woven on the wind, phrases only intermittently heard were dependent on the caprices of the air to carry to Morgund and his company.

"That man has the gift." Morgund called out to his friends with a pleasant look of appreciation. "The sound is close now. I wonder how many come with him? Seward, ride up on that hill and convey to me numbers."

Upon the site nominated Seward made great show of looking, hand shielding his eyes. Finally, he shouted down to Morgund. "One piper." After a bit, Seward repeated his earlier statement. "We have one piper."

As the piper neared him Seward cheerfully called out to him. "Good day to you." Faced with the silent man glaring back at him Seward took a moment to accept that he had been affronted. Expecting to be answered this time in harder tone he said, "I wished you health."

"And to you," the man replied coldly.

Seward knew an ill wind blew in with this wanderer from the woods. Morgund, unaware of Seward's misgivings approached the man with goodwill. "Will you share a cup with us?"

A scowl flickered across the new-comer's face, his brow creased in a hundred lines. The man said something Morgund had not expected to hear him say and had Morgund on the back foot when he said it.

This said the piper: "Aye, do so and be quick about it." As if Morgund was not stunned enough there was even more consternated at what came next. "The dead they do not drink, and amongst them thee is soon to be." The piper's hard eyes met Morgund's nervous ones. "The portents are full of foreboding for thee Morgund. War is coming, and death is coming with it. Many who breath now will be food for the worms when the swords sing."

Morgund gasped in reply. "Be thee mad?" Taking in the look in his eyes Morgund had in his mind that he was.

"I see darkness for thee Morgund. Morgund you have the look of death on you. A year hence you will be gone from this earth."

Morgund's hand went to his sword. "Thee will die before I do. My blade tells me such a thing will come to be."

The newcomer said without a trace of fear, "The specter of death is but a blink of an eye away for you, as it is for me and for us all."

Morgund was unimpressed with him. "What brings thee with such grim tidings?"

Rather than reply, the piper came forward until he was eye to eye with Morgund who shoved him back. Eyeing the sword on his hip, Morgund wondered if he was going to draw it. Morgund's hand already was on his own, and now he withdrew it. In response the hard-starrer made to withdraw his own. "Don't," Morgund warned him." Morgund's sword was near the mage, Morgund had decided he was one.

The man who could see beyond all others stood confidently. "This sword inches away from me it will not end me."

It was a game prediction given that Morgund's blade almost touched his skin. With a smile Morgund took a step back. "Should I cut you down?" The question hung in the air. Regardless of the fact the piper kept his own sword sheathed, Morgund drew forth a slight red from the predictor's chest now by cutting him. "What are the portents for death for thyself, now?"

The piper stared without saying a word. "I suggest you stay away from any warlike acts towards me," he finally said.

"Such wisdom." Morgund took another step towards him and decided there and then to end his life. He was going cut him down. When the piper remained motionless his sword still in its scabbard it prompted Morgund to say, "Why keep thy sword sheathed?"

The man responded, "If thee does not do as I foretell, thee will die. Desist from warlike acts towards me and yet there might be a chance for thee. Small though it be."

"Is there nothing else thee can do but bleat of ill tidings?"

The piper turned his back walking away almost immediately swallowed up by the wet-green. As the others watched the direction he went in, Morgund remained locked in his dreams, thinking of the mistreatment he had had at the hands of that witch who held him hostage and committed such barbarity upon him. To think of her at such a moment was curious and Morgund did not know why he did, something about this man who had accosted him with dire warnings of things to come brought that foul woman back to the forefront of his mind. The piper's appearance amongst them in itself gave Morgund pause for thought. Someone put him up to it. Scotland's monarch was reputed to be the cleverest man in Europe, what better way to unnerve a man than foretell his death. With this in mind Morgund walked to where he last saw the piper. Once there, looked for him. The lushness of the forest surrounded him on all sides but no sign was there of the piper.

Seward appeared beside him and Morgund asked his friend, "Did you see where he went?"

Seward could not believe what Morgund had just asked. "I would not follow him."

"Thus you say, but I want the truth of it, why he came and who sent him."

Paten then appeared and brought up, "Perhaps he does talk of the future."

This grated on Morgund nearly as much as had the piper. He turned his eyes away from Paten. He would not have him see how displeased he was with him. Looking into the trees he thought he saw movement. For a moment he saw a rustle in the leaves. Morgund set off at once into the green. Seward looked at Paten but as neither saw anything in the woods they assumed Morgund was going into the forest to relieve himself.

In the forest, the huge pine trees glowered down in the filtered morning light like ogres. A slight breeze shimmering through the leaves as Morgund walked past them. In the dark shadow of the woods Morgund met again this odd man full of prophesy. The piper did not seem surprised at all that he had been found. He stared back at Morgund then let his eyes travel to where Morgund came from. "Those two, your friends, are no friends at all. Friends without hearts are they. Neither one will do you any good in the end."

"I think King Alexander sent thee to undo my senses. Did he not?"

"Sometimes the future speaks to me. Shows me that which is about to come. A blessing or a curse I know not which. I speak to forestall the danger I see coming for you. If one path leads to death, perhaps another can lead to longer life and success. Perhaps my coming is to thine good fortune and if thee takes heed of me good things may come of it."

Just then an eerie whistling wind hit Morgund in the face opening a grin from the man who spoke and thus it seemed that he who stood before Morgund had some kind of power over the elements. "The wind blows. Out of nowhere. Just like that. Listen hard to it. Hard to understand what it says, but listen hard enough and perhaps you will know what it tells thee, it too knows thy fate. Perhaps it gives thee warning."

"Forget that. Where did you come from?"

"Away south."

"Why come to me?"

"To warn thee."

"I do not think so. I believe the king sent thee, and thy insights are nothing more meaningful than washer women's gossip that rises and falls and means nothing."

"But you know otherwise. In your heart, you know I have the second-sight. I believe thee knows the truth of it." The piper fixed an unnerving gaze on Morgund as he pealed back his robe and revealed the charm hanging from his neck. The charm had a goat on it. It was the symbol of the witch's coven that had enslaved Morgund, they who had taken from him everything but his life.

Morgund gritted his teeth. "I know thy kind. I do not want to speak another word to thee."

"Then thee is cursed. A year of life that is all you have left."

Morgund, could not contain his rage, was but a second away from running him through. "Does thee want my sword in your belly?"

"I have a sword too. And here it is in my hand."

Both swords were out now. The piper remained calm, sure of himself. Carried himself like a swordsman. Legs apart, well balanced, sword to the fore. Suddenly, he screamed, his words directed at a greater power, his eyes turned in his head, only whites shone out. "A friend will bring thee down. That and thine own pride will be thy undoing. All who love thee now will have cause to hate thee then. Seward the best of friends shall become the worst of enemies. All eyes will mock thee when thine child is known to be not of thine own making but in Seward's likeness. And Seward, like you will of him, regret the day he ever set his eyes on you. Despite any friendship professed between you, one day his blood will be shed by you." His words came from deep well inside him from an obvious place of prophecy, or, so it seemed. "On farther shore, the tide shall go out, taking Seward's body with it. On the tidewater will go Seward. Seward will be floating in the water that will be stained with the red of him. And Morgund, I tell you this, kill me and a curse be on thee and on all of thine name until the end of your line, not long in coming." Continuing to shout out his hatred he intoned with deep conviction. "Death to all who carry the cursed name, MacAedh." His manic voice settled into the tone of a sane man but was no less frightening for that. "It has ever been thus. There is a curse on the MacAedhs." His spasm or fit or whatever it was gripped him again. He raged on and on with curses, one such: "Everything of thine will be taken from thee, a dank, drafty croft, is all thee has to look forward to, dying there alone and in poverty if thee does not make war. No escaping a cruel fate. If thee makes war, a more dreadful fate."

Then he vanished like he was never there.

Morgund raised his voice. "The MacAedhs are not cursed. Not by you, nor any other. That I have survived despite all odds it means that some blessings are bestowed upon us."

Hearing Morgund shouting Seward came to investigate, when he found his friend it caused concern to crease his face. The excitement Morgund showed at seeing Seward bordered on desperation.

The words Morgund spoke were these, "Seward, my stalwart friend, my friend beyond all others." Seward began to think Morgund was from his wits dislodged when he heard him say, "That is your reward for years of faithful service to lay face down in the water, slain by me." Morgund tried to clear the image of his dead friend from his mind. The water becoming red with his blood. Dead eyes staring up at him. Seward's dead face appeared most white. Seward's death he could see it in graphic detail before his eyes. The others who had appeared by now witnessed that Morgund had something before his eyes that disturbed him greatly.

Morgund eyed Seward. "Seward, you will be cast down by me. By my sword."

Paten could not help but feel dread mixed with a fascination at the sight of Morgund. The man who told Morgund this was a high priest of some kind Paten knew that from the moment he set eyes on him. When Morgund escaped inside his mind Paten somehow caught a glimpse of Seward's body mixing with the sea. Paten could see through Morgund's eyes, the sight he had was what Morgund had in the future, altogether a very strange thing. As soon as it came it went. Back in his own skin, he tried to make sense of it. It was hard to, a lot happened since that prophet made his appearance. Something very important had just occurred. To his mind, that was undeniable. Unlike Seward, Paten had come after Morgund earlier and had heard something of the exchange between Morgund and the piper. Paten felt that the piper foretold the future. He also felt something inside him stir, something awaken. The future was just foretold with the kind of certainty that made him want to hear and know more of it, know what his own fate might be. Paten thought of the prophecy, he could feel his heart beating inside his chest at the power of it. Morgund would slay Seward. He saw the piper in his mind's eye his face full of wisdom. The seer's words rung out with disturbing resonance. His mind dwelling on this on the way back to camp. The day passed with his mind full of it. When the others had gone to sleep, that night, still his mind was on it.

From out of the dark from his dreams he heard a voice: "Thou shall come to me! Thou shall come to me! Thou shall come to me!"

There was no doubt in Paten's mind the mage was summoning him and waiting for him in the forest. Visions of a glade pulled on his mind, pulled on his body. Before long Paten inched away past his companions, followed a path written out in his mind until he broke through low greenery to the glade that had been brought forth into his mind by magic, and now, it was revealed for a real place.

A laugh followed by a voice he knew only too well. "I see my friend has come."

In the firelight the piper's teeth flashed silver. At first the two of them did not talk at all and Paten thought they wasted precious time for the piper seemed more intent on making a brew stirring tiny leaves in a pot which he seemed to like to stare at. Both watched the whirl of the leaves amid the current. The concoction that swept around gave off a vapor that had a herby, pleasant, smell. But as the sun threatened to bring the new day and Paten saw the ivy-choked limbs and roots take the sunlight, the piper's eyes turned on his, he stared at Paten intensely, from very far away came the sound of his voice.

"Satan is majestic in all things, he is the light in the dark. Normally hidden, but if you give yourself to him bright beyond belief he will reveal himself to you and you shall share his power." Paten did not interrupt, did not frown, nor nod. The red-gold of the fire waxed and waned adding to the mesmerizing effect of all this. When the piper started speaking again the fire responded shooting up engulfing the piper's face in an otherworldly glow. "He will guard you from harm protect you when no others can."

Paten had small recollection of the next few minutes, how he came to serve a new master, to wear the goat image on a necklace was a vacant space in his recollection, in truth, to have a memory there needs to be time for reflection and he had not had time for that. He needed a place to settle and take it all in. The strange thing was, he felt bigger, stronger, taller. His heart pounded with a strange power. There was much to learn, all he had to do was commit himself to Satan to share in his eternal glory. The others his former friends seemed small to him like a memory. Recalled one thing on the way back to the camp, noticed, there was something strange about the light in the glade and surrounding forest, the trees both bright and dark by turns, light seemed to come from beneath the ground, from the underworld. The height of the trees was breathtaking, they were all so tall, so grand, they were grandiosely luminous, lavish, and surreal, they were not of this world. It was a very special place that stood on its assets a part of different plane of existence, easily distinguished from surrounding areas, yet he knew that if he went back there and tried to find it after he left it, he never would.

With a new day Seward lent his sword to a young fellow from a poor family who had never possessed one and taught the youth how to parry and thrust with it. Alarmed by his ineptitude Seward stepped in. "You are in danger of being cut with that sword, give it to me."

"No, I am not," the youth objected. "How long before I can be as good as thee?" Said he who wished to be.

Seward insisted and took the sword from him. "I will show thee the use of it well but for now a wooden sword is for thee."

Again the youth's words flew with anger. "How long before I can beat thee?"

"It will be a cold day in hell before that happens."

"Truly I will be as good as thee? I will test thee soon enough."

"Never. Whoever seeketh to better me must be prepared to wager their life on it, their life, remember it well. And remember well that I am the greatest swordsman in all Scotland."

Indeed, it was true that Seward was one of Scotland's greatest swordsmen. Morgund knew it true. Knew too that Seward loved to proclaim it. For the first time Morgund did not like to hear him do so. To Morgund it sounded oafish. All men know their worth and few need to remind others of it, to do so, earns whoever does so the tag of fool. It is often the taunt directed at such men. Discomfortingly Morgund was aware that there was something to dislike in his old friend. He caught Seward's eye. Reading Morgund's expression Seward met the look of displeasure with one of his own. Something in that exchange altered their relationship. Before the best of friends now between them something subtly uneasy had begun, something that said one was a stranger to the other, that things were not as they were.

Morgund sent out word for all men of fighting age to hear him speak. He chose a wild and isolated place where there was little risk of drawing MacCainstacairt's attention. Few if any had any connections to him here in Ross. Once Ross had been the bastion of MacAedh power. Those days were long gone.

One man in particular was scathing when Morgund outlined

his plan for the Celtic revival in Scotland. Morgund had only just started and hardly had a chance to get a word out of his mouth when the man said, "I am no follower of lost causes," the man then, directing, a sneering gaze on the subject of his attention, said, "Morgund MacAedh you are a fool." Thinking the man had finished Morgund began again and scarcely got started when the man raised his voice interrupting him, "I would not put my confidence in Morgund. His manner and speech alone tell me he is loosened from his wits. King Alexander is a very clever man. As is MacCainstacairt a worthy protector of us all."

Morgund retorted, "If he is such a rare wit, of such cleverness, this king, why are all the highlands all rent asunder with all manner of strife?"

"That thee does not know tells me what an idiot you are because you and people like you are the cause of it."

Morgund ignored that to say, "I doubt he is so clever?"

"You know him not then." The man levelled his disdainful eyes on Morgund. "Because men like thee seek to fall on rightful men, rightful earls, to advance themselves despite all the ill it does to the kingdom, Scotland is a land of blood."

Addressing others, he said, "Green foliage and good things that is what I like, to keep my cattle safe. Unattended cattle are like to go a wondering when those that own them, go on silly adventures with silly men."

Morgund waved his hand dismissively. "I look for men of courage, willing fighters, not those with craven hearts."

Again, Morgund heard the man's voice, "The MacAedh stupidity is legendary."

"... As I said ..."

"... Like a cock he makes a noise to the annoyance of others."

Morgund waited to make sure the man had finished, convinced he had, and that he could continue he began again, "The Normans ..."

Another interruption. "... I see a man with a head destined for the chopping block."

Morgund had had enough. Morgund called the man out. "Stay thy tongue. Thee is obviously a coward and a thief. Not the kind of man I seek. Go, or else I will take my sword to you."

A smile appeared at the corner of the mouth of the man full of contempt. "If you can, do so." The Rossman stepped forth sword in hand. "Test me if you dare. We will see if thee is a better swordsman than a speaker, for as a speaker, woefully inept."

"I came to win friends not shed blood."

A sneer came with the reply, "A cowardly response that. I would expect nothing less from Morgund MacAedh."

Laughter arose from those around him grating on Morgund making him grip his sword the tighter. What drove the man? He was disturbingly calm. Faced with the greatest danger the superior man feels the most at ease. A difficult thing to attain as Morgund knew only too well. Thinking he had learned how to amid the maelstrom of combat Morgund realized he had not, realized this listening to his racing heart. There was the dampness of sweat on his brow. This loud mouthed man must be possessed of great skill for fear was totally absent in him, or it might be that he was ignorant, unaware of the gravity of the risk he took.

Morgund wondered why he felt such dread? Had he not changed, left such fears far behind him? Telling himself it only existed in his head made his response to it even more real. He remembered his boyhood, the would-be murderer who would take his head. Recalled, how near death was then. The sword hovering above his head was about to take him into eternal and everlasting darkness. A part of him was still in that moment. Still, to this day, the swordsman's face leered at him from his nightmares. How familiar it was that face full of hate. It was going to debilitate him if he wasn't careful. He reassured himself with the fact that he was now a man and a truly formidable swordsman. A determined cast took hold his face, he would show this oaf who did not know it that he was someone to be reckoned with. This man's relentless glare in a way was a blessing because it created anger and made Morgund itch to begin combat.

The man had the nerve to display his even white teeth. Liked putting them on display did this son of a whore. When Morgund drew his sword it felt unusually heavy in his hand which he thought a strange thing. It made no difference, heavy or not, it was the weapon he was going to kill this man with. Fear relaxed, and hardihood increased for in moments he would find out if his arm was strong and true, discover, if his heart was still full of courage. Suddenly forcing down another moment of uncertainty. Whatever was wrong with him today, despite it, he would fight, and fight well and die well if he had to. His mind was nowhere and everywhere at the same time.

Having dealt with fear of dying on many occasions, it was a comforting emotion the familiarity of this situation thus it relaxed his tension. Every fighter knows death's twisted ways, that it can see into the soul, that it feeds on your fear. A fighter must defeat that sly slayer of the soul before defeating any enemy.

Seward called out, "Morgund, good luck."

Morgund did not respond lest his concentration desert him. As his opponent came at him, as their swords joined, Morgund, was outwitted, was brought down, however, rolling away from the next expected killer blow. Without this anticipation his head would have flown off his shoulders. On his feet again Morgund was forced back. It was only a matter of time before his opponent tried again to take his feet out from under him as he had before. Morgund would be ready for it next time. Though starting sluggishly his timing had gotten better, his judgement, also, his ability to read the man in front of him, too, steeply improving.

Winning fights is mostly about winning moments in fights, and crucially making those winning moments, happen. Morgund made himself the embodiment of this when he flung out an apparently misdirected thrust at the Rossman who thinking he had his man thrust straight back at where Morgund was, was, being the key word, because the Rossman struck thin air, Morgund was to his side. The Rossman who had his sword out in front of him was left wide open and defenseless. When he realized he was about to die all his swagger fell away from him. A long, long moment when death was the noose which had tightened around his neck, he took a breath, held it.

Morgund could quite easily of slain him, instead, sliced his hip open. When the Rossman fell to his knees wounded Morgund put his sword to his throat. "One so brave does not deserve to die." For a moment Morgund kept his sword on his neck before telling him, "I spare thee. For no other reason than to prove I am a better man than thee thought me to be."

To Seward, he said, "I have not devoted the time to keeping my skills sharp and by not doing so nearly got myself killed." As an afterthought, "We have both seen ourselves a hairs length from death. I stood witness to you fighting for your life. Now, you have seen me one heart-beat away from death. Curious, is it not?"

Seward gave thought to the prophecy of this man before him

bringing about his own death. Seeing a sword in Morgund's hand gave Seward cause for thought. Would he, he wondered, ever again look at Morgund holding a sword and not feel the prospect of his own death.

THE FUGITIVE

AFTER A LONG cold winter spring should be a time of rejoicing, it was not. On one of these early spring nights the high table lacked in conversation since all its occupants were sorrowful. Finally, after a dreadfully long stillness her father, Lord Argyll, declared she would regret every day of her life willfully riding out to warn Morgund MacAedh that someone from Argyll's castle meant to harm him. Such an act generated from Argyll's castle could be considered an act of war and therefore put both Argyll's honour at stake and put him at risk of Morgund returning to seek revenge. All because Morgund took her fancy. Her father could not believe that for so childish a reason she had betrayed him. Daughters were expected to obey their fathers. To fail to was to forgo all parental support. He told Edana that he would see her damned in hell for her dishonour of him.

According to Argyll he would sell Edana in bondage to the Irish. No good was coming to her that much was true enough though she doubted her father would go that far. In reality the Irish were not getting a new slave, whispers between mother and father told her so. That said, Mother could not bear the shame of having Edana in her house. Edana knew her father's mind and some kind of retribution was at hand. Something awful impending that she knew. Fretting over the prospect of what was in store for her sleepless nights ensued. Whilst all others were discussing her in whispers her father took himself off to the lowlands. Argyll had the solution on how best to deal with his wicked daughter. When he returned from the south he continued to be cold and distant to her. The coldness and the detachment did not prevent him imparting this with a menacing smile, that she was no longer of the nobility, she had to forget that. He deemed her lower than any simple goatherd's daughter. She was a girl without status or protection, not yet a slave but she may as well be. No longer the daughter of a lord, she was a girl awaiting the judgement of her father because although she was no longer a lord's daughter he was still her father and he had complete power over her. Argyll made it plain to Edana that if she was the king's offspring and had acted like she did, the king would have had no compunction in evicting her from the royal castle to beg for her living. All and sundry knew what manner of low slut she was, thus, she was surrounded on all sides by judgmental eyes as she performed menial tasks fit for a lowly servant. Her mother now looked at her with the narrow eyes of suspicion. A slut, they called her a slut, highly ironic given that this slut was a virgin. She was full of fear as she waited for the axe to fall. Father would make some profit from her. She belonged to him and he was a thrifty man as she knew only too well. Night after night Edana lay awake tortured by fears. Tossing and turning in her bed, furthermore, crying to the silent walls until she was weak from the effort. In her nightmares that she was to be sent to Ireland to live a rough life amid a charmless race forgotten by all who once held her dear. Some Irish men came to talk to her father and given her the sorts of looks that had made that fear great in her.

    The dread day of reckoning finally came. Edana learned she was to be wed to the Norman knight, Sir Richard De Sourules. Sir Richard was notorious in all Scotland for his cruelty. Argyll had found a man suitably nasty to curb her ways, he told her. This man Sir Richard De Sourules was the heir to Lord Floors, the Norman heir of Floors, would turn her into an honest woman or kill her is how her father described it. That he would kill her she took to be an exaggeration; no father would accede to that. Reputed to be the vilest of all the Normans and she knew their acts of brutality shamed all Scotland.

    After a hasty breakfast Edana rose from the high table and bid farewell to her mother who refused to speak to her. The woman who had given birth to her did not give Edana the barest glance. None in the tower bid her farewell as she left. On the road to

Edinburgh accompanied by her still wordless father who looked anywhere but at her. It all passed in a blur the travel across what would otherwise have been a wondrously beautiful landscape, but none of it registered, nothing dispelled her foreboding until the sight of Edinburgh. There was excitement at visiting a town. She had never been in a town before. Entering the gates there was an uplift in her spirits followed by another moment of good cheer meeting the surprisingly good-looking Sir Richard De Sourules. If there was evil in him his favorable looks belied the fact.

"Edana may you plague him less than you have me," were the last words her father spoke to her on the day of her wedding.

A brutal rape followed the hasty ceremony. A very brutal rape it was with acts committed upon her only a fiend would commit. An endless night spent in pain and degradation was her lot. Brutalized in intimate parts especially humiliating. Edana passed out from the pain of it. Having been curious about what it would be like to have a lover, this was far from what she had imagined. It wasn't a dream come true it was a nightmare.

In the days that followed Edana's wedding she was dragged from one tower to the next across leagues of land before coming to her husband's castle, castle Floors. Castle Floors was never meant to be called, castle Floors. Originally designated Castle De Sourules, to the Scots that surrounded the castle De Sourules sounded like Floors thus De Sourules castle became castle Floors over time. The De Sourules, prevailed on their tenants to pronounce the name correctly, but despite their best efforts, the name stuck, it became castle Floors to one and all. A charming story. Edana would learn it was the only charming thing about the place. Edana had dreamt like all girls do of marriage but never in any of her dreams had she imagined herself married to a brutal husband who raped her almost every night. Her dowry was the only reason this Norman knight had wed her and now was given license to inflict more pain and humiliation upon her than he would have been allowed to on a simple serf. Over his cups he unlaced his breaches prior to an act which preceding which she had never even heard of. Pulling her head onto his prick he used her head to sate his lust. Filling her mouth with his seed, after which he poured the contents of a cup of wine over her head. If only she could say this was the worst thing that happened to her, it was not. Far more horrifying things were done to her, things that only a deranged mind could think of.

It was a lonely existence in the castle frequenting the long hallways trying to stay out of the way of the unpredictable heir of Floors, her husband, Sir Richard, as well, Lady Floors, her silent disapproving mother-in-law was best avoided. Nor did the last member of the family Lord Floors make her life any easier. Lord Floors, her father-in-law, cast his eye onto her whenever he had her alone making her feel as if she were naked. Responding to her discomfort he enjoyed the impression he made, and fixed his gaze on her with much salacity. As if all was not bad enough, none of the servants dared talk to her adding to her loneliness. All this was as nothing compared to what her husband did to her at night. He would turn her over onto her stomach with cruel intent. He came to bed late at night with the stink of alcohol on his breath. This abominable man laid into her with his fists, pummeling her before he pressed his horrid thing into her ass, or, thrust her head down upon his prick, feeding her his engorged mass until it made her sick. The stink of the substances he evicted and the feeling of the slime slinking its way down her throat was unspeakable. It was vile. Sometimes he would pull her hair until it came out by the roots. It was the stuff of nightmares.

Even worse when particularly drunk and violent he endangered her life. One night she was sure he would kill her. On one of those occasions he made her lay face down then thrust a blunt instrument into her anus. She cried thereafter but not for long. She tried not to let him know how much he hurt her because of the satisfaction he got from causing her pain might drive him on to kill her.

Many were the times with no cause he hit her. Not to mention the blood which came from her anus all too frequently because of his cruel and vile acts of degradation. Beatings, constant rape, instruments stuck up her ass, as bad as all this mistreatment was, Edana endured it, seeing no other way to live, no other thing to do. She reckoned such was her lot until something happened which forced her hand. What she discovered was truly shocking. They were going to kill her. When a servant warned her dumbfounded by it, she had wandered aimlessly wondering what to do about it. The last time she had acted independently it had meant the end of her world as she knew it. That what the servant girl told her might be true caused her mind endless torment. Talking herself into the proposition that it was some flight of imagination by a servant girl lost in whimsy, such was her reasoning until more dreadful warning did she have. Her sadist husband Sir Richard was away and with him gone she took to wandering the hallways like a ghost. Wandering all night because she could not sleep with worry. On one of those occasions at night seeing the two detested figures of Lord Floors and her mother-in-law approaching, Edana faded into the shadows. What she overheard took her ignorance away from her and revealed the true dire necessity of an escape. Edana was startled but realized almost immediately that this was what the servant girl had warned her about.

Hiding and listening, she picked up on the faint suggestion of mockery ever present in her father-in-law's speech, "The girl needs a good knocking on the head."

"Too messy," from Lady Floors. She heard her mother-in-law, then say, "The girl has not quickened with a child these many months." Thereafter, a moment or two of silence until she heard, "... Perhaps an accident. There are many stairs to fall down in this castle." It was her mother-in-law who said that.

Lord Floors, venomously, "At least she knows better than attempt speech with me the foul bitch. Do but say the word and I will go ahead and thrust her down a stair, or else have some other folly overcome her."

Her mother-in-law said this on the subject. "Any night will do, any night at all."

Edana would love to appear from the shadows and to confront them with their villainy. She realized it would gain her nothing she would only fall prey to their unpalatable plans. Was it her failure to fall pregnant that caused them to hate her so? Her husband's rough treatment was more than likely the cause of it. He preferred her ass and mouth to that part of her body that could result in a child.

Lord Floors interrupted her thoughts. The depth of his hatred was only too apparent. "Her dowry is ours to keep despite her death."

She could not believe it, they were talking about her life like it was worthless, a sheep would be of more worth to them, according to them she was already dead. Their heartlessness was beyond belief.

Lady Floors in only what could only be described as the definition of evil, said, "An injured bird once landed on the battlements, Richard, small boy though he was, picked it up very gingerly. Then wrenched its neck and looked for all the world like he had committed an act of great kindness."

Both of them laughed heartedly, and it seemed to Edana, proudly. Lord Floors, gleefully. Then from his lips did come, "In the village they say he has the cloven hoof."

Edana immediately thought of the cloven hoof of the devil. Remembered she had heard it said of him by the servants that he had hooves instead of feet. Although it was only a tale, she could understand why it was believed. If ever anyone was a devil in human form it was he. Only because she had seen his feet could she attest to its untruth.

She heard Lord Floors again. "He teases them that he will take his boots off and show them it is true." Lord Floors laughed again before saying, "Perhaps we should allow Richard to enjoy himself at her expense and abuse her to death."

It immediately occurred to Edana that if the son had not a cloven hoof, surely the father must have after a statement like that.

Lady Floors again, "Such would make it impossible for Richard to find another wife. I want her gone. By the end of the week. While Richard is away."

This was indeed her death they were talking about, she had to remind herself of it, not routine matter of domesticity, not a washing or putting down new rushes.

Lord Floors let the question hang in the air. "How do we get rid of her?"

It could be from the tone and nature of their discussion were discussing how to fix a leak in the roof.

"An accident," Lady Floors said, "It has to be an accident."

Panic seized Edana and had her hands gripped tightly together in an effort to control her rising terror for at that moment Lord Floors stated staring seemingly straight at her. Edana stilled her breath and listened to the sound of her pounding heartbeat. His head finally turned causing her immense relief. Soon she heard their departing footsteps and breathed easier. Her husband was visiting another castle and would be absent for the full week. They wanted to kill her while he was away so it did not seem Richard had murdered his wife. Although the perception of murder did not hang over him there were enough stories to dishearten any woman from contemplating marrying him. Alone, in her room, Edana tried to tell herself that what she heard meant little but deep in her heart knew her parents-in-laws were planning her murder. It was the most dreadful predicament.

As bad as it was, it was about to worsen still. The door opened and through it stepped Lord Floors. Motionless, too afraid to move, she lay on her bed terrified. A hand swept through her hair caressingly. Edana tried to not to shake in terror. A voice above her said, "What a fool I am to have frightened you."

His hands drifted down her body. Edana's eyes glistened as she felt his hands on her breasts, then lower down, on those parts only a husband should touch or for the sake of cleanliness of the person a woman herself.

"I desire you, move your legs apart."

It was kind of a relief to know he did not plan to immediately murder her. Alas, that solace was taken from her. Her heart skipped when she saw his hand come to rest on his dagger then she knew this was to be her last night on earth. She managed to ask, "Are you going to kill me?"

"Stupid girl. What would give thee such a fancy?"

"I pray to God that I do not die."

"It is beyond belief. Put the pillow on thine head so I don't have to look at your ugly face. I do not want to look at you."

He was making sure she did not see the dagger thrust coming, she was certain of it. Edana lay there waiting for the deadly stab. Full of the agony of expectation she slid aside the pillow. Looked up at Lord Floors and noticed he was in a rage. That beyond doubt her death was not his sole consideration was made clear, his naked prick was tense with rigidity. That it was was revolting. A moment later she was subjected to still another rape. When he had finished with her he dragged her to her feet and out the door. "I much prefer to kill you and have it look like an accident. I thought about stabbing you. It would of given me much pleasure to do so. A fall is better."

Edana ran when his grip on her loosened for a moment. Lord Floors in his cups could not keep up with her. Edana disappeared from his view almost immediately. At least one good thing about wandering the castle alone at night, it gave her a good guide to its layout. Tonight, she was leaving, finding her way out. In all her wanderings she remembered a long tapestry. If she threw it from a window it might take her to the ground. Then she realized how far down to the ground it was and knew that would not do. Only one way in, one way out, by the gate, shut at dark and not opened till morning. The key was kept secure. An alarming idea occurred to her, Lord Floors might call one of his servants to assist him in murdering her, or, more than one man. A man like Lord Floors would have many servants capable of any depravity. Like goes with like as the saying goes. If one was not bad when they came here the absolute darkness of the place would seep into them turning them to the ways of evil or else the devilment of the place once known would prevent anyone with good intentions of remaining in such a lodging. That there was a flaw in her opinion occurred to her, some, like the servant girl who had warned her, had good in them. Thus, despite the wickedness in this place there was also some good here. The kind servant girl was a shining light amidst the darkness. So perhaps there was some hope for her.

The slow realization came that she would have to slay Lord Floors, there was no other way. By morning Lord Floors would have the gate well-guarded preventing any escape. She would have to kill him and hide him. Often in his cups it would be assumed he had fallen asleep somewhere and his absence would not be commented on until mid-morning when someone went to find him to wake him. This would work in her favor. If all went well she would be long gone before Lord Floors was found. Would ride out at the crack of dawn when the gates first opened. Although it might be thought strange no one would stop her. Going for an early morning ride was common enough, although, she had never done it, the porter would not dare waylay her without his lord commanded it.

Lord Floors called her. "Edana come, I have something for thee. It is thick and hard."

Coming to the dining hall, a knife was left on a table. Soon such would have another purpose, cleaving a different kind of meat than the hams and roasts than it was usually used for.

"Edana! Edana!" Floors was close by. Then right by her side. "There you are my dear."

"I am at my lord's command." Her arms were down by her sides, hiding the knife.

When he came forward to take her into his arms she slid the

knife under his breastbone, thence, his leer turned to stone.
Exhausted at the effort to drag him through the door to a room,
Edana fell to her knees panting. Poured a cup of wine all over him
then turned him away. If he were seen it would be assumed that he
was drunk and asleep. The wine she spilled on him was a deep
burgundy thus if any red was seen it would be taken to be wine and
not blood. A servant seeing him would fail to come close lest they
find themselves the object of his wrath.

    Edana ran to her room where she washed the stench of the
blood off her, whilst still there, dressed warmly. Took a blanket
from her room, picked up a long man's cloak from the floor in the
central hall. The central hall was empty at this ungodly hour thank
God. Gathered, all she needed from the main kitchen. A large
flask of water and a flask of wine completed her escape kit. In the
stables Edana mounted a fleet looking beast and crept out of the
stables thence to the gate now just being opened by the porter as
the dawn had just newly broken. The old gatekeeper never even
gave her a glance. That he did not notice the tears streaming down
her face amazed her. Beyond the gates she rode for her life,
keeping to the road briefly before riding into the woods for cover
in case riders pursued her. They would think her to be on the road
and that was where they would seek her.

    Waking, for a moment Edana wondered where she was.
Noticing she was slightly wet realizing then that it had rained
overnight. Beneath a tree most of it had missed her. Then it all
came back to her, all of the dreadful details, saw herself running
down the corridor of the castle. Lord Floors lying on the floor a
knife skewering his breastbone. The porter not even looking at her
even as she passed through the gates with all manner of distress
upon her. Edana tried not to condemn herself for doing what she
had to do. They were conflicting the emotions she felt because it
was necessary to save her life the murder of Lord Floors, but the
pleasure she felt when she drove the knife into him gave her much
shame. Bitter tortured feelings welled up inside her, so many tears
falling down her cheeks at the shocking memory of it.

    Despite her lack of hunger, she ate, for the sole reason that
she would need strength to keep going. After eating, attending to
her bodily functions. That done, she led her horse to a nearby
meadow where it grazed peacefully. A long rope tied to a tree to
prevent it wandering off. Another thing she had remembered to

bring with her was the rope, all in all, she had done well given how fraught with stress she had been undertaking her escape. Edana knew herself to be many miles from Floors castle, and anywhere many miles from there was a great place to be.

A female voice was lifted in song, by virtue of it, for the first time in a long time Edana felt uplifted. The singer must have a wholesome heart because it was a hymn that she sung and with such delight and love that Edana thought God himself would proclaim it worthy of Him. Edana had to find the source. The devotion with which this woman sang touched Edana deeply. It could only be a sign from God that such a wonderful, pleasant and religious song was heard here in the middle of nowhere. Peeking around a hawthorn bush she stepped past it to see who it was who sang so beautifully. Standing in the middle of the field was the singer. Edana guessed by her pleasant expression that she had nothing to fear from this humble servant of God. Because that is what she indeed must be, no other creature could produce such a melody. Large in the hips but otherwise attractive was she of the Godly voice. As a humid haze rose from the lush earth, Edana gazed at this agent of Our Lord in Heaven. The singer in a fine wool gown noticed her. The singer, examined Edana briefly, before walking towards Edana with a warm open smile.

Edana could not keep the wonder out of her voice. "You sing like an angel."

The singer noticed the younger girl's eyes touching on her wide hips. However, her tone had no anger in it. "I carry some weight on my hips. I never did when I was your age."

"You are blessed with a heavenly voice."

A good-natured chuckle was the answer.

"A gift to sing so," said Edana.

"I am filled with a love for God and how could I not sing well with Him inside me. Can you feel a particular blessedness here? The flowers are colorful and delightful, the bees going about their business with much gaiety. I am not the only singer, here, listen, all God's creatures sing this morning."

The grass, and trees, tuneful, by virtue of the wind. This and the buzzing of the insects created a soothing cocoon of sound. How fine it all was. To be here was like entering heaven after being in hell. This woman who had a gift for singing had a gift for words with them revealing the splendor that was all around them.

"Last night rain fell, and now the sun is out. The droplets of rain with the sun shining on them are like kisses from children?" A moment later realizing she should introduce herself she did just that, "My name is Emma."

Realizing the singer was studying her with an unspoken question on her lips Edana gauged what this question was and answered it. "Edana is my name." Almost immediately understood that giving her name was a poor idea given that a pursuit would come after her and this could put them on her trail.

"What troubles you child? I will do thee no wrong nor pass on thy name to another. For all that, I have not seen you."

Edana bowed her head and tried to explain herself. "I did not wish to disturb you I but heard you sing and had to see you."

A smile in reply, followed by, "And you did. Furthermore, it was no accident that you came to me. In need you came and thee will not go without my help. Edana is a lovely name by the way."

Edana contemplating the dangers that lay ahead decided it was time to leave. To thank this kind woman for her offer of aid and to go. To have her aid could be to endanger her.

Emma had an acute mind and with it discovered what went on here, looking at the travel stained clothes brought the comment, "Thee has been on a long road thus getting away from somewhere."

This had Edana in tears.

"Oh dear I have said that which I should not."

On Edana all her misfortune plain to see in every aspect of her person and what Emma had said was merely a statement of fact.

"Is it that obvious?"

"Never mind dear. Your accent is of the north. Hardly here. I would say thee is bound for the north. That thee has some mud on thee, indeed has all the tempers of travel on thee and is alone in quality clothing makes me think there is a place of residence gone from under duress, and that thee is of the gentle class. The sadness in you, another sign that from someone thee is fleeing and has been wronged."

"Wronged ... indeed so," replied Edana. "Of the north ... "Edana stopped and thought about it. "Emma you are acutely cleverly minded to see my plight and work it out at a glance and have placed me."

"Come child, you can share my morning with me in my kitchen and in my garden."

Edana retrieved her horse and followed Emma. Whilst a part of her would seek the road and be from this place gone, that said, she needed some kindness and contact with someone who was not a devil. Soon the trees closed in around them as they climbed. The air became cooler, with the crisp snap of the heights in it. Arriving at the yard there were barking dogs and chickens flying up in alarm. Edana gazed at the two-story manor house with admiration. The fragrance of fresh herbs saturated the yard. When across the threshold of the house fresh rushes strewn on the floor made her decide it was the grandest most welcoming home she had ever stepped into. The fresh flowers on the table a sure sign they were warm people who lived here. Sparsely furnished, the house bespoke of good taste and wealth.

Emma joked with Edana, "The mistress and lord of the house are away leaving me here alone therefore I am the lady of the house. You may bow to me and call me, My Lady."

Edana did a little curtsey to her. As for Emma she was aware how admiring Edana was of where she lived and could not help but take some pride in it.

Edana suddenly had a wary look which brought forth this comment from her host, "Don't worry we are all alone?" Emma noticed Edana looking right and left. "Put thyself at ease, no harm will come to thee, here. The others are gone."

"How long for?"

"A week. I can get you fat in a week I am sure of that."

Edana asked her, "Who are they this lord and lady you serve?"

"The lord and lady are Sir John De Lay Hay and Lady Patrice."

"De La Hay, a Norman lord!" De La Hay was obviously a Norman name, Patrice, likewise. In the highlands the Normans were one and the same with the devil.

"Not so fearful, he is a good man," Emma reassured Edana.

"The others?" asked Edana.

Emma answered that with a smile. "Servants, the grooms, some squires."

"So many?"

Emma was curious. "Were there not many where you were from?"

"Aye, but if they knew what was good for them, they stayed hidden. Every honest man was at risk from Lord Floors and his son, Richard De Soureles. Not to mention, Lady Floors." Anxiety in her darting eyes when she said, "Where is he this Norman lord who is you tell me a good man?"

"At Stirling castle paying attendance on the king. I bid thee into my kitchen."

The kitchen like all else was functional. In this sun-lit kitchen Edana was fed a feast of hot eggs and butter with fresh bread. A change of clothes and a bath took Edana to a place of contentment unknown for many a day, perhaps, never before in her life had she felt so good. When one has been on a tough road to take a turn in that harsh road and then see the fire-light of warmth and comfort, makes the heart swell with happiness, thus it was with Edana.

Having pushed back her curiosity until now Edana's hostess held it back no longer, would have the truth. "It is obvious thee slept out last night. I can see that thee art very weary. Come Edana tell me what manner of misfortune has befallen thee?" Emma reached down and touched Edana's hand. "There is nothing wrong in telling me child."

"Too much has gone on that I could tell of it." Terrible pain was obvious in Edana.

"Say no more of it. Keep it to thyself child if thee would have it so."

The depth of kindness that flowed from Emma to Edana felt like a mother's love, the mother's love Edana realized she had never known. Nothing more for the moment was spoken of the cause of Edana's sadness.

Chores made up the majority of the rest of their day. When shamed in her father's home Edana had assisted with similar work. Found such tasks calming to her mind. In pleasant company with frequent breaks it was as good a day as Edana could remember.

Dinner that night was a broth of pigeon so delicious it felt sinful to eat it. Edana felt now she could tell what had had happened to her. Trusted Emma enough that she felt it was safe to do so.

Edana started her tale: "Misfortune has been my lot since the day I offended my father, thence, was married off to the heir of Floors castle." Thinking back to what happened anger overcame her. "Does thee know castle Floors?"

Emma replied, "A good few hours ride away. There is communication between my good lord Sir John De La Hay and Lord Floors."

A tremor ran through Edana. "I hate them all, all, that devil's brood."

"The Lord God asks us to forgive our enemies."

Edana ignored that. "I will be executed for my crime."

A deep silence nervously entwined the two amidst the flickering light of the candle. It cast on their shadowy faces, recesses, unreadable emotions. Edana trusted this woman but wondered if it was a good thing that she did. Telling herself that someone who sang like Emma did must have a good heart, then again when she first looked upon Richard De Sourules, indeed, saw how handsome he was, Edana found it hard to reconcile that with his fearsome reputation, alas, what was reported failed to tell the half of it. So to trust in someone's appearance was a proven folly. Emma sang like God was within her but as she knew appearances were just that. They meant nothing.

Was she right to trust Emma? Was it a mistake that would cost her her life? Whether it was wise to do so her lips ran away with her. Edana imagined the furore her act had caused at castle Floors. Her tortured voice rang out with the dreadful fact: "I am a murderess."

Edana knew only too well a woman of God would find herself unable to forgive this mortal sin. Not immediately condemned Edana spoke again. "I shall die alone. Loved by no one. Abandoned by my parents. If a wife is judged by her husband as folk say they are, I must be a very wicked woman for my husband Sir Richard De Sourales is a servant of Satan if ever there was one."

Edana leapt over a deadly precipice telling Emma so much. It would be easy for Emma to send word to her enemies, if so, then, so it must be, for she could not remain silent on her ordeal any longer. The poison must come out. Her face was flush and tense. "I will be judged and hanged for the murder of my father-in-law, Lord Floors. I pray I will be hung for I deserve to be for I left him lying in his own blood and took joy from it."

Silence engulfed the room. The flickering candle light cast shadows on Edana's face, turned her into an older woman, into a wicked woman with blood on her hands. Although it was Edana's voice the face that spoke out of the half-dark was that of a wicked killer, made so by virtue of the half-light and the guilt she felt. "I rode for my life. I had to. In defense of my life I did it. Lord Floors would have me dead. I defended myself and so now it is he who is dead - and I will go to hell because of it."

Emma sensed that Edana was no murderous hellcat, a child still although her body was beginning to outgrow its childishness. Her remorse spoke of a kind heart.

As Emma considered Edana, Edana said something that was completely understandable given it all. "I carry such a weight."

From nowhere came a breeze to stir the formerly stable air, and to blow the candle out.

"Who will you absolve me now? Even God deems me unfit for the light."

"God does not judge you child. It is the wind that blows and nothing more."

Edana was introspective. "God have mercy on my soul."

Edana was glad of the dark, it made her anguished eyes hidden from the force of Emma's assessment. Such darkness ended all too soon when Emma relit the candle bringing back the shadows on the wall and the strain on Edana's face, which brought forth a verbalization from her. Again, in the light, Edana felt she had to justify what was done, justify the deed that hung so heavily in the air. "He was going to murder me. I had to do it."

"Well I believe it."

Edana felt compelled to add. "I took a horse and slipped out the gate at first light." There was so much left unsaid. The terrible silence was too terrible to bear. "Murder is not an act where peace of mind is gained." A slight shudder came from her. "Now I sit before you and have eaten well and bathed and am still a murderess with a cold and black heart."

"No, you acted in defence of your life, as God permits."

"I never thought to get out of there alive."

"Apparently God watched over you and with his aid you did."

Edana thought that no one should say God watched over her. Then the thought came to her that this woman knew more than she did about His mysterious ways having more learning in the word of God. There was a slight reassurance thinking that. Perhaps He did watch over her. Although she was a sinner, all under God are sinners. The flickering candle had Edana mesmerized for a moment, made her feel calm. Enough had been said of grievous things for now Edana would speak no more of it. Deeming she had said enough.

Emma reached the same conclusion. "I think that is enough for tonight. I suggest we say goodnight."

A restful sleep Edana had being very tired after the rigors of the day before. For Edana, little did she know it but this would be her last night in a bed for many months.

Morning, and oatcakes and porridge warmed her. Emma anticipated that Edana would seek the road as soon as the light of the new day shone. Emma reassured Edana that her horse was well rested and well fed. A roast chicken wrapped in cloth given her, together with the oats, and boiled eggs. Edana went well supplied, some men's clothes as an extra precaution to disguise her. After many kisses and hugs and prayers for her safety then off she went. Her intended direction was north. Morgund was to her north and she hoped he would help her. At first, she stuck to the road to ensure she got through mountains rising in the direction of travel. The steep, uneven lay of the land prevented getting off the road. Although men might be looking for her on the road there was no alternative but to ride upon it, to go to the forest might be to be lost in the mountains where she could fall victim to the dangerous beasts or die from the weakness of starvation and if her horse stumbled and broke a leg she would be left stranded. At the foot of gently sloping woodland cutting cross country when a castle appeared amid the trees. Edana did not want to go anywhere near castles, castles were where men might stop her and perhaps question her. After leaving the castle behind her she returned to the road as it offered faster travel and avoided the prospect of getting lost in the great forest that lay either side of her. But soon enough she had to enter the forest again on the approach of heavily armed men. Praying they didn't see her racing for the cover. It was not an easy ride navigating between the great oaks and avoiding low greenery that filled this part of the country. Finally, exhausted, Edana halted.

Resting, when far off shouts and shrieks wrenched her to her senses. The noise became quieter until finally fell silent altogether.

Riders, suddenly bursting through the trees, immediately she realized that to try to mount was to risk capture or being struck down by one of them.

Riders were on every side of her forcing off their hands grabbing at her. Edana ran towards closed, dense, woods. She soon found herself in amongst dark heavy leafage. Here amid the deep woods praying that she was safe. They were determined to capture her, calling out to each other seeking her through the woodland. It came to mind that perhaps trusting Emma was not such a good thing, for them to be here they had information on her whereabouts. They came closer these men who would make her pay for her crime, forcing her deeper into the depths of the dark woods. She had no option but to be draw herself further and further into the shady darkness, treading in amongst the leaves and roots, and bright orange lichens that inhabited this waterlogged place. Here it was dimly lit, so dimly lit that there was hardly any light at all. Breathing hard, hobbling with exertion, for by now, she had walked many a mile.

Falling into the water. It had expectantly appeared at her feet. Felt like to take her breath away the severe chill of it. Then, again she was back under the water. This new dunking because her feet slipped out from under her on the far bank. By the time she clawed her way up the wet earth, the dark cloak of night had fallen. The woods were totally silent and so dark now she could not see her hand in front of her face. That night she slept poorly in the complete blackness, wet, with teeth chattering from the cold.

Gormlaith had once been like a sister to him, though, it was no secret that she had more than sisterly affection when first he came to live with her family. Despite the years that had passed she still had her looks. It also did not escape Seward's eye how eager she was to see him when she met him at the door. Greatly contented in her marriage despite the lack of a child that was the version of her life she gave to Seward who doubted it. Her husband John, farmed a plot on some hills not far away from a

small village. It was said that her husband showed considerable bravery and ability when the Earl of Buchan descended on this locality. The Earl of Buchan was a savage young man lately given lands not far from here. That savage young man, Buchan, had come on heroically, just as heroically got going once John and others fell upon him. When first they spoke, Gormlaith, the woman he came to visit asked after Morgund. Seward told her how near death Morgund had been just when engaged in single combat with that man from Ross, the smug smiler with all manner of derogatory words for Morgund when Morgund spoke in front of others. As things went it was a very near thing. Swordery was a matter split second timing and Morgund's lack of timing nearly cost him his life. That Morgund recovered was down to his experience. Seward doubted Morgund even recognized how near a thing it was. The blink of an eye, at times like that that is all there is between life and death. Now Seward brought himself to the reason for his visit, it was not Gormlaith alone he came to see.
"Suanna, do you remember her, Gormlaith?"
"Aye, I do."
"Tell me what became of her?"
"She was always curious about you too. I remember her eyes followed you wherever you went."
Seward remembered that as well, it brought a smile to his lips, not something Gormlaith wanted happy to see. It took him many years to understand the power he had over women and to use it to his advantage. His inability to draw Suanna close to him back then was something he would rectify now. She was still in his heart after all these years.
"So you have ridden over here for her sake?"
"I am just curious what became of her."
Gormlaith was outraged. "I see."
"I came to see you, too."
"Of course you did."
"It is the truth."
"I very much doubt that." Giving him a very sarcastic laugh then she said, "Here is your answer, married, and very much in love with her handsome husband. And in no need of visits from strangers, however handsome they may be."
Gormlaith rushed on, "Suanna may of cried for you once long time ago but that was long ago." Gormlaith noticed his demeanor

when he learned Suanna was married, how downcast it made him. Despite herself it made her feel sad for him and she reacted to his forlorn look. "Seward if you did not go off with Morgund when you did I am sure you would both be married by now. She cried long and hard when you left."

Gormlaith was mature enough to understand and sympathize with him, all the time realizing how horrified she would be if learning of this as a young infatuated girl.

Oblivious to how it might make her feel he revisited his old love. "My first sight of her in the great hall I will never forget it. That smile of hers. I have a flutter in his heart at the memory of it. What a game little fighting cock she was." A suppressed smile remembering those days of long ago. "I remember her shyly trying to hide her pleasure when looking at me."

When Gormlaith looked at Seward she saw he was far away. Heard this from him, making her eyebrows rise: "When last I saw her I was seventeen and taking Morgund to supposed sanctuary with the king." In a tone of melancholic memory, he said, "That was long ago."

Gormlaith offered the comment, "Fortune never favored that king with no son to rule after him. A toll for Alexander's sins I say. Although, King Alexander came too close to ending the MacAedhs. Despite the king's malice and intrigues Morgund survived and flourishes, in no small measure thanks to you."

Gormlaith spoke and Seward sat there moping not really listening to her. That he did not listen was beyond Gormlaith's sufferance. So much for him coming to see her. She may as well talk to herself for all the notice he took of her. That Suanna was wed caused deep heaviness in his heart, that was one thing but to ignore her like he did was rude and not worth bearing. In all the time he had been back - it had been many years - he had never stopped to see her until now, itself, a cause for her anger. He was with her because it was Suanna he wished to see.

He drove her to distraction when he said, "At least she found someone to love."

How could he fail to miss how irritating this was, his self-pity about a past love. Gormlaith decided to ignore him. Seward sought the road after getting the silent treatment for long enough to let him know he had outstayed his welcome. Alone riding with his disenchantment he mulled over this sad news told him by

Gormlaith of Suanna's marriage. Just the thought of it took his happiness away from him. Small items of household gossip told to him by people with families about what things they did together, all in all, it made him yearn for a house and wife of his own. He had thought that somehow it would have been possible for him to be Suanna's husband, and for them to have a family together. To see Suanna's lovely face again, he decided would be a wonderful thing. His teeth clenched together in determination, he was going to do just that.

There was something Gormlaith failed to tell him. Gormlaith in a fit of jealousy once long ago bade Suanna put Seward from her mind. Told Suanna, that Seward considered her nothing only a servant and a lowly one at that. In love with him as she was it engulfed Suanna's heart with heartache. Gormlaith's revelation was the bitterest disclosure in Suanna's life. Further to that, Gormlaith told Suanna that Seward had no affection for her, none at all, in fact, the opposite. As much as he wanted to, tried to tell her of this, his natural kindness prevented him from doing so.

To see her as nothing but a servant, how dare he. From that day forth Suanna told herself she did not love Seward at all, in fact, hated him. Although telling herself this in reality her love for him never left her.

Suanna lived near the village of Forslie. Committed to seeing her again, Seward rode towards it. Finding a woman collecting wood who knew Suanna he learned of a forest Suanna liked to visit. This forest was close by.

The heavy foliage he sought now enclosed him within its shady peace. He picketed his horse in a secluded area further away in case its presence gave him away. Now all he had to do was sit and wait. He did. She did not appear.

More than sick of waiting for her he took himself into the village where a fair was ongoing. There, he and Suanna nearly came face to face. It was a near thing. He did not want to see her with her husband so turned around and took himself back to the trees. After a while he felt compelled to sneak back into the village keeping his hood close about his face hiding his features.

Suanna, often found peace and serenity amongst these giants that cast themselves up from the ground and branched out above her head. She cast her eyes up into the limbs as she walked past them, her fruit picking basket held in her hand. Like so many of

Pictish ancestry, she felt affinity with trees. So large and stately to her mind many had more personality than most humans she knew. Suanna patted the wood of the trunks for luck as she passed them by.

Taking in the subdued wistfulness all around her, whilst someone, was very close by, watching her. That he should step forth and take her in your arms hammered away in Seward's heart with an intensity that was almost overwhelming. Not long before he had almost done it stepped out and grabbed her. No, no, must bide his time, think how to talk to her without causing alarm. This stretch of woodland near her home was where she often wandered for hours.

The clouds that had been threatening all morning dropped wetness down upon them. When it started raining Suanna moved deep under the trees to gain cover from the wet. When she did, Seward lost sight of her. Seward remembered earlier in the day, in the village packed with people and livestock, Suanna had browsed, eyeing the beasts. And he had watched her. She had caught sight of him for a moment, he was almost certain of it, then had turned away from him and then hastened off deep into the woods. Soon after he had trod in her footsteps that led away from the village to the dense woodland. To his mind, she had pretended not to see him. Remembered her half turn her head and smile before departing further into the green. He found a spot where he could watch her from the verdant foliage, until she fell from his sight getting out of the rain.

The rain stopped and she came into sight. Turning around as if looking for him. That smile again, as if it was meant for him. She patted the massive trunks before vanishing again among the towering giants.

He thought he had lost her until she reappeared beside him, to say, "It is a good place to sit. as any. If you wanted to spy on someone this would be the perfect place to do it."

His face reddened. "The fair is a place of merriment and entertainment perhaps I came to this place of quietness seeking some solitude after its revels."

She held a lingering gaze on him, the corner of her lips trying to stay tight shut in case she openly laughed at him, not a good thing to do after not seeing him for so many years. He looked so serious it made it hard to keep a straight face.

"It is many years since I last looked on you," he finally stammered out.

It was then that by some irresistible instinct he kissed her. She pulled away, surprised, but delighted. Her eyes were on him attraction dancing within them but she spoke to him like one would to a little boy who had had done something he was not supposed to yet it is no great offence.

"It is a shame you did not do that fifteen years ago. I have not seen you for fifteen years, I know I have counted them." A smile lingered with a thoughtful expression. "I thought you might be bald and fat by now." Seemingly without caring she asked, "Have I changed much?"

She knew herself to be, back when Seward first knew her, pretty, and wondered if she still was. She saw men and boys gazing at her often back then but it took her a while to work out that they had done so because they found her fair to gaze upon. In her mind that attempted kiss put it beyond all doubt that he desired her. Of course he did, had he not been watching her. It was written in every expression on him that he wanted her.

Holding his eye she smiled. "It is a wonder thee remembers me at all, after all, I was but a lowly servant?"

Suanna was goading him for what he had told Gormlaith. Could not help but feel slightly furious at what he had told her. In fact, no such thing had ever been said. The anger did not last long, how could it when he was so strikingly handsome and so near with such obvious interest in her. She must get away before something silly happened. She had a husband she had to keep that to the forefront of her mind.

A strange formality was in her tone when next she spoke. "So after a very long time thee has come to see me now after so long. Why?"

Not content to wait for permission he took her hand. It suited her to let him hold it, for now.

A dappled sunshine rained down on Seward through the trees. A golden-white halo was on his head by virtue of a sudden burst of sunlight shining down upon him. If she was religious person she would see it as a sign from God that his head was lit up like this. Telling her it was right that they should be together. That could not be because what was ongoing here could have no sanction from God for sin was on her mind as much as it was on his. She was terrified she might lean over and kiss him. Kissing him was a thing she had wanted to do since she first saw him enter her village when she was a very young girl. No one would not of condemned her if she did back then. That was then. To do so now would be unforgivable in a married woman.

Again, she was struck with what a remarkable face he had, such pale hair, so bright, with brilliant blue eyes. All in all and considering the halo, he was godlike. She moved away, broke eye-contact, she had to, or else she would reach out and begin that which could not be un-begun. Suanna knew she had to get the silly girlish expression off her face. That she had not changed much from that young girl who had pined for him so long ago was only too evident to her. His handsomeness was robbing her of her self-control.

It was obvious that he knew how attractive he was pulling her closer ready to plant another kiss on her lips. With his eyes letting her know he was about to push her onto her back. Knowing herself she would fall back with full compliance, forced herself to break away, breathing heavily. If he tried to engage her in intimacy again she would not have the will to resist him. Like a fair magician pulling out his white teeth to disarm her. Betraying herself with her own. She was helpless before him. All at once their lips met. Seconds later in a totally bewitching fashion his arms held her and gently forced her back.

Gazing at her he decided she had the most perfect face, furthermore, only a highly virtuous soul could possess such flawlessness of both face and body. It was duality that existed in her, God, and the Devil, was one in her. Her body was an instrument of the devil creating in men lust, an almost overwhelming sexual desire. Create it she did, but she did not have a shred of evil in her.

It was God after all who had given her that instrument to draw men to her and woman to curse her and to commit the sin of envy, and perhaps in Suanna herself commit the sin of pride. As her body drew his eye it was her wonderful hair that now drew his admiration. Each strand of it had a deep honey color. With the light reflecting off it he marveled at the multitude of sheens created by the interaction between light and tresses.

Her resolve weakened by Seward's continued presence prompting her to distance herself, to say, "I must be going. I have a husband, Seward."

"Yes, I know." When he said it he found himself alone in the forest for she had left him.

CLASH OF ARMS

VILLAGERS REMIANING APART from others traced their descent to the mythic Pictish king, Drest. Morgund had come to visit them after spending time with clans he sought to align himself with, stopped briefly with them on his way to the hillfort as one would with the intent to get to know a neighbor. He came in peace, and they welcomed him seemingly with hospitality. Something did not ring true however Morgund determined very quickly upon his coming amongst them. There was something false in their manner. Deciding their goodwill was an attempt to lull him into carelessness he kept a wary eye out.

By killing Morgund Drest's descendants sought to send a message to all others who sought to intrude upon them like this forward fellow did. Ascertaining their true intentions Morgund took his leave of them. All was well until Morgund neared the gate, there well-armed men, ill intent written all over them blocked their way. It was then that one of Morgund's men was cut down. Morgund was forced to leave his friend behind, barely escaping with his life. As if it was not bad enough his friend was slain they now placed his head on a spike. Seeing this Morgund pledged they would pay for this with their lives. As he fell back the ghastly sight appalled him. He felt the tears at the sides of his face brushing them away and avoiding the eyes of his companions as his heart was full of grief. He rode for home silently, full of terrible anger.

Within the hillfort Morgund saw Frida briefly before deciding he must be away. He hurried off taking with him all the men he could muster to have his vengeance on those who had fallen upon his friend, in addition to which, had stuck his head on a pike and displayed it like a trophy.

At the village lately came from Morgund descended upon them laying waste to them and thus by a consequence of his great and ruthless vengeance Drest's line perished. Having defeated them Morgund decided to attack the Earl of Buchan. Apart from the Morays, Buchan, was Alexander's most northerly placed supporter. He, newly given lands here. Morgund crossed the Moray lordship with no martial intention. The Morays were men he deemed himself indebted to and thus were free from his martial actions. There was an element of logical purpose to his decision to have at the notoriously impetuous Earl of Buchan. Morgund knew that all highlanders must be at their most aggressive to prevent the Norman tide of acquisitiveness.

The Morays were bypassed as Morgund's small army's progressed south. Though, they were the king's men, the Morays, they had proven themselves to be Morgund's good friends. They too had won land but showed some humanity and nobility and sought not to take more than the king had granted them. So easily they could of taken much much more. The other Normans knew no limits to their greed and would take all they could. As Morgund knew a weak neighbor draws a stronger neighbor upon them, a strong neighbor keeps those around him with ambitions from fulfilling them, thus, to act aggressively, making the statement, come further into my lands and you will pay a high price.

Small parties were sent out to harass and burn in order to draw a response from Buchan. Buchan, by Morgund's reckoning was long overdue to learn the price of his recklessness. The Normans considered none their equal and Morgund intended to use that against them. In the remote north so far from the center of Norman power Buchan would want to display his martial prowess.

Just as Morgund supposed he got the quick response he had planned on, scouts reported heavily armed Norman knights approaching. The ground had been chosen well by Morgund who took a lot of time choosing it and deciding how to position his men with special consideration on how he would counter the Norman charge.

Looking every inch the warrior Morgund stood to the forefront of his men and addressed them, "They will come on with ill-considered haste. Let them. We will shatter their conviction that no man is their equal."

The young Buchan was the perfect knight, a famous tournament fighter, said to be rather stupid, but Morgund acknowledged that he was still nineteen therefore took no heed of that, after all who at nineteen is wise. The native Scots in this part of the kingdom took him to be a corner-stone of Alexander's rule. Although Morgund did not know it Alexander had a quite different opinion than the one most men thought he had - as was said of him, he was as wily as a fox - he considered Buchan dangerous and with that in mind someone to be watched. His ambition and opinion of himself was of a kind that made Alexander wary. Feats of arms gained a man respect. When such men spoke others listened. The king spent much time considering Buchan's loyalty. He had much to gain from it as he had much to lose with the lack thereof.

Wisdom alone does not hold kingdoms just as true that with swords a kingdom can be won. The king knew that those with the sharpest swords were to be watched the most closely. Alexander sought to bring the Earl of Buchan close to him, also sought to temper his audacity. Morgund by his actions this day would bring the king what he wanted, a humbled man, and by the by, this unwieldy subject and the king would come into accord and as much as could be said of a king and of a subject, one would be friend to the other.

In due course, the Normans arrived on the field. Men of Morgund's army men signaled to the mounted knights who had appeared in front of them with obscene gestures. Over on the other side impressive Norman pennants flew, the sun struck the Norman silver-grey armor, coats of arms displayed on shields and surcoats splashed color across the field. A sight indeed compared with the two hundred or so seemingly ill organized highlanders. Smug glances passing amongst the armored host showed what they thought of this rabble they were about to fall upon. The knights high in their stirrups and in resplendent armour and heraldic devices had contempt for the men who dared throw obscene gestures at such splendid men as themselves. Buchan was itching to charge at these highlanders and put the force of his mounted knights straight through them. Those shouting abuse and gesturing obscenely were fools and soon would be dead.

At the moment the ground between the two sides was tranquil enough, inviolate gentle downs, flatter in parts, unbroken by streams or marsh, thorns in sections, but few, for the most part it looked the kind of land fit for a ramble. It was no accident that the ground near the Celts was more boggy than it looked.

A heated mind can miss the most basic of things. Morgund planned to provoke Buchan to act without due consideration. Serious things require serious thinking, not much of the kind went on amongst the Normans. Show thyself a fool and people will see one. As Morgund had predicted, so it was. There had been no reconnaissance, a testament to Buchan's inexperience.

There was much shouting as spirited horses were brought into line for an attack. The knights seethed to charge after being exposed to the shouted slurs that carried across the field to them from the ragged highlanders. Buchan readied his men, shouted instructions, encouragement, his heart beating rapidly, a wetness tinging his eye. Buchan had entered tournaments often enough that he should feel almost comfortable here, admitting to himself he felt nothing of the kind. Buchan took his helm from his squire and put it over his head. For a stunned moment Buchan studying the scene before him felt a pang that something was wrong with it, his eyes became hard with anxiety. He told himself it was natural to have some nerves in his first battle and to ignore this feeling of uncertainty. Hundreds of men waited on his command.

Before him were the ranks of the enemy, in plaid, hardly any in body armour, simply armed. Whilst with him were all the armour that glinted and sparkled in the world, knights on great war-horses, who were esteemed in all Christendom for their feats of arms.

Their great destriers snorted and stamped, raising dust, and brilliant pennons blazoned with the colours of knightly houses quivered and flapped in the breeze. Besides his own white and black of Buchan, there was the dark red of Lindesay, the gold of Bisset, the dark blue and yellow of De Colville, black and yellow of Cunningham, shields and surcoats repeating these colors, splashes, shades, giving a vitality to all the field. Above all rose the buzz of excited voices as friends called advice and jests across the field. It made Buchan proud to look at these knights. What a wondrous, magnificent sight it was. Buchan wondered how the Celts could stand their ground faced with such an amazing array of chivalry.

Buchan raised his arm and let it fall. The signal given the knights cantered forward, further on, began to gain speed. At the gallop in an arrowhead formation they lowered their lances. Faced with this gallop thundering Buchan wondered how smug the damned highlanders felt now.

Morgund's men were anxiously anticipating the coming clash. A few found it a most disturbing sight, it made some back away, others simply ran as the space between the two hosts narrowed. The dominant feature of the landscape, the Normans, who shook the earth with their thunderous charge. The Normans looked forward to dispersing this unruly mob, using their horses and weapons to make a killing field of it, only an alert few wondered why most of the Celtic seemed so calm and stood their ground.

When the ground ahead showed itself to be more treacherous than it at first appeared that was the first setback. For Buchan, stranger still, men started popping up in front of him from where he did not expect them to be, men formerly hidden. They were bowmen shooting arrows at him. For a fleeting moment, Buchan realized he had ridden into a trap before such thoughts were taken from him, instead focusing on the arrows on every side of him and on horses stalling, rearing, falling sideways, moreover, knights falling heavily. Many were knocked senseless by meeting the ground. It took all Buchan's effort to stay in the saddle. Lucky were those few who rolled clear. Several Normans trapped underneath their mounts made excellent targets for the archers as did those who remained mounted, stymied by felled or blocked horses. That Buchan was not one of the dead was down to luck alone.

Richard De Colville dropped out of his saddle seeing better prospects afoot, faced the enemy battle-axe in hand raining down death left and right on his foes. When his axe imbedded itself into his enemy and he could not get the axe back out again, when stuck in wood it irritates, here, it spelled his death. Because of that stuck axe the Celts closed in around him burying him under an avalanche of steel. A cousin of the man just killed with a number of arrows in him staggered in ever smaller circles until he finally fell, only wounded, he rose again, he begat yet more stumbling until a final arrow hit him square in the forehead and then he was truly from this world gone.

So many others had by now been hit it was impossible to count them some so arrow-ridden it was like they were hedgehogs. Two of the leaders Cunningham and Buchan in their first major battle had blood and guts all over them however none of it was their own. The younger of the two by two months, the Earl of Buchan, cleaving an open space around him took a moment to look either side of him. No comrades stood with him now thus he was surprised to learn he was quite alone among his enemies. Even though none stood by his side to carry the battle with him; those in opposition to him gave way remarkably easily before him. This was down to his heavier armor and particular skill at arms. With violent thrusts, he disabled the last man who stood between him and the open countryside. Buchan looked back as he had done before, far away were the pennants of his own army a wall of steel between him and them.

Vanity has no place on battles field. Those who deemed themselves invincible with no need of lesser men, had made a fatal mistake. That the armoured men without due care and consideration for how badly things could go went ahead without their close infantry support. It proved disastrous. The Celtic foot, saw the folly and retired from the field. It was readily apparent that the battle had been badly mishandled. Considering what had transpired the Normans exhibited great grit by remaining disciplined. Had they not, it would have been a massacre. Buchan, good tournament fighter though he was showed himself to be no general.

There was something the Normans could be thankful for, a few pikeman with closer personal ties to their lords appeared trying to fight off Morgund's men, attempting to create an escape corridor for the armoured knights. This was done with some success. A very few knights rode to safety, thereby.

Blankness was on the face of lord Bisset. Bisset in charge in Buchan's absence had a dilemma. The dilemma being this; could he depart the field without the Earl of Buchan? By remaining they put themselves at more risk and the battle was clearly lost. Falling banners on all sides of him made the matter urgent. The fate of the young earl was uncertain, he could be dead, just as easily he could be fighting for his life somewhere close by. Bisset did not know what to do, so did nothing. He did not want the blame for abandoning Buchan to his fate to fall upon him.

For Cunningham, the mayhem took a deadly turn. Cunningham fighting in earnest just to survive had steel on every side of him. A man went down with a choking cry as Cunningham's sword caught him between neck and shoulder.

As the highlanders hacked, hewed, and hammered the Normans, the young Earl Buchan took himself up a hill, and watched all from afar. Felt safe within his armor standing high above the highlanders although in full view of them. If a group of them broke off and came towards him he could easily find cover in the trees. He noted Cunningham by his surcoat and him afoot drenched in blood swaying on his feet. Buchan acknowledged that all hope was lost for the young man from Ayr. Cunningham had done well to fight them off for so long. The men surrounding him were too many. Witnessing the caliber of the man he now had a deep respect for his fighting qualities and his courage. Buchan not wanting to witness the slaying of Cunningham turned away. All that was left to do was to take to the trees and go around highlanders to his men if he could get to them.

Cunningham fighting for his life knew it would soon be over. Swords hitting him from all sides only his armour saving his life. One good thing had come out of this by his reckoning. He realized he was able in the direst circumstances to hold his composure, to stay in the fight despite all odds. Handy to know, save for without a miracle he would be dead. Perhaps his head would lay upon the ground without a body to hold it up so that knowledge that he gained would be of no earthly use. Despite all, he would keep trying, he told himself. Then it struck him, just learning what he was made of when about to die was so very futile. That, with the grave prospect of his death almost robbed him of the will to fight on.

His despondency was overcome, thus, he had not fallen, yet many others had, it gave him heart that simple fact. Perhaps God had a greater plan for him than that he die on some field slain by highlanders in a place that no historian would remember. As if God looked on and appreciated his bravery his luck turned. Arrows shot from afar somehow fell wrongly, to benefit Cunningham. It made those around Cunningham shy away from him. That still more arrows continued to fall close by made his enemies move even further away. There were gaps around him now that had not been there before. On into one of them until he collided with a man who got in his way, sent him down with a sword thrust to his side. Stepping over him he wasted no time in killing yet another with bitter intent facing him with a sword and baring his way. Yet a third joined the fallen, although his mouth was closed he was not silent for there was a clang and crunch as Cunningham's blade bit through his head and brain. All was well until a swinging shield caught Cunningham's arm and head. Red began to fall into his eyes from a head wound. That it would be over all too soon was obvious to him as he staggered away. His arm hurt terribly from the collision with the shield. Even with an aching arm, Cunningham managed to fend off more attackers until he was away from the fight, somehow having put distance between himself and those who would kill him. Many were the men he had wounded, he knew not how many, there were perhaps over twenty of them. How many he had killed, he did not know, at least three. He trod on the wet soil until he came to a small stream that came to his ankles. A riderless horse was on the other side of the water.

In another part of the field seeing no other option and completely surrounded on all sides but one, despite this, the Normans chose to sell their lives bravely. They rallied briefly under Bisset. Bisset the only son of the chancellor of Scotland was known throughout the land as a swordsman and a singer. His singing voice would never be heard again in Scotland, for this reason, when suddenly his horse went down an arrow in its side, then men came from all sides raining steel down upon him. They hacked at his neck until his head fell off and rolled away. His beheading unnerved his comrades.

Just as all hope seemed gone Buchan reappeared on a new mount, although blood smeared, his helmet dented, he was calm and took control with a canny head. Cunningham was by his side his useless arm hanging down beside him. Buchan was relieved Cunningham had showed up but could find no rational reason to explain it because he had seen how hot the fight was he was in. When he saw Cunningham he could hardly believe he was not a ghost. Reached out and grasped his hand to reassure himself he was a man and not a spirit or a phantom in his mind, convinced then that he was human he bade Cunningham ride beside him. When this was over if they got away safely he would have

Cunningham tell how he managed to get himself free of his ring of steel and overcome overwhelming odds. He knew nothing of the arrows and the fortuitous circumstances. To coincide with Buchan's reappearance, and with Cunningham's, between the Normans and the Celts a gap appeared wider than it had been and those Normans who survived fell back through it.

It was obvious to Morgund that to attempt to attack over open ground given that the Normans now had a new level of organization would be pure folly. He thought about what he would do next. His thoughts interrupted when he heard a voice calling out to him across the field, it was Buchan:

"The day is yours highlander. Thee has shown thyself to be sage and wise. I will fight thee again though and next time I will not be beaten so easily. You have my thanks for a good lesson and in time I hope to give thee a lesson but a fatal one."

Buchan pulled his mount around raising his hand to Morgund as he did so. Buchan put scatterings of reliable men throughout his remnant host to steady the line as the Normans withdrew. Like his friend Cunningham, Buchan found he had resources within himself that he never knew existed. Discovering this, learning what to do with it opened up a whole new possible future. His father had a reputation for cunning of the political kind but not the kind that won battles. Buchan, even though he had lost a battle recognized in himself traits that would stand him in good stead in war or statecraft.

Morgund saw Buchan shepherding men protecting them as best he could. That Buchan valued them enough to risk his life for them an indicator that Buchan was well suited to leading men. Any man seeing this would feel a sense of reassurance that Buchan was a man worth following. Cunningham himself followed the example of his stalwart leader. Injured though he was and even though he could not use his sword and the pain was greater than it had been, although he realized he could do nothing for the moment, despite this, he pretended otherwise, that even with his injury he would fight on till his last breath and sell his life bravely was the image he portrayed. Part of being a soldier is playing the part of a soldier. It was something learned from Buchan, deemed Cunningham, as Buchan deemed he had learnt it from the man beside him, Cunningham.

Buchan was one of the last Normans to leave the field.

Before he did, that these two, Morgund and himself, would meet once more was reflected in the young earl's eyes. As he had earlier, he called out to Morgund. "Enjoy the victory it is yours Morgund. It will bear thee bitter fruit."

By his behavior, by his words, Morgund realized Buchan was a dangerous opponent. Buchan was in no way cowed and Morgund had seen him grow this day. If he was a boy in the morning he was a man by noon. Morgund had put his hand in the hive and survived the sting. Buchan was extremely dangerous and how their next meeting would go was unknowable but Morgund had no doubt it was coming. He had a welcome distraction from considering Buchan for a soft breeze washed his face. It felt pleasantly cool. Calming was this motion of the wind. It was not until he heard Seward that his sense of introspection left him. He kept eyes closed as he listened to Seward:

"We can catch them, some wounded men are scattered throughout the fields we can strike them down."

"Kill as many of them as you can," Morgund replied.

Seward and Paten a'horsed sped away to find any of the enemy who still lived and were apart from protection. Phail now just turned seventeen although full of warrior excitement stood by Morgund's side ready to protect him. Phail, because he had guarded Morgund found little opportunity to bloody his sword this day and Morgund could tell he would have it otherwise however he had the maturity to see where his duty lay. Even though he was young bloodshed was not new to him. It was said of him that he was a born killer. Morgund knew for all his likeability that he was justly deserving of that reputation.

The young man so admired by Morgund asked a question, "This will surely bring a response from the king?"

A thoughtful Morgund musing on this, said, "Perhaps ... he is not much for fighting king Alexander." Morgund did not expect the king to react he would have others act for him.

Phail was not content with that. "What will thee do it he does come?"

"Hit and run, and avoiding tactics. There are many intemperate places in the highlands, by drawing him on into them he will find campaigning wet and miserable, hopefully sickness will stalk them all. The Normans used to travelling on horseback will be forced to lead their horses. It will be frustrating and draining and tired men make mistakes. When they are at their lowest ebb I will fall on them. I will fall on them like a hammer falls on a nail."

As he said it Morgund smiled and so did Phail.

THE UNICORN

FOR MANY DAYS they rode through the wild dark mountains. They rode down steep valleys with roaring waters through mountain-clinging forests. Leaving the mountain behind them, they were out of the mountains, out in the open moorlands. Riding forth, the sun just lately having showing itself after being stifled by clouds, Fergus Cunningham's mind was on the queen, how sick she looked when last he saw her. When he last set eyes on her he knew she didn't have long to live. Her death would allow the king to sire the heir Scotland needed. Whilst riding along mulling all this over when he was pulled from his horse by outside forces colliding with him. Shouts, horns, galloping steeds. The suddenness of it was hard to fathom. A riderless horse had crashed into his and sent him flying. On the ground he was only coming to his senses when there was another jolt given him by a rider casting him again into the earth. Pulling himself up from the ground the noise of the melee was all around him. A strange object was on the ground in front of him, a sword. A sword in itself was not a strange thing, but a hand still held that sword, an ornate ring worn by the hand, again not so unusual that a hand had a ring on its finger. What was unusual was that that hand before him was not joined to any body. A man somewhere was without a hand, without a sword. In all likelihood was without a life.

For a moment Cunningham with compromised powers of perception wondered where he was. Before the fall had he not ridden beside the new man, Ewan of the Black Spot? Argyll,

Marshall of the Western Highlands, rode with them. He was sly that Ewan of the Black Spot. He did not trust Ewan at all. They were making a progress through the West Highlands proclaiming to one and all that Alexander king of Scots was their lord and that Argyll was the king's new agent in the West Highlands. That was why he was here and how he came to be here, in the West Highlands, if not on the ground. He had come here after recovering from his injuries in the recent battle upon receiving such advice that he should do so at the behest of the king. A messenger had found him and told him to. This matter of the severe hiding they had taken by Morgund MacAedh, Cunningham would leave it up to Buchan to tell His Grace of that. No doubt it would displease Alexander and thus very little urgency did he note in Buchan to inform the king.

Well at least he could stand with no injury on him. Standing, swaying slightly, snatches of imagery came to him. Early on, Ewan trying to engage him in pleasantries. To Cunningham's mind Ewan was a social climber. A very new man. Indeed, he was of an unknown family. As such it could be said of him that he had no right to speak so freely to someone of such a renowned family as Cunningham.

The Cunninghams had served Scotland for over a hundred years. Ever since Warnbald had the good sense to save prince Malcolm from the savagery of Macbeth. That Macbeth had murder in mind with regard to the young prince was without doubt. For the sake of a crown newly won he would have the prince's blood. Macbeth had done in King Duncan, therefore, his son must die as well, otherwise winter would give way to spring when that young man took to arms and beset the older Macbeth with his youthful vigor. Warnbald, for pity's sake alone he hid the prince. For this, when the prince became king - when he returned to Scotland - Warnbald was rewarded with the lands of Cunningham.

The only reason Fergus Cunningham bothered with Ewan was because Alexander deemed him worthy. Obviously, the king saw something in this man, Ewan. Therefore Fergus deemed it his duty to be civil to him even though he did not like, nor trust him. Fergus noticed the fundamental pursuit of power resident within Ewan of the Blackspot, and that he would fulfil any purpose to advance that power. Alexander was quick to notice any usefulness in a man. Argyll, now he was not so sure how he fitted into the king's plans. A dullard was he. So stupid he doubted he was much good to anyone let alone himself. Knowing how the king's mind worked perhaps his stupidity was the reason Alexander had chosen him. Lucky in this state of muddled senses that none had slain him suddenly occurred to Cunningham. Still, the cloudiness of his mind was heavy on him.

Trying to fathom recent events he remembered that the morning had started out well. In his mind's eye he could see fine figure he had cut, very proud and athletic of carriage. All that seemed a lifetime ago now. Pulling the shroud of stupor from his mind he saw horses right and left of him in headlong gallop, mounted men astride them at arms. He saw arrows falling nearby. Cunningham looked up responding to the sound of someone calling his name. Where the voice came from he could not say. His eyes fell upon Ewan of the Black Spot who fell hard upon the enemy, valiantly, sword in hand.

Not to be outdone Cunningham waved his sword about as heroically as Ewan did seemingly moments before. However, with no one now close it was vaguely ridiculous; more time had passed than he realized. Things had moved quicker than his mind could absorb, one moment war was near now there were only the debris of battle past. Obviously, he must move to play his part and had not recovered his senses. The noise of the melee came from over a hill to his right. There was nothing for it but that he must get himself there. When he charged sword above his head he felt unbelievably stupid. Falling again, struggling to negotiate the heavy wet-ground. It was a considerable misfortune being unhorsed and hitting the ground hard enough to knock the sense out of you. By his reckoning it was the worst day of his life. Flat on his arse again, it occurred to him that this battle would be memorable for all the wrong reasons. At least he still breathed, he consoled himself with this until a second notion entered his head, if this level of bad luck held he soon would be dead. He recommenced advancing on the enemy this time watching his step. It was immediately apparent as he advanced that the sounds of battle were not in the direction he was heading in. It seemed the battle had disappeared altogether from the face of the earth. Not knowing what else to do he picked a direction and walked in it. A discarded spear and some arrows, a dead horse, which he walked past, otherwise no sign of a fight did he see.

A small peaty stream arose before him, in the still-water he could see a rainbow reflected on the surface. Pausing, admiring the beauty to be found here. It was a mistake to stop and bide his time. On the far side of the stream finally the battle found him, three swordsmen eyed him from not so far away. Without thinking about it Cunningham turned from them and ran.

Demoralized after his falls, and knowing to take on three men was to die he considered that he had no other option. He was not in heavy armour today thank God so he could run. If he was in heavy armour he might of stood a chance of winning, and running would have been out of the question, the armour slowing him down. He slipped, again, this time hurting his knee. Fergus Cunningham lamented all the calamities that had befallen him this day. Then an idea held his mind, in Celtic lore the number three has magic, further to that, he had fallen three times, or maybe more but he thought it was three. Luck and three went together. Three enemy swordsmen came to kill him. Musing on the significance of this when he was unexpected lifted to his feet by his hair. Whoever had him had a handful of his hair and it could be only moments before he was slain. He felt for the blade at his side. His dagger nor his sword was to hand. He had dropped them somewhere. Indeed, this was the worst day of his life and that it was his last, there could be no doubt of it. As quickly as he thought death was a heartbeat away suddenly there was hope. The man's sword was there on the ground near to hand, his assailant had dropped it, no doubt in the struggle. Fergus Cunningham got his hand on it then drove it deep into his enemy's side. Blood dripped from his attacker's side as he stumbled away. Fergus saw him fall to his knees clutching at that wounded area of his body.

A sword nicked Cunningham's head from his rear. He should have expected it, he chastened himself for relaxing. He was not right in the head. Stumbling away, unsure of his footing into heavy undergrowth, swerving through bracken and hazel bushes using these leafy plants to shield him from any sword thrusts that might come his way. Never far from his mind that he could meet the enemy at any moment right in front of him.

Again falling, again rising, for the fourth time this time, if it was, in such a state of befuddlement he could not say and now was limping heavily. Despite all that had gone against him this day the assailant's sword dropping as it did near to hand was worth all the other bad luck he had had. Coming to a stream he grabbed at handfuls of reeds and with them pulled his way across it. His injured leg began to hurt so badly, on the other side, he was forced to use his sword to advance his steps. Treading through the waist high grass until he lay down exhausted. For a very short time he rested because it was ever present in his mind that as much as his leg hurt that his enemies could be looking for him. With this in mind, he regained his feet and brought himself to some oaks. In amongst them he leaned against one of the trunks and his eyelids printed themselves onto his eyes in tiredness.

    He woke with a start wondering how long he had been asleep, essentially helpless. However long it had been it was time to go. Hopefully whoever was chasing him was not near now. Not much further on in the waist high prickly grass his bad knee made his progress slow. A thought occurred to him making him truly scared. He could die here. Not from an enemy killing him, it could just be he was too tired to continue. That he could lay down and never rise thus his bones would lie forgotten, his parents never getting word of what fate their son had suffered making a mystery of it to all who had ever known him. He had wanted to make his parents proud by coming to the royal court. He had failed, failed, his parents and himself.

    His clothes were rags and the only thing that marked him out as a man of wealth was his belt, in addition the sword he had taken from one of his attackers, and his boots. The sword was not his own and far inferior to his own. He was a remnant of his former self. His hair once so admired by the court ladies was filthy and knotted. So it had all led to this, his attempts to improve himself, to this current state of degradation.

    His lover Beth had laughed at him for coming to the royal court and thinking to serve the king. According to Beth, Fergus deserved to fall on his face for putting himself at the forefront of national affairs when he was unsuited to anything but to stay at home and look after her. It made Fergus love her all the more for saying it because she only said it because she wanted him to stay with her in Ayr and because she loved him. Fergus was meant to be by her side she told him again and again. Now he wished he had abided with her.

    Coming to a slightly higher place that was not so wet he slept.

The hours of darkness crept upon him by subtle increments until a subtle shift of light meant a new day had begun. When he opened his eyes the bristles on his neck made their presence felt. It occurred to him that it in a day or two he would look like the beggars one meets on the road. With passage of more time those beggars would deem him, beneath them. So little separated him from those men it showed how meagre were the artefacts which made one man a king and another a vagrant and despised.

Sighting the mountains he had crossed preceding his entry into the West Highlands, it was his intention to go back across those same mountains, make his way to where civilized men had their homes, moreover, to where men who spoke a language he understood, lived. The barbaric blather these folk here called speech was the jabbering of monkeys. It was subtly different to the Gaelic he knew to the south, the accent so strong he understood them not. Further to that, he wanted to be in a place where men were loyal to the king.

Although he never had thought to stray into the West Highland wilderness here he was in that very same wilderness. Before he had entered this disturbing place there was a land he loved. At home there were large shady woods, clear streams and tranquil lakes, in those places it was easy to find his way. If only it was one of those well-trodden paths he was on now, and not this stark deserted land.

In the bright of the morning light he trod on and on and before long dense woodlands surrounded him. Frustrated to see them, these dense woods were between him and cultivated, civilized, climes. Thinking he had no other alternative he entered the forest and made slow progress in the heavy undergrowth. Came across a broken branch which he thought he had come to earlier. Fighting his way through the dense greenery until confusingly he saw the broken branch there again. Without another option he trod forth hopefully progressing forward and not circling. So much of this woodland reminded him of where he had been before that he did not know if he had previously come this way or not. Picking out a new direction he continued on and in time came to a hanging branch he also recognized as having come to earlier. With a heavy heart, full of dread, admitting that he was lost. He had been walking in a circuit. What else to do but bound forward looking for patches of light ahead, for in those places, not surrounded by so many trees he was more able to tell if there was any newness to the sights around him.

Somehow, he knew not how, he came out to the low grey sky having escaped that green hell that had swallowed him body and soul. It was almost like a religious experience coming out into the open and escaping the trees. Congratulating himself too soon he realized when topping a rise and there was another green hell that seemed to have no end. From where he stood to the horizon nothing but trees, furthermore, this new forest was frightfully dense.

Fighting his way through it until coming to a small water meadow where he lay down intending to close his eyes briefly. The next thing he knew, the brightness came forth of a new day. It had seemed like only moments with his eyes closed.

As he did before, he picked his way forward with no clear idea if he was progressing or circling. Making many stops now in his tiredness. Another long sleep he had during the middle of the day. Fergus Cunningham found it difficult to get up, thereafter. As he plodded forth each step was more heavy, tiring, and painful.

Beth, his sweetheart woke him, was urgent in his ear. "Wake up Fergus. You fell asleep again."

Waiting for her to say something else he waited in vain. His beard felt heavy on his face now, how long since he had last shaved he knew not. His heavy eyes began to drop.

She stood in front of him, Beth. He found himself gazing into the same hazel flecked eyes that he always found it so hard to look away from. Responding to her urging he rose and continued on. It did not matter if he walked forever he would not get anywhere, it seemed his life was endless walking now and nothing else. He was not going anywhere, he was already dead and was in hell, not a fiery hell, but an endless green hell.

Beth called out to him again from where he knew not. "You only went a couple of steps and fell down again."

She was right, he had fallen down. Without her telling him he would not have known it. He was at the point that he did not know if he was standing or not.

It was her again. "Fergus wake up!" He guiltily realized that he had closed his eyes again. "Fergus, if you sleep you will not escape this place and return to me."

How he loved the sound of her voice.

"You only went to the royal court to escape me. Admit it. You went there to find pretty girls."

That was far from true. As beautiful as some of the court girls were there was only room in his heart for Beth no other girl made him feel like she did or had that most special smile she had. He tried to shake Beth from his mind but could not. She laughed at him for trying to. He felt saddened she was with him; he did not want her to see him like this, on the point of death, looking like a beggar.

Beth laughed. "Look at the mess you have got yourself into."

"How have things come to this?" he asked her.

She did not reply.

A few steps more he took and then she said, "Have you had no thought of me at all of me since you left me?"

"Every day I have thought of you."

That laugh of hers when she was not happy with him she made it now. "I doubt that!"

"You are always with me in heart, in my soul," he replied.

"I am now in your thoughts as we both know." A happy laugh which made him feel better. "I have thought of you so often Fergus."

"As have I thought of you often, Beth."

Then she appeared just above him, he could almost kiss her she was that close. Beth spoke. "Take care of yourself. Find something to eat or you will never come back to me. Keep walking, or you will die. You must not of missed me too much that you give up so easily. Do you want come back to me?"

"I am on a journey, a walk, and soon will come to my father's hearth, and it is nearly supper time. Father, and mother, must wonder what is taking me so long. I do wonder that myself."

He looked around for the light of home.

The way Beth laughed was not pleasant to hear. "Home is far away and thee will never see it again or me unless thee stands and walks."

He felt her arms around him lifting him to his feet. Then a moment later he looked for her but she was not there. Fergus was sure he was walking home for dinner. The door would be open. Mother would be there.

She sighed; she was back and not happy with him as ever seemed the case at the moment. "You are slowing down again, keep your stride up no slackening in your pace slow boy. Show me you want to come back to me."

He had always sought to make her happy. "I hope to meet you again one day."

"I hope that too," he heard her say. "In the land of the living."

He lay motionless in the darkest recesses of the forest and felt for his sword. He still had it which was a relief. He thought perhaps he had let it slip from his grasp in his tiredness. Somewhat later something woke him. It was almost dark. He realized he had slept for many hours. He looked around for Beth, expecting her to be angry with him but he was alone. He withdrew his sword from its scabbard reassuring himself it was not part of a dream that he had it. He was thirsty but when he went to his flask it was empty. Quietly thinking about this for a while until he fell asleep. With the first light, hearing noises he melted into the shadows that were on every side of him.

Something or someone was coming. Moments later, men were in between the trees, a word here and there passing between them, highlanders by the sound of them, heavily armed, he could tell all by the sound of their metal weapons, a sound all fighting men recognize. He heard one of them say that they were after the Norman. It infuriated him that they thought him a Norman. He was not, he was as Celtic as they were. The forest became silent. Listening in case they came back until finally he fell asleep yet again.

The periods between him waking and sleeping were becoming shorter and shorter. Somewhere in his mind, in that state between sleep and wakefulness, he had a conscious thought that he must have been many days lost because now he could feel his beard heavy and thick. In that place of semi-consciousness another thought came to him, he knew that very soon he would die. It seemed that all he could do now was sleep and soon he would sleep the eternal sleep. Then Beth called his name giving him joy waking him. "Fergus don't give up now you are so close to food."

"Yes sweeting."

"Return to me and marry me."

He rose, with renewed vigor, walked.

Behind his eyes he was a boy again. It was the height of summer of his fourteenth year when something unprecedented happened, he fell in love. She was a slender twig of a girl with hair like gold. Every boy his age, or older, was held in the palm of her hand, despite this, he was well aware that her eyes lingered on him more than on the other boys. She made it plain her body was known to men, and could be known to him if he so chose. Her father Robert was her father's liege man. Robert, his laughter and good nature shot goodwill at all who knew him. As lively as that man was his lively attractive daughter, Beth, was livelier still.

That day Beth made love to him there was a summer storm. He remembered the heavens were firing. When he had his eyes on the flashes in the heavens she had leaned forward and kissed him, her eyes lingering on his long enough to make his heart jump. Those pointy tits of hers were very close to his chest. They were angling over him just above him. He reached out and cupped them in his hands gently squeezing them.

"Be careful with those."

"Oh, yes."

"I have other attractions besides them."

He could tell by her smile she was going to tell him what he could do with those other attractions. He could easily guess what means of entertainment she was talking about. Just then a few children ran past them making them realize they were not as alone as the thought they were. When they found another quieter spot, away from everyone, Fergus expected then to be joined with Beth in sexual bliss. But after promising so much he only got another kiss. He was delighted to get that as it was from a such a wonderful girl. Running his hand through her hair he admired its softness. Fergus was wondering how to get her on her back and enjoy her to a greater degree.

He saw her eyes on his penis which called out for her attention. Beth made fun of his thing sticking up. Fergus did not really know what to say to her about it. He felt like telling her it was her fault, it was, but was not sure if he told her that that she would not laugh at him. Part of him wondered why she chose him instead of all the other boys and young men. He was handsome, he knew that because his mother told him so. He would have known without his mother telling him seeing the way people looked at him. People admired him rather like they admired holy pictures in church, almost with a sense of awe.

Before this day, whenever Beth saw him she had paused

studying him. That she liked what she saw was written plainly on her face. Because of his good looks, he decided. It could be for no other reason, he lacked the cleverness of conversation so often found in fellows admired by girls. Despite his lack of lively remarks, she had chosen him above all others. Even though Fergus considered himself not so very worthy he noticed he was good at making Beth laugh. He seemed to do it so very easily yet he did not know quite how he did. And now she was laughing at him again because his thing had gotten big. That was no reason to laugh at him, because she had done it, she had made that happen, by her closeness, by how she had nudged him with her tits. He felt like telling her that it was her doing and thus she should pleasure him. Now feeling a rush of desire his composure prompted him to make something happen to challenge her to do something with this sticking-up-thing that she found so funny. This mischievous girl must do something about it or felt he would go mad with desire. Yet he dared not say so.

Beth took his hand and led him further away to the darkness of the deeper woods. This time when she looked at his penis she did not laugh. He could see he had a hunger for it. She sat on his lap and rubbed herself along him until he felt ungovernable excitement rising. She turned her head slightly, giving him a knowing glance. So straightforward was she, she said, "I will lay face down so no child can start in my belly."

Groaning with pleasure for she had him fully planted inside her. Heart thumping, because it was lodged where only husbands did lodge, so the church said, where only they had any right to be and even then not how this configuration was for where he dwelt would create no child and was not sanctioned by the church, only by the devil.

After it was over she told him, "You know I didn't want to fiddle with you but I did." She smiled her enchanting smile. "I am your girl now?"

He could not quite believe what had happened.

She was staring at him with a look of dreamy-contentment before she let out a short laugh and said, "I have to go." Then she turned and ran away.

His heart was hammering when he called after her, "I love you."

She skipped away happily calling back to him over her

shoulder. "Do you?"

    Suddenly he felt a sense of wonder sweep over him at the fact that he was no longer a virgin. Her expression when she looked back at him he would cherish it for evermore. Her mirthful, beautiful eyes were dazzling. He woke up expecting her to be beside him, however, dreams, she was only dreams, dreams and memories.

    Amidst the fine larches were two apple trees growing almost seemingly placed like trees in a garden, like they were put there by the hand of God. The apples on the branches were bathed in the glorious sunshine. Each bite was delicious when Fergus swallowed it. There he lay back entranced by what surrounded him. The lush quiet luxuriance, the ferns he laid on were moist, soft and lush.

    Over the highland line, many Celtic nobles who once held that Morgund was of no use in aligning with, belonging as he did to a family that was almost mythical in its list of failures, notorious for them in fact, had now decided to support him. Morgund's warlike nature had brought their favour. If he had friends so too did he have enemies, MacCainstacairt foremost amongst them. MacCainstcairt, thought Morgund and all these traitorous men in the kingdom were men of clay. That lineage meant so much to them and that they took so much pride in their blood made MacCainstacairt despise them all the more. Their families had existed, in some cases been noble for hundreds of years. Some put Trojan warriors in their glorious past which was beyond belief. That they considered MacCainstacairt whose father was a wandering monk beneath them earned them his undying hatred. In stark contrast to MacCainstcairt's humble origin, Morgund's great-grandfather was the son of a king, which explained as far as

MacCainstacairt was concerned why Morgund MacAedh was so enamoured of himself, that also explained why, those who esteemed ancestry and were obsessed with such a ridiculous notion as richness of blood favoured him, his was even better than theirs.

Whilst prominent highland lords brought their loyalty to Morgund, as heartening as that was to him, on his mind was the girl he had left behind in England many years before. That she had been pregnant with his child when he left her gave him much guilt. If there was blood of his in this world, he had in mind that he would meet the holder of it.

In furtherance of this ambition he set forth into England. He told few others including Frida where he was going; for the reason that for some time he had not been as close to her as he had been in the past. When he reflected on the cause he thought it was her failure to give him an heir. Without knowing it this was something he had in common with Alexander king of Scots. In each case the need to have a child to ensure a name lived on drove a wedge between a husband and a wife. When he reflected on Mirium, the girl he had left behind in England, he recalled her deep love for him. Such memories kept him confident of a warm response. Not a happening in the world could make him gladder than to see this child who was of his blood.

When he started for England the air was full of the joyousness of early spring. The season was very cheering to him. Morgund was alone with this thought whilst crossing the territory of MacCainstacairt. Despite the delightful surroundings, as he rode south painful memories fell heavily on him. He recalled MacCainstacairt's deadly hatred for his family. Should like to meet that former tormentor of his and show him what he could do with a sword as a man. He was not a boy as formerly he had been when he was MacCainstacairt's victim. With an angry grimace, he remembered MacCainstacairt was said to be something of a swordsman. If their steel met, Morgund had no doubt of the outcome considering himself a better man than MacCainstacairt who was much older. Realized the waywardness of his thinking, for, although he was alone, doubting, MacCainstacairt would move throughout the land as he did without a bodyguard. Thus having determining if they did meet it would be to his misfortune, therefore pulled his hood close around his face to hide his features.

Reaching England little more than a week later where strangely the spring awakening was behind that of the more northerly kingdom. He made good time soon getting close to the place he sought. Riding through the tall timbers where once he had raced he remembered Simon castigating him for his slowness. A mile or two further on, rushing water, such good memories here as well. Recalled sitting with Cristo beside this stream, relaxing, calmed by it. The colours and patterns of the mossy stones of the stream jolted his reminiscence. Once he had known every twig, leaf, and rock face in this place. These things he looked at were gradually taken from him by the fading light. Too dark to continue he rode no further. He lit a fire and before wrapping himself in his plaid for the night, he threw some fresh wood on the fire, which, crushing down upon the hot embers, sent up a scintillating shower of sparks that ran a mad race in and out of the trees. Although wrapped in his plaid and warm and comfortable he could not sleep. There was too much going on in his head to sleep. Rain drops alighted on his skin and hair so he pulled his hood and plaid closer and moved further under the trees. The sound of hard rain was all around him as he took his mind to what tomorrow might bring. The prospect of meeting Mirium again caused his heart to race faster than this moisture that fell from the heavens, now a good shower. Finally his eyes closed and he had his rest.

When dawn broke, on he rode. He met the cliff-face above which lived Cristo and his family. Considering that he was close to them emotions rose in his breast of such magnitude that tears were in his eyes. This, he decided, was a moment in his life when all things might change. If Mirum loved him, if she did, if his child lived, perhaps the life he left behind him in Scotland would be no more, perhaps ...

Walking under a green canopy that had not been here when last he was here telling him how long ago it had been since he had been in this place. Once, long ago, this area was a field of wheat. Whether to take this as a sign of ill consequence that now it was not, he did not know. Ducking under a limb, stepping over roots and rocks, he proceeded in the amber morning light. In the sky over his shoulder it was grey and dark a sure sign that more rain was coming. A good thing that he arrived when he did, and could rest inside and have a fire to warm him and dry his clothes. Such could be the case if all turned out to the good. A slight pale smoke arose from the chimney of the house. Coming closer he could make out the individual pieces of thatch. His heart leapt, a vibration existed at his throat, a nagging feeling to turn back came, a shallow, normal inhibition to avoid those who he had not seen for a long time but he forced himself to continue to set himself free from the ghosts of the past. The door which stood near was unlocked and when he tried it it opened.

No two people could be closer in affection than Simon and Mirium were. Simon was Christo's son and when Christo sheltered Morgund when he first came to England, Simon and Morgund had spent many hours together. And he had her now, Simon, now it was Simon who was with Mirium and showering his affection upon her. They were like two peas in a pod, these two. He eyed Mirium at a cost because she looked back at him with an expression he did not expect to see, the look on her face told him she was happy and that Morgund was not wanted, that Simon was her man now. What was worse Simon smirked at him. Simon had never liked him, never more obvious than at this moment. Morgund had thought that somehow there was a place for Mirium in his life, knew, now, that there was not and never would be. Seeking to avoid humiliation he slammed the door and departed. Running it over in his mind, it was hardly to be wondered at bearing in mind how they met. It had not been love that she felt for him. What she felt for him he decided was base lust. It left Morgund with no regard for her. Feeling even more gutted at the glaring truth that she had replaced him with a simple woodsman.

Behind Morgund Simon came out of the hut and sank his eyes deeply into the highlander's head as he departed. Simon wanted to taunt Morgund for his abandonment of Mirum, reprimand him for his return with a mind to begin that which what had been over a long time ago. As for her sake Mirum wondered what Morgund had wanted from her. She had not known if he would ever return so what did he expect? They were a lot alike she thought. Like Morgund she had suffered many indignities and cruelties. Not least of them was that Morgund had left her. With that in mind it turned her heart cold. Eleven years had passed, too long, far too long. Away in a corner lay the boy William who was never to know his biological father. Yet to wake, but for this fact he might have met Morgund.

Morgund was not far from the cottage when a ferocious wind

tore through the trees. The wind blowing all around him felt to his mind like a suitable companion to the bleakness of his heart. Inside these thick woods Morgund had a measure of protection. Mirium, he remembered was in inside, and warm, and loved, and he was not. When he was at the foot of the cliff, after climbing back down, Morgund, despite the weather rode on deeming nothing could make him feel worse than he felt. The wind ripped at his skin as he rode however he was impervious to it for such a thing like everything else related to this day and his life was ill-omened, was full of darkness. In the wind, a voice spoke, causing him even greater agony for he heard over and over in a mysterious composition of words woven on the wind. "I love Simon. I love Simon."

Incisive rain fell on leafy ground, the moon shone through luminescent grey fastening onto him between the branches as he rode on, giving him the appearance of a ghost. Checking his visage through a small copper mirror he held he saw the face of an old man, a tired old man, an old man who was sick. An old man who was also very sad. At the most direst extent of his despair he realized how little in life he had that was meaningful. He rode on into the night and into the rain and into his own despair.

On the way back, Morgund learned that Lord Floors had been stabbed to death within his own castle by his own daughter-in-law no less. A murderous tale told all over Scotland. The murderess herself, Edana, had disappeared none knew where to. Morgund did not condemn her realizing how little there was between murder and self-defence. Like so many others Morgund was aware of the De Sourules reputation. Little did Morgund know it but when he was told this by a forester that very girl herself was not so very far away.

Frida, fell pregnant to Seward the previous autumn and had lost the baby. Morgund never knew that she had come so close to disaster. What happened before should have been warning enough that she should not enter into an act that could put her at risk of a terrible event again. Despite that whilst Morgund was far away in England, and none knew where he was, such was the level of distress that dwelt in Frida's heart that she again took Seward into her bed. Frida missed her monthly cycle three weeks later. Again, she tossed and turned, felt guilty, as did Seward. Still, despite that, when he came to her door she let him in. Upon Morgund's return they relented in this passion for each other. Nobody caught them together, thus, for now they got away with it. Some servants were eager to tell Morgund of their suspicions. Telling Morgund could prove dangerous, thus, as it fell, Frida and Seward's secret remained a secret. Seward finally looked for his sport elsewhere and Morgund showed a renewed interest in Frida when he learned she was with child. Poets talk of love, they rarely talk of animal lust. One is celebrated and the other abhorred. An adulterous wife, with a close friend the culprit, poets do not talk of such things, tragedarians do.

Edana, was like a leaf on the wind, blown this way and that. Exhausted, dirty, Edana needed to obtain food and shelter to regain some vigour if she were to continue on her way north. These pressing necessities forced Edana to a country door. Her heavy footsteps echoed on a stone flooring adjacent to the doorway. With desperation she knocked until the door opened and a large man with callous eyes held her gaze, with a sneer when he looked down at her current state of dishevelment. "Yes, girl?"
"I am looking to serve for food and lodging."
"I see." He looked her up and down before saying, "There is naught of such here, be on your way."
"I am skilled in needlework, sewing. I can do calculation."
He held nothing but contempt for her. "Obviously a runaway

you have no such skills."

Edana held out her hand. "Just something to eat?"

"Serfs who think to find prosperity other than under the management of their masters must suffer as is only right. Be on your way or I will set the dogs on thee and give thee a beating to learn thee who thy betters are and that thee must not presume to bother them."

Edana was too hungry to give up easily. "Ask me a sum? Test me. Art thee a man of learning? Test me?"

Something told him she did know something of numbers. If she did she had fallen far below her station in life. He decided to use this to wound her. He gave her a look like a cat gives a mouse that is cornered. "If you understand figures learnedly what art thee doing here looking like this, and so far from your heathen barbarian tribesman. You are one of that barbarous kind. As I said, a runaway, worse, a highlander. That thee knows numbers is the work of Satan for no girl of thy ilk can have come of such knowledge by Christian means."

He turned his back on her. Edana wasn't going much further without food thus she watched the house from the trees taking in when the servants came and went. Persistence paid off, a pie was left on a windowsill to cool and caught her eye. That and some eggs from the yard went into her gown as she edged warily away from the house having stolen them. Safely back in the trees she ate what she had been taken and then traipsed off into the darkness, off into the shadows, ever deeper into them, hoping to hide and put a lot of distance between herself and the house.

She felt a lot better having eaten. Perhaps she thought she might have even better luck at her next stop. She would clean herself up a bit make herself more presentable which might influence them to take her on as a servant. More walking and then little else did she contemplate but her tiredness. Ahead of her was nothing but wilds, here, only the creatures of the forest. Little did she realize it for these lands looked no different from those behind her where people had their living and there was something of sustenance to be had.

Admiring the clean freshness of the early spring sun imparted to the king's skin a fine feeling of warmth, all so enjoyable until the queen walked up beside him. It seemed she could never leave him be. That ugly head of hers cursed his mind, it made him shiver with repugnance. She wore the usual bewildered look he was accustomed to. The paleness of her skin was a deathly shade unfortunately she was alive despite her clammy look. She just stared as she ever did. Thank all the saints no hectoring voice yet. Alexander felt a deep sense of revulsion at the very thought of hearing it.

Queen Joan had been married to the King of Scots since she was ten, once so very pretty and an ornament to the court now she was a repulsive crone, old before her time. Her face appeared so white it looked like a death mask. Her lips were so often puckered in displeasure at him that he could not remember a time when she had looked happily upon his person. Once, and could not believe it, he had been deeply in love with this hideous wreck of a woman. The love he felt for her had long faded. Joan constantly sought his attention which created weariness in him. Her attention-seeking, ill judgement, childish rages, her failure to bear him a son, condemned her as a wife and a queen. Appearing when he tried to escape her often sent him into a towering rage. Wherever he was, she would appear. How he could have any peace beset by this woman with her peculiar talent for tracking him down he did not know. Take himself somewhere she could not follow him that was the solution, far away, out of the castle. Such unseasonal warmth would not last long it was too early in the spring for it, another cold snap there would be before true spring. Whatever the reason for it, Alexander decided to enjoy every particle of what the day had to offer. He ignored the staring woman, instead, concentrating on where the sun rested so gently upon his face. Opening his eyes for a moment he saw that Joan had gone. Now that she had he could relax. The stillness and the sound of everyday things came from far away. This joyful sun made him fall into a kind of reflective torpor. Where else could he feel so at home but here in Edinburgh castle. From the cobblestone courtyard, through to the portcullis, bastions, the crenulations, there was no doubt in his mind this was the most perfect castle in all Scotland. Edinburgh castle, it brought to mind Camelot. He realized he was doing just what old men did, sitting around and not doing much of anything. He was not old but on his next birthday he would be thirty-seven, not old, certainly not a youth, and still there was not another of his blood, a prince to wear the crown after him. Only this morning he had seen a vision of himself in the mirror and saw his father staring back at him. He was becoming his father. Aware the family likeness emerging so blatantly meant he was no longer a young man. The worry of it made him start pacing. After pacing up and down he moved away from the battlements. He was profoundly anxious and blamed it on the queen. After all before her appearance he felt in good spirits. That hideous expression she wore so often it was enough to cause any man unease of mind. She always did that, made a good thing bad, for had not the pleasant sun brought a calmness to his mind before she came. He retraced his steps. Why should he not be where the sun was most pleasant? On the battlements again he tried to pacify himself. He looked down on the many oaks and pines with the barest hint of grey just remaining where some had been struck by lightning. Footsteps coming his way it could only be her, she would not disturb him this time he would command her to leave his presence. It was the queen, of course it was, moreover, she was displeased with him, no surprise there. How had she changed so much since she first met him was a constant source of wonderment to him. Whereas once she brought joy into his heart now only discontent.

Taking him in, it made her smile caustically. His behavior sorely wounded her. When she saw him she saw a man in his prime, a noble looking man, the very picture of a ruler. He used to smile at her but no longer did. She remembered how he used to gaze happily at her - so long ago now. She retired hastily intimidated by his severe expression. The way he looked at her made tears flood from her eyes. Her weeping and running off was the last straw for the king. He could not stand another moment near her. He intended to spend the rest of the spring alone without the queen.

Queen Joan watching him go with his retinue out the gate equipped for a long stay elsewhere felt very much unaided in this hostile place that felt like it was a prison. She knew how much the king and his fellow Scots felt about Edinburgh castle, considering that it stood alongside the greatest castles in Europe, as good as any of them, according to themselves. They knew nothing and

had been nowhere. She felt the same away about this castle as she did about her departed husband, a great deal of hatred.
Accustomed to the castles of France and England, this showpiece of Scottish architecture impressed her not a jot. The castle itself was desolate; it was a wasteland of cold stone. The loss of her good looks and the king's contempt for her which had replaced his affection turned her heart as cold as the cold stone that surrounded her. She was so sick of this place, and of the king, furthermore, sick of Scotland itself. Although he could put some distance between them, she would put even more.

In the days following she refused to speak to any but her most inner circle. Putting on the airs of an English highborn lady Joan refused to speak to the other Scots telling them the language spoken here was so uncouth she did not understand it. Perhaps that was part of the reason she had lost the affection of her subjects and the king because she could not adapt to their ways. She was a foreigner and always would be and foreigners in this backward country were considered only one step away from Satanists in the measure of dislike dealt out to them and no foreigners were hated as much as the English. She got away with it whilst she was young and fair and not proven to be barren. Alexander had a bastard or two to prove his fertility. No matter, she was their queen and deserved better than she got from them. As they hated her so did she hate them in return. But to be honest she knew not why her husband disliked her. That she had remained barren after so long no doubt contributed to it. It was a matter of the gravest concern to him as it was to her. He listened to men who told him she was not suitable as she could not produce an heir. Constantly told for nigh on twenty years that she must produce a prince caused such concern to weigh upon her mind that she suffered and it had aged her. She shuffled along awkwardly, casting malicious glances on all who came into contact with her.

Mulling all this over, in her room amid her cares, she cast her mind back to an idea. If Alexander could vanish so too could she, at the notion of it for the first time in a long time a sly grin replaced her almost perpetual pout. Joan felt worse remembering her most recent humiliation. Some time ago she had written to the king beseeching him to restore her to his favor. The king summoning her to his private chamber forbade her to correspond with him again. She could not of been more hurt. How could he treat her so cruelly? Now she could not ask to talk to him, nor could she write to him, before too long he would command her to stop breathing. It was insufferable. Joan bolstered her courage when with her lord the king that night and discussed the matter with him.

She asked him if he was sleeping with someone else, he denied it. Then sleep with me, she pleaded and to that too he said no. She asked then how she might please him and bear him a son if he did not sleep with her?

His reply was, "Oh how do I know!"

Then he flicked his hand dismissing her. He had no respect for her to dismiss her like that. As if she was nothing, a nobody, like nothing else he had ever done to her it earned him her hatred, seared a hole in her heart that would never heal.

Only Simon, her unicorn, her pet, who she had basically kidnapped as a child really loved her. No man, no king, could love her like Simon did. Joan made up her mind many years ago that she would never seek friendship with the courtier wives. Those wives hated her, their sham sophistication turned her stomach. It was the servants she had turned to for comfort. Those very same servants and Simon would rescue her from this hateful life, help her escape to her brother, Henry, king of England. She was going, humiliating Alexander in the process. Often in the past she had retreated to her room for days and seen no one. Days … that is how long before anyone questioned her whereabouts. It would arise, certainly, someone would want to know where she was, eventually. Perhaps not, they were so used to forgetting and ignoring her. Conceivably Alexander would not notice until years had passed, maybe never. Perchance that was a good thing, her frequent absences had accustomed the court to their lack of a queen. If they did not notice for several days it would be enough to get her over the border into England. Surely they would assume it was a reaction to Alexander leaving her that she was not seen. Those that hated her would assume that she was away sobbing somewhere. Let them think that. Her mind quickly went through the steps she would need to go through to escape. She would need help and who better than the person who loved her more than anyone, Simon, her lucky unicorn, he would help her. She needed time to think. When it was all worked out she would call for him.

The walls of the queen's room were hung with tapestries

depicting Jason and Medea. They were horrid scenes of murder and revenge. Alexander commissioned them and Queen Joan could not help but think that the tapestries were meant to depict her. Medea was known as an enchantress, often depicted as a witch. Medea slew her two children. Jason her husband, too, died by her hand. In Queen Joan's opinion Jason, because he left Medea for a younger woman, got the death he deserved. The way the light from the brazier glinted on the tapestries gave them an unreal light. As Queen Joan stared at the flickering light it brought the scenes to life. These scenes before her had a message for her. That Jason underestimated the danger of Medea was very meaningful. As he paid for the scorning his wife, so too, would Scotland's king pay for scorning his. The tapestry gave Joan heart. Art often imitated life. Why not life imitate art? Again the sly smile sprang to life overwhelming the scowl that had become her constant companion.

Alexander's neglect of her was frightening. His need for an heir endangered her. Joan knew he possessed enough resourcefulness and ruthlessness to commit any act, even murder. Alexander needed her gone. That man liked easy solutions to problems so why not kill her? With her gone he could seek a younger, more fertile wife. She knew the pressure that Alexander was under to solve the succession crisis. This very night the king might be in the arms of a younger woman who he had promised to make his queen. As soon as this other woman fell pregnant, a crown would be hers. That another already held it was a minor consideration, and easily solved by murder. No one got in Alexander's way for very long. The indifferent attitude he had towards her signaled her end. King Henry, her brother would understand, he would accept that she had to escape to ensure that she lived. She did not know how long she had, and with this in mind decided that she had to go as soon as possible.

The next morning found her high up on the castle walls from where she gazed down on the plain of Edinburgh including the township. The town that once had loved her now despised her. In the beginning they had flocked to see Joan and thrown flowers in her path. She hated the sight of that ugly grey town now. She took heart in the fact that there were blue skies all the way to Melrose. That was where she was going to Melrose. From there, still further south, all the way to England. The king no doubt was with his mistress in Stirling. He would not even know that his queen passed out of Scotland whilst he with his illicit slut and was trying to solve the succession crisis or more likely satisfying his urge to enjoy himself with a younger woman. A very young girl, more likely.

She remembered how things used to be, his unconcealable arousal when he was near to the child-queen as she was. Had not turned eleven, she was only a wisp of a child, and the way he gazed at her made her turn red from embarrassment. Alexander, back then, with his hungry eyes reminded her of the big bad wolf. He was big, and rather than a wolf, a fox, in fact, called, 'The Fox,' although not bad then he had turned bad to her great personal cost. She had also found at great personal cost what he had liked about her. Nothing pleased him more than her little tight vagina into which he rammed his ample adult member shooting pain through every atom of her body. The whole castle heard her screams, which propelled further assaults on that tiny space. It was a space barely able to fit a full-grown man's penis. It seemed he had no pity for her, for the more she screamed the more he rammed it in with even more conviction till her gasps threatened to choke all the breath out of her. He could scarcely sit still beside her without she must be led to the bedroom. All the woman at court looked at her with compassion in their eyes. She was so small, so hurt, so terribly afraid. Despite the agony he inflicted on her he won her over with his charm and wit, with his good looks; he loved her more than life itself he told her. Joan could not help but love all his romantic phrases, his deep and honest regard for her. Although his physical love hurt dreadfully she bore it as bravely as she could. Alexander made her believe it was sign of his love for her. He called her his Well Beloved sometimes she dreamed she was still his Well Beloved. That is what they had all called her back then, her subjects, Queen Well Beloved. Scotland took her to its heart. Joan had loved the ancient northern kingdom back then. It came as a bitter surprise when that love for her turned to hate. It came to an end when after so many years the queen failed to fall pregnant. It was certainly through no lack of trying on her behalf or her husband's that her womb did not stir. The king could not be accused of being a neglectful lover. He had delighted in her. That was long ago, the woman they saw now they took no delight in. She remembered perhaps two months past she had cornered him and put it to him that he did not love her.

"Do you wish me to speak frankly?" With Alexander sometimes one did not. Nonetheless, she nodded. "You are Scotland's queen but Scotland needs an heir and you cannot give her one. The day you die I am set free of you and can solve the problem of the succession."

Joan was overcome with emotion reeling struggling to regain her balance thinking she must fall after hearing that. From then on, her behavior became the talk of the court. Dressed drably, often in stained gowns, she haunted the corridors like a ghost. Always seeking Alexander and wanting to be with him despite his contempt for her. Her only joy was Simon, the son she never had, her unicorn.

That Simon had come to be her unicorn came about in the following fashion. Whilst still a child-queen Joan rode away into the Scottish wildwoods as yet new to her. Joan wanted to get as far away as possible from the castle, to somewhere wild and untamed, perhaps to spy a unicorn. In her childishness she still believed in the deep green they were apt to play. If she found a unicorn at frolic she intended to keep it. Although she did not find a unicorn she did find an angelic child. Coming to a sunny glade where children played one boy had the most beautiful hair she had ever seen, it was like sunshine. He smiled at her with a smile that melted her heart. That he directed it at her gave her so such profound happiness it almost felt magical. As a result of it she gave him her own expression of joy. Meeting who she thought was his mother Queen Joan learned this delightful child had no mother or father, the boy lived with his grandmother who had five other small children to care for, which was a great burden to her. Joan who was exultant and told his grandmother she would take him with her to the royal residence, to bring him up as a royal prince. The grandmother made a clumsy curtsey and the queen finally had her pet, her unicorn, her son, the only one she would ever have.

There was astonishment at the castle when little Joan returned with this pleasant boy. Being a peasant he had no surname. Simon was his only name. He soon obtained a surname. Those in the castle took to calling him MacQueen, son of the Queen. Although Alexander was somewhat aghast at this foundling boy, Simon MacQueen, he was in no way harsh to him and often gave him minor tasks as one would give to a young squire. Simon was always by Joan's side and popular, as strikingly good looking children often are. Queen Joan brought him up like her son. Simon learned to read, learned to wear amour, was taught to fight with knightly weapons, instructed on behavior suitable for a boy of rank. He grew into a worthy knight who won many tournaments. Had crossed lances with the Earl of Buchan himself, no less. Was cast onto the ground by that very same earl, famed throughout Scotland for his prowess. After defeating MacQueen, Buchan assisted him to his feet to the acclaim of all. Buchan was a gracious winner, how he would take a loss no one knew as he had not had one. Queen Joan knew nothing about his defeat at Morgund's hands no one at court did as yet. He was in the north, sulking delaying telling the king of his defeat. An early heavy snowfall the previous Autumn prevented word from getting out. The mountain passes were still blocked. Queen Joan found Buchan like so many of the Anglo-Scottish knights very full of himself. The queen decided he would do well in tournaments in England after witnessing his abundant ability in Scotland. Alexander too found Buchan arrogant, this outweighed her dislike of Buchan, thus she always took the time to bid him good day, tried to be pleasant to him for no other reason than because the king took objection to him.

 At the moment the young earl was far to the north on his estates. Upon his return she would favor him as she always did to nettle Alexander then abruptly she remembered the king was elsewhere, with his slut, so she could not nettle him. The queen decided in that moment of bitter resentment to be gone from Edinburgh before the turn of the week.

 When Simon MacQueen came to have his meal with her that night as he most commonly did, she told him that she thought Alexander was planning to murder her. Made Simon privy to her plan. He was so sensible, so competent, she was proud of him as he listened patiently to her explaining her fears and determination to escape and flee to her brother king Henry, in England. He asked the occasional relevant question. When she had finished she waited for his response. Thinking about what she had told him, she worried lest he think her a fool or mad for thinking Alexander could wish her harm.

 Simon put his arms around her. Pulled back from her then, after wiping the tears from her face, he said, "Getting out of the castle without being seen that is the hard part."

He did doubt her for a moment.

Heartened by this fact it gave her the confidence to put it to Simon, "Simon, for the love you bear me, help me."

He responded as she wished him to. "Yes, my queen."

Two nights later, it was a dark night, no moon, ideal for what was to transpire. Everything was quiet. The castle slept. Simon MacQueen's energetic mind working fast as he waited for a signal crucial to their endeavor. When it came, a torch-light in a meadow, detecting it he went straight to the queen. Joan was ready and immediately closed the door to her room behind her hopefully for the last time. The guards on the gates were easily fooled to let them pass no idea it was Scotland's queen who passed them. Joan wore the robes of a priest with a hood close around her face. Once out the gates they stepped carefully in the dimly lit streets listening out for the sound of approaching night-watchmen whose job it was to assure the safety of those out after dark and to deal with evil doers. They passed, without incident, through those parts of the streets that they had to pass through to make it to the meadow, Simon lighting their way with his torch.

A wagon drawn by four horses was in the same meadow where earlier the torch light had signaled to the castle. The horses were soon under the lash as they gained as much speed as possible as they left Edinburgh behind them. Simon took his turn driving. They were constantly moving, and by dawn they were south of Melrose. Only stopping to change horses. This operation was organized by Simon. After many hours with this new team they spelled them. The horses ready again they sped south ever southwards towards England. Simon's contacts did not extend any further therefore it was not possible to change the horses with discretion and stopping seeking new horses might attract attention thus had to be avoided. Day became the night and still they kept going devouring the miles. Catching sight of the endless night the queen rejoiced that all the while Scotland was ending for her. On the rough stony highway bordered with leafless scrub and ragged woodland they sped, with the queen looking out at the twisted limbs that seemed to reach out after her attempting to prevent her escape. Thick woods stretched ahead as the rising sun reddened the sky. The queen stretched her neck to see outside. Above her skeletal branches groped at the cool, still, air. Suddenly, through the bony branches she saw a glint of light, a solid circle of silver-yellow hanging in the depths of the woods. When the ground began to slope gently downward they passed a lake which gave off a pale glimmer as they passed it and then it was seen from afar. As the wagon labored painfully up some hills it was obvious that the horses needed a break. Coming to a chain of even more cumbersome heights which slowed them even further. Joan all but gave up on getting any further. Stretching her legs, she walked as did the others to take a load off the horses. Only the wagoner remained to manage the horses on. When it rained, forcing them to get back on again, given that the horses were completely played out they did not get far. When they stopped, Simon went to find replacements. Later he came back with a new team. Pieces of royal jewelry had paid for them. They sped as best they could on the slushy roads until they were no longer in Scotland.

Alexander struggled to hold back his tears. Torn with bitter contempt for himself for feeling such an unworthy emotion, anger at his wife. Acknowledged that poor Joan had only done what he had forced her to do. '*As ye sew so shall ye reap!*' That biblical passage resonated in his brain. The king had to acknowledge that he had neglected her to such an extent she had no choice but to shame him. Of course, given the depth of her hatred for him Joan could only humiliate him.

Joan had not been gone from Scotland long when news of the battle to the north where Morgund trounced Buchan and Cunningham came to the king. The two forlorn figures all the fatigue of defeat upon them appeared at the castle. Cunningham had after the defeat, spent nearly a week lost in rough country somewhere in the highlands, much hardship suffered by him there.

This matter of the rising of the Celtic north came at a most inopportune time for the king, his mind was elsewhere, given, he was a deserted husband, the ultimate shame for a medieval monarch.

Gathering men, responding, Alexander unlike himself acted

without due consideration. His personal attempt to deal with this was a complete failure. The frightful rain. It was unimaginably. It was impossible to make headway. It was as if God himself barred his way. Such rugged country at this time of year was not fit for any man let alone someone used to a roof over his head and a bed to sleep in. The wet bedraggled Alexander arrived back at Edinburgh castle having had enough of it.

It did not take the king long to put together a more effective response. The king decided this weather would be second nature to men accustomed to it. Highlanders, they would push through it. The king decided to leave it in the hands of such men. The Earl of Ross, Feachar MacCainstacairt, who was at court could speed himself to Argyll with a directive from the king that Argyll give MacCainstacairt all aid to suppress the rising. Ewan of the Blackspot who as yet had played no part in anything to Alexander's benefit must prove himself worthy of his confidence. If these men could not deal with this notorious highland traitor, Morgund MacAedh, the king himself would fall upon him, come better weather, perhaps in the fullness of next summer if the weather was suitable. This summer was out of the question given the matter of the queen's absence.

A minor lord, young and stupid, offered to go with MacCainstacairt, however, Alexander gauging he would be more trouble than he was worth waved him down. "As much as I appreciate the offer young man, men of age and experience are what is required."

The young lord Crawford young and stupid though he was made a good marriage and his ancestors would play a large part in Scottish affairs, the Crawfords were closely related to the Wallaces. Great patriots they proved themselves to be and well-endowed with intellect were the later Crawfords when they supported William Wallace.

The king had a private audience with MacCainstacairt before MacCainstacairt left Edinburgh to subdue the miscreant, MacAedh. "Take my written order to Argyll, he will raise the West Highlands and place such men as he has under your command." Alexander addressed MacCainstacairt with narrowed eyes. "Fall upon this traitors, MacAedh, and bring me back his head."

"I will sire."

MacCainstacairt had every intention of doing so.

The king hailed the two Buchan and Cunningham whenever he saw them. By all accounts they had done well despite their defeat. Buchan's late father was known well to the king, and although never a worthy swordsman he was good at politics. The king now saw his canny son might well excel at both. It was obvious that Buchan held Fergus Cunningham in great personal esteem, unusual for Buchan, who was a formerly distant, difficult and arrogant youth, often at Cunningham with scornful words. After Alexander had spent time with Buchan and Cunningham he recognized the immaturity that had defined them previously both was a thing of the past, they had become men, and good men at that. Cunningham, the kings liege man, had always been loyal to the king. This being the case he was full of respect for the man who sat on Scotland's throne and he often shared his high opinion of the king with Buchan. Thus, Buchan was inclined to share his friend's attachment to the king.

Cunningham and Buchan were with the king one night when Alexander said to Buchan, "Buchan, slow down look at how others have thrived thus may thee. Ask why they have profited and so may thee too. There is a man Sir Hugo de Montgomerie. There is a reason Sir Hugo has won so many battles. Seek him out and talk to him. Learn from him."

A week later when the king saw Buchan again, said the king to Buchan, "Montgomerie has told me that thee has heeded his advice. That thou is a clever learner." The king's smile acknowledged the good conduct told to him by his friend, Montgomerie, and because of the said good conduct, the king said, "I will take thee into my personal library that thee may read books on ancient battles."

A companionable silence followed until Alexander said, "Half intelligence is learning from others, that is a good thing to remember, and in books there are many clever men to learn from."

Buchan appreciated the king's counsel. Alexander's efforts to bring Buchan close to him worked. Buchan saw in Alexander a wise man. That he could be ruthless was only as it should be with a king. The king in return was satisfied that he had Buchan as an ally. It was in Alexander's best interests to develop both Buchan and Cunningham, they were powerful lords and the king needed such men to help him rule the kingdom.

A tournament scheduled for the First of May went ahead despite the disturbance done to the kingdom by the absence of the queen. Alexander was in attendance with many of Scotland's gentry, and of course, many of the low folk were there. It was here that a new man made a name for himself, Dugalad, he, of later legend, who was reputed to have all manner strange powers.

It happened that Buchan rode past this serf called Dugulad - as Buchan would later learn his name to be - proclaimed long and loudly this Dugulad, "Given the proper weapons and armour I myself could best any Norman knight."

To put it beyond doubt that Buchan was included in this, Buchan turned his head to hear the following comment directed at him, none too pleasantly:

"Yes, Norman, thee too."

The flat look that followed was full of contempt for Buchan. This was highly unusual, serfs did not address lords thus. Buchan propped ready to slap the man hard in the face. Part of him found it hard to believe a serf would be so forward as to address him in this way. Eyeing this lowly man who did not know his place Buchan sneered, "I would not trouble me if I were you."

Dugulud dropped none of his spite. "He stops acknowledges me a simple serf, all praise to him."

Buchan scowled, typically it frightened all who saw it.

Not this time. Dugulad laughed. "Half or more of your success is down to your expensive armour. With it, I would be your equal, if not better. Ride on if thee deems it a true statement and too risky to refute, or else, refute it by force of arms."

Dugulad was more enterprising and intelligent than most of the villains Buchan had come across, that was instantly clear. Surrounding himself with cleverness fostered it personally —

according to Alexander - so Buchan decided to engage this serf and see what came of it.

More sharp words came his way. "I see thou art tongue tied as well as lack witted and slow at arms."

This man made Buchan laugh. He actually liked this serf so much he was going to teach him the hardest lesson of all, how to fight.

Buchan dismounted, said to the serf who would cross arms with him. "Let us see how good a man thou indeed art?"

Came the peasant's reply, "Oh we will see alright as will others see how feeble thou art on equal terms with a villain and not covered in armour."

The low folk witness to all took to this language and their pleased eyes and grins indicated they would like nothing better than that a villain beat the man of high rank. These looks Buchan was getting made him realize an act of civil disobedience and social disorder had just occurred so extreme it must be punished or it would undermine the class structure which kept him above these very men who took his orders. If he had wanted to he could have Dugulad whipped.

Buchan decided there was a better way to punish him and show him the superiority of the noble class. Buchan cast a wary glance in the direction of Alexander who was nearby in the royal pavilion. Alexander's eyes fell heavily on Buchan, eyes like fire, telling Buchan he better know what he was doing or he would suffer the king's displeasure. It was highly unusual to contest a peasant in single combat and if the outcome displeased the king Buchan would pay for it. Buchan put a high price on his honour, and could not ignore a challenge to his courage and skill. He decided Alexander could dislike it if he chose to. Encouraging a peasant to get above himself was a crime against the privileged class, yet, he did not care about that. It was more out of curiosity at how good this man was more than anything else, that he would fight Dugulad.

He also had a certain amount of admiration for the man's fighting spirit. There was a bit of anger there too. He had something in store for Dugulad, something unpleasant. His sergeant of arms tried to catch his eye. He could easily have signaled to the sergeant to club this man down. There were many reasons to, but he would not. To see what his opponent had to offer and find out if he could deal with it, that was the main reason he chose to fight. He had fought in many tournaments but never against a common man, equally armed. The prospect of it was fascinating. Buchan detected a real willingness to fight in Dugulad a rare quality, one that as a fighting man he admired, and valued.

Dugulad spoke once more. "Thou would have no hope without weapons and armour."

Buchan proclaimed, "We are trained from boyhood in the use of them. So I will use mine and soundly beat thee for thy impertinence."

The outraged peasant stood before Buchan. "With me in no armour, and thee cloaked in mail!"

Buchan revealed his previous statement was only a jest, "Never, I seek no advantage I am to go uncloaked."

"What?"

"I will shed my armour. A quarterstaff is a common enough weapon. Art thee familiar with it?"

"Aye indeed, I have bashed in many heads with it."

"I will train thee in its use."

"That is preposterous. Train me!"

"I too know its use. A simple weapon in case I had to face one armed with it. I have learned to use it well."

The peasant's heartbeat was racing and his aggression rising. "A Norman without armor against a man of true worth and with my favorite weapon the quarterstaff, you are in for a beating."

Buchan smiled sweetly as one would to a silly child. "Thee is in no danger from a head strike with thine very thick head. With each word from thee it doeth proclaim thee a dolt."

More numbers came, already there had been a crowd, most of them looking forward to the rare sight of a knight being beaten with a quarterstaff by a common man. Someone handed Dugulad his quarterstaff and he stood proudly with it.

Buchan took the same weapon from another hand. The crowd roared for although Buchan was slight and pretty as a maid, he was a redoubtable fighter as his exploits in tournaments had shown. Buchan's eyes were lit by merriment. The serf's, Dugulad's, lit by an incandescent flame of rage. He pushed back his hood to reveal dark hair plastered to his skull with sweat. Dugulad's hand closed tight on his weapon.

Buchan said with a smile that infuriated Dugulad as he knew it would, "Keep a firm grip fellow you will need to." It provoked Dugulad into action as Buchan had predicted. Buchan struck Dugulad's wrist as he came in. A smirk from Buchan. "Not much good with the staff I see."

Dugulad proclaimed, "I know thy arrogant kind. The staff is my weapon here is how I use it."

Dugulad swung at where Buchan was a moment before. Missed him by a good bit.

"Not quite." Buchan's lazy smile infuriated Dugulad.

When Dugulad lunged again Buchan stepped aside from Dugulad's strike and met the peasant's thrust with his own, striking Dugulas to the chest making him gasp for breath.

Thereafter, said Buchan, "You are strong lad but lack finesse." A second lunge to Dugulad's mid-section left him staggering and gasping. Buchan made his opinion plain. "We are ill-matched, put the staff down and surrender, no harm done."

Dugulad was deflated but did not give up and plunging headlong met more painful blows. Though he had received some nasty whacks he stood steadfast.

Buchan looked concerned. "You look a bit pained did those whacks hurt?"

Another rush, another failure. Dugulad arms now had many dark bruises, as did his legs and torso.

Buchan decided to end it. "I believe this contest is over." With that Buchan spilled Dugulad off his feet and struck Dugulad's staff from his hands. Because it was over now Buchan felt he could be magnanimous. "By my troth thee is determined."

Dugulad looked confused. "I thought I was going to win."

Buchan looked down at him and replied with a smile. "I thought so too."

The comment brought much merriment from the onlookers. Seeing the hurt expression on Dugalad's face Buchan struck him on the back in comradely fashion with his hand after helping him back up. "If thee wishes to learn to fight I will teach thee. Swear to be my faithful man and I will take thee into my service. Determination like yours, I would have it serve me." Buchan looked out into the crowd. "If any other man here wishes to serve me he can. If he can prove himself like Dugulad has. Challenge one of my men and if thee beats him, thee is my servant and the beaten one, is no longer. But remember well each of my men has been trained by me."

Buchan sat back to watch the fights. There was always room for another good man and it would provide entertainment for the afternoon and it would keep his men on their toes. Knowing this could happen at any time in the future, it would require them to be at their best at all times.

Though much merriment went on this day, the king found none himself when news arrived that the Earl of Strathearn was exerting his power with other prominent families in Strathearn against him. Alexander thought as many others did that he could easily crush Strathearn, a noted fool. Given his other worries, his wife leaving him, Morgund MacAedh's rebellion, all in all it seemed like an avalanche of disaster. With so many issues Alexander could do little to address his absent queen. Besides those issues mentioned, there were others, raiding on the borders not the least of it. Scotland always known to be a dangerous place had become a kingdom of blood.

The same day that Buchan fought the peasant Dugalad, Alexander busied himself with a delegation into England to sort out this mess with queen. Even as busy as he was, a messenger arrived with news that brought other business for him to attend to which made the king think that if Scotland had two kings they could still not keep up with all the matters there was to deal with. Dealing with these affairs was the king when word arrived of the queen's death. In Dorset she had fallen gravely ill. Just as she breathed her last her brother Henry got to her bedside. King Henry himself had been ill and gained much credit for coming to her side. The exertion of travel in terrible weather was put down as the cause of her death. Some said she died of a broken heart. No one dared tell the king that.

In the summer of 1238, twenty couriers wearing the king's livery passed out of the gate of Edinburgh castle at full gallop even as bells of mourning peeled loudly throughout Edinburgh signaling Queen Joan's death. The riders had no rest before dark, and for many days thereafter they galloped, some east, some west, and in either of the other directions to announce in town and village that the kingdom was in mourning for Queen Joan. Throughout the land and in England the death knell tolled for, Queen Joan of Scotland. For all the tragedy of her passing, since her departure from Edinburgh she had been happier than she had for many a year. For seventeen years Joan had been Scotland's queen.

One in particular missed her, her adopted son Simon MacQueen, her unicorn. Simon MacQueen founded a family that has descendants today. King Henry gave him a bag of gold for his faithful service to Joan and a warhorse and rig for a fighting man. Alexander rewarded him with a small holding of land.

LEAVES ON THE WIND

PHAIL WAS MARRIED to Granoc MacNicol. Granoc, was slight and freckled, spiky haired, also four years younger than Phail. Although with kinky hair that defied all art Granoc was pleasant to look at. She knew she was fair and loved to be noticed. That was her problem, she needed to be admired by all the good looking young men around her. Not only was this desire for admiration by handsome young men an undesirable trait another failing that boded ill for the future of her marriage was this, although wed to the very handsome Phail this silly girl was fascinated by Morgund and his illustrious descent. Morgund made gentle mockery of her when they happened to find themselves alone together. He noticed the willingness in her eyes. In truth he had no interest, apart from the reason that she was Phai's wife, Frida was with child, as a consequence of that, Morgund was as close to her as he ever had been.

    Under different circumstances Granoc may have learned to know her husband and have respected him, perhaps, if he had talked to her things may have been different. If Granoc expected to get to know Phail through conversation she was thoroughly disappointed. He never had much to say, never was especially warm. Granoc was surprised he had so little to say. Consoling herself with the thought that she had the rest of her life to get to know him. The only notice he took of her was once night fell then unquenchably he rode her that hard her teeth rattled in her head. He did not seem to care much where he put it, he was big for his age and at fifteen and with no previous experience of a man he caused her great pain. It was obvious to her that he did not care about her at all. In short order, given it all, she had an oaf for a husband and unlike Phail, Morgund always had a clever answer to any question she asked him. He could make her laugh. Phail made no effort, to.

Granoc spent days following Morgund around looking for an excuse to talk to him. When she could, she stole off, placing herself where he might appear so he could gaze at her pretty eyes. She also hoped her nubile body would appeal to him. Frida was much older and wide in the waist and getting wider every day now that she was pregnant. Granoc always ensured her gown was tight across her chest to accentuate her budding bosom. Swaying a little to ensure these assets were noticed.

Frida caught on quickly, and her and Morgund laughed about it. Frida made the comment, "A pretty girl. Fifteen and with good looks."

Morgund replied putting his hands on his wife's pregnant belly, "I don't want her. I want only you."

The coming child gave Morgund great pleasure. Frida for her part knew the child was probably not Morgund's, prayed, it took after her and not Seward. Her thoughts ran to Seward who was so distinctively white-haired, if the child looked like him, that would be a disaster.

Finn lived with his parents on a farm two miles from Morgund's hillfort. Finn although he was slow of speech was not slow of mind. His mother Leirdra was fond of saying what little he did say was the equal in cleverness to a thousand words from another but he said it with ten. At seventeen he never won any great name as a warrior-to-be, was too clumsy, earning the nickname scatter-limbs, for his lack of coordination. He was the younger brother of Colla a large bad tempered fighter. Finn more than of an age to go to war had not done so yet. That was down to his mother. Leirdra, worried lest his ineptness at arms would be the death of him. Even though Finn lacked dexterity he had plenty of spirit and looked forward to fighting. He knew he was very ugly which angered him, no girls looked at him and he wanted them to and do more than look at him, to give themselves up to him. His brother on the other hand was much admired by pretty girls.

Although that was the case with his brother that he could take his pick of the girls, if Finn wanted a wife he must win renown by combat. Morgund might arrange a marriage for him if he proved his worth. That was a belief that Finn held. Being noted as a warrior brought many benefits. Famous swordsman were pursued by woman. This accounted for Finn's willingness to risk himself. When Morgund went to war Finn would be at the forefront of it and give a good account of himself or die in the attempt was the promise he had made to himself. He was ready for a wife, needed an outlet for his passions and frustration. That thing that woke him up every morning told him he needed a wife or he would go mad. As if in answer to his prayers the Earl of Buchan landed two ships on the coast not far away.

The air smelt of pine. Finn noticed that deep in the woods it was very silent. The quiet of the woods was unnerving. Not accustomed to it, every branch looked sinister. A peculiar kind of unease existed here, he felt. The pitter patter of rain made its presence felt in the forest. The sound of it was softer than a distant memory. The sun poked through the branches at times but mostly the air was dank, inhabited by the slate-grey drizzle, and the sweet aroma of the conifers.

Morgund signaled for quiet. He thought he heard something. Those who listened, heard the rain falling and nothing more. In all likelihood the rain and the wind caused the sounds. Again, there was the murmur of wind through the trees. It seems that nothing was here but the those sounds mentioned above. To give the lie to that, a young deer trotted into the clearing and flitted away again. The deer was most likely the cause of some the noise Morgund supposed. Most of the men relaxed. Unlike them, Finn felt his frustration grow, knew without a chance to gain fame his yearning for woman would go unfulfilled. Finn wanted something to happen.

Morgund kept concentrating on the undergrowth. He was sure he had heard a metallic sound, on considering it, the kind made by men with weapons. Ancient Scots pines, lulled his eye, gentled his mind. When the whispering winds got louder, Morgund watched the trees groan under this assault from the air. Looking into the gloom Morgund saw only dim shadows, tree-limbs rocking in the air currents. Morgund finally urged his mount forward drawing the advance on with him having decided his fears were groundless.

His worried friend Seward stayed behind. His sixth sense warning him that something was out there, something human and threatening. Suddenly, Seward heard a sound that curdled his blood and stilled his heart. A war horn cried long and low, Aooooooh! Aooooooh! An arrow meant for Morgund thudded into another man's eye. The man with the arrow protruding from his eye had got himself between Morgund and the arrow, unknowingly urging his mount forward at the crucial moment. As this man toppled from his saddle a stream of arrows followed. Finn, near Morgund, witnessed the man he had shared a joke a with moments before on the ground with an arrow protruding from the center of his eye. Too stunned to move, his arm felt the breeze of another arrow which stirred past him, expecting yet another, despite that, he could not make himself stir. There is no glory in war, he realized, war is death.

Seward, found himself beneath trees striking right and left at those who leapt out at him swinging swords. Seward pulled his horse around climbing the slope he had just descended meeting many enemies on the way up and lucky not to have an arrow find him. Out of the corner of his eye he got a glimpse of Phail. Phail was returning to the more open country as Seward hoped to.

Finn had not moved since the attack began and now had bowman on all sides of him. An arrow passed before his eyes. His heart in his mouth for a moment seeing a feathered shaft that he thought was about to hit him. It lodged in a tree behind him. Finn knew to hang around was to invite death, yet, he could not move. Seward, not so very far away wondered why Finn stood there like a statue waiting for his death, ensuring it by his immobility. An arrow thumped into the wood beside his own head, seeing another about to fly, Seward set his spurs into his mount. As Seward rode, Paten who was running in amongst the trees caught sight of Seward and tried to get his attention, calling out his name. Grabbing Paten's arm pulling him up, thence Seward and Paten rode away together.

Morgund's mount, two arrows were in its side and that was the end of it. Once Morgund rolled off he found himself with armed men on every side of him. He met their steel with his own and they felt his sword whilst he did not feel theirs. Rounding a tree, an axe came at his head. The axe stuck fast in the living wood. The man who moments before was armed, now was not. Thus, Morgund put a sword through this man who had held the axe and kept going.

In the darkness, in the deep forest, organizing survivors, ensuring arcs of possible attacks were covered, Morgund conducted an orderly retreat. Collecting men as he trekked through the soaked vastness; for what had been drizzle had turned into a drenching downpour. Tramping through this dense, saturated woodland, Morgund saw the trees on every side of him watching his defeated army pass under their heavy branches. Their brooding looks gave the impression they would have these men be on his way and leave them be.

The downpour ceased and the silence was total, until, the wind picked up, making it easy to believe that armed men were on every side of them. They pulled together ready to defend themselves. After enough time had passed Morgund realized the wind in the trees was all that it was. As he made his way again, sword poised, eyes watchful, Morgund could not help but think someone he trusted had betrayed him, how else could they have been waiting on his line of march? Returning again and again to it with that question in his mind, who was his betrayer. It got to the point that he hardly saw what was around him so taken up with this matter was he, if the enemy erupted through the foliage now little hope would they have, Morgund weighed down with his heavy musings. Finally, he came to his senses. He had already been caught unawares once. Morgund decided, once was enough.

Darkness crept on the land early with the sun stifled by raincloud skies. When night came they halted and simply rested, sleep too hard to come by given the nature of their ordeal and by the rough, damp and uneven ground that they were upon and how very wet they were.

With a hint of bird song at dawn thereafter they stumbled on in the somber woods over roots and rocks until at last the trees thinned out around them, kept on walking until the hillfort appeared ahead of them. Banners snapped in the breeze, Seward's blond head was there on the wall, Phail's blond head was there too. Along with them were many of the men Morgund had last seen in the forest before the attack, vastly relieved at seeing them alive. A horn signaled Morgund's return. As he entered the gates cast an eye on the weary men who had returned with him.

Seward standing in front of him, said, "Good to have you back Morgund."

"Seward my friend there are hardly any of us left. Many men left in the forest, dead."

Seward indicated others high on the walls or in the courtyard, men who had arrived separately, before Morgund. "Aye some are dead, some are not."

Morgund replied, "Aye, a few."

"More than you think." Seward indicated from whence Morgund had come. "Look behind you."

Morgund did and saw others coming across the same field he had just crossed. Men who had not been a part of his escape party but obviously nevertheless had made it back.

Morgund gave vent to his feelings. "Many are dead. Too many."

Seward did not reply, for indeed there were many dead. An idea came to him. Even as he thought it he thought it unworthy of him. The sounds in the forest, Morgund rode on despite them, he was careless, thus, because of that they had suffered defeat. He realized that it was not good to blame Morgund. In war men made mistakes, thus, it had ever been, thus, ever, it would be.

All that day Morgund waited for an army to come and besiege him, none did. Nothing happened. That night setting a careful watch Morgund went to bed. Rather than a restful sleep, he was tormented sleep. All night he dreamt of arrows and screaming men, feathered shafts stuck deep in human flesh. Wave after wave of arrows came out of the dark to invade the peace of his mind.

Just before dawn the alarm bell rang from the highest tower. An attack force led by the Earl of Buchan, Cunningham by his side, attacked the gates. Morgund's running footsteps echoed on the slate floor as he took himself to the action. From the walls Morgund returned arrow for arrow. Those shot from outside were fiery and much work was spent in putting them out. By dawn this attack had ceased.

That day, and again, that following, nothing, and the day after that, again, nothing. During that time Morgund restlessly patrolled the walls with his stalwart friend Seward by his side. On the fourth day after the first attack on the hillfort, with no attack, thinking how strange it was that there had been no further attacks, Morgund sent out a scouting party who disappeared without trace. The fifth day brought rain and a continuation of the assault. When the second attack came Morgund knew it was Cunningham who led it by his livery. After a few hours of combat the night became very still, heavy with the prospect of rain.

The next evening they were back. Those outside the walls made it plain a much larger force was coming. To hear them say this Morgund thanked God for the warning and knew that he must strike the enemy before more attackers arrived. Gathering all his close comrades together, Morgund put it to them that they should attack. Phail almost always for aggression was not on this occasion. Phail felt that having experienced the enemies cunning in the forest, and aware, that it would undoubtable suit them to fight outside the walls, was concerned, that Morgund was going to do just what they wanted, leave the safety of the walls, thus, thought it was unwise. Morgund looked to Seward, Seward's intuition often had served him well in the past. Unfortunately, on this occasion Seward had no sense of what would serve best and Morgund was torn with indecision. Taken away from his troubling uncertainty by the alarm bell ringing yet again signaling another attack.

Fire arrows. Standing on the walls Morgund watching Buchan's men roaring their approval thought it is extraordinary what heat and flame can do for jaded spirits, ecstatic acclaim bespoken at the sight of the orange and yellow in the cool night air. The pitch for the arrows was protected from the wet - Buchan's doing that. The substance on wrappings affixed to arrows after which they were sent off streaking through the darkness like comets. As if in answer to the prayers of those besieged the skies cast forth wet darts of sufficient quantity that the flames died as if quelled by an unseen hand. Just at such an auspicious moment for the defenders one of them caught a fire-arrow and tumbled from the walls pierced through the neck his screams cut short when he hit the ground.

All the enemy gained by defying the elements and Morgund's walls was disappointment. To Buchan, this proved beyond doubt that it was imperative to get Morgund outside to defeat him. Buchan and Cunningham, out in the rain, were thoroughly demoralized, the weather, and their failure together gave them nothing but regret. Buchan remembered something the king once said, that the best weapon a man has is his mind. He would make use of the wits God gave him, however, luck would also play a part in Morgund's fall.

After many days of little sleep Morgund was in the land of dreams whilst still on his feet, in that world where what is around you is perhaps of this world and perhaps is not. Though extremely tired he had a very good idea, that idea was, given, that Cunningham and Buchan had landed on the coast, supplies would have to come to them via these ships. It should only take a small number of men to raid and destroy their supplies. Buchan, by firing his infernal arrows of flame inspired Morgund to do the same to Buchan's ships. With no easy means of withdrawal and unable to resupply themselves Buchan would find it hard to keep going. Deep in enemy territory, consequently, would realize how vulnerable he was thus be forced to retreat.

Morgund was again with his close confederates. With Seward was the new man, Finn. Morgund knew him as the young man whose mother did not want him to go to war, the young man who wanted a wife or go mad because of his lack of one. It was said he had been like a scared rabbit when facing the enemy. A riderless horse had erupted from the forest scattering those bowman about to shoot Finn, but for that Finn would of died amid the trees skewered by an arrow. This Finn, despite the gossip about him, had somehow impressed Seward. For his part Finn had already noticed Granoc, who was briefly with Morgund before the council began and he thought she kept her eyes on him a moment longer than she had to. Telling himself that he must find a way of putting his body upon hers and to fill her with his seed. His hunger for her was obvious in his eyes when he swept his eyes up and down her body. They had shared a secret smile. He did not know if anyone else noticed, he hoped not. Something in the look she gave him told him she would be up for any mischief.

Presenting himself to Morgund, Finn said, "My lord I will give my life to your cause. Every inch of my heart and ability is yours."

Morgund gave him no answer. These were shallow words; the boy was yet to prove himself. All Morgund saw was a spotty youth notably ugly of face. Ignoring him Morgund explained to William MacRuarie, Phail, his longtime friend, and to Seward, known to one and all as his greatest friend, and to Paten a longtime companion and swordsman, to them, he described the plan he had in mind, which was a quick raid on Buchan's ships. One, must stay behind to manage the defense of the fort. Which caused much debate for some time until Phail and William MacRuarie eventually agreed to. That meant Morgund would have to put up with Finn, Seward's friend, so seemingly willing to shed his blood for him, his sword so ready to strike the enemy as he made clear to all. These were ready words of his, Morgund deemed he would soon see if they had any power of truth behind them.

They snuck out after dark and rode with all possible urgency. An uneventful journey took them to their destination. Bonfires were lit at the Norman camp. From the shelter of the heather Morgund could see the enemy. The bonfires showed men hauling and carting stores. Morgund fell upon them and committed great slaughter upon them. Finally on the beach Morgund and his cohort loosed fire-arrows after the ships. Arrows arcing into the air towards the dark shapes in the water, thence, one of the vessels pulling out to sea was in flames, sails burning. Just as one ship caught fire so did another. Morgund, recognizing the ships were now beyond arrow-range put a stop to it. He got busy taking food from the pile of stores. What was not taken was burned.

"It is a notable victory." Seward said. Finn by his side.

The boy irritated Morgund. Finn looked very pleased with himself. His sword, unbloody, which came as no surprise to Morgund.

Seward noticed the look of distaste on Morgund and asked,

"Morgund art thee pleased?"

"I am, but we must ride back to get back inside the hillfort before first light so we are not facing a wall of steel upon our return. Where is Paten?"

"I do not know," was Seward's answer.

Just as Morgund inquired of him Paten erupted out of the dark towing two captured horses behind him.

Paten addressed Morgund. "A great success."

Morgund felt very tired and closed his eyes for a moment. Behind his closed eyes he heard the waves crashing on the shore. Seward again said something. Just what it was he could not say, therefore he asked, "What?" Not waiting for a reply, "We must go."

The fires now were burning brightly bringing a mosaic of red and yellow to the sky. Morgund liked the way the wind drove the flames, liked the sound as the fire climbed higher into the heavens, liked the way the embers merged with the blackness being pulled into infinity. As Morgund kept his eyes on the fire spilling forth filling pieces of darkness with light he heard again the waves exploding on the beach. The sound of the waves came from far far away they barely penetrated the haze of his exhaustion. His eyes were so heavy he just felt like lying down somewhere and sleeping. Was on the verge of doing just that.

Seward took him by the shoulders his face was very close to his. "We must go now. You said so yourself."

Morgund shook off his exhaustion to say, "I agree. It is time to go."

And they did, rode like devils until they rode through the gates just before dawn and started handing out bags of oats, of wheat-flour, and hard salted fish which did much to lift the spirits of the besieged as did the description of the destruction of the Normans on the beach and of their burning ships.

Inside, beside the warmth of the flames, Morgund's eyes felt so heavy he could barely keep them open. He let them fall shut. Briefly he gauged he had slept when he first awoke but it must have been for a considerable time for it was already night when he woke. Morgund realized he had not moved from the fire the day long. Surely much had happened but he could not recall a moment of it.

Seward's voice to sounded like it came from an eternity away.

"I think Morgund more than anything you need to sleep. You have not been in your bed for days. Sleep in it and you will feel better."

Following his fiend's advice Morgund departed to his bed.

Seward must sleep himself for as tired as Morgund was he knew he was no less so himself. With Morgund gone, his heavy, tired footsteps took him to his own bed. Later, he had a disquieting dream, in it, he was dying and the fort was full of flames. As his lifeblood was leaving him out in the courtyard cold rain hit his face mixing with his tears. He awoke covered in sweat. He lay on his back until sleep overtook him once more. What went on behind his eyes had no pleasantness. His dreams took a new turn; Seward led a futile charge until he was cut down. As he had fallen, so too, had Phail. Seward gazed upon Phail's pale dying eyes as he lay beside him. Phail was like a son to him. It worried Seward enough that he opened his eyes. Many hours thereafter he spent staring at the walls.

Frida had no liking for Phail's young wife, Granoc, whose flirting with Morgund was well known to all. Even without it it would have been hard to like her. The feeling was mutual. Granoc thought Frida was exceedingly dull. On one of the few occasions Frida talked to Granoc, the subject came up of Phail's near maiming by Gregor's beast-dog. Frida took her mind back to the Bard who was on the one hand clever on the other hand an utter fool. Frida decided that this strange girl would of liked that miscreant who caused so much mischief. At least he would not bore her like Frida knew she did. Frida thought it decidedly odd that Granoc put her nose into this business of the demon-dog which near killed Phail. Granoc seemed to enjoy hearing of it immensely, had to stop herself from laughing out loud when it was recounted how grievously it had set its jaws upon Phail like a monster.

A large brass key stood on a hook. When Granoc learned it belonged to the Bard's room which was vacant and away from any other quarters, never used, her interest was unmistakable. Even though Frida and Phail were dullards Granoc was in no doubt there were others who were not and she could use this room to entertain them in complete privacy. Frida told her that it was believed to have a curse on it, this room. Because of this reputed curse, it remained unoccupied since the Bard's death. Nothing else would do than that Granoc must have the key and visit the scene of this mischief done to her husband. Granoc began to nag Frida about getting the key so she could visit the room. All this did not surprise Frida, it was in keeping with the girl's general stupidity. Obviously, the girl lacked sense and sought excitement. As far as Frida was concerned Granoc could go there, and go to Hell too if she so pleased. Frida became very sick of hearing of this room and how much Granoc would like to see it. So much so Frida handed Granoc the key. Once Granoc had the key she told Frida she would return it soon, however, she had no intention of doing so. Frida did not care either way. There is a saying which Frida thought of, 'Someone looking for trouble always finds it', and as another saying goes, 'Those going to Hell find others to take with them', as much as it applied to Granoc it could be said of herself, Frida decided.

Granoc thought it was splendidly insolent of Finn to stare at her like he did, to put his gaze on her breasts and linger his eyes down her body. That he dared to intrigued and excited her. Although he was not handsome - she was being kind, he was notably ugly - his build and audacity pleased her. His athletic body, the wicked way he engaged her with his eyes made her want to giggle out loud, made her want to put her hand out and touch his prick to see if she could cause him to spit his seed. She would abdicate all modesty with him and succumb totally. He could do anything he wanted to her and she rather hoped he would make her do forbidden things. Her intention was to have him soon. By his look she wondered if he would be rough with her, if he would force her to do things she did not want to, and if he did, whether she would enjoy doing them. Phail half-raped her as it was. Although her husband forced her to do things she initially did not want to, she found that she liked being dominated moreover had decided Phail alone was not nearly enough to satisfy these delicious urges which had stirred within her.

In an empty corridor, passing a quick message onto Finn in a whisper, "Come to me tonight, meet me at The Bard's old room. I have the key."

Finn made his way to the room that night. Pushed on unlocked the door to find Granoc lazy eyed upon the bed. There she was her legs spread out wondrously. Her pale white thighs took the light as she leaned back giving him an even better view of that which he came for. Short breaths came from him so excited was he.

He smile was spreading as wide as her legs. "So here we are," she said.

"Here we are," he replied looking down at her entrancing gateway to heaven.

Moving to the edge of the bed she unlaced his breaches and he felt her hand on his manhood pulling it out and towards her mouth. She looked up at him and smiled and then settled her head on it. He sighed. Hearing that, she stopped and said, "Does it please thee?"

He clipped off an answer. "Aye. Very much."

Those eyes of hers had a challenge in them that he wanted to meet. She had the nerve to ask, "Shall I continue?"

Rather than answer her forced her head back onto it. She did not seem to mind and took it very deeply in her mouth. Abruptly she took his penis out of her mouth and laid back legs askew, eyes hard, an eroticism in them he was almost afraid of. Just as she wanted him to he drifted down on top of her with his handsome erection. Madness without dignity overcame them both. In his eyes a kind of rage, Granoc, had tears of passion in hers.

Seward and Morgund stopped talking and watched heavy rain falling. On the battlements they wore heavy cloaks to keep out the chill. Morgund looked blankly into the void, the prospect of a stormed assault upon the hillfort meant he had slept little since the first attack. The heavy rain falling lessened the chance of this.

"I am so tired." These words escaped from Morgund in barely a whisper. Had no energy to produce more than that. He had to sleep whether he liked to or not, for he was not much use to anyone in this current state.

Beside him, his friend said, "Nothing will happen, go to bed."

Morgund did not say a word when he departed, too tired even to think about talking. As Morgund made his way to his bed, soft gentle rain fell but nearing the outer courtyard the speed of the rain turning heavy forced him to hurry on to avoid it.

After midnight Phail took over the watch. Just turned nineteen he was deemed sufficiently able. Many of the men on the walls had slept little, were wet and cold and many of them hated the discomfort of being stuck outside. Phail was as miserable as any of them. He deemed it safe to go inside to pour himself a cup of warm milk. What was meant to be minutes inside became hours. Seated near the fire he expected someone to come and tell him if anything noteworthy occurred. Like most of them he had slept little and was very tired.

A white scorching lick of flame touched the ground and signaled the start of an even greater downpour which sent more men scurrying off the walls. Like Phail, they longed for where it was warm. Some of them went in their beds. As it got colder and wetter still fewer and fewer men were on the walls until one man alone stood there, Paten. For all his observation he was not one of the defenders. With the heavy rain, the ground had dissolved into a sludgy mess. With no one near him, under the cover of the watchtower he grabbed a burning brand and waved it back and forth signaling to those outside the walls. Amid the gloom a fiery light appeared in reply. Seeing this, Paten went to the gates and opened them.

An unseemly pounding on Morgund's door made him rise stiffly from his bed to answer it.

"M'Lord!" The voice was wild, full of alarm.

Morgund blinked his eyes looking at the panicked man before him. Morgund looked out the door and though his eyes were stinging with tiredness he tried to concentrate on what the man was saying. Standing in the doorway was another retainer smelling of smoke. Morgund thought he heard screams. "What is going on?"

They wore the expressions that left no doubt that something terrible had occurred. What was said next confirmed Morgund's worst fears. "The enemy has come through the gates."

Morgund's face was full of terrible confusion. "Come through the gates. How?"

"They were opened M'Lord."

Morgund's mind struggled to process this. "Through the open gates?"

"Treachery. The gates were opened and thus armed men came through them," said the retainer.

The other man butted in. "They will be here soon M'Lord!"

"Very well." Morgund turned his mind to how best to deal with this. "Find Seward and Phail, have them come here to me at once."

When the warriors darted away Morgund turned to Frida. "Find clothes and bread and cheese, bag them and be ready to leave immediately. Hopefully, Seward and Phail can get here before we are forced to depart without them."

With regard to Granoc, the fact was, that she was trouble, unspoken between them that they did not want her with them. Unstated also that a bad piece of judgement by Granoc could have them all killed. There was shouting out in the hallway, it was Seward. Morgund ran to his friend's side fighting off several swordsman intent upon killing his friend. Seward gasped for breath as Morgund stayed alert for new enemies coming down upon them. Thankfully, for the moment the corridor remained empty. A part of Morgund could not help but think it all reminded him of the story of King Edgar and his Queen, Margot. Long ago, an act of treachery brought about their downfall. The heads of the two monarchs were cut off. Morgund had liked to hear Gregor tell of it. The king even with his head cut off spoke and he condemned the men who did such mischief to him and his queen,

Margot. Queen Margo renowned for her beauty had her beauty no longer, her head was upon the floor, beside Edgar's. Morgund recalled this act of villainy, knavery and treachery, as a piece of lesemajesty extraordinary for its savagery.

More of the enemy appeared thus Seward's and Morgund's swords rang hot in contest with them. When they were heavily engaged Phail came to their aid. He killed three men by coming up behind them with his ever ready sword. His heavy blade doing as good work as it had ever done. For all his worthy swordsmanship more enemies came running at them thus the three of them, Morgund, Seward, and Phail, stood their ground, fought, and spilled as much blood as they could, knowing if they did not repel this attack Morgund's pregnant wife would die, and so would they all. In the confined space the three of them prevented the enemy getting behind or to the side of them.

For a moment Morgund thought it was his last moment for the odds were great and terrible weakness overcame him. Stunned at the thought that Frida and the child to be might be losing their lives within moments of his own death. If he failed Frida could expect a terrible fate. With that in mind rather than feel weakened by that prospect Morgund fought like he had never fought before and never would again. It was like he held three swords and not one. The men he met with his steel did not live to tell of it. Morgund arced his sword down and sliced open a neck and scarlet pumped out in a fountain spraying right and left, to the floor. It went everywhere. Almost overcome by blood lust then put another man down with one clean strike.

Seward noticed he was bleeding from his arms. Just as well Morgund fell on the enemy like he did because Seward was overcome with dizziness. The ground tilted one way and then another. Seward knew that although they had fought well, the narrowness of the corridor had saved them.

The enemy were not entirely gone. Those men who would shed their blood were at the other end of the corridor, seemingly waiting, probably, for someone to lead them forward again. Without a leader they were not game to face such men as Morgund and his comrades had proven themselves to be.

In the room, the fretful Frida waited full of concern. For all she knew Morgund, Phail and Seward, all of them could of been killed. Frida's terror was not solved by their reappearance. It could not be resolved according to Frida in their favor by any means. They were trapped in the hillfort which was full of murderers. Her nerves were not going to be spared, for, from the corridor there came the sound of more advancing men. The last thing any of them should do was face the enemy again, there were too many of them, but Morgund could not ignore the plea of a man who served him worthily for many years, William MacRuarie.

As William MacRuarie wrestled his way forward with his sword out towards the invaders, alas, steel drove into his stomach, a fatal wound. Hearing his screams, Morgund pulled himself out of Frida's arms and ran to William. Seward knew he could not let Morgund deal with this alone, thus, his battle-weary steps took him from the room, those weary steps of his more so with each one of them. Suddenly, Seward was aware of how cold he felt. His sword dropped from his trembling hand, a moment later he followed it down to the floor.

At the same time Morgund fought back men intent on Seward's death, Phail dragged Seward back behind the onslaught. All the while, William was bleeding to death. Not content with the wounds they had already put on him several blades pierced William's body one after the other. This done to him even though there was no life left in him. Through no fault of his own Morgund had to take steps back or share William's fate. At this rude assault upon the dead man's body William's blood stained the walls, the floor, every surface had his blood and gore on it. The way his neck hung was not a posture of the living.

Behind them, Seward staggered back to the room. Once there, looked into Frida's eyes. He knew as she did that these were last moments of their lives. Frida held her belly protectively, full of sorrow that the life within her would never get a chance to see the light of day.

Morgund and Phail spilled into the room. Once inside, Morgund slammed the door shut and bolted it behind him. Morgund looked across to Frida. "Time to go."

Frida's trembling lips, "Go where?"

Men began breaking down the door. They did not have much time. Morgund went over to a spot on the floor. By pushing on a stone a trapdoor opened. Seward until that moment had never seen it, nor had Frida, nor had Phail. Frida who had resigned herself to death a moment before thought she was witnessing a miracle. Seward and Phail were amazed beyond words. There was no time for reflection, however, once, years before, Morgund had seen the stone when the light was on it slightly lifted above the others and wondered at its purpose being in an otherwise level floor. He had pushed on it and discovered the trapdoor and from that day till this, kept it to himself. Secrets like that were not likely to remain secrets if spoken to another, so no word to another did he say and a secret it had remained. Steps descended down. Morgund led the way with a lit torch taken from the wall.

As he led them Morgund said, "It leads beyond the walls to a small patch of woods. Be careful it is damp and slippery under foot."

Seward put it to Morgund, "They will find the trapdoor and follow us."

"Get in front of me Seward I will pull it shut behind us. It might take some time to find the door and it is harder to open than it seems. They might not find it at all. They have set fire to the fort, I smell smoke. If the fire is not in the room it is near to it and the fire is certain to spread."

Slowly negotiating this narrow crypt whilst keeping the torch still in case it went out was not an easy thing to do. It would obviously be impossible to see if the torch died, if it did, they would be like rats in a trap. It would take time to re-light. It might be the difference between life and death, the time it took, to have the flame spring forth once more. The heavily laden Morgund handed Phail the torch to help Frida along.

Morgund offered his encouragement, "I know it is hard, but keep going."

Part way, Frida sank down.

"Frida!" Morgund's horrified face was inches away from hers. "Do not stop!"

"I can't go on it is too hard for me."

"You must stand and continue."

"I am pregnant, remember?"

Morgund thought that being pregnant would drive her on, not cause her to halt. Her stopping confounded him. The enemy would not care about her being pregnant. If they entered behind them then death was certain for all. For Frida, for all of them it would be a slaughter. Frida must of taken leave of her senses to stop now. Morgund did not wish to upset her but they would kill her, as, they would kill them all. Not knowing what else to do Morgund spared her a moment. If they could see his eyes they'd see dark pinpricks of anger. "We will wait and rest for a minute or two," Morgund told them all.

Morgund passed her a flask of water which she emptied in a series of gulps. As the moments passed by the light of the torch waved back and forth casting an unearthly glow upon all. To Frida's mind making it look like they were already dead. These people around her could be members of a ghostly race. Strangers, people she had never known.

Morgund, finally said, "Sweetheart, if you do not get up we are all dead." Frida made no reply. The tide of silence was a trap Morgund realized and he would not fall into it. "That child you carry, it will die. I do not want its life over before it has begun. Nor, ever to see my child, nor to have its love. Get up. I am not dying down here and neither are you, and neither is our baby." When she still did not rise, he berated her with, "Selfishness and cowardice are things I never thought to accuse you of."

Cruel things to say, perhaps, but he would do anything to get her moving again. Conceivably he thought a moment later it was not heartless enough because Frida still did not move. She just sat there head hung low. "Is it fair that all our lives depend on you whether you stand or not? And whether you stand or not I will carry on." Morgund looked down at Frida, her head still low and in her hands. "I do not want to condemn you too sorely but within moments our enemies could appear and death will surely come with them." Mulling over what to do until finally anger overcame him. "Frida any moment that trap door will swing open and men with swords will come down to kill us. That baby not yet born will die." He had to say something to shock her into continuing. "Go to hell. I am leaving you behind, die then if you want to, here, alone, amid the darkness."

If he had thought to shock her into action it worked. Frida took her hands away from her face. "I will have some more water, after that, I will continue."

Morgund looked down at her more sympathetically. "My flask is empty." He turned to his friend and asked, "Seward?"

Seward's reply came, "My flask is full."

Seward handed it over to Frida and it went the same way as the earlier one, emptied quickly.

Frida got to her feet and shuffled forward. A few moments later she faltered.

Morgund spoke to her kindly. "We are nearly there, keep going my girl." He smiled in a way meant to lend her energy and strength. "We will come to no harm now, just keep moving."

Frida felt a terrible sense of guilt. This child Morgund spoke of was probably not his but Seward's. That was one of the reasons she faltered, not believing she deserved to live, however, as Morgund had reminded her, if she died all the others died with her. Part of her knew all this was down to her, a punishment for her sins. Frida avoided Morgund's eyes. If this child was ever born, it was damned, and so was she. Morgund, poor man knew nothing. Hopefully, the child would take after her, or possibly was in fact Morgund's, she had a minor hope that somehow it was.

When they came to the end of the passageway Morgund pushed on the heavy stone slab that entombed them and it moved as it did they came out into the moonlight and found the air heavily hung with smoke. Climbing out into the night air Frida saw that no one was within sight that the fort was a mass of fire and destruction not so far away.

On their way, at dawn, the temperature dropped. The sky was slate-grey. As it usually does with the sky that color it started pouring. In amid the teeming wetness they found a hidden place, safe enough though near to the fort. Morgund thought it best to lay in hiding for a day or two before trying to move further away. Patrols could be out. Luckily potential hunger was solved when a duck with more ill humor than sense challenged them and became dinner. There was plenty of smoke in the air from the destruction of the fort thus they risked a fire.

Continuing on in the blowing gale two days later, it was obvious that Frida was much distressed and that her mind was full of apprehension. Morgund put it down to their obvious hardship, to their recent defeat. The truth was that Frida was worried lest her child when it was born was like Seward thence her secret be revealed. Phail would feel the shame of having a slut for a mother, a slut, the thought of it made her hands shake. Whatever way this was to fall was about to be decided because the baby was coming. A thought, came to her in her pain and distress, so often early births proved fatal and if the child did not live, it would prove fortunate. With no woman to help her, Morgund managed what was a calm, relatively easy birth of a son who Morgund named Constantine after one of Scotland's greatest kings.

At a small farm, Edana left the horse she had stolen from rich folk with the people who had sheltered her during the course of the winter months. The horse as payment for her food and lodging. This would help that poor family. With the coming of the spring knowing how little they had to eat Edana took herself away. Stayed off the road as there she might be discovered. Her accent alone would draw attention. By avoiding the roads she found herself deep in the woods, ever denser, until God knew where she was.

    Enclosed in the vibrant spring growth to her right there was a cliff. A gentler downward slope beside it led her to the sound of rushing water. The small stream that ran out of the trees dropped over the cliff to the valley below. The valley was not so very far below her, not too steep to get to. Navigating het way down at one point her feet kept moving and she went down and down and came up with a sore head. As if God looked down on her and had her in His keeping as Emma said He did, blackberries appeared in front of her. She knew they were edible because birds flitted on the branches of the bushes that were heavy with fruit and were at them with a ferocious appetite. She knew what a bird can eat so too can a human. This piece of forest lore is commonly known. A moment later she pushed the berries into her mouth feeling the rush of sweetness and flavor. Eating these berries made her thirsty and she continued on to the stream. Fell to her knees and had her fill of it once she got there. Breaking through some small trees further down two deer fled at her advance.

    Approaching the area where the deer had been there were hundreds of nuts strewn on the forest floor. She unshelled them with her dagger. They tasted good. She already had the berries in a twirled blanket hung from on her shoulder, now, she put in it a large array of nuts. Following the watercourse further down into the valley the steep banks were heavily overgrown forcing her away from the water. When she was in those denser parts away from the water full of trepidation expecting to get lost and not find the stream again. Despite her fears the lay of the land helped her reconnect with it.

Frothy rapids appeared in front of her, in amid them, salmon leapt clear of the water working their way upstream. Edana wondered if she could catch at least one of them. She did, with her hands. A flint, a parting present from Emma, now using that flint given her by her friend, striking her dagger on it to make a fire. As a consequence orange flame spilled forth wonderful heat. With a fire going everything felt so much better. To the flame then went the fish. The white flaky flesh when cooked was the best meal she had ever eaten, decided Edana. Edana fell asleep with a full belly listening to the soothing sounds of the flowing water.

In the morning, Edana had the idea to use her dress as a net to catch more fish. Standing naked with her dress draped across a narrow funnel of water, her dress weighed down with stones at the bottom, also the dress was partly out of the water, held up with two sticks at the top. Using her hand to chase the fish into it. In no time at all she had a dress full of fish. She scooped them up and ate them soon after.

Feeling very clean in a now clean dress, having cleaned it thoroughly with a soapy plant, one she was familiar with from home. Having eaten, being clean, Edana felt better than she had in many a day. Laying back Edana put her mind to what sort of welcome Morgund would bestow upon her and smiled to herself that all would be well. With the sun out, and at her ease, her hunger satisfied, it was not difficult to believe only good things could happen to her.

To the north, an uneasy winter passed in a cave far from others. Although it was calm and quiet for now, the tempest that was coming that would cover them all in grief was not far off. All was well until one night Frida caught Morgund staring at her. Staring at her with consternation and anger. She knew then what he thought, could see it in his eyes, he knew Constantine was not his. After much more of this kind of staring, she asked him what was wrong.

He answered her, thus: "I stare because unmistakably there is something of Seward in Constantine."

Hearing that, she felt gripped by panic, calmed herself as best she could and told him not to be silly. Later, when Morgund was out of hearing she warned Seward to be on his guard.

The days got longer and warmer and as they did, Constantine grew, and as he did, who his father was became more and more obvious until one night Morgund met Frida's eyes with a blatant accusation in them. Frida brazened it out and told Morgund he was seeing things that were not there. She resumed what she was doing but could only guess what would happen if Constantine grew to look even more like Seward. Despite her worst fears, he did. Phail also noticed a similarity between Constantine and Seward and quizzically frowned at his mother, the unspoken question on his lips how had a thing such as this happened. The word slut reverberated inside her mind her as her worst fears were being realized.

Frida acknowledged with much regret that the seed of disaster planted, was now bearing fruit. As the days of midsummer came the distance between Seward and Morgund grew into an unbreachable chasm. Morgund disappeared for days at a time. Hunting the meat they needed to sustain them he said. It was obvious to all that he did not find them fit company, particularly the child who looked back at him with Seward's eyes. Expecting Phail to side with his mother if all this exploded Morgund eyed the youth with hot eyes, as he did his two betrayers. Each day brought a harder stare for Frida and a harder one yet for Seward. The white haired Constantine he too had Morgund's hate-filled eyes boring into him.

The blond haired Frida told Morgund Constantine's paler shade was common in her family with younger children. Frida herself was a blond, Phail was blond, a blond son born to Morgund and Frida could only be expected. Still Phail and Frida had hair with a tint of yellow, not pure snow white as Seward did, however, as Morgund told himself - with the same words Frida told him - that he had not seen either of them, Phail and Frida, at Constantine's age. Frida stated that when she was very young, as with Phail, her hair was as white as Constantine's. Morgund felt guilty for a while that he held such a level suspicion of Frida and his friend Seward.

The reprieve in the violence that was coming lasted very briefly. By late summer Constantine's likeness to Seward had grown even more noticeable. By and by it was beyond doubt who his father was. Morgund confronted Seward with it finally after suffering it as long as he could. All he got in reply was silence when his accusations fell heavy on his former friend. Seward could not meet Morgund's eyes. When Morgund's hand went to his sword there was no turning back, the dye was cast. Soon after that the sword that Morgund faced was the Seward's own.

Although Seward's sword was out he wished it was otherwise. His worst fear was to face Morgund in combat. To Sewards mind, it was beyond doubt that someone's blood would be shed, and for what, a few moments of madness, a madness, which had caused a life, and now could just as easily could bring about a death. At this point it was hard to believe that one would kill the other. Such doubts, would prove incongruous with reality and prove how love can turn to hate in a moment no matter the degree of former close affinity between people and that man is made to kill. As they stepped out on the sand so as not to harm others, the others wondered how far they would take this. None believed one of them would slay the other, or if they had such thoughts they hoped and they prayed otherwise.

Muted were the sounds of the ebb and flow of the water as it lapped at their feet. Seward looked at the naked steel in Morgund's hand, at the naked hatred in his eyes, something that he never expected to see and felt great grief in his heart at it. Seward felt no hatred for Morgund they had been friends too long for that. That now they were enemies was almost beyond belief. For his part, Seward felt barely a part of the here and now.

With his heart besieged with terrible anger Morgund brought the accusation to his lips. "You betrayed me!"

When Seward heard it the hurt in his heart was beyond a sword thrust.

Morgund exploded into action striking, drawing first blood, a nick under Seward's left eye. That Morgund drew his blood was a barb that struck Seward's heart with even greater pain than any words of accusation could. What hurt most of all was that it was true that he had betrayed his friend and really could not say why he did. Hating himself beyond measure and because of that his body was drained of energy. Speed, usually his greatest asset, there was no semblance of it today. Luck could always play a part and Seward knew without it his death was certain. Despite his shame and the friendship he felt for Morgund he wanted to live and he could not do that if he could not stop Morgund so he gave his all to prevent this onslaught.

To no avail. A new onslaught came upon him with such terrible power blood was gushing out of his arm from another wound.

Seward did not know if he could kill his friend but was absolutely certain Morgund would kill him and was a moment away from doing so if he did not engage all the senses that had brought him fame as a swordsman. The lesson taught by steel is that it is absolutely unforgiving. An old swordsman's saying that. He realized how true it was when he felt the blood dripping down from another cut under his other eye. There was a high price to pay to have your body penetrated by steel, and, as if he didn't know it well enough, learnt it again. This last wounding he did not even see it coming.

Seward stepped back and looked down at the thick blood spilling out of his side. Something was wrong with his insides. He felt maimed for life. Consoled himself with the fact that it was not likely to last long this excruciating pain her was in. Very shortly his life would end, and with it, his pain. Because of the nature of his wounds he was almost defenseless. Morgund stood watching him bleed. It lasted a heartbeat, this reprieve, for a moment later Morgund cut Seward under the eye again, a particular nasty gash which bled freely.

Morgund almost felt sorry for his once-friend, but not sorry enough to prevent slicing off one of his hands. Not his sword hand though mores the pity.

Damn him thought Morgund: *"I'll slice off his other hand if I get the chance."*

Morgund stepped back gloating and said. "You are a sore sight."

The one handed man said, "I taught you well did I not?"
Morgund had no answer to that.
Seward asked, "How have things come to this?"
"You dare ask …"

"Does this have to happen? That you kill me?"

Morgund bided his time. Let him talk. It would tire the blonde haired betrayer. He noticed how very pale Seward was. His sweat darkened hair was the darkest he had ever seen it. That he did not look handsome now was very apparent. Morgund just stood by watching him bleed to death. Another blow did not need to be struck. Just as this thought occurred to Morgund, Seward tottered and fell face first into the surf.

"I am dying," escaped Seward's tortured lips as he raised himself to his feet.

It took a supreme effort to do so. Why he bothered was beyond the man with the sword who had put him down in the first place. By rising, all he did was make butchers work of it.

Seward lifted his sword and came onwards towards Morgund. However feebly it was done when next their swords met Seward's slipped past the one it faced, and drew some of Morgund's blood. After this sudden burst of energy Seward had none left. He readily acknowledged to himself that his life was almost gone from him, that these were his very last moments. Seward felt the gaping hole in his side, almost he felt his inner organs would fall out of him. He looked at his missing left hand. Where once it had been his lifeblood flowed out of him. Again he fell to his knees.

Seward did somehow with a supreme effort rise once more, and to his former friend and current murderer, said, "I will die sword in hand, on my feet."

Surprising himself Seward managed to stand and get yet another glancing blow on Morgund and shed some more of his blood.

Seward looked into the eyes of his murderer. "Some of your blood has fallen too."

Morgund gave a sigh. "Not much of it." It was time to end this.

As Morgund's sword arced down from the heavens for a moment the light on it was in communion with the infinity above yet for all that it was not a thing of light it was a thing of darkness. It fell on Seward's sword-hand and severed it.

Seward said with resigned eyes, "Friends should not murder friends."

It did not seem to Morgund that they were murdering each other, only that Seward was dying by his hand. With the both his hands missing the outcome was a foregone conclusion. Although many times after Morgund regretted not speedily sending Seward to his death it was impossible to find it within him to strike him down fatally. What was happening was not consciously cruel, Morgund took the targets offered. Seward's hands had been there and he had taken them, his side too, Seward had given him that target and so it had felt his blade. Seeing Seward's remaining hand cut off pity rose in Morgund's heart. Some part of him did not want to see this man who had been his friend, die. Even as he realized this he considered it too late to do anything about it. To the end Seward was a valiant despite his terrible wounds.

Morgund stepped back, lowered his sword. "It is over you will die. I will not strike you again."

Seward felt the terrible sting of salt water in his wounds. Although there were too many to count, he did not now remember receiving a single one. How he had taken them was beyond him yet he identified where they were. He knew that he had lost a lot of blood, had lost two hands, that from two places in his side blood was flowing plentifully, knew, that somewhere near one eye was a small gash and near the other two significant gashes bleeding furiously.

Though he was about to die he cast a jest at his former friend, "Despite these wounds I may yet still win this."

Seward's words prompted a rather sad smile from Morgund.

Seward's eyes closed. Finally this courageous warrior fell crashing down into the rising sea. A part of Morgund felt the need for absolution; it seemed like it was a dirty deed had been done, a murder. Morgund felt the cool rain washing his face as if to wash away his guilt. Closing his eyes it felt like the caress from an angel, like an act of forgiveness, like God's messenger telling him that what he had done was not a foul deed. Understandable, given the scared contract of marriage and that whoever breached that sacred contract deserved vengeance. Then his eyes sprung open. The air turned colder. He had killed a man who was more than a friend to him, a man who had been his savior, a man closer than any brother could be. He had loved Seward. He had genuine affection for Frida also but that was behind him now. Morgund noticed the water turning red with the stain of Seward's blood.

Phail stood near, sword in hand, prepared to sell his life dearly. Morgund had no intention of killing Phail. Was done with death. There was no room in his heart for more killing.

Thinking that, as Morgund had killed Seward, that his mother would be next, the youth was prepared himself to defend her to the death and therefore stood alert, sword out and ready. Despite what Phail thought the killing time had ended. Morgund demonstrated his intention not to shed more blood by throwing down his sword. "Too much blood has already been spilt. I will spill no more of it," rang out along the shore line.

Seeing Morgund's sword on the ground Phail was lost for how to deal with this event that had changed his life forever.

Not far away and within sight of them fearing for her life was Frida. That Morgund had thrown down his weapon had escaped her notice. She fled into the forest holding her son Constantine in her arms trying to put as much distance between herself and the man she believed would kill them both. The foxgloves pressing flat along the forest floor as her running feet thrust down upon them. As she ran, the stark gloominess of the forest gave way to open marshes and the smell of salty sea. Skirting the coast until she came to a wide but shallow river. With the tide rising it was deepening by the second. If she got across it she would be safe from Morgund until the tide turned again because no man could safely get across without a boat with the tide in. The grey-shining water caught her mid-way across making it an easy thing, fortuitously dragging her to the farther shore. When barely winning clear of the sand and saltings she came out to an old woman gathering wood on the riverbank. This woman helped her up the bank. Frida and Constantine had food and drink by her hand and warmth and safety also given by that same kind hand.

To Frida's mind there was little comfort to be had inside this woman's shelter that night. Too tormented to feel relaxed under her roof, thus, when night descended and the terrible events of the day fell heavily upon her she felt like she would choke from a lack of air under this roof, felt, that she needed to go somewhere else or go mad. Such suffering upon her that Frida left Constantine behind and departed into the darkness. Wandered the cliffs that aligned the coast until she fell onto the rocks below which made a ruin of her beauty.

This was where Phail and Morgund found her in the morning at the foot of the very same cliffs. Morgund assured Phail that he had not meant Frida nor Constantine harm and it pained him more than words could say to see Frida come to this end. Her comeliness spoilt like it was woeful to behold. Because she was dead like this they assumed so too was Constantine, that the water had carried him away. Whereas, Frida landed on the rocks Constantine had fallen into the nearby sea. The sad fact of it caused immense sorrow in them both. The sharp rocks made a mess of a once beautiful woman. How long they stood there they did not know but eventually the tide rose and the water began to claim her until she vanished beneath the waves.

There was a lot that had ended but one thing that did not was Phail's love for Morgund. Morgund saw Phail's love and admiration for him and it gave him some solace for he had lost the two people closest to him. Morgund continued to mourn Seward his life long, he also mourned Frida. World weary after this, never did he regain the power and vigor he had before this terrible series of events. Notwithstanding his heavy heart, Morgund eventually found another wife, Christina. By her, he had two sons, who would carry on his name. They was a comfort to him. Like their father, they were more than able with a sword and earned their fame and living by virtue of it.

The old woman who rescued Constantine did not know who his father was, thus, could not tell him for Frida had not told her, nor the baby's name. The woodswoman named the baby, Bredain. Bredain is salmon in the Erse and naming him this because he came out of the water like a salmon. To her, it was more than apt. Bredain had the same gift Seward had. Like his sire Bredain was very able with a sword. It was obvious to many he had Scandinavian ancestry however none for many years related him to the celebrated hero Seward. Finally, an old warrior who had known Seward well, mentioned the likeness to Bredain many years later, and told him, that the way they handled a sword was very alike, one to the other. There had to be more to this than mere coincidence remarked the man who knew them both. From then on Bredain took the surname Gunn, Seward's surname. Bredain did not know if Seward was actually his father but given their similarity, confirmed by tracking down other men who knew the famous Norse warrior, and their similar ability with a sword and the same way of handling one he felt in his heart it was true. Gunn, as a name exists still and is even now associated with men who carry arms and use them well.

Granoc, Phail's wife, to tell of her one must return to the night Morgund's fort fell. That night the pounding on the door to the Bard's room was such that at any moment those inside expected it to fall apart. Granoc's face was haunted and staring, was almost witch-like. For a while Granoc and Finn pushed against the door trying to prevent forced entry but when the pressure was too much it crashed open and men with swords burst in. They killed Finn immediately. Where he had been was nothing but a bloody lump on the floor. Granoc went from terror to arousal in a second when she realized they were not here to kill her, that they had other intentions, eyeing her feminine allure with great admiration, thus, she looked back at them with high excitement. Even though her beauty was in disarray it was obvious.

They had her from one end to the other. Their naked lust made her heart leap in her chest and familiar sensations exploded in her groin. Where moments before she had felt horror and tension now a calm came over her. Some of them were young and were not bad looking. What came next reached a new level of depravity, rather than being forced her lust was no less than theirs. She pulled one of them onto her. Even if the whole roof burned above them it would not burn harder than the fires that were burning in their soulless lustful hearts.

Granoc was under the thrusting power bearing down driving her to ecstasy. Other men stood waiting their turn, their faces to her were black smudges in the darkness. Beside them, on the floor was the dark figure of Finn. Granoc did not mourn him. He was just a plaything. Although he had sacrificed his life in an attempt to protect her it made no difference to her opinion of him. She considered him an oaf, he was not as oafish as Phail of course, but vulgar all the same. Not thinking about him for very long, for the rhythm of sex enslaved her again as the man on top of her made her gasp with the power of his relentless onslaught.

When all the cattle and booty was rounded up Granoc and many other young women, along with the cattle were driven towards the coast. Closely guarded initially, there had been no chance to run away. They camped early in the evening in forest near the site of the earlier battle where Morgund was ambushed and arrows flew like hornets. It was here she heard talk of the burning of Morgund's bedchamber with all trapped within it. Hearing that, Granoc decided Morgund must have died amid the flames with his boring wife Frida, Frida of the wide hips, she thought with a smile. Phail must of died then too since no word was had of him. They were all dead she was certain of it. That made her a widow which was something to be thankful for. A girl with her looks could find a rich husband easily, all she had to do was get away from these men who held her.

When the windy night became still intruding on her senses was a sharp bitter smell that was very unpleasant. The hounds with them grew restive at this smell. So much so, the dogs leaving them, roamed freely this way and that and she could hear their distant howls and barks. Two of the hounds came back with parts of limbs. Realizing there was nothing they could do to stop her with the dogs gone roaming looking for dead bodies, Granoc fled. She ran and ran as far as her legs could carry her. Was found starving and half dead two days later by a family, two young boys, a little girl, and their mother and father. They were out harvesting nuts and berries. This family who found her were the poorest of the poor. Even as ugly and poor as they were they had humor and took great joy in each other not that Granoc could see there was much to take joy in, given their poor clothing and lack of material comforts.

Granoc, at sixteen, was waxing lovelier every day. Men had been glancing at her since she first had breasts to show off. It was as vital to her as air to her to have the admiration of men, to have them commenting on how pleasant to the eye she was. Granoc must be admired every day. Donald the husband of Katrine was the only candidate. There were no other men here, so him it had to be. The two older boys were in her thrall, but being only ten and eleven were not sufficiently manly to be worthy of her. At first, the whole family liked her. It was natural to pity her. They were very curious about how she came to be with them. But despite all efforts they could not elicit much of her story other than she spent days wandering in the forest. Granoc did not want word of her escape to reach the men who had lost her. Her previous captors might seek to reclaim their prize if word reached them of her whereabouts. Of course, Granoc considered that she had been an especially valuable hostage.

By the family's reckoning the only certain fact was she had been somewhere where great danger was and a great killing had been done. She told them she was lucky to be alive which they believed after seeing the state she was in when they found her. It was said of Granoc before the attack by those canny in such things that there were none to compare with her anywhere for saucy looks given to men and soon Donald found out that she could indeed look saucily, and despite the horrified observance of his wife, Donald returned saucy look for saucy look. His wife, Katrine, took in Granoc's interest in her husband thus told the saucy-looker it was better to continue on to some other place. Go from them she must and far. After being insulted by Katrine as she thought herself to be Granoc decided she would not stay where she was not wanted.

Granoc found no admiration, rather a cold, hateful glare from Katrine as she parted from her. Katrine's parting word of advice were, "If thou finds another safe haven, do not try to lure a husband into sin for if thee does a hard time of it thee shall have."

This riled Granoc no end. Despite the rage it caused her she would not dignify a peasant like Katrine with a response. With many provisions generously given to her by these folk, who, she had nothing but contempt for, Granoc sought the road to what perils she knew not, and cared not, for, had not she endured much privation and danger of late despite which she had managed to survive and triumph. She had no doubt that she would overcome all hardship again but perhaps fall in with better people than these peasants who she had the misfortune to make the acquaintance of. A girl of rank did not need the help of peasants. Although these were the thoughts in her head such did not occur. A day later on the road she met a bandit who raped and murdered her. Granoc did not even get a chance to pass him a saucy look.

Paten's end is as dark as any tale told, as dark as Satan's heartless soul. Promised Satan's reward by Eachadh, the piper and seer who was a close supporter of the king. This man, the piper, Eachadh, had predicted that Morgund would end Seward's life. He was instrumental in Morgund's downfall. Paten was lodged in Edinburgh in a small place paid for with the money he had earned by betraying Morgund. When Morgund made his attack on the supply ships Paten had slipped away and made contact with the enemy, amongst them was Eachadh, thus, between the two of them they formulated a plan. If an opportunity presented itself Paten would open the gates. As we know an opportunity did present itself which resulted in horrendous misfortune for all within the hillfort. Eachadh promised his stalwart friend a great reward, one that would be very worthy of his loyal service to His Dark Majesty, to the king, and to himself. Those who seek communion with Satan and expect to benefit from it fool themselves for no man may trust he who is he but a murderer and stealer of souls.

On a day of unruly weather Paten felt great excitement knowing the time for his communion with this higher being had come. It seemed a moment later after a brief meeting with Eachadh and drinking a cup of wine given to him by Eachadh that Paten lay on a floor somewhere he had never been before as a million flecks of light danced before his eyes. Paten felt like he was floating back to that glade where he had first met Eachadh long before when he Eachadh had first predicted Seward's terrible fate.

A good-humoured voice spoke. "We have not moved, we are in your room."

Paten did not believe it for a second. "We have moved."

"No, we are under the same roof where you made your bed last night and the night before that."

"But we have moved." The smell of clover and grass was unmistakable. From his side a woman he had never seen before entered his line of sight. She spoke to him. "Tell me of the other worlds. What do you see?"

The words that came from that dark unholy cavern that was her mouth seemed to be unearthly as if spoken by a being only half human the other half in the world that existed elsewhere of the land of ordinary mortals. Paten was mesmerized by the way the moonlight flashed off her teeth. It was night, somehow, he had lost hours and the rain that had been falling so heavily on his roof fell no more. By some weird alchemy frogs were croaking near him. So he was outside. How? Did not know if he was outside, or whether overall his senses were adrift and the frogs were in his mind. Then voices came one on top of the other. Heard more and more of them. They were outside in a field now he was sure of it. Could feel damp grass under his neck. Something important went on and he wanted to make sense of it. His mind was befuddled and it was impossible to concentrate and decide and reckon with all this.

He heard a girl's voice. "Do you want a kiss?" Her face appeared before him. She was a very beautiful.

He did kiss her. Kissed many others. Old, and young, all merging into one until they were not many people but many lips. A spread of figures all in black surrounded him. A strange light glowed in the field. No logic existed here tonight. The sliver of a silver phosphorescent light was not moonlight, it was like the light he had seen that time in the glade and never saw again after that, until now. The field he thought he was in now had turned into a forest. Trees were growing and falling, growing and falling, and growing and falling. And something else rose. There was a massive rise in his penis. A member of no regular appearance made its stalwart introduction. It was obvious to him, as it was to all others, that it was like the appendage of a donkey. Everyone stared at it. He liked that they did. It felt good having something of such magnitude. Enjoyed, having a penis this big and that they all stared at it. He wiggled it to have more attention on it.

"It is very big," said the woman who had spoken to him earlier, the one who had asked him about the other worlds.

Another woman whispered in between rubbing her tongue along his shaft giving him a feeling of ecstasy beyond belief. "It is a gift from Satan this thing you have." She sucked on it for a while then withdrew her mouth. "To feel something so big inside my mouth is like trying to get my lips over a barrel."

A body was pressing against his, it was a very young lass who was trembling with desire. He could see something in the young lass's face. She stared at him eyebrows raised. It was like she wanted to tell him something. Then, an older, much uglier woman with no teeth, disgusting in every detail of her body, evil beyond belief, now she was on top of him. No one could earn such a disfigurement by good conduct. And what she told him left him in no doubt she was totally shameless. "Do you like me, not my face, but down below, you would not if you saw it. He does not care," she cackled. "My other lover. He loves every deep crevice and bulbous nodule, and pussy sore."

Even assaulted with such wretchedness his manhood took no note of it if anything his penis became even harder. It felt like his body was not his own and betrayed him. After her it seemed there were another twenty woman one after another taking from him that which he no longer wanted to give them. His penis had a mind of its own and worked despite the horrific flesh it fell upon. His heart was pounding with absolute abhorrence.

There was something strange about his surroundings. He was back in the glade where he had come to meet Eachadh on that occasion many years before when Eachadh predicted Morgund's downfall. He was almost certain of it. Wherever he was it was both bright and dark by turns. The trees all around him grew to such heights that they rose to the heavens themselves. Then as if by some form of mad alchemy he was looking at bare walls and inside a room, his room, however subtly different.

Eachadh, who had played the pipes so beautifully the day they first met brought himself to Paten's side. Looking up at him, Paten noticed that Eachadh took on differing looks, part, pithy black, part orange. Then he became totally black with red glowing eyes. There was a figure behind him. That figure behind him was blacker than black, blacker than a man's worst imaginings, no human figure could be so without lightness.

"Is he real?" Paten's question was directed to Eachadh, no one would dare to speak to that massive figure of darkness behind him.

Although not addressed the massive figure addressed Paten. "Does thee know who I am?"

"Aye." Because suddenly Paten realized who it was. He felt a lump of terror in his throat.

Eachadh thrust his hand out suddenly and Paten found blood dripping from his arm. "That is your blood Paten. I cut thee to see the blood of thee, but I need more blood to keep my lord satisfied. He is hungry for it."

The dagger moved swiftly along Paten's other arm. What had been white was streaked with crimson.

"I did not feel anything why is that?"

"The blood we take from you will go painlessly for a while. When the inebriation wears off, which it will, then what we do to you will be such that you will wish you were never born."

Another quick slash released more blood this time from his shoulder.

"Why do this to me?"

"We are only given one life to sacrifice. Yours, you must give to us. Paten we need your heart to gift to our lord who feeds on such carrion. We cut thee at first in little parts to make magic of the blood that flows."

The sexual ecstasy of earlier felt like it happened to someone else, certainly not to the him. Paten felt himself break out in shivers.

Eachadh spoke again. "When we first met, you wanted to share yourself with us and so you shall share yourself with us."

Paten realized that he had been deceived there was no reward, his reward was to be murdered. Paten managed to gasp out between anguished breaths, "I just want to go home."

This did nothing but make Eachadh laugh. He mimicked Paten to the black one. "I have things to do, I want to go home." His next words were, "You sound like a child." A grim and hate filled expression formed itself on Eachadh's face. "There will be pain, a great deal of it."

Paten did not reply, he knew anything he said could not prevent what they were going to do.

A ceremonial dagger was poised high and despite his desperate situation Paten could not help admiring the beauty of it. Eachadh noticed his expression and stayed his hand. "Is it not a work of art? It is Roman and it was old when Jesus was born. Our ways were old even then." The dagger rather than stab down dropped down by Eachadh's side, remaining there, harmlessly. "We are all here to honor you. It is a great honor we do you. Do you realize that Paten?"

"If I am ... to die ..." It was confusing. Paten felt there was something missing from this unfolding event.

Before Paten could make sense of it Eachadh turned away.

Paten did not know if that was a good or bad thing. It was better than being stabbed of that he was certain. Orange faces flickering in the diffused light, through clouds of smoke. *"What ... what ... was going on!"* He could not see them through the smoke, all was sepia-toned, twisted lips, figures moving with no discernable change of position, frozen expressions, arched eyebrows, piteous looks.

Meanwhile, the fire sparkled higher. Paten was studying it with rapt awe. Bits of burning light crept into the sky. A touch of grey meant dawn was near. It was locked in his mind that dawn meant something to these he was amongst.

Paten noticed a dry taste in his mouth. Moved his tongue around trying to gain some moisture in it. After yet more time he listened to the rapid beat of his heart with a clearer head. Chanting went on all around him. He noticed his legs felt more real like they were connected to the rest of his body and under his control. He realized that if he could move his legs that he could escape. His head was clearer now, he was regaining his senses. With more time still he would be able to rise up and run, perhaps, escape. Obviously he had been drugged and was starting to come out of it. They were all shouting with excitement. He was about to be killed. There must be something he could do to stop it.

Quickly, they spread around him and now were within touching distance. Daggers touched him but did not draw his blood. The numbness was leaving him. He felt his legs shaking wanting to get up and run. They bunched up obviously overcome with excitement. He lifted his arms to protect himself. The daggers for the moment stayed up high. He looked up at the black figure standing higher than all the rest and at the daggers shining high in the night air. They could go no higher. As one they would fall and his death would come with it. With the terror bubbling up inside his throat he started screaming when he saw the first dagger drop. That only brought the others down faster. Someone cut his arm off. He saw someone holding it.

Paten appealed to the Highest Power. "Help me Almighty Lord of Heaven!" erupted from his bloodstained lips. Blood filling his mouth preventing any further speech.

God who is all around heard him and answered his prayer but not how he had expected. Suddenly in amid the whirling faces above him Paten saw the one he loved above all others, his mother.

She did not hold a dagger, only a calm beatific smile. The stabbing continued however he felt calmed knowing he was going into her loving arms.

Finally the daggers stopped. Paten's heart went into Eachadh's hand, this, his gift for Satan. Paten's side was hollow and empty. The liver newly removed was passed around and bites taken out of it. All the best organs gathered and supped on, two of them were sacrificed to the Great One who ate them with ravenous hunger. Then what was left of Paten was tossed on the fire as a worthless carcass. The man known as Paten disappeared in a black ruin of smoking fat. That was Paten's reward for choosing to follow the path of darkness and choosing to betray Morgund and open the hillfort to his enemies. All trusting in Satan, trust in the ultimate betrayer.

Edana came over the hill to what was left of Morgund's hillfort, riding a horse stolen from a man who Edana thought could afford the loss of it. Not approaching any closer for to do so, would put her close to those who had made all this happen. An old man, mounted, stood near watching like she was. Then her focus turned inward. Edana struggled so hard to get here just to find it like this, a smoking ruin. It seemed to her like her whole life was cursed. All this and more beset her mind with heavy woes.

Breaking into her thoughts the man spoke, "Morgund was burned to death in a terrible catastrophe with his pregnant wife. No trace was found of either of them but they were trapped in a room that was destroyed by fire. Apparently he gave a good account of himself before dying, killing several of his enemies."

Gazing off into the distance wondering what to do, from far away she heard the man say something else which she did not pick up on, having little interest in it. Finding that his words were not listened to silenced him. Her lack of interest was no reflection on him, or on what he had to say, Edana was thinking about her own troubles and where else she could go. It was a most pressing concern. That she could not find a place of safety here with Morgund was a catastrophic blow. After struggling so hard to get here, here, she was, nowhere, resonated in her mind. Despite all the misfortune that had befallen her she had to find a way to survive somewhere, somehow. Here, it had to be, there was nowhere else to go. The old man was still near so she asked him, "Can you tell me if any seek a servant anywhere hereabouts?"

If before she did not want to speak to him he would not bother to answer her now he decided. He was like that apt to sulk. Not being listened to was a pet hate of his. His wife was a great one for it. Unconcerned by his refusal to reply Edana spoke to him again. "Morgund was my friend." As true a statement as that was so much of her misfortune was down to him. "What did you say happened to him?"

He could not resist relating of this great event. "Burned to death inside the hillfort as I told you before." Slightly peevish in telling her that again made more obvious when he said, "I hope you listened this time. I said it earlier and I may as well of spoken to the wind." The old man continued on, "Morgund was a worthy man, full of vigor, a swordsman. This was a great event in these parts. He incurred the displeasure of the king who set his wolves upon him."

Edana gave him her full attention now. "Who were these wolves?"

"Buchan and Lord Cunningham," he replied

Her interest could not be hidden when she inquired, "And Argyll?"

"Not Argyll."

"Has thee heard of any event dealing with Argyll? No doubt a man known to thee, as to all in the highlands."

She hung on his every word now he noticed. "I have seen him once or twice." The old man was reading something into this.

She held an unwavering gaze on him when she asked, "Heard good things of him?"

She was very interested in Argyll and he thought he knew the reason. "No," he said in answer to her question, "I have not heard good things about him."

The old man knew that this girl had travelled far. That she was of good family was plain. All this asking about Argyll brought forth an idea. Could she be Argyll's missing daughter? The one who killed her father-in-law, who murdered the Norman lord, apparently as close to Satan as a man could get, even said of him that he was known to have a cloven hoof as did his son, thus both were of Satan's bloodline and full of his evil.

Looking at her closely he decided her looks spoke the truth of it, she was Argyll's daughter. Then again she could be some bastard of Argyll's or in some other way related to the Warden of the West Highlands. If she was important - he had the impression she was - he could benefit from it. She was without the benefit of protection, a runaway. A plan started to work its way through his mind, if he took her in then he could figure out who she was with certainty. If she was Argyll's daughter he could contact Argyll and earn a reward for bringing her in.

The old man gave her his best effort at a smile. His gaze fell on her with such interest Edana began to distrust him, to feel uncomfortable. It was the kind of look that a potential buyer might give something he was considering buying say a horse. In fairness he could just be wondering why she was unattended.

Pre-empting this she told him, "I am out for a morning ride and got displaced from my companions. Unfortunately, I fell into some briars too."

That made him smile. "Oh that happens."

She did not like that smile of his it seemed to say that it seemed very doubtful which made her angry. "Yes, it does happen often, to people, to me, often."

Away from her father, at large, because no gentle girl would be out alone like she was, or in such a state of dishevelment however angering her would not put her at ease so he told her with his best effort at humor, "Forgive me. The briars are bad this time of year."

Light snow flurried down, early for it, but nonetheless, and reminding Edana that she must find shelter with the possibility of bad weather always present in the far north. The cold weather would be fast on its heels of these first snows. The south was too dangerous for her and in the north, in winter, death would be certain. Perhaps she could get through autumn, but certainly not winter. Although she had come a long way and survived, now her energy was low, and things looked bad for her.

As if reading her mind the old man shot her a look that showed his teeth however it was no pretty sight with so many of them missing. "Come thee with me I will feed thee."

Edana given her circumstances decided that she had nowhere else to go.

"It is a good place, you will see."

"Very well," she agreed with resignation.

A stone croft stood in an empty field, on three sides surrounded by a line of trees. A lake shone silverish somewhere off in the distance. To the south a steep rocky hill almost bare of trees. As they rode a spring of fresh clear water appeared as if by magic. Riding along its edge until they came to a croft where they dismounted. Inside the croft, the old man sat very quiet, his wife was equally reserved but as she made Edana a meal and sat gazing at her, Edana could tell that this woman liked her. Muire, for that was her name, told Edana she was welcome to stay as long as she liked. As Edana knew people were not always as they seemed thus did not know whether to trust this feeling of affection she got from Muire. One thing however she did know she did not trust the old man. Remembered, Edana, the story of how king Duncan was murdered late in the night when his guard was down, affected by strong drink. His host with the key to his room entered it with a dagger and stabbed him to his death. With that thought in mind her own dagger was never far from her hand as she lay on a pallet of straw which served as her bed.

Despite the bloody act committed so close by little did it impact the farming folk living here. The attackers of Morgund's fort had soon gone on their way after destroying it and the previous mode of life had then resumed its former serenity. Angus, that was the old man's name, spent a good deal of time hunting, and fishing. Hereabouts, there was a good yield of berries, with groves of hazelnuts. Here, too in profusion edible mushrooms grew. All this made for a good living but when the chill cold hand of winter was felt here no comfort would there be.

If Edana thought she had come to a quiet place she had not. Surprised at the active social life, equally surprised by how much she enjoyed it. Edana found she preferred the living to be found here amongst those she had the good fortune to find herself amongst, people that her father would have called the low folk, having met them both, having lived with them both, she knew who the low folk were, not these kind and gentle people.

Visits between neighbours, dancing, and drinking the lively

water, the uisce beatha, were all a feature of the local frolics. Although the social life was loud, loquacious, that was not the case when she was with only Muire and her husband, Angus. Living with these two quiet people who never said much, but the little they did say forged a link of affection between them all. Angus despite his initial intention to take Edana back to her father Argyll came to like Edana so much that he put that idea away from him. Muire's sister, Inna, who lived across the loch was as full of love for Edana and became like a mother to her, like Muire was. Inna, like her sister Muire had no children so for all of them Edana was a blessing. Edana came to consider all of them her family and they considered her their gift from God.

WALTER OF GUIYUCK'S CURSE

SCOTLAND'S KING HAD himself a new wife, the fairest of France's daughters, Marie De Coucy. Many thought the king would have a good time of it getting her with child as she looked as a princess should, clear-eyed, high-breasted, white of skin. Although narrow of waist, pleasantly broad of hip. If she had been a farmer's daughter some wealthy lord would have had her for his mistress at once. One of the servants leered at her like a hound and got cuffed around the ears for it. Men found it very hard to turn their eyes away from Marie. This beautiful girl was twenty-one years old. Several of the guests came from far away places, England, France, the duchies of the Netherlands. Her father Lord Coucy was the greatest baron in Picardy.

When all had eaten their fill of the best of meat and tasted the finest drink, the two most famous jesters in all the lands near and far sprang forth with leaps and hand walking and such acrobatics as were amusing and stunning to the eye. Those in earnest conversation stopped mid word and with mouths hung open were amazed at their antics. One of the jesters Domnal was Scottish, his fellow artist Edwin was an Englishman. Many of the child guests made haste to get as near as they could to gaze at them. For a long while they held the gathering alternatively dumb with amazement and helpless with laughter. They turned somersaults both backwards and forwards without the help of their hands, landing always on their feet, played ditties on small pipes.

They made merry of the newlyweds telling the king, "With your new bride watch thee doesn't get something stuck in a hole and pulling it out, it fall back in again, and have to pull it back out again." Drinking proceeded merrily and a'pace until just past midnight, with that, the king took the hand of his delightful new bride and led her to the bedchamber where all manner of pleasures were taken each of the other.

After an uneventful pregnancy Marie did deliver to Scotland a fair prince who took after his mother in looks and coloring. A blond was the young Alexander heir to the throne of Scotland. There was much of the mother and little of the father about the child. A delight to all was this clever and handsome prince named Alexander, after his father and great-grandfather. The king did not enjoy his young son for long dying when Alexander Prince of Scotland was just seven.

A joyous successful reign had Alexander MacAlexander king after his father, Alexander MacWilliam, until a terrible event cut short his reign. Alexander the Third at the age of forty-four, sought pleasure with his young queen who he was newly married to. When most men were inside and away from the elements which were dire, in the dark, the king rode over a cliff. It brought an end to the line of Margaretson. That last Alexander of Scotland had no issue.

The young Earl of Buchan became one of the leading political figures in the kingdom during the minority of Alexander the Third, the king who rode over a cliff to his death. As opposed to his father, the previous earl, this Earl of Buchan, Walter Comyn, was generally popular in the kingdom and with the highlanders. Walter Comyn governed the kingdom for ten years over the course of King Alexander's minority, with the Earl of Atholl, co-ruler.

Buchan died suddenly in 1258 in a horrific accident when in his early thirties. By then, his son Henry was dead, taken from this life by one of the common ailments so often fatal but today do not exist or are treatable. The Earl of Buchan's wife Isabella remained countess of Buchan until 1260-1261. The countess remained countess of Buchan until, Walter Stewart, the son of the previous king's High Steward, also Walter, took the province from her. The Lordship of Buchan passed back into Comyn hands again when her nephew Walter Comyn, another Earl of Buchan went on to hold it thirty years later.

The Comyn power in Scotland eventually ended when they opposed king Robert the Bruce during the wars of the Scottish succession in the 1290's and the early thirteenth century. As a result of this, the Buchan lands passed into the hands of clan Macpherson.

The Macpherson clan tradition is that in 1309 Robert the Bruce offered the lands of Badenoch - part of the lordship of Buchan - to the chief of clan Macpherson on the condition that he destroy the Comyns. The Macpherson chief acted as the king would have him act and thus the former Comyn lands became MacPherson territory. The modern version of the name Comyn, is Cumming, or Cummings, and is common today. For those with the name Cumming or Cummings they should remember that once their family were contestants for the kingship of Scotland, and very nearly kings. Those few Comyns who survived after their initial defeat by the MacPhersons kept to the deep forests. In these lonely areas none bothered them and in time they rose again but never were they to attain the high offices that they once held.

Walter Comyn, Earl of Buchan, is primarily remembered in the proverbial expression Walter of Guiyock's curse, encountered in Sir Walter Scott's, *Rob Roy*. under the English and Lowland form of his name, Walter Cuming, where it appears in chapter 29: The saying being in old Scots is foreign to modern ears but essentially it relates how he died and describes him perhaps somewhat unkindly, for although aggrandizing himself, he protected the young king Alexander from many who would do him great harm, even of murdered him. Sir Walter Scott noted, I believe somewhat unfairly, "A great feudal oppressor, who riding on some cruel purpose through the forest of Guiyock was thrown from his horse and his foot being caught in the stirrup was dragged along by the frightened animal till he was torn to pieces." Thus the expression, 'Walter of Guiyock's curse,' is proverbial.

And what became of Buchan's friend, Lord Cunningham? Cunningham, married his lovely bride Beth, and rarely, for those times they both lived long lives just as unlikely for the medieval age their three children survived into adulthood and led equally long lives. Fergus's son Harvey fought for Alexander the Third, at the battle of Largs with great valour. The Cunningham family has thrived to this day. My friend Larry Augsbury is the Chairman of the International clan Cunningham society based in Chicago, with regard to my first novel, Celtic Blood, Larry, was especially helpful to me. Here's to you Larry! Without Larry this novel would not of taken the course it did, because, for Larry's sake I included the doings of clan Cunningham. With that, I will mention another illustrious holder of the name, the publisher of the Harry Potter books, Barry Cunningham.

Of those two men who were subjected to king's displeasure so openly at Edinburgh castle, Muieadach and Gillesbaig; and placed in the king's dungeon, which, it must be said the king allowed them to escape from, Gillesbaig came into the king's peace and made himself useful to the king. Muieadach in time also came into the king's peace but just as often was his enemy. After many years of good conduct and valuable service Gillesbaig was rewarded by Alexander the Second. This being the case Muieadach was much in anger towards his former friend which caused him to commit an act of murder upon him. The jealous man Muieadach hated that Gillesbaig had made his fortune and was favoured by the king whilst he was not. From within four walls to an open field was Gillesbaig brung by means of sly artifice. As it is said of it, one of the descriptions of what happened is as follows, one description, there are several:

'Because of envy inveigled out of his house through the device of looking at a horse, once past the door four men, Muieadach, foremost of them murdered Gillesbaig on the spot. Getting his revenge then did Muieadach for Gillesbaig's preferment by the king over himself.'

A second account has it: This account claimed that, *Feigned craftily by the ungodly disposition of Muieadhach was Gillebaig coerced out of his heath and comfort to a field where they were supposed to see a horse. No horse did he see but a sword which struck him down.'*

In both these accounts a horse is mentioned so perhaps a horse was involved in this mischief. If there was a horse then there were also men with swords and anger and strife and murder in their hearts. By what kind of slyness Gillebaig's widow could not say that Muieadach convinced Gillesbaig to be from his hearth gone to be with them, the words were spoken outside her hearing, however, the tone could be implied by the reaction one on the other, that it was one of cheerfulness.

The murder may have been carried out with the king's connivance. Gillesbaig was employed by the king in the inspection of weirs and water wheels. According to some Gillesbaig was taking money by rights due to the king. If the king was aware of this, it is possible, and given more credence by the fact, that, Muieadhach subsequently received the king's pardon as according to Alexander, there was insufficient evidence to find him guilty of any crime. Before this, very event, much merriment going on between the king and Muieadach as if something of common purpose was planned between them.

According to the king, had not the widow been seen talking to men of evil repute just days before her husband's murder. Much quietness in the speech going on between them, perhaps, because of this, might he find her guilty and put a rope around her neck and hang her for the crime of murder.

By the king's reckoning, "Is it not the case that wives would have husbands dead, with all manner of goings on in secrecy, unknown to others in marriages with one spouse in deadly enmity of the other though on the surface happy times are being had by both."

According to the king, what the widow had seen on the day of the murder was precisely nothing, no act of violence, just one friend talking to another, in itself, no crime.

The king subsequently addressed the court on the matter. "With regard to this," said the king, "many are the men who are Muieadach's defamers, themselves, men of infamy with much to gain by Muieadach's downfall."

Whether Gillesbaig's death was orchestrated by the royal hand is open to question. As the widow herself said despite the ill doings and ill words of certain individuals more or less with blood on their hands none felt the hangman's noose, this was down to the king.

In rebuttal, the king had this to say in relation to this accusation, "Based on what the widow knows it is meaningless to level suspicion at anyone, because she knows nothing. Her ill words against Muieadhach are well known to be motivated by the fact that she was once enamored of Muieadhach whilst he was not equally enamored of her."

The king discounted her accusations on the basis of that. Sympathizing with the harm done to Muieadhach by comments made, that put him as last known conversationalist with the dead man. That did look bad, the king conceded that, but that could happen to anyone that they be the last to speak to a man subsequently murdered. Such a thing had happened to him the king told them. That was no cause to hang someone. The king made the case that it was, of itself, not evidence of murder. The king put it to others, would they, if it was themselves be witnessed in like circumstances would they like to be hung on those grounds. All agreed that they would not. The king did well, had them feel the tightness of a rope round their own necks. With his canny head and canny words king could bring people into agreement with him with consummate ease.

Muieadhach was known to be in great hatred of Gillesbaig, was seen with him moments before his murder, an idiot could see who had done this, thus, spoke the widow. By the widow's account a lot knew what had happened and if pressed would tell who the murderer was. "As if the king does not, know!" Spoke the widow.

Again, according to the widow many had lots to lose if the truth came out. It was very unlikely to, because, once more, according to the widow, the king was up to his neck in it. In her opinion the king, would not, scrutinize the crime diligently for the very good reason he himself was behind it. So said the widow. Alexander had as much blood on his hands as anyone, more even, than Muieadhach, for without the king's nod to carry the murder out no murder would have been done. He was wrong to do nothing. With this in mind she sought the king's attention in Edinburgh and as before on several occasions belaboured the point, even taking the king by the arm when he ignored her.

"A shaky kind of premise with which to hang a man," said the king shaking her off. "Did you see Muieadach murder your husband?"

"I saw nothing of the kind as you know very well."

"Nor where they went, or even if they went together."

She knew not where the two men who spoke at her door, one of them being her husband went. She knew though where his body was found. She told the king how horrified she was to find his slain corpse.

"That he is dead has been established," the king answered her.

"It was Muieadach who coaxed him out to his death."

"The proof being? Before we hang a man we must have proof." Asked the king of her, then, "And what words did they speak together?" Said the king responding to her silence, "Not one word of it is known to thee!" He sneered at her and walked on.

As for the matter of the king's involvement all knew he was a man wily and full of trickery. Regardless of all suspicion, after Gillesbaig's death, Muieadach was held high in the royal favor. He lived many long years and many were the instances of his feuding and his disturbances with others. He did not disturb the king's peace again he had at least grown wise enough to not venture there. Muieadach's unruly nature was finally ended when he was brought down by a man long in hatred of him, as was this hatred mutual and known to all. This man, one John of Inverlochy, much affected by strong spirit was subsequently thrown from his horse as he rode away leaving Muieadach with a stab wound and soon to be deceased. Whether by accident or some spite of Muieadach's spirit as he rode off John fell from his horse and snapped his neck. Thus from beyond the grave the wreckage of other lives did Muieadach still make, ensuring, his enduring fame. Famously known that his hatred was so powerful it struck someone dead from beyond his mortal life.

Of Dugalad, the young man who challenged Buchan, fought him with a quarter-staff, and went into his service after a heavy defeat by the said earl there were many strange happenings. He found ill fortune in a small melee and had a heavy blow to his head. Perhaps this was the cause of his subsequent strange behavior. If so the change in him had been very great. It took him from the normal man he was to a man feared and avoided for his oddness. So odd was he that if he saw a holy man he would accost him calling him a false prophet. As his strangeness grew and he did not wash people forbade that he come near them. It was said of him after his head-knock that he could cure toothache, and had healing powers. Where he housed himself none knew. The tales told of Dugalad became even more weird. He was nicknamed "The Mad," for reasons that are clear. It was said if he walked in the dark a light sprang up beside him. By this strange light strange small beasts would hover near to him as if in speech with him.

If the weather was good he would appear and say, "It is I who bring this good weather."

People took to leaving offerings out to him in areas he was known to show up in.

He took to calling himself the Earl of Buchan and said that the actual earl was an imposter. He showed up to the gates of the Buchan castle demanding entry and that he be served as if he were the earl. He was whipped for that. Dugalad told one and all that was not the end of it that the imposter would rue the day he ever put a hand on him. It is said that the man who laid the whip on him was left with a black mark on the whipping hand that never left him. Soon after he sickened and died, all put down to witchcraft. Somehow Dugalad on a night soon after got inside the castle and entered the dining hall to put a curse on Buchan in front of all, as a result, not long after a terrible death overcame Buchan. He fell from his horse, his foot caught in his stirrup, in the forest of Guiyock and was dragged to his death as is related in *Rob Roy* by Sir Walter Scott.

THE END

ABOUT THE AUTHOR

James John Loftus is the author of a previous novel, Celtic Blood, a play, The Trostsy Sisters In The Haunted House, co-writer of a film, Underdog's Tale, and lots of things that will never and should never see the light of day. In a past life he was a Police Officer.

Made in United States
Troutdale, OR
10/13/2024